SEVEN DEADLY SINS

FURRY CONFESSIONS

EDITED BY THURSTON HOWL

A THURSTON HOWL PUBLICATIONS BOOK

No part of this work may be reproduced or transmitted in any form or by any means, electronic or mechanical, including photocopying and recording, or by any information storage or retrieval system without the proper written permission of the copyright owner unless such copying is expressly permitted by federal copyright law. Thurston Howl Publications is authorized to grant permission for further uses of the work in this book. Permission must be obtained from author or the publication house. Address requests for permission to make copies of material here to Jonathan W. Thurston, at jonathan.thurstonhowlpub@gmail.com.

ISBN 978-1-945247-09-5

SEVEN DEADLY SINS: FURRY CONFESSIONS

Seven Deadly Sins: Furry Confessions © 2017 by Thurston Howl

Edited by Thurston Howl
Book design by Thurston Howl.
Cover illustration and part illustrations by Joseph Chou
Cover design by T. Thomas Abernathy

First Edition, 2017. All rights reserved.

A Thurston Howl Publications Book
Published by Thurston Howl Publications
thurstonhowlpublications.com
Knoxville, TN

jonathan.thurstonhowlpub@gmail.com

Printed in the United States of America
10 9 8 7 6 5 4 3 2 1

Acknowledgments

"Click" and "The Collection" by T. Thomas Abernathy. Copyright © 2017.
"Richard Cory" by Tristan Black Wolf. Copyright © 2017.
"A Voice Not Spoken" by Stephen Coghlan. Copyright © 2017.
"Lucy" by Dax. Copyright © 2017.
"The Music on the Street" by NightEyes DaySpring. Copyright © 2017.
"Victuals" by Dwale. Copyright © 2017.
"Devil's Snare" by Faolan. Copyright © 2017.
"Bones" by Searska Grey Raven. Copyright © 2017.
"Black Fur" by Gullwulf. Copyright © 2017.
Interludes by Thurston Howl. Copyright © 2017.
"Repository" and "Stay" by Hypetaph. Copyright © 2017.
"Those Three Letters" by Rayah James. Copyright © 2017.
"The Bear Necessities" by Bill Kieffer. Copyright © 2017.
"Down in the Valley" by Billy Leigh. Copyright © 2017.
"Relations" by TJ Minde. Copyright © 2017.
"Migration Season" by J. A. Noelle. Copyright © 2017.
"Listmember Lost" and "Runaway" by BanWynn (Suta) Oakshadow. Copyright © 2017.
"Don't Judge Me" and "For the Sins of the Father" by Sisco Polaris. Copyright © 2017.
"The Beauty Regime" by Evelyn Proctor. Copyright © 2017.
"Fun at the Mall" by Teiran. Copyright © 2017.
"Shelter" by Avin Telfer. Copyright © 2017.
"Drop Tower" by Varzen. Copyright © 2017.
"I Burned the Bridges to Heaven" by Weasel. Copyright © 2017.
"Anthrophagy" by Zarpaulus. Copyright © 2017.

CONTENTS

LUST

Don't Judge Me
Sisco Polaris — 9

Down in the Valley
Billy Leigh — 25

Click
T. Thomas Abernathy — 48

Fun at the Mall
Teiran — 60

WRATH

Bones
Searska Grey Raven — 77

Those Three Letters
Rayah James — 85

For the Sins of the Father
Sisco Polaris — 92

I Burned the Bridges to Heaven
Weasel — 116

GREED

The Collection
T. Thomas Abernathy — 131

Stay
Hypetaph — 137

ENVY

The Beauty Regime
Evelyn Proctor — 160

Richard Cory
Tristan Black Wolf — 167

Lucy
Dax — 188

Devil's Snare
Faolan — 196

Black Fur
Gullwulf — 212

SLOTH

Repository
Hypetaph — 237

The Bear Necessities
Bill Kieffer — 246

Relations
TJ Minde — 260

A Voice Not Spoken
    Stephen Coghlan   270

Listmember Lost
    BanWynn (Suta) Oakshadow   282

GLUTTONY

Victuals
    Dwale   302

Anthrophagy
    Zarpaulus   307

PRIDE

The Music on the Street
    NightEyes DaySpring   319

Runaway
    BanWynn (Suta) Oakshadow   337

Shelter
    Avin Telfer   357

Drop Tower
    Varzen   366

Migration Season
    J. A. Noelle   374

AUTHOR NOTES   402

> "When you realize your guilt in any of these, you shall confess the sin that you have committed."
> —LEVITICUS 5:5, NRSV

> "LUCIFER. Do so, and we will highly gratify thee. Faustus, we are come from hell to shew thee some pastime: sit down, and thou shalt see all the Seven Deadly Sins appear in their proper shapes.
>
> FAUSTUS. That sight will be as pleasing unto me, as Paradise was to Adam, the first day of his creation."
>
> —CHRISTOPHER MARLOWE,
> *The Tragical History of Doctor Faustus*

Seven Deadly Sins

INTERLUDE

Derek's fur stood on end when he felt a paw on his shoulder. Wheeling around, he stared into the grinning face of a tiger. "Damn it, Zinc!"

The shorter tiger nearly fell down the stairs laughing, his paws wrapped around his stomach. "You should have seen your face!"

Feeling the heat rise in his face, Derek was glad he was German shepherd and not a human. He crossed his arms in front of his chest and growled back at the tiger, "What took you so long anyway? I've been waiting here for over half an hour...and the place is creepy." He cast a sideward glance back to the obsidian double doors that led into the cathedral. The Gothic designs coupled with gargoyles that stood watch at the bottom of the stairs both mystified and terrified him.

"Aw, poor Derek," the feline mewled as he walked closer to his boyfriend, hips swaying. He traced a paw up Derek's side and reveled in the dog's shiver. "Were you starting to get scared of the big, ol' church?"

"No." He removed Zinc's paw and replied forcefully, "It's just that you know we're not supposed to be here. The place was abandoned for a reason."

Zinc waved a paw dismissively. "Yeah, yeah, it's haunted and all that crap."

Derek shook his head. Despite being scrawny as fuck and more feminine than a lot of girls Derek knew, Zinc always seemed so dominant. Derek's eyes glanced over Zinc's short pink shirt that revealed the tiger's white belly, down his skinny jeans, and marveled at the silver-painted tail that swayed behind him, giving Zinc his chromatic moniker. "And the place is labeled a danger zone."

Leaning forward, Zinc tugged at the belt loops at the sides of Derek's jeans and pulled him close so their chests touched and Zinc's mouth was inched from Derek's. "Yeah, but we promised Barba we'd be here. Besides, I want to see if he's really as good at this card reading thing as he—oh, hey, Barba!" He had turned to look over his shoulder, still holding Derek close.

The horse was moving up the stairs wearing a long purple robe as if he were a priest, mage, or worse, a role-playing gamer who was trying to dress up as both. "Sorry I took so long, guys. I was missing a few cards."

Derek smiled over Zinc's other shoulder and started, "You're fi—"

"Well, this had just better be worth it!" Zinc interrupted.

Derek glared at the back of Zinc's head and removed the tiger's paws from his belt loops. "Let's just get this over with." Convincing himself that this would just be a few minutes long, he turned to face the cathedral doors, swallowed, and pushed the doors open. He was not the only one arrested by what he saw inside.

Splintered pews lined either side the spacious nave. Shredded Bibles and hymnals littered the floor. And high against the back wall, the fading light of the sun beamed through panels of stained glass to tint the flying dust with shades of crimson and gold. The window depicted seven figures, bordered with different colors, seeming to struggle against their panels, beseeching freedom from the artwork. The dusk's light revealed a podium in the center of the chapel.

"I told you this place was the shit," Barba said as he stepped past the two gaping lovers. His purple robe swished behind him as he walked straight down the center aisle. "I'll just set up here at the podium. You guys can grab a chair from the sides of the room or sit on the floor. I don't care which."

Derek felt a claw-tipped paw slide up his back, and he shivered again. "What's the matter?" Zinc asked. "Cat got your tongue?" Derek rolled his eyes at Zinc's back as the feline walked toward one of the walls to grab a chair.

Following, he grabbed his own and went with Zinc to sit before the podium where Barba was already laying out cards. Derek noticed the cards were taller than standard playing cards and seemed to have hand-drawn art on the backs of them, but he didn't comment. He had never actually seen Tarot cards in real life, so he had no idea what to really expect.

"Alright," Barba said finally. He turned the podium so that its slanted front faced Derek and Zinc. "Usually, you're supposed to do this on a flat surface, but this is the best we've got." He started shuffling cards on top of the wood panel, their ornate backs catching Derek's eye once again.

"So, how does this work?" Zinc asked, leaning back into his chair with his legs crossed. "You're going to read our futures, right?"

Barba nodded hesitantly. "The past, present, and future technically."

Derek looked around the dusty cathedral, his tail twitching as he said, "Sure, and how long is this going to take?"

With a smile, Barba replied, "You don't like being here?"

Now having reason to glare at both of his friends, Derek said, "No, I don't. It's creepy, and we're not supposed to be here. Why couldn't we do this somewhere else?"

"Because," Barba continued, "this place has all the right spirits. It is a holy place, but it has its own dark history, too."

"Let's just get this over with," Derek repeated.

"Alright," Barba said. "I need you two to together pick out seven cards at random."

Zinc leaned forward immediately and picked a couple at once. "Can I look at them now?"

Barba shook his head as Derek grabbed two more. "Try to pick the last three together now."

The canine and feline paws managed to decide on three final cards mutually, and Barba separated the seven from the rest of the deck, which he placed on top of a broken table near his hooves.

"Alright," he started. "This is going to be the relationship spread. In theory, it will say something about each of you, how you met, what your strengths are, and what your goals should be."

"Wait," Zinc said with a smirk, "so you won't be able to tell us the winning lottery numbers from this?"

"No, Zinc."

"Then, what's the fucking point?"

Derek sighed. "C'mon, are you ready or what?"

Zinc sat back with a frown, disappointed that he was being scolded. "Yeah, I'm ready. Go for it, Barbie." Zinc emphasized the taunting nickname.

The horse swished back his robes and clasped his hands together in prayer, "Oh God and gods above, guide my mind well tonight. Give me the power to interpret your signs." He spread his hands then and held one hand over the first card. "Zinc, this first card is yours. It should represent your true essence, what makes you tick, and what makes you *you*. It portrays your main essence and how you thrive in this world."

Barba watched the tiger's silver tail swish with amused excitement. Then, he flipped the first card over.

Emblazoned on the white card face was a nude human male with the head of a fox. Its eye were wrought with fire, and black tail-like shapes protruded from its rear. Its body held a feminine pose, but its cock was present though flaccid. At the bottom of the card, the thing's feet merged together into darkness.

With a smirk, Barba explained, "Your essence, Zinc, is Lust."

Derek burst out laughing, bending over in his chair as he roared.

For once, Zinc glared at him. "What's so funny about that, dogbreath?"

"It's just…it's just so *true*," he managed.

Zinc felt heat rise in him, and he turned to Barba. "You know what? Since I'm so *lustful*, let's make a game out of this damn card reading."

Derek stopped, fearing what was about to come out of his cocky boyfriend's snout.

"Why don't we trade stories about lust?"

"Why on Earth," Derek started, "would we wanna do that?"

"It'll make this night a little more interesting...but let's have a twist. Whoever tells the least arousing story has to sit the rest of the night nude."

Derek flushed. "Hell no!" He gave Barba a sideward glance, hoping the horse would get them out of this situation, but Barba only smiled at the suggestion.

"Sounds good to me," Barba said.

Derek fell back against his chair. "Damn it. Fine. Fuck both of you."

Zinc folded his arms behind his head, much like the fox-human was on the card, and reclined. "Alright, who wants to start?"

Barba nodded his head toward Zinc. "You do it, Mr. Lust. It was your card."

"Well," Zinc said with a toothy grin, "if you insist. I'll try not to leave you both wet by the end though."

Derek rolled his eyes again as Zinc began.

Seven Deadly Sins

DON'T JUDGE ME
SISCO POLARIS

The third street gym, steamhouse, and sauna, I know it intimately. A well-run, well-maintained establishment and one I have a membership to, not that I let anyone know that because, as well-maintained and clean as this place is, it's well known to be a gay hookup spot. A place for any guy looking to empty his balls or wet his pipes with some thick cum.

Humans and furs are welcome, and many people frequent it every night. However, I rarely visit, only when the need is high, and that night my needs were so very high. My balls were aching, my cock was begging, and my ass was singing its siren song *"Just once more, one last little fling, what could it hurt?"* I can never resist its song: I lack the strength of will and had no friends to whom I could confess and have them tie me to the mast. Of course, if I had, I would have found the act of being tied down only adding fuel to the fires that burned inside me.

I'm not much to look at, a human, six foot-ish, broad shoulders; my chest is actually quite strong and fit, and my stomach is round and pert. My mid-thirties are in the rear view mirror now sadly, and yet I still retain the passion in the eyes that I used to have. My blue, green, and yellow eyes, tri-color if you look close, and there are a few who have looked beyond my glasses. A scruffy brown beard to match my unkempt brown hair.

Walking in the door that night, just like any other patron, I signed in, grabbed a towel, and headed to the lockers. A lion and wolf were in there; well the wolf was certainly *in* the lion, pressed up against the lockers, the golden fur on the black, hips swaying the slap of flesh on flesh, the whine and moans of sexual bliss filling the air.

Watching them, I stripped quickly, my cock understandably coming to full attention. Still, they were busy, and I had my own needs to see to; watching would make me jerk off, and I'd done that a lot lately as I tried to resist the call of this place. Closing my locker and putting the keychain around my neck and my white towel over my shoulder, I strutted through the place. I had the body of a bear, a gay bear not an anthro, although I would trade my right nut to be an actual anthro bear; fuck me, they are sex on thickly muscled legs. You could tear the thing off with your teeth if you wanted: it would be worth any pain to be one of those plush wonders.

Sadly, it's not possible, and so I strutted my thickly haired belly and strangely fit ass through the halls as I headed to my preferred spot. The sauna, nowhere better in this place to get hot and sweaty, to bathe in the musk of others and do things that I can tell no one else about. I walked in, and the heat hit me, and I started to sweat in an instant, filling the air with manly musk; the air was already thick with it anyway. So thick that it nearly choked me; while the heat baked me, I walked to the bench, sat down, grabbed a cupful of water, tossed it over my head, and then a second cupful onto the coals.

That night, I was the first to enter, which suited me fine. I was a bit early, and I knew it wouldn't be long before this room was filled with furs and humans; then I would be filled by furs and humans. In fact, I waited less than five minutes, just long enough for my body to adjust to the heat and my cock to soften; then in walked a man mountain. An orca, over seven feet tall and so broad he had to turn sideways to slide in the door. His shoulders were like giant tightly packed hams, his black and white skin glistened in the steam. Looking at me, he nodded and then took a seat, spreading his legs so I could see his mammoth cock; it was flaccid and yet almost a foot long, wide and just beautiful. I wanted it the second I saw it, I looked from it up to his face; my hungry eyes met his, and there was a slight nod of agreement from him.

That was all I had needed: I was on my knees in front of him a heartbeat later, my sweaty hands grabbing his cock, my bearded mouth open as I swallowed his meat like a starving man swallows his last morsel of food. Only this was far from the last morsel I would get that night; fuck, the need was strong in me then. My hands grabbed his nuts: they were huge and red hot in my palm. Glancing up, I saw him leaning back, his arms behind his head, not even looking at me. Like me, he didn't come here to meet someone; he came to satisfy an itch. He didn't care who I was, where I was from, what I did for a living. I was there, and I was willing to suck his cock, and that was all either of us cared about.

Wasting no time, I began to suckle on his meat. I've worked many, many cocks over the years, and I was good with my tongue. Plus, I had a rather nice tongue stud that he hadn't noticed, but he felt it as I dragged the round metallic tip over his glans and meatus, then ran it over his slit. Oh his flaccid cock was suddenly at attention, and he was moaning and gasping. Smiling smugly, I continued to work his cockhead, teasing around the corona with my piercing and then just lapping his glans with my tonguetip, making him groan desperately as he wanted to feel the metal again. Oh, I may have been the one on my knees, but he was the one begging.

Not that I made him beg for long: his cock was too wonderful for me to hold myself back. I thrust down as far as I could go—gag reflex is something I left behind years ago. I pressed forward until my lips kissed his musky crotch. My nose detecting powerful notes of sweat and grime; the orca hadn't washed before he came to the sauna. From the rank attacking my nose, he had just come from a workout, or maybe he'd been rutting in one of the other rooms. Somehow, this man had built up one hell of a sweat, and that suited me down to the ground. Sweaty, dirty, filthy, fucking men, that's what I craved more than anything. No please, no thank you, no flirting, no hitting on someone slipping them your number and hoping they call. Just cock and ass, and plenty of both, and I was going to get my share of cock that night. Ass, well that's not really for me unless you want me to lick you out, then just bend over and I will go to town on you like a fucking Alsatian on peanut butter. I will lick you out as deep and nasty as any guy. I may not have the tongue of an anthro, but, damn it, I had the will and sexual desire of a thousand rampant fucking wild rabbits.

While he was gasping and groaning in delight, the door opened, and I glanced back, pulling off his cock for a moment to see who had arrived. A mouse with a nervous look on his face, his white cheeks blushing, the towel wrapped around his waist tenting. Skinny and nervous, white fur covering his trim frame, an office worker's build if ever I saw one. I returned to my orca meat treat, sucking faster and returning to the deepthroating of the wonderfully musky meat. One hand reaching out blindly to the small tray between benches, grabbing what I hopped were lube and condom packets, and flicked them in the direction of the mouse and then slapped my ass, grabbing it and pulling the cheeks apart. Subtlety wasn't needed here; it wasn't welcome as far as I was concerned, and my body language said it all, *"Here is my ass, now fuck it."*

At the same time I gorged myself fit to burst on orca meat, I felt trembling paws on my ass. I was grateful he got the hint, but a little doubtful he would be up to giving me what I wanted, still a cock in my ass, any cock in my ass, was better than no cock in my ass. It's that simple; besides someone like him to open me up before some of the big boys took a turn was not a bad idea.

Pulling off the cock, I began to lick the tip, long languid laps as my metalwork teased his meat. My friends and family had said the tongue stud was an early midlife crisis; if only they knew the real reason I got it. I could hear him huffing, my hands rubbing his thighs, feeling the tight skin and the muscles under it flexing. Knowing that the orca was ready to blow and that so far I had no other partners to turn to, I didn't want him to cum yet. Worshipping his huge phallus, I kissed and licked down the whole length, burying my face in his huge leathery orbs. Using my hands to keep him near the edge, to keep him pleasured and pliant.

Mouseboy behind me finally decided he was a mouseman and pushed his cocktip to my pucker. Preparation was key to being a good slut; I'd fingered my ass properly with a good deal of lube before I got out of my car, knowing that in this place sluts rarely get properly prepared. Guys were here to dump their load in you: they didn't want to spend time fingering you. All they wanted to put in you was their cock. Stretching around his cock easily, I moaned deeply for the first time, and mouseboy had some girth to him. Noticing that I could feel flesh on flesh and that the bastard had decided not to rubber up, I clenched around his cock making the cheeky cunt squeak in pleasure. My well-trained ass could crush his cock if I chose to, yet he was in now, and truth be told every time I was in this place I broke the condom rule. I never turn a guy down, so what the fuck, I just decided to let us both enjoy it.

Sadly, he was pushing in so slowly and hesitantly I knew it would be an age before this boy got up to speed in my ass. Hell, if he ever got up to speed. *First timers, come on boy you are a few inches deep in a slut, grow a pair*, I thought to myself. Sighing, I was about to break one of my rules about coming to this place and speak to tell him to speed up. Thankfully for me, the orca saved me from it: he leaned over and in a deep voice rumbled, "He's a fucking slut, boy, don't be gentle; give it to him hard! Believe me, he will be grateful, cause after I fill his mouth, I'm taking his ass and if you ain't out of his ass by then, I will fuck you instead."

Mouseboy paused for a moment while he struggled internally, blushing deeply at the challenge of another male. My guess was it wouldn't be long before he returned to the place as a fully-fledged slut, but that day he decided to at least try to be a man. With him slamming forward with all his might, my ass sang when it was taken at last, and I moaned out deeply. Girth he may have had, but length he was lacking and his technique and aim were appalling; still, it was a cock, and it was fucking my ass, and that was a good thing.

Thanking the orca with the return of my lips and throat, I deepthroated his cock with wild abandon. Feeling mouseboy going feral on my ass, thrusting wildly once his paws gripped my hips, finally showing some dominance as he lost himself in my ass. I know how to work a cock in both ends and love it when I'm doing both at once. The big and beefy orca began to moan and groan, he actually reached out to grab mouseboy and pulled him in for a kiss, not a gentle lover's kiss, but a passionate deep, dominant one, the orca's tongue delving into the boy's mouth and taking what it wanted.

That was when it all became too much for the rodent. Squealing and squeaking like only a mouse can, he broke the kiss, and I felt a small jet of warmth shooting into my ass. I redoubled my efforts on the orca's cock, the mouse out of the way. I wanted me some real male meat, some whale meat in fact. Desperation is a good driver, and it wasn't long before I got my wish.

His cock was so wide it made my jaw ache, and it throbbed wider, just a heartbeat of warning. Enough that I was able to pull the tip out of my throat. That bulbous cocktip just erupted like a fountain on my tongue, floods of thick orca honey coating my mouth. Guzzling like only the best cumsluts can, I drank as much as possible, his jets far too powerful and copious for even my well-trained mouth to contain. Cum dribbled out of my lips, getting stuck in my beard, soaking the hair on my chest and stomach.

Pulling my lips off with a groan, the last few weak jets of seed splashed on my chest. The big strong orca lay back on the bench, panting heavily fully spent, his cock softening. Nodding down at me, he grunted, "Need five." Disappointed, I glanced at the mouseboy who was on his knees behind me, cock totally deflated as he panted.

Stamina you never miss it until it's gone; fortunately for me, at that moment, the door opened, and in walked a blonde rabbit along with a large brown bear. Taking one look at the human on all fours cum dripping from both ends, the bear gave a large predatory grin looking to the orca he asked, "Slut?"

"Yeah, mouth like a vacuum, and he can breathe through his damn ears. You guys want to cut in while I regroup?" Offering me up like he owns me, I should have been mad at him. However, my lusts were up, and I had come there to be stuffed and mounted as many times as possible, so who was I to complain? I simply looked at the pair, stroking their cocks, and licked my cum-coated lips. A real bear, I loved being the bitch of a real, big, shaggy bear, and the muscled lug standing in the door was like my wettest dream on legs. Tall, broad, huge muscled chest and then just a bit of belly, enough to feel warm and snuggly as it ground down against my back.

Glancing at the rabbit, he wasn't bad, bit too fit for my liking, his body toned and trim. A real twink, but sluts can't be choosers, and I knew that seven-inch wonder pointing at me would taste and feel good. Praying that the bear would want my ass I stayed put, quiet, hoping and praying to the god of sluts that I would get my wish. A few seconds that felt like hours passed, and then they both moved.

The orca slid to one side, and the rabbit took his seat in front of me. I was so excited he didn't have to touch or look at me. My mouth was around his cock, and my tongue was teasing his cocktip. He squealed with delight at the feel of my smooth piercing teasing his glans. Two paws grabbed my head, roughly, oh bunnyboy liked to be in control, fingers ran through my hair and then gripped. I didn't resist, fuck, I never resist. Who would want to resist a thrusting cock, the taste so good, the feel oh so good? Oh god, I was just desperate, and he was horny as fuck. Musky juices flooded my mouth: the bunny was preing heavily, and I swallowed happily. Spirits you sip, ale you chug, wine you drink, pre you swallow, and cum you guzzle: a guide to how any slut should handle his fluids.

Grunting deeply, he began to thrust, holding my head tightly, almost dominantly, as he fucked my willing face. I'd have held still for it anyway, but hell, I loved the feeling of being held, being forced to swallow his cock over and over while his hips pumped rapidly. Of course, a few seconds later, I felt two paws, two huge rough calloused paws, grab my hips, and I was in heaven far beyond anything I had ever known. The paunch of a large bear resting on my buttocks and then a thick cocktip pressed to my ass. I'd seen the bear's cock seven inches and some change; however, it was also thicker than a beercan and, when it thrust, he made that mouseboy cock feel like a finger. Squealing around the rabbit's cock, I was lost in hog's heaven.

Gentleness, tenderness, patience, the bear had none of those traits; he fucked me with brutal savage power and speed. Forcing my face deep into the rabbit's crotch with each thunderous thrust, the slap of his hips on my ass echoed around the room, along with my moans and squeals. My cock was screaming at me to play with it, begging for release when the thick ursine maleness tried to rip me apart. Spreading my ring wide around it, the sensation of the thick pole sliding in and out of me was unbelievable; he didn't need to aim for my prostate: with a cock like that, he just got it inside me, and he assaulted it brutally. Fuck, what I would have given to have that kind of brutal fucking every night.

Gasping around the rabbit's cock, I did my best to suck on it, but my attention was definitely on the sensations inside me. I resisted the urge to jerk myself off. I didn't want to just cum: I wanted an orgasm fucked out of me with brutal raw aggression, and this bear was the kind of male to do just that. Huge warm balls slapped off my ass; fuck, they felt full, and all I could think of was how badly I wanted them emptied inside of me. I had intended to ask for protection; the mouseboy had blown that, but now I didn't care. A series of tests for one night of brutal savage fuckings, it was worth the risk.

Next thing I knew, my mouth was filled with warm cum; sucking it down hungrily, I milked the bunny boy dry. The bear behind me suddenly picked up the speed and power of his mating, which made my cry out. I have been fucked by dozens and maybe hundreds of males, but I have never felt anything like the brute strength of this ursine when he took me that day. His paws so tight on my hips, claws slicing into my flesh a little so I could feel a light trickle of blood on my thighs. Not that I gave a crap: I was in nirvana, heaven, fucking hell. I was in a place I have never been before and always want to get back to.

I screamed out louder and longer than any male has ever made me, before or since, my cock spraying my unimpressive load onto the floor. As he roared like a beast, snarling and screaming into the hot sweaty room, his cock throbbed hard, and I felt wave after wave of thick seed being pumped into me. Those thick balls danced on my taint and jetted everything into me.

A few seconds later, I fell onto the floor, his cock slipping from my ass, a flood of cum leaking out. Panting heavily, I tried to regain some strength and composure when I heard the orca moan, "Aww man I had next. You better not have burned out the slut."

Thoughts of that orca meat getting inside of me were enough to pull me out of my stupor. I pulled myself back up to my knees and turned my ass, cum dribbling out of ass and down my thighs.

Burned out? I was a true and proper slut. I didn't burn out off just two breedings, even if one was one of the best of my life. As the orca grinned and got into position, the door opened and in walked the black wolf and twinky lion he had been fucking.

White, thick orca meat began to slide into me, and I reached out to the newcomers, grasping their cocks and pulling them close, I licked and sucked them both, teasing their tips one at a time, a hand stroking each shaft to ensure they were never left alone. The wolf had a good solid nine-inch cock and the knot at the base was impressive. I eyed it hungrily. It would rival even the bear's cock for thickness. However, I never got knotted in this place: the others wouldn't allow it. Knotted sluts are out of action for half an hour or more, well mostly. I still had a mouth and two hands which I could use to great effect.

Moans of three males I was servicing filled my ears, and I felt the orca cock bottoming out inside me. While the bear had girth, the orca had length, and he also had technique, his thrusts finding their mark on my prostate every time. His thrusts were powerful and fast, but each time he pulled back, he paused, making me whimper and push back, like the wanton cock-hungry whore I was.

Taking the wolf cock deep into my mouth, I began to suck him properly, keeping the lion in my hand, stroking the feline cock quickly and eagerly. A few seconds later the light was eclipsed by the shadow of a bear who wandered over, pointing his cock at me opposite the lion, a grin on his face. I knew what he wanted, and I wanted it just as much. Wrapping my free hand around his cock I began to stroke them both off at the same time. This was the pinnacle, the perfect score for a slut like me, a cock in my mouth, ass, and one in each hand. For a moment, I cursed that I didn't have more hands, mouths, or asses to serve the rest. Or someone taking a video of this so I could enjoy it again later.

Musk, sweat, cum, and pre, the scents of so many aroused males flooded the room. With me right in the middle, the slut servicing them all and any other who would follow them, I whimpered as the wolf pulled me off his cock, the black canine stroking his own meat, grabbing my hair with one paw while his cocktip rested on my nose. The lion and bear followed suit, pawing themselves rabidly. I waited like a good patient slut while the orca mated me with growing speed and strength.

First to blow was the lion, streaks of white landing across my face and hair. Next was the wolf tugging on my hair and mashing his cock against my cheek, and he jetted his watery cum over my face. Last was the bear, thick and musky fluids spraying over me. I was drenched in their mixed fluids, cum dripping down my back, chest, and arms.

A slap on my ass from the orca reminded me that he wasn't done yet and neither was I. With rivers of cum running down my cheeks back and shoulders, I gasped out loud as huge leathery orca balls slapped against my perineum. His thick shaft speared me faster and faster, damn that whale knew how to fuck. To be beneath an expert like that was everything I wanted, everything I needed, and the entire reason I frequented the place.

Hot, panting breath flowed down my back, drops of drool splashing down to mix with the sweat and cum, and I dripped with moisture. Gasping and crying out, the air was so thick with the musk and rank of males that I almost choked on it. I pushed back onto the shaft wantonly, wanting only to be bred, to feel that long thick cock while he rammed me full force. My balls were dancing with each thrust, my cock sang, and I knew it wouldn't be long before I spilled my second load of the night.

"Cum for me bitch. Give me a tight hole to fuck!" It was a grunt and a command, one that my body knew only one reaction to. Never refusing the orders of someone pounding your ass, I grabbed my cock and with just one stroke I began to cum, jets of human seed splashing on the floor. My ass spasmed, and if I'm honest I made sure to clench, giving him as tight a hole as possible to fuck. That bear may have stretched me out, but I still knew how to work a cock inside me.

With a deep grunt and then a gasp, the orca buried his cock as deep as he could inside me and then held still as his balls convulsed; his cock throbbed and his fluids flowed into me. My third fucking of the night and yet I was hungry already for the fourth, fifth and sixth.

Looking around, I could see the lion bouncing in the bear's lap, cock-stealing bitch-slut that he was. The mouseboy had slipped out, and after he pulled his dripping cock out of me, the orca left as well, taking the bunny by the arm as he did so. Leaving me on all fours, cum dripping from both ends, horny, slutty, and desperate.

That's when I felt two paws grabbing my sweaty cheeks, looking back I could see the wolf, a predatory look on his face, along with a grin. No others were currently around, and he had a need. Mounting me fully, his furry chest and stomach pressed down on my back, his fur soaking up the sweat and cum while his cock found my well-used hole. His muzzle found my ear and whispered, "Lion boy wouldn't let me knot him, but you seem like the sort of bitch who knows how to please a wolf."

Asking permission to tie, how gallant of him and how desperate of me that I nodded my head halfway through his request. Growling with predatory lust the wolf began to rut, there was no need for slow build-ups, the last two fuckings had left me stretched out and flooded with cum. The door opened again, and he growled deeply when in walked another patron. A boar, giant tusks poking out of his mouth. His body was similar to mine in many ways, his skin a dark brown, but with a wiry mat of hair covering everywhere. The porcine fellow took one look at the scene and pulled the towel off around his waist.

Clearly, he was here for the same reason as the rest of us. While the lion squealed through an orgasm behind me, I eyed up the thick corkscrew cock in front of me. I had only ever had one other boar before, and the guy had lived up to their reputation. Opening my mouth and sticking out my tongue showing my tongue stud, I invited him forward.

Growling dominantly, the wolf fucked forward suddenly extra hard and fast, the challenge of another male making his feral side take over. He wanted to knot the bitch under him, and the boar was not going to stop him.

My knees were aching, and yet I had no intention of complaining of looking for a more comfortable position. Discomfort was nothing when there was cock to be serviced. The drooling boar cock was presented to me, and my lips sealed around it hungrily. I heard the wolf snarl, "I'm tying this bitch!" It was a statement, a demand and a threat all in one. The boar just shrugged and thrust forward, his belly touching the wolf's nose as his corkscrew meat slid down my throat.

Growling and snarling, the wolf began to fuck like a male possessed; I could feel his knot ramming against my ass, my well-used and lubricated ring stretching easily. Knowing it wouldn't be long until I was locked to a wolf stud and my guts were flooded with his seed, I focused on the cock in my mouth. My hands caressed the huge nuts he had, twice the size of any I had seen that night. Of course, he would need them, pigs and boars were well known for how long their orgasms lasted and how much they could cum in a single fuck.

Smiling around the meat, I let my tongue slide around the corkscrew length, my stud teasing around the curve as it thrust, making him grunt with approval. Giving full oral to a boar, serving him throughout his orgasm, that was a challenge even for a slut like me, one I was desperate and oh so willing to face. The rough rutting got faster and heavier while I bobbed my head, suckling like only a real slut can, cum still glistening on my cheeks.

With one extra rough thrust, I screamed out once a knot was forced inside me, the wolf yipping with triumph as he felt his knot swell, locking him inside me. Growling, he licked and bit my shoulders, making me whimper and moan while he knot-fucked me with abandon, shoving his knot back and forth just an inch. The huge bulk squashing my prostate bringing me so close to my third orgasm of the night. A furred paw grabbed my cock, and I was so shocked I gasped and moaned out loud. I could count on one hand the number of reach-arounds I had gotten in that place.

Piggy was on the edge already, a deep throating was all it took to get him hot and ready to blow. With my ass locked to the wolf for the next half hour, now was a good time to start the boar oral challenge. With my body shuddering, my cock spasmed, my ass crushing the knot inside it while my cock sprayed the already wet floor with more cum.

"You'd better be able to finish what you started," the boar grunted, closing his eyes, rutting my face faster and faster, those huge nuts mashing my chin and cheeks. I could feel them beginning to churn as his orgasm built inside him. My tongue renewed its efforts, and with a groan I felt the first jets of watery cum begin to flood my mouth. The boar kept fucking while I drank jet after jet, guzzling the cum greedily: the full boar challenge was on.

He kept fucking and cumming; I kept sucking and swallowing. The floor in front of us became a puddle with the juices that escaped my lips. My back ached, my jaw ached, my arms ached, and my knees were screaming in pan. Huge boar hands had grabbed my head, pulling my hair while he fucked back and forth. After a few minutes of rutting and cumming, I couldn't believe he was still going; the last time a boar had been in my ass, it had seemed so easy to just lay there while he rutted and seeded me for a full thirty minutes. Swallowing jet after jet of seed it was becoming a bit much, even for a slut like me. The wolf above me sniggered, and I heard a chant begin, "Chug slut chug!"

The bear and lion were both watching with grins on their faces, and as the three of them chanted, the door opened, and a few more turned up to watch the show. Human slut on his knees, wolf knotted to his ass while a boar fucked his mouth cumming endlessly into the human cumdump.

It was one hell of a night, I managed to complete the challenge, must have drank a whole pint or more of boar cum. Afterward, I got really lucky and a pony arrived, my stretched ass just perfect for the tree trunk he had between his legs. There was at least a half dozen others. I sucked them, let them fuck me, wanked them off, did anything and everything I was told or asked. My balls were drained again and again until I could barely walk.

After several hours, I finally had had my fill, and I returned to the locker room. A hot and powerful shower to clean their seed off me, four fingers deep into my ass scooping out the cum of at least nine different people. While I dried myself, I couldn't help but smirk at the sight of the orca and mouseboy: the black and white beast had the mouse pinned to the bench, his huge meaty leg right by the mouse's head as his hips thrust up and down slowly. I got a great visual of the orca cock slowly taking his ass, the rodent squeaking and squealing begging for more. A slut in training, I knew it; someday soon, he would be a pro just like me.

Still, he would need lots of training, and, getting dressed, I heard the orca moan, "I'm taking you home...mmm sexy little squeaker." Smiling widely and nodding at the pair, I left, knowing that mouseboy would soon be mouseslut.

Getting into my car, every muscle ached, and despite the shower, I felt dirty and used, yet at peace with myself. Turning on the ignition, I drove home; it was late by then, and I entered the dark house, not bothering to turn the lights on. Dropping my car keys in the bowl by the door, I climbed the stairs to bed. I stripped in silence and slipped under the covers.

A soft moan came from the bed, and my wife rolled over to frown up at me, "You're late. You really shouldn't let your boss work you like that. I missed you."

"Missed you too," I lied and then kissed her, with lips that had sucked at least twenty cocks. Her hand trembled a little when she slid her fingers down to my crotch. Wincing a little, I sighed, knowing I had to do my husbandly duty. Thoughts of that bear and his cock, the orca and his stamina, the wolf and his savage knot. All served to make my cock react to her touch, it engorged as her legs parted.

No need for a condom here either; we were trying for a second child after all. I guided myself down, and my cock found her silken folds moist and ready. Keeping her locked in the kiss so she couldn't spoil my fantasies with talking, I thrust forward. She moaned loudly when my modest length slipped inside her, making small gentle thrusts as I began to fuck her. After more than a decade together, I knew her body well, and I knew how to pleasure her. A hand slipped to her clit teasing her gently, and my cock rocked back and forth, spreading her silken labia, making her cry out in pleasure.

Knowing her well, I broke the kiss, licking her delicate neck and kissing her smooth shoulders. Some would say I had done well for myself: after all these years, my wife still held her figure trim and pretty, her breasts pert and perky despite years of service to my son. My parents introduced us, a nice Catholic girl for a nice Catholic boy, or so she thought anyway. Her breasts were my next stop; nuzzling them, her delicate scent filled my nose, washing away the scent of maleness. I had to keep my thoughts on what I had done that night to keep myself hard.

Piston-like, my cock rammed into her again and again, my fingers teasing her sex and clit as I nibbled on her perk nipples. She was lost in a world of bliss, crying out my name, her hands scratching down my back. Amanda always said I was a generous lover, and thought it was good that I always made sure she came first. Little did she realize I was always desperate for her to cum, that to hold myself back, all I had to do was focus on her, and I could last forever.

Panting and moaning, she was getting close. I picked up the pace, my musky, recently emptied nuts smacking off her nether lips, and I drove myself home like a real man. I bred her like I knew I wanted to be bred, the slap of skin on skin and soft feminine cries filling our bedroom. Then, I felt it, her folds tightening around me, a warm wetness gushing out of her while she clawed down my back. In the morning, she would spot the bear claw marks, and I would blame her, and she would believe; she always swallowed my lies. As she came, I flooded my mind with images of the night, of orca cock, bear rutting, cum bathing, and for the first time, I felt something. Just enough that I did too, shooting a small load deep into her. Hoping that this time, my seed would take root, and I would have the perfect excuse not to fuck her for a year or two.

I rolled off her, barely panting as she lay there gasping for breath; a few seconds later, she cuddled up to me. Now, I know what you're thinking: *What a bastard. Why don't you just tell her you coward?* and you're probably right. However, you don't really know me, and you don't know what made me this way, what forced me to hide. It wasn't you who was committed, strapped down, and shocked until you begged for forgiveness, begged for some fake deity to save your non-existent soul. So, I suggest you keep your piousness to yourself and just whip out your cock; it's all I really care about anyway. I'm a good husband, a good father, and, when the urge calls me, as it does right now, I'm an unbelievable slut.

DOWN IN THE VALLEY
BILLY LEIGH

It is possible to get what you want, but it comes at a price.

That was what I discovered during my fateful trip to Africa.

My name is Ralph Walter Travers. I'm a Fennec Fox serving as an officer with the King's African Rifles. My regiment is about to go into a fierce battle in Italy, and I can't deny that I'm scared. My paws shake as I try to load my service revolver while my ears are filled with the sounds of machine gun fire and the explosion of mortar shells.

I have come a long way, from London, to the African Savanna, to end up here.

After leaving school in London, I took a civil service entrance exam and worked for the British colonial administration in Africa.

I was single and cubless. Not having a family enabled me to travel more freely, and I claimed that my unmarried status was due to my work. In reality, I chose not to share the actual reason out of fear of imprisonment.

By 1939, it was becoming obvious that war was about to rage in Europe, but I had been shipped to Kenya to continue my work for the colonial office.

I received a posting in Nyeri. It was a picturesque town, surrounded by orange savanna and towering green mountains. The locals were mostly Lions and Wild Dogs, but hearing British accents was not uncommon. I often observed British furs being chauffeured to the social club opposite my office.

The females wore expensive evening gowns, and the men were clad in suits.

My work was far less glamorous. I was stationed in a small office no bigger than a broom cupboard. It was hot, stuffy, and dull. I sank into a routine of working at my desk then retiring to bed as the sun went down. Wireless reports detailing the invasions of Poland and France provided something interesting to listen to, but the war felt far away at that stage. The only contact I had was with my surly feline secretary who disappeared at the end of the day without saying goodbye. I soon grew bored and considered requesting a new posting.

However, the situation got interesting when I plucked up my courage and went for a drink at the social club one evening.

The interior of the club was a jumbled contrast of wicker chairs, worn wooden tables with a polished tiled floor, and art deco lighting. The ceiling was hidden by a stratospheric layer of cigarette smoke. Jazz music crackled from an old phonograph in the corner.

I spent the first half of the evening sitting alone at the bar, nursing a whisky. I was about to leave when a trio walked in. I turned and saw a tall and handsome white tundra Wolf with brilliant blue eyes. He glanced at me with curiosity before he took a seat nearby.

He was followed by a red Fox with a female black Cougar hanging off his arm. She was talking loudly as if to announce her arrival. I was intrigued to hear that her accent was American.

They sat behind me, laughing and chatting.

"Excuse me," I heard the Fox call.

I turned to face him.

"Join us!" he said.

I hesitated before smiling and taking a seat at their table.

"You're new?" the Fox inquired. "I haven't seen a Fennec in here before."

He spoke with a drawling, upper class accent.

"Yes. I arrived last month," I explained.

"I'm Hugo Marlish," he said, extending a paw.

"Ralph Travers," I replied as I took it.

He attempted to clasp my paw in a firm grip, but his pawpads were clammy.

The Cougar introduced herself as Lois Donoghue and the Wolf as Giles Lockhart. I noticed her paw brush against the Wolf's thigh as she spoke.

I studied the three of them. Both Hugo and Lois were dressed formally. Hugo sported a gray, double-breasted suit with a black knitted tie. Lois wore an expensive-looking blue dress with a string of pearls around her neck. She inserted a cigarette into a holder and puffed smoke up at the ceiling. She was glamorous and would not have looked out of place in a Hollywood feature. However, her shrill laugh and over-the-top manner soon began to grate on me. There was also a rather intense expression in her black eyes. I sensed there was something wild lurking beneath the pretty exterior.

Giles was dressed in a beige linen jacket and a white shirt with half the buttons undone. I could see his furry, muscular chest. I hoped he had not caught me looking, but I remember glancing up to see his bright blue eyes gazing back at me.

"What brings you here?" he asked.

Like Hugo, he sounded well-spoken, but his voice was a resonate baritone.

Hugo and Lois were no longer paying me any attention and were laughing raucously at each other's jokes. I told Giles about my work as a civil servant, and he nodded with interest. I asked what his business was. He explained that he had originally moved to Kenya to help manage a tobacco farm owned by his father. He grew bored of that and found work as a bush pilot.

I could not help but stare right into his deep blue eyes. They seemed to change like an ocean tide as he spoke about his experiences flying in Africa.

"The endless savanna is so awe-inspiring, you feel like you can touch the crystal blue sky, and the mountain ranges are so tall you can't help but feel dwarfed by them, even from above," Giles explained as his eyes shone.

I was captivated by his stories and was consciously aware that my heart was beating faster as he spoke. I felt glad that I had gone out for a drink.

Lois spent the evening hanging off Hugo's arm, but I thought I saw her sneaking glances at Giles, too.

Giles explained that he maintained a plane nearby and that he could take me on a flight sometime to see the sights.

"You've never taken me!" Lois exclaimed, putting on a tone of false outrage.

Although she had tried to pass the comment off as a joke, I remember her tail twitched while her eyes carried a hint of malevolence.

Eventually, Hugo seemed to remember that I was sitting opposite him. He announced that they should leave but insisted that I spend the weekend at a ranch up in the Aberdare Range owned by their friends, Mr. and Mrs. Gilmartin.

"Oh, I don't want to intrude," I replied.

"Nonsense! We always enjoy having guests. A new face might liven things up," Hugo said with a grin.

I glanced over at Giles. His eyes were trying to tell me something, but I was unsure what.

"That's very kind. I'm on leave this weekend in fact."

"Splendid. I'll have a car sent to pick you up," Hugo explained.

With that, Hugo gave me a rather effete wave and walked away with Lois in tow. Giles looked back and smiled warmly at me before making his way out.

I can't say that I was taken by either of Hugo and Lois' personalities, but I'd been craving a chance to get away from the confines of my office. I was also determined to see Giles again.

Something drew me to the Wolf that I could not put my paw on.

The next morning, a white Rolls Royce Phantom III showed up outside my quarters with an Ethiopian Wolf behind the wheel. He introduced himself as Bandile and took my suitcase.

The drive up to the Gilmartin's place took twenty minutes. Initially, the landscape was flat, but as the road began to ascend up to Aberdare Valley, I could not help but marvel at the sights. The road twisted through a vast expanse of greenery. The hills towered up on either side of the road, and the sun illuminated the lush foliage.

The Gilmartin couple lived on a white painted ranch that was nestled in the hills. It was a beautiful yet isolated spot that offered glorious views over the valley basin that lay below. The lawn was typically English, neatly manicured with a croquet lawn and bed of roses near the front door. The lawn sloped down, ending with a sheer drop into the valley. A pair of Lions were cutting the grass while another Wild Dog appeared to retrieve my suitcase from the car.

A Border Collie couple were standing on the veranda, watching as I climbed out. The male Collie walked down and took my paw.

"Welcome to paradise! You must be the Fennec that Mr. Lockhart was telling us about. I'm Denys Gilmartin," he introduced himself, "and this is my wife Elizabeth."

Like Hugo, Denys spoke with a drawling voice, but the grip of his paw was firmer. He was dressed in a linen suit and a crisp white shirt. I remember Elizabeth as a pretty and petite canine who smelled strongly of lavender. However, she looked down her muzzle at me as Denys introduced us.

"And what do you do, Mr. Travers?" she asked.

I explained that I worked as a civil servant.

"Oh. I see," she replied, forcing a polite but unconvincing smile as she struggled to say anything diplomatic.

Denys led me into the house. The interior could have been transported from an English country estate. There was an Axminster rug on the living room floor, floral oil paintings on the walls, and a large fireplace guarded by two stone lions. Denys explained that Hugo, Lois, and Giles had already arrived. Out of the corner of my eye, I thought I saw Elizabeth scowl at the mention of Lois' name.

"We're expecting other guests to arrive later," Denys had continued. "I like to hold social gatherings up here. In the meantime, do make yourself at home".

Little did I know what Denys' definition of a "social gathering" was.

A shy looking female Lioness in a maid's uniform showed me to my bedroom. It was a bright, airy room at the front of the house. It had a window overlooking the valley, and I threw the shutters wide to take stock of the view. The sunlight streamed in, and I felt glad to have accepted Hugo's offer.

Once I had unpacked, I made my way downstairs to find Hugo, Lois, and Giles waiting in the front room. We walked out to the garden, and Hugo suggested that we play croquet together. We played for an hour and spent the rest of the afternoon sitting in lawn chairs, drinking iced lemonade.

Hugo threw back his head and brayed with laughter as Lois joked with him, but I also noticed her glancing surreptitiously at Giles. I decided that Hugo was too drippy for my taste and decided to stay closer to Giles for company.

As I sat next to Giles, Lois' eyes fixed me in a hard and piercing gaze. It was as if the mask had slipped, and I could see something lustful and dangerous lurking behind the pretty irises.

I noticed the Rolls Royce coming and going as it ferried new guests to the house. I watched as a white Ermine couple arrived followed by a pair of Brown Labradors.

Eventually, the maid returned and announced that dinner would soon be served in the house and that Denys would like us to dress formally. I made my way to my room and changed into a tuxedo I'd brought with me. My shirt was a little crumpled, but it had to do.

Downstairs, the men were also dressed in their tuxedos, apart from the male Labrador who sported a green military parade uniform. The females wore evening gowns adorned with expensive jewelry.

Giles was sporting an elegant white tuxedo. I couldn't help but marvel at the sight, but I noticed Lois casting him a lovestruck glance, too.

At the table, I was introduced to the Ermines, James and Edith Blythe. The Labrador was called Major John Norton (he was keen to stress "Major" to me). His companion turned out to be his fiancée, Dianne Haigh, although I thought she looked young enough to be his offspring.

We were served dinner by the staff. I noticed they wore nervous expressions and avoided eye contact with the guests. The conversation at the table was polite and refined at first, but the atmosphere grew louder as more drink was consumed.

Major Norton clearly thought himself the Alpha male of the group and ensured that his booming voice was heard above everyone else's. Lois continued to shriek with laughter, downing glass after glass of wine. I noticed that Elizabeth shot her irritated glares whenever she laughed.

Lois never seemed to notice. Her eyes were focused on Giles.

I tried to block out the sound of laughter and kept my attention focused on the Wolf, too. He looked back at me, and I was sure he gave me a smile which conveyed more than friendliness. I was so lost in the depth of his blue eyes that I did not notice Major Norton had asked me a question about my work. The brown Labrador was gazing at me suspiciously. Feeling flustered, I told him about my job at the colonial office and then kept my eyes focused down on the floor until dessert was served.

Once the meal was finished, Denys told us to congregate on the veranda.

More alcohol was served as we sat to watch the sun set over the valley. The deep blue melted into an intense shade of red. The twilight set in as the moon peered out from behind the hills, bathing the valley in a soft, silvery glow.

I was so transfixed that I'd failed to notice everyone had gone back inside.

Eventually, I made my way back into the house to find everyone drinking and laughing in the front room. I sensed the mood was taking a bizarre turn.

Dianne was clearly tipsy and flashed her cleavage at Denys, seemingly not bothered that Major Norton was sitting nearby. Meanwhile, Mr. Blythe was unwrapping a package of shisha, boasting to Elizabeth that he had brought it all the way down from Tunisia.

There was a *crash* as Elizabeth dropped her glass to the floor. She giggled without a care. Hugo tipped back his head and laughed. He threw his glass into the fireplace before pouring himself and Elizabeth more wine, allowing the empty bottle to roll across the floor. Denys and Dianne were walking out of the room arm in arm. Her eyes were gazing at him hungrily.

Above the din, I heard raised voices in the dining room. I peered around the doorway and saw Giles arguing with a drunken Lois. She screamed something incomprehensible and stormed off.

Mrs. Blythe had been standing by the fireplace, a glass of port in her hand. She grinned slyly and beckoned me over. I backed away. Hugo, Mr. Blythe, and Elizabeth were smoking a hookah pipe and reclining in their chairs. Elizabeth was fixing Hugo with flirtatious looks through the haze.

I tried retreating upstairs, wanting to get away. I heard noises coming from the bedroom next to mine. The door was ajar, and I glanced in. I saw Dianne lying on a bed, moaning as Denys thrust into her.

I hurried down the steps and raced out onto the veranda, gasping at the night air as if I had just surfaced from deep water.

To my surprise, Giles Lockhart was standing outside. He was gazing fixedly out into the night, as if trying to take his mind off what was going on in the house. He turned as I approached.

"Welcome to the mad house," he sighed.

"Is that why they invited me up here? To join in their sordid activities?" I asked.

He shrugged.

"Why aren't you inside?" I asked, thinking the question sounded silly.

"If you want the honest answer, I only socialize with these individuals as I grew up with some of them. My father is a friend of Mr. Gilmartin. But I hate it up here. They have no sense of shame. They have nothing to do but indulge in drink and sex to pass the time," he explained. "When they're not making love to their mates, they're sleeping with each other's. Yet if I acted on *my* feelings, I'd be considered abnormal," he added bitterly.

I walked over and stood by him, clasping the railing with my paws. We stood in an awkward silence; the calm night air was occasionally interrupted by a squeal or cackle of laughter from the house.

"Why don't we go somewhere quiet?" I suggested.

He hesitated, but nodded and led me down the front lawn.

"Lois keeps trying to start an affair with me, but frankly, she's chasing the wrong canine," Giles explained with a wry smile.

"Does Hugo know about this?" I asked.

"Probably," he replied nonchalantly.

"How did an American feline end up here of all places?"

"Hugo found her in Paris. She had traveled to Europe from New York and was working as a muse for some artist friend of his. They went to London together before going on holiday to his father's place in Kenya. Since the war began, they've been trapped here. I think it's driving her mad. Her way of releasing her emotions is to join in these *parties* the Gilmartins hold, or flirt with me."

We walked until we reached the very edge. The ruckus in the house had faded, and suddenly we were in peace. A full moon shone down on us like a giant mirror. I remember a cool breeze blowing up through the valley, and I swished my tail into Giles'.

I paused, thinking the gesture was too forward, but the Wolf smiled and brushed his tail into mine. A flurry of emotions gushed through my mind. Surprise, confusion, and then excitement. Giles turned to face me.

"Whenever they invite guests up here, I warn them not to come. But with you, I sensed something different. I wanted to get to know you better. I just wish the circumstances were nicer, but I got a feeling you were..." he struggled to find a word.

I didn't say anything. Instead, I took hold of his paw, closed my eyes, and kissed him in the moonlight.

Giles broke off as we heard drunken laughter from somewhere behind us. I took his paw and led him toward the very edge of the garden.

Giles still looked hesitant, but my burning anticipation to see his naked and athletic body was growing.

I unbuttoned his shirt before removing mine and pulled him to the ground. The hesitation disappeared from Giles' face, and his muzzle broke into a grin.

Giles straddled over me, his blue eyes glimmered, and his soft white tail wagged. Holding my arms gently, he went down for a kiss.

I closed my eyes as his tongue stroked the roof of my mouth. I reached up and slipped a paw under his slacks. Giles broke off and looked surprised for a moment, but he relaxed as I stroked his balls and sheath. I had not felt this sort of pleasure in years. Giles moaned as I continued stroking. He lay down beside me as I grinned and unbuttoned his slacks.

I began licking his balls and member. I savored the musky scent of his genitalia as I licked intently.

My initial revulsion at the party had completely vanished. For the first time in years, I felt like I was in heaven.

"Giles! Are you down here?" a voice called.

We sat bolt upright and tried to pull our clothes back on. I looked up to see Lois storming down the garden.

"Should we hide?" I whispered.

However, with Giles' tall and white form, it was almost impossible to crouch down, even in the darkness.

Lois had seen us and was tottering in our direction.

"What...what are you doing?" she asked. Her speech was slurred and barely coherent.

She stumbled, and Giles lurched forward, stopping her from falling over the edge.

"Let's get you back to the house," he said.

He cast me a regretful glance as he carried Lois away.

I sighed in frustration, sat down on the grass, and continued to gaze up at the silver moon. I wondered how I'd stumbled into such a surreal situation.

The next day, I made sure I was thoroughly clean and wandered outside to find everyone taking breakfast on the veranda. The food was served by the unsmiling house staff. After last night, I could understand why they looked unhappy. The conversation at the table was civilized and polite as if the drinking had never happened.

"Anyone seen Miss Donoghue?" Denys eventually asked.

Everyone around the table shrugged and claimed they had not.

"Maybe she's still in bed?" Dianna suggested.

"No. Lois never came to bed," Hugo replied. "She's probably wandered off somewhere. She's done that before but came back after a couple of days."

I was surprised at how blasé he seemed.

"I saw Lois in the hallway with Giles. He was helping her indoors," Major Norton said. The Labrador fixed Giles and I with a hard and scrutinizing glance.

Casually avoiding our intimate moment on the lawn, Giles claimed that he'd taken Lois up to her room and sat her on the bed to sober up. He had checked on her again ten minutes later, but she had wandered off.

After breakfast, the staff sniffed about the garden to no avail. Denys, Hugo, Major Norton, and Giles went off for a quick search of their own but came back with nothing.

"She'll be back. I'm sure of it," Hugo remarked with a shrug.

With that, everyone had continued on with the day as if nothing were wrong. I was sure that I heard Elizabeth muttering, "I found that girl far too brash anyway," as she left the table.

I asked Giles if it were still possible to go flying. I still felt uneasy and wanted to get away from the house. He hesitated, but said yes. We had done all we could for now, and everyone had hoped that Hugo's prediction of Lois returning would come true. I promised Hugo that I would keep our eyes peeled for any sign of Lois, and he shrugged impassively.

I rushed upstairs to get ready and passed Major Norton on the stairs. The Labrador shot me a suspicious glance but said nothing. I felt unnerved and couldn't wait to get away from the ranch.

Giles was waiting for me by his Chevrolet convertible. We drove down the valley road and as soon as the ground leveled out, the Wolf planted his hind-paw on the accelerator and we sped along with the wind howling over the windshield. I remember feeling bewildered at Hugo's indifferent manner to Lois' disappearance but also intrigued by Elizabeth's apparent dislike of her.

However, as Giles and I sped along the dusty road, my worries momentarily melted away, and I looked forward to our flying excursion. I turned to him and grinned. His blue eyes shone back at me as they reflected in the glorious sunshine.

If only that moment of bliss could have lasted.

What happened later turned my blood to ice.

Well, I guess you want to know what happened after the party?

We think the enemy are on the run, but the rattle of machine guns and the distant *boom* of shells exploding continue to ring in my ears.

I'm still waiting for the command to move forward, so I have time to finish my tale.

Giles took me flying as he had promised. It was a wonderful distraction from the atmosphere back at the ranch. The drive to Nyeri airfield did not take long. The airfield itself was ramshackle-looking, but Giles' bright blue eyes were full of enthusiasm as we drove in. He parked the car and led me over to a yellow DH Tiger Moth biplane.

A Cheetah technician was tinkering with the engine.

"Ah, Mr. Lockhart!" he called as we walked over.

"Morning, Amani. Would it be possible to take her up? I'd like to show my friend the Aberdare from above."

"Of course, Mr. Lockhart. I'll get her ready."

Giles disappeared into a nearby building and emerged a moment later, carrying two pairs of flying goggles and a padded jacket.

"You'll need these. The sun might be out, but it'll be cool up there. I sussed out your size so this should fit."

A minute later, the Cheetah announced that the plane was ready for take-off. I climbed in feeling somewhat apprehensive. Giles offered me a reassuring smile before he pressed down on the throttle.

The fur on the back of my neck stood on end as the nimble little aircraft sped down the grass runway. My stomach lurched as we took off into the clear blue sky. Giles was hunched over the controls, but I was gazing excitedly over the side as we left the ground.

Soon, we were passing over the town, and the houses were as small as building blocks. Furs scurried along the roadsides like ants. I was sure that some were pointing and waving to us. We flew over the outer suburbs, and soon the endless orange expanse of the savanna stretched out before us. The plane climbed higher, and I felt a childlike sense of happiness and exhilaration. The cloudless blue sky continued on for as far as the eye could see. I felt like I was in a small boat in the middle of a calm ocean. The green hills seemed so comically small compared to how imposing they had been from the ground. Giles flew the plane even higher. He'd turned to me and grinned before pulling on the controls. I yelled with surprise and excitement as Giles performed a loop. The sky disappeared and was replaced by the savanna before he righted us. I was grinning from ear to ear and whooped with joy while Giles howled in response.

I was still grinning when we touched down, and I climbed out of the plane.

"I've not had that much fun in years. Actually, that's the most enjoyable thing I've ever done!" I exclaimed as my tail wagged happily.

Giles smiled back.

"It was a pleasure to take you up with me. Hugo certainly wouldn't have found it fun!" he chuckled.

The exhilaration was still gushing through me as we drove off. However, it was soon replaced by a feeling of foreboding as we neared the hills. I sensed by Giles' body language that the Wolf felt the same way. His ears drooped, and he sunk down in his seat.

I turned to face him.

"Why don't you just fly away from here if you hate it?" I asked.

He didn't reply at first.

"Look, I'm going to request a new posting. Come with me," I continued.

The Wolf's eyes glimmered as he mulled the decision over.

Without a warning, he suddenly pulled the car off the road and parked on a bare patch of scrubland.

"Why are we here?" I asked, gazing around in bewilderment.

Giles did not reply but instead gestured with his paw. We were parked in the valley basin, and the green hills towered up on either side of us. The red savanna stretched off into the distance, eventually merging into the sky. There was no sound, nothing but a gentle breeze blowing down from the hills.

"I loved this place," Giles sighed before turning to face me.

"I'll come with you, but I wanted to appreciate this view one last time."

"It's beautiful," I murmured.

"This is the first time I've stopped with someone to look at it," Giles explained.

I smiled and leaned over to kiss him. We closed our eyes and enjoyed the sensation of our tongues exploring each other's mouths. Giles held me in his strong arms as the warm sun shone down on us. I felt all my troubles drift away. His paw reached over and began stroking at my crotch.

I wanted to pleasure Giles to make up for the interruption at the party. I reached over and unbuckled his belt. He pulled his slacks down so that his genitalia was exposed. His blue eyes encouraged me to continue. I took hold of his balls and kneaded them as I ran my tongue over his sheath. I tried slipping it into my mouth and sucked at the tip. Giles groaned with pleasure. His member soon emerged, and I continued sucking earnestly, working my muzzle up and down. Giles closed his eyes and stroked the fur in between my ears.

"Oh Ralph..." he moaned before ejaculating into my muzzle.

I swallowed the warm load as he sat back and panted in ecstasy.

We spent another minute sitting in silence, gazing at the view while I leaned against Giles' shoulder. His rested his muzzle upon my head and gently nuzzled me.

"We should head back," Giles eventually sighed. He retrieved a handkerchief from his pocket and cleaned up the remaining mess.

"We'll get our belongings and head back to Nyeri," he said.

As we drove up to the ranch, the sun retreated behind a cloud, and the valley suddenly felt gloomy. There was an uneasy feeling in the pit of my stomach.

We rounded the corner to see a black police car parked outside the house. My sense of disquiet grew.

There were two Cheetah police officers standing at the front door. Their expressions were grave. They were flanking a tall, brown Rhodesian Ridgeback dressed in a pinstripe suit.

"Mr. Lockhart?" he asked in a clipped, authoritative voice.

"Yes?"

"My name is Inspector Roland Finch. I would like to ask you some questions regarding Lois Donoghue. Could you follow me to Mr. Gilmartin's study please?"

Giles fixed me a worried glance but nodded to Inspector Finch.

"If you could wait in the front room, I'll send for you next," Finch then said to me.

I waited until both canines had gone to the study and quickly ran up to the bathroom. I washed myself at the sink and smeared some toothpaste into my mouth, hoping to mask any lingering scents.

I returned to the front room and sat in a wicker chair by the fireplace. I observed that the house staff had cleaned the room thoroughly, no doubt in anticipation for the visit by the police. The scent of lavender filled my nose, and I looked up to see Elizabeth Gilmartin standing in the doorway.

The Collie's face was fraught with anxiety. She glanced over her shoulders before hurrying into the room.

"Have they found her?" I asked.

"A local Lion found her body at the bottom of the drop. She fell apparently. We're being questioned one by one to determine what happened," Elizabeth explained.

I remember she was breathing heavily, and her eyes were wide with fear. Checking that no one was at the doorway, she walked over to me and pushed her muzzle right into my face.

"Listen. On pain of death, you are not to mention any details about our party to the police. Do you understand me, little Fox?" she growled.

I could smell alcohol on her breath. I swallowed and nodded. Elizabeth backed away and took a seat opposite me. I tried to avoid eye contact with her.

Inspector Finch reappeared a minute later and led me to the study.

Like the rest of the house, it was a large and airy room with a window overlooking the garden. Finch stood behind Denys' desk and gestured for me to sit opposite. He began by explaining the discovery of Lois' body. His face was deadpan yet his green eyes bore right into me as if they were searching for any hint of guilt.

"When did you last see Miss Donoghue?" he asked.

I stated that Giles and I had been talking in the garden when Lois had appeared. Giles had stopped her from falling and took her back inside. I repeated his claim that he'd put her to bed, but she had somehow slipped away.

"There was a bottle of whisky on the grass near to where she fell from," Finch explained.

"It's possible that she was intoxicated, wandered out of the house, and fell by accident. However, according to Mrs. Blythe, Miss Donoghue was shouting at someone in the garden."

"I see," I replied.

"Apparently, she had been quarreling with Hugo and Giles. You don't know about the nature of their friendships. Could they have potentially harmed her?"

"I know that Hugo and Lois were mated, but I didn't speak to either of them much. Giles was not fond of her, but he's not the sort of canine to wish ill on anyone," I replied carefully.

Finch wrote something down in his notebook.

"Did she seem depressed or insane? Would she have wanted to take her own life?"

"She struck me as quite a character, but I'm not sure if she was depressed," I claimed.

A vision of her intense black eyes flashed before my mind. Beads of sweat broke out on my muzzle, and my heart pounded unpleasantly in my chest.

"What is your connection to the Gilmartins?" Finch continued.

I replied truthfully that I'd met Hugo, Giles, and Lois at the social club. Wanting to get away from my office, I'd taken up their offer to spend the weekend at the Gilmartin's ranch. Something close to a smile spread across Finch's muzzle as if he had found something significant.

"This gathering that took place last night. What exactly went on? Were narcotics and alcohol consumed by the guests?"

Heeding Elizabeth's threat, I claimed I had not seen much as the atmosphere, had been too loud for my liking. I'd spent most of the night outside. Not mentioning the shisha, I told him that alcohol was drunk, but no drugs were taken. I was aware of Finch's pen scratching ominously against his notebook as I spoke.

The Ridgeback gave me a scrutinizing look as I finished. Slowly, he had reached into his pocket and pulled out a small glass bottle.

"Do you recognize this?" Finch asked as he slid the bottle across the desk.

I'd picked it up and examined it closely. It contained a white powdery substance.

"I found it in her suitcase. Were you aware that Miss Donoghue was taking this?"

"No," I replied firmly, "this is the first time I've seen it".

Although it explains a lot, I'd thought to myself.

"Very well. I'll let you go for now, but I have the address of your office, and I'll be in contact with you. Are you likely to be leaving the country any time soon?"

"No," I replied, although in my head, I was still formulating my plan to get a new post.

Finch had then gestured for me to leave before calling Elizabeth into the office.

I made my way up to my room and pressed my ear to the floor. I'd worked out that the office lay directly below my room, and I was intrigued to hear what Elizabeth had to say.

"What were your thoughts on Miss Donoghue?"

"Honestly? I could not stand that Cougar. She was an urchin from the backstreets of New York who had no business associating with furs like us. She formed a relationship with Hugo so she could help herself to his money. I think she used to thieve out of my bedroom! The last time she came here, my diamond ring went missing."

Elizabeth had ranted for another five minutes before Finch interrupted her.

"So you would have been happy to see some harm come to her?"

"*Certainly not! I disliked the girl, but that's a ghastly thing to wish on someone.*"

I'd suppressed a snort at the irony of her statement.

I listened to Major Norton, Dianne, and Denys' interrogations. They all claimed to be equally clueless as to what had happened. Once Finch had finished his questioning, I packed my suitcase and made my way downstairs.

I was waiting outside for Giles to appear when I noticed Hugo standing on the veranda, smoking a cigar.

"I'm sorry for your loss," I said apologetically.

The fox shrugged. "I think it was the only way out for her," he'd mused, puffing on his cigar.

"What do you mean?"

"She wasn't happy. I'm not surprised it came to an end that way," Hugo said.

He gazed impassively down the garden to the spot where Lois had fallen.

I felt rather unnerved. The drippy Hugo that had been braying with laughter the day before had vanished.

To this day, I cannot decide if he was in shock at Lois' death or simply did not care.

I made my way down to the lawn and turned to see Major Norton gazing at me through the study window with narrowed eyes. There was something in his expression which suggested he wanted to stop me from leaving. I turned my back and pretended not to have seen him, but I could feel his eyes boring into the back of my head.

I was grateful when Giles appeared at the front door and beckoned me to the car. I climbed in with my suitcase.

"Finch is going to question me again. He reckons Lois' death was accidental, but I was the last person who saw her alive. I'm named as a fur of interest in this case," he'd explained. "Look, what I said about Lois was true. I had no idea where she had gone when I tried to check on her," he added. His blue eyes were wide with concern.

"It's alright. I believe you," I replied firmly.

Giles forced a smile, and we drove off together. I was glad to get away from the ranch and vowed not to run into Hugo or the Gilmartins again. Once we reached the bottom of the valley, Giles reached over and clasped my paw reassuringly in his.

I continued my work at the office, listening to the wireless as the war grew worse. Much of Europe had been taken, and the conflict was spilling into North Africa. I spent my nights at Giles' house which was a couple of streets over. He continued his work as a pilot, disappearing off for a few days each week while I tried to contact my superiors.

Finch came to the house and questioned Giles again but seemed satisfied that the Wolf's story was legitimate. He left us alone after that.

Two days later, I got a call from Finch explaining that one of the house staff had been taken into custody. He had been caught with Lois' pearls in his pocket. This particular Lion had also been accused of violently assaulting and mugging someone in Nyeri before working at the Gilmartin's place. Finch explained that if anyone had pushed her, it must have been him.

The case was closed.

That same night, I received a new posting in Cape Town and convinced Giles to come with me. We packed our belongings into his car and drove south.

My new office in Cape Town was an improvement on the stuffy, box-like room I'd had to put up with in Nyeri.

I was also given a spacious, modern apartment on the seafront that was delightfully fitted with art deco paintings and furniture. The bedroom window offered an unbroken view over the white-sanded beach and the sparkling blue ocean beyond. Giles moved in and immediately declared that he loved the place.

I settled into my new job with renewed enthusiasm. My secretary was a cheerful Leopard who never failed to greet me in the morning and say good night when she went home.

I listened to the occasional newsflash on the wireless as I worked. Britain had thwarted an invasion and claimed a victory in North Africa. I was also surprised to hear that America had entered the war.

Unlike Britain, South Africa was not subjected to food rationing. Giles and I would head out for a meal together before drinking at the bars and dance halls near the quayside.

When the weather was fine, we would walk along the sand as the blazing red sun set over the water. We'd brush our muzzles and swish our tails if the beach was empty. Other evenings, we went home and made love on the bed, not bothering to close the curtains. No one could see into the apartment, and I'd gaze up at his blue eyes as they reflected the sunset through the window.

Giles made one trip back to Kenya to retrieve his Tiger Moth. He maintained it at an airfield just outside the city, and we continued our flying excursions every other weekend. I'll never forget a sunset flight we took one evening near Table Mountain. I marveled as the night sky turned a curious yet impressive shade of purple and the stars appeared one by one.

I felt a giddy sense of happiness and freedom. I'd gotten away from a dull posting and could spend my free time with the canine I loved.

I wish I could end the tale there, but I can't.

There's a mantra that says the universe has a funny way of rebalancing itself. I guess that was what happened.

The bliss was shattered when a set of call-up papers arrived on my desk one afternoon. They had been mailed personally by Major Norton who had traced me to my new office.

As British subjects, Giles and I were to be recruited into the King's African Rifles to join in the efforts at retaking mainland Europe.

With my background, I was quickly promoted to officer rank and placed in charge of a small regiment of furs. Giles was taken in by the air force when it was discovered that he had a pilot's license. He promised that we would be back together again.

So, here we are.

Giles is now flying sorties over Belgium and Holland, towing gliders of furs to be dropped into battle. We write to each other as often as we can, although we can say very little.

I'm about to lead my furs into a muddied battle in Italy. I've managed to load my revolver, and I'm sure my command to advance will be given at any minute.

I feel the same fear that had gripped me when Lois had returned to the garden.

I had been sitting in the moonlight, feeling frustrated that Giles was away taking care of Lois. I looked up and saw to my horror that she was storming down the lawn toward me. A bottle of whisky was clasped in her paw. Her eyes were narrowed with revulsion. She hissed through gritted teeth before shouting that Giles and I were disgusting, depraved individuals. She had seen us kissing. Her senses were clouded with alcohol, and her eyes became crazed. I felt terrified that someone would hear us and gestured with my paws for her to calm down. This only made the situation worse. She shrieked and beat her paws against my chest, causing the whisky bottle to fall to the ground. She began ranting that everyone would find out, and I'd burn in Hell. I grabbed hold of her, trying to stop the shouting, but she kept punching and scratching. I pushed her away, and she fell, giving a small scream as she disappeared into the darkness.

I stood still. Completely frozen in shock.

My mind could not comprehend what had just happened. I peered over the edge, but it was too dark to see anything.

I realized with a sickening sense of dread that she must have fallen all the way to the bottom. She was either dead or seriously injured.

I knew I should tell someone immediately, but I did not.

When Inspector Finch asked me what I knew, I played dumb.

My initial reaction of horror turned to relief once we had left Kenya. I no longer had Lois to interfere with Giles and me.

Here comes the command. I'm about to charge into a bloody fray with my regiment. The enemy are retreating, but I pray I come out in one piece.

I got what I'd wanted after I left Kenya. Giles and I were free. I feel conflicted: part of me wishes I never went to that party and done such a horrible thing, but then I'd have never met Giles.

Call me selfish, but if given the choice I'd rather survive the war and live with the guilt so I can see him again.

CLICK
T. THOMAS ABERNATHY

Jack pressed his back against the stainless steel door of the small restroom stall. His heartbeat was pounding in his ears loudly, almost drowning out the buzzing drone of the harsh fluorescent lights overhead. He slowly reached out his hand, and steadied himself against the cool tiled wall. As far as hiding places go, this wasn't the best in the world. He knew that. Someone could come in at any minute, but he didn't have anywhere else to go. He needed to get away.

click

The handle turned, and the door to the restroom swung open. Jack slid away from the stall door as a pair of work boots shuffled heavily over to the urinal. He heard the sound of a zipper, and then a grunt of relief as this intruder began to relieve himself. Jack stood perfectly still, almost not breathing, as if maybe the thin steel walls would completely hide his being there. After what seemed like an eternity, he heard a flush, and the work boots shuffled back out the door. He let out a shuddered sigh, and quickly unbolted the stall door. He crossed the tiny restroom, and pushed the small button on the door that would bar any further interlopers to this small sanctuary.

click

He sank to the grimy, stained floor, his back against the door. *Get a hold of yourself, Jack,* He thought to himself. *Nobody noticed. Nobody will even notice you're gone if you go back now.* But he couldn't; he knew he couldn't. Not in a state like this. No matter how cool he played it, they would know. That was the thing about working with those animals—they could smell it. Call it anxiety, fear, whatever you'd like. They could smell it coming from across the room.

click

He jumped at the sound. An automatic air freshener sprayed a cloud of what was supposed to be flowers across the room. Chemical flowers that barely masked the stink of days-old urine. *And now you're sitting in it*, he thought sarcastically to himself. He'd never been forced to work with the beasts before. Not that he'd ever call them beasts whenever they were in the same room, no. To their faces, when they were in the same room, they were Mark, Dan, or Bill. But behind closed doors, it was a different story. Most people accepted these beasts into society, were even friendly toward them. Why couldn't they see? They were different. Strange. Dangerous.

Emma always agreed with him. They'd crack jokes about the bears and wolves that came to the bank where they'd both worked. Once, he was sure that a middle-aged vixen overheard them joking. He remembered glancing her way. She had met his eyes for just a moment, and he was sure that he saw a spark of anger, or was it hatred in her gaze? It didn't matter to him. After that fleeting glance, her eyes filled with sadness, and she lowered her gaze to the floor. *Good*, he thought to himself, *At least this one knows her place*. He didn't give her a second thought after that. To be fair though, he was distracted that day. That was the same day that Emma told him to wait in the parking lot for her after work. She'd told him that there was something important that she wanted to tell him.

He'd waited for what seemed like an eternity, nervously playing with a pen someone had absentmindedly dropped. He rolled it between his hands, stopping every few moments to press the nub on the end in and out rapidly.

click
click click

"Pregnant." he said the word out loud. His voice sounded strained, almost unfamiliar. He shifted his gaze around the still restroom. Sink. Mirror. Toilet stall. Urinal. Nobody there.

Nobody who could have heard, but it still unsettled him. He wondered how long he'd been gone. He stuffed his hand down into his pocket, and pulled out his phone. He was planning on checking the time, but something stopped him. His finger hovered just above the power button, but wouldn't go lower. He looked at the blank screen, at his reflection in the black glass. *What the fuck, Jack. Just turn on the phone.*

"Pregnant," he said aloud again. This time though, there was anger in his voice. He thought about how careful he'd been. How careful they had been. But, here he was. Working a second job to support this child. An overnight job. A fucking manual labor job. A job for the lowest of the low, the animals. And they were everywhere here. Tigers, otters, lizards. A whole goddamn menagerie. Sure, there may have been a few other humans like him, but in this place, humans were clearly the minority. Even his "supervisor" was an animal. A black bear, his shoulders huge from moving the crates full of who knows what across the warehouse floor all night. On his first shift, Jack was speechless, simmering angrily as the bear (who called itself Robert) walked him through basic safety procedures, and showed him how to use the timecard punch machine. The bear fumbled slightly, picking up the card, and Jack tried not to roll his eyes. "Robert" hadn't noticed. "So, once you have your card, you slide it into the machine like this, and—"

click

Timecard. Time. how long had he been in here? He tried to look at his phone again, but felt the same hesitation as before. Jack growled with frustration at himself, and tossed the phone away. It skidded across the floor, coming to rest underneath the sink. He wanted nothing more than to be out of there. Out of that tiny bathroom, and out of the building. He thought of Emma. At that moment, she was probably asleep. There was no way that she knew that her man, the father of her child, was cowering in a filthy bathroom because he was too scared to face his coworkers. Jack felt his face flush with a mixture of embarrassment and anger. *It's not my fault*, he thought. He stood slowly, and caught his own reflection in the grimy mirror hanging over the sink. He said it again, out loud this time.

"It's not my fault! None of this is my fault! It's all her!" He stopped, shocked at what came out of his own mouth. It was her. That fucking animal. That fucking deer.

click

The air freshener again. What did that mean? That 10 minutes had passed? 30 minutes? It didn't matter. No amount of flower smell was going to cover this up, and Jack knew it. But it was not his fault he was in here. It was the doe. It was her fault that Jack couldn't get on with this awful job, and go home to Emma. He closed his eyes to picture Emma sleeping again, but now all he could see was that damn animal.

It started his first week on the job. He was new on the warehouse floor, sure, but it didn't take a rocket scientist to load boxes into a truck. He was wheeling a dolly that was loaded down with boxes toward the back of the warehouse, completely absorbed in his own thoughts. Suddenly, a figure cantered by, smashing into the dolly, and knocking the boxes to the floor.

"Watch where you're going!" he shouted. He looked down at the figure that had fallen to the floor, and was met with a pair of bright blue eyes on the verge of tears.

"I...I'm sorry, sir!" the voice that came back was small and quivering. Jack tore his gaze away from those piercing eyes, and sized up his assailant. She was a small doe, covered in a soft, almost velvety cream-colored fur. Jack snorted dismissively.

"Whatever. Don't cry on me, just pick this stuff up." He stepped back from the dolly, and gave her a small "after you" gesture. She shakily got to her feet, and Jack caught himself sizing her up. His eyes slid slowly down her long, shapely neck and down to the small curve of her breasts as she started reloading the cart. He felt a twitch coming from his pants. Emma was always asleep when he got home, and they didn't have the time to...it had been awhile since they —No. He shook his head to try and get rid of those thoughts, and addressed the doe, "I've got the rest of this. You're moving too slowly anyways. Get out of here." The doe tilted her muzzle down in shame, and walked away without saying another word.

A loud banging on the restroom door snapped Jack back to reality. From the world outside he heard a muffled voice saying, "Come on, man, I've got to take a leak!" He panicked. "Get out of here, man! It's occupied!" he shouted back. The voice outside grumbled, but he couldn't make out what it said. His mind raced. He had definitely been in there too long. Consequences or not, he needed to get out of there. He steadied himself, and walked toward the door of the bathroom. He reached out to open the door, but as soon as his hand touched the handle, he heard a soft buzz. A text message. His phone. He turned, and looked back toward the sink. The small black box was still there. He wanted to just turn and leave. He wanted to run, but...what if that was Emma? What if something was wrong?

Things at home were growing steadily more stressful. Sure, whenever Emma asked what was going on, he would just say he was tired, or make up some other excuse. In his mind though, he knew why. He couldn't get that doe out of his head. He would lay down to go to sleep, and all he could see were those incredible blue eyes. At the bank, every animal that he saw made him think back to those soft curves. It was the worst at this warehouse. He would catch himself glancing around the room, trying to catch a glimpse of her. He didn't know which was worse: the looking, or what happened whenever he finally was able to spot her. He hated the way his eyes traced her legs, following their smooth and slender form up her back to her ass. He hated the way it made him feel.

He'd try to rationalize it. *Come on Jack, she's just an animal, and you're lonely.* It never stopped him though. He couldn't get her out of his head. He would think about her muzzle wrapping itself around his hard member, fitting him perfectly as he pushed in and out while he looked down into her blue eyes...

Maybe that's why I did it.

He remembered earlier that night. He and Emma had fought before he left the house. It was a stupid argument; he couldn't even remember what it was about. She wanted him to stay, and work things out, but he left anyway. He sped to the warehouse, letting his mind wander, as it did so often these last few weeks, to thoughts of the doe. He imagined what it would be like to press himself naked against her soft, furry body, relishing the feel of her against his cock before he pushed it into her. He was still dwelling on the fantasy as he made his way to his workstation.

He spotted her immediately when he walked in. His fantasy was working right next to his area. She'd never been this close before. At least, not since the first time that she knocked off those boxes. She noticed him approaching, and gave him a small nod and a polite smile before returning to her work. Jack tried to ignore her. He threw himself into his work, trying so hard not to think about all of the things he wanted to do with her. To her. *Damn, she smells good.* His hands were clammy. He was nervous, and he could tell that the doe was noticing. She kept giving him curious glances as he loaded and unloaded his boxes. Even when he wasn't looking, he could feel them. *I have to do something about this.* He felt his phone go off in his pocket, and breathed a sigh of relief. Finally, a distraction. He pulled out the phone, and opened it up to a text from Emma.

"Sorry about tonight. Can we talk about it when you get home? I love you."

Jack started to type a reply, and then deleted it. He needed time to clear his head. He started to turn the phone off, then he noticed something out of the corner of his eye. The doe's back was turned. He quickly closed out of his messenger app, and tapped on the screen to open the camera. Almost in a trance, he aimed the camera at the doe, getting a perfect view of the smooth curvature of her ass. His finger twitched.

click

The sound rang out above the usual din of the warehouse. *Fuck.* He looked up. The doe had turned, and was looking at him. Her blue eyes weren't questioning at all. They were angry. Jack felt his face flush. He stuffed the phone in his pocket, and ran off the main floor into the men's restroom. It was the only place that she couldn't follow.

But that wasn't true. He stared down at the phone on the floor, and slowly picked it up. She was there in his mind, and wasn't that just the same as her being there? He pressed the power button on the phone. The screen came to life, displaying the last thing he'd done. The picture. He stared at it. He stared at the smooth, cream colored fur on her legs, the outline of her backside in her shorts, and the soft little puff of a tail that poked out under her t-shirt. He felt his pants grow tighter as he grew hard.

Why not?

He looked over to check the door. It was definitely locked. He reached down with one hand, and slowly unzipped his pants. His erection sprang out, fully hard. He kept his gaze focused on the picture as he gave his member a firm squeeze. It had been so long...it felt so good. He imagined pushing her against the sink of the restroom, and bending her over. He envisioned himself pulling down her shorts, and rubbing his erection against the soft fur of her tail. He sighed with pleasure at the thought, and slowly began stroking himself.

In his mind, he reached around the doe, gently squeezing one of her soft, supple breasts. He wondered what her small, quivering voice would sound like as it moaned his name. His breathing quickened, and he let out a small groan of pleasure. He let himself get lost in the fantasy of placing his hand on her furred back, and bending her over further so he could enter her. He would slide himself in gently, letting her get used to the feeling of having a real man, a human, inside of her. He stroked himself faster and faster, intoxicating himself with her imaginary scent.

In his mind, he picked up speed, thrusting into her harder, and harder. She moaned with pleasure, sliding and bucking her hips back to fit even more of him inside of her. Jack grunted. He was close now, and he pumped himself faster and faster as his orgasm approached like an oncoming train.

In his fantasy, he pulled out of the doe and spun her around. He pushed her down onto her knees, and began thrusting himself into her muzzle. She tried to pull away, but he held on to the back of her head, his fingers intertwining with her fur. He gave a last thrust, and came into her mouth, emptying his week's' worth of stored cum down her throat. As this last thought ran through his mind, he surrendered to his orgasm. He let out a low moan, closed his eyes, and came hard. His spunk flew onto the mirror and the sink counter of the restroom. He was dead to the world, lost in his fantasy, completely unaware.

Completely unaware of the sound of a manager's key sliding into the keyhole of the restroom door. Unaware of the handle turning, threatening to unleash his sin on the world. The door to the restroom popped open.

click

In his haze, Jack barely registered the door opening. It was only when he heard a soft clear voice that he turned his head.

"That's the guy!"

Standing in the doorway was Robert, the bear manager. Peeking out from behind his large, furred shoulders was a pair of bright blue eyes. It was her, the doe. Even after what he had just done, Jack felt his cock twitch at the sight of her. The bear surveyed the room, his eyes landing on the cum splattered all over the sink.

"Jesus Christ." His voice was like gravel. He picked Jack's phone up off of the floor. The screen still showed the picture. The evidence. The bear turned to the doe.

"Well, Robin, it looks like you were right. This pervert was taking pictures of you." Jack could hear the anger in his voice. He tried to stand, and defend himself.

"I-I'm sorry, I didn't mean to—"

Out of nowhere, the bear's foot connected with his chest, sending Jack back down to the floor, and knocking the wind out of him.

"You get up when I say you can, human." Jack groaned, and tried to curl up into a ball. The foot came again, pressing down on his chest. The bear's voice came again, like ice.

"Don't. Fucking. Move."

Jack heard a giggle. The doe moved closer, peering down at him.

"Damn, Robert...the guy's still hard." She took a step back, and nuzzled against the bear's large, sinewy arm. "What are you going to do to him, babe?"

The bear looked angrily at Jack. "Do you have any ideas?"

"Pick him up."

Jack started to protest, but the bear leaned down and pulled him into a standing position. Jack felt himself being pressed forcefully against the tile wall. Jack felt his raging erection subside as the doe picked up his phone, looking at the screen.

"Hmm...one missed message. Who could this be?" She made a few deft gestures. Jack yelled out in anger.

"Hey! That's my personal—" He was cut short by a smack across his face. The doe glared at him.

"You don't get to say what's personal to anyone." She looked back down at the phone. "I miss you, baby, and I love you." She laughed. "Aww. That's sweet. Does this Becca know what you've been up to behind her back? Maybe I'll let her know."

Jack struggled violently against the strong paw that was pinning him to the wall. How could these fucking animals make him feel so helpless? His voice came out strained, and weaker than he'd hoped.

"No, don't...please…"

They both laughed this time. The bear shook his head.

"He's not so confident when his bitch is involved, is he?" Another laugh.

"I'll make you both regret this. You stupid animals, you have no idea who you're fucking with!" They went quiet. After a moment, the doe responded.

"You think you're better than us?" Jack went silent, and then yelled out when a burst of pain ripped through his chest.

The bear had extended his claws. Jack felt a slow trickle of warmth roll down his chest. Blood.

"Answer the lady, human. Do you think you're better than us?"

"No, I—"

"Don't listen to him, Robert. He's just going to say what we want to hear." The doe spit at him. "Racist bastard." Jack noticed a gleam appear in her eyes. "Hey, babe...put him in the stall."

The bear gladly complied, and roughly pushed Jack into the stall. He could feel the cold metal again, but this time, it was against his bare ass. The doe whispered something to the bear, and he burst out laughing.

"Go for it, babe." The bear moved around behind Jack, easily pinning his arms with one paw. The other moved to Jack's throat. Jack felt the bear's claws graze lazily over his jugular. The bear's breath was hot and humid on his neck as he growled.

"Try something, human, and it'll be the last thing you do." Jack stiffened. The doe moved close to him, staring him in the eyes. She leaned in, and Jack shuddered as he felt her soft tongue lick his neck. She knelt down in front of him, and Jack could feel her warm breath on his exposed cock. It twitched involuntarily.

"N-no, please don't, I—" The bear cut him off with another growl and a soft squeeze to his throat. The doe moved in closer, and wrapped her muzzle around Jack's cock. It throbbed, and slowly, unwillingly sprang to life. Jack let out an involuntary moan as her lips worked up and down his shaft. He felt his back arch into the bear's warm fur as his body tried to force his erection more into the doe. He closed his eyes. *Maybe this won't be so bad.* The doe's mouth slid all the way down, taking him all the way inside. It felt so good, better than he'd ever imagined.

click

Jack's eyes snapped open, and looked down in horror as the doe took another selfie.

click

The doe stood, and walked over to the sink to rinse her mouth out. She glared at him.

"Disgusting." Jack looked at her in disbelief. "Keep holding him, Robert." She slowly sauntered back over to them both, Jack's phone in her hand. She pulled up the pictures she had just taken, and packaged them into a text message. Jack realized what was about to happen.

"Oh, god, no. Please don't...no. I'll do whatever you want!" The doe's gaze turned cold.

"Sent. Let's see what 'Becca' thinks of that." Both animals laughed. They were laughing at him. Jack tried to break free of the bear's grip. He didn't care anymore. Not about the claws, not about the consequences. All he could see was red.

"Let me go, you motherfucker! I'll kill you! I'll kill you both! I won't—"

He was cut off by the bear effortlessly picking him up by the waist. His screams of anger turned to panic. The bear roughly forced him up next to the stall door, pinning him again between the door and the cold metal wall. They both were laughing again. The bear turned his head.

"Babe, would you like to do the honors?"

Another laugh from the doe. "Gladly, love." Jack was confused. What were they going to do to him, what would they—

His thoughts were interrupted at the doe forcefully pried open his jaw, and stuffed his phone in his mouth. Then, there was nothing but white-hot pain. The doe smiled as she slammed the stall door on his erect member. Jack let out a primal scream that was stifled by the electronic device in his mouth. The doe slammed the door again. And again. She kept on until nothing remained but a tattered, frayed, and bleeding lump of skin and tendon. Jack's vision blurred from the pain, and he felt himself slipping into unconsciousness. The bear dropped him. Jack hit the floor facedown. His jaw slammed into the floor, and then through his phone. He felt his teeth shatter. As the world faded to black, he heard a tearing sound as the bear ripped apart his shirt.

"Towel, love? You've got some human blood on you." The animals laughed again, and made their way to the door.

"Should we call someone about the mess?"

"Nah, leave it."

The doe reached for the light switch, and didn't look back. The last thing Jack heard as the dark void claimed him was the sound of the buzzing fluorescent lights finally being extinguished.

click

Fun at the Mall
Teiran

The fox browsed through the little shop's aisles, picking his way through the various leather contraptions and kinky toys. A slim, feminine-looking dog bounced up to him, "Hey Wildfire, you going to pick anything out for me today?"

The fox grinned at the little dog. "Yeah right, Jimmy, you couldn't handle me."

The dog grinned up at him. "Oh come on, you'd be surprised what I can take, fox."

Michael "Wildfire" Fox chuckled as he fingered a ball gag and raised an eyebrow at the dog. "Oh, trust me doggy. I'd break you." The fox grinned, "And so, so many of the guys would hate me for that." The dog just grinned at him.

Jimmy was the clerk at "Yiff R Us," the sex shop in the Haden View mall. Its entrance was around a corner, as far off the main hallway as you could get, so it was hidden from the rest of the mall. It was one of the mall's largest stores, and each day, hundreds of people would walk casually down the hallways of the mall, look around them to see if anyone was watching them, and then casually skirt their way down the little side hallway that led to the store. Jimmy's boss was quite understanding about people's need for privacy; for a while he'd even used Toys-R-Us bags, at least until the owners of the Toys-R-Us on the other side of the mall found out. Jimmy had personally tried every single thing they sold, either with his boyfriend or one of the customers themselves. The little dog was really popular with the crowd of gays who hung around the mall. So for that matter was Wildfire. Though they flirted shamelessly with each other, the fox and dog had almost nothing in common, except for their love of dick, of course.

Wildfire was almost a foot taller than Jimmy, and easily twice as large. Jimmy was an eternally slim and lean type of guy, able to break the hearts of any man who came through his door and wear a dress better than most women could. While Jimmy blurred the gender lines like nobody's business, Wildfire was all male. He was muscular, strong, and built like tank. His slim fox body was covered in muscle, mostly because he worked out every day at the gym. Of course, because he was a fox, Wildfire's body didn't really show his strength, but that only served to make him fast as well as strong. At one time, there had been some debate about whether the fox was all talk or not, but no one was willing to say anything after he came to the defense of two young wolves that a couple of gay bashers decided would be easy targets. They'd gone home in ambulances, and no one had ever messed with Wildfire again. At least, not like that. More than a few of the guys who frequented the Haden View mall had been drawn to him because of the incident, intrigued by the danger. If there was one thing classically "fox" about Wildfire, it was his sex drive.

Wildfire grinned as a group of cute twinks whistled at him as he left Yiff R Us. He twirled the small bag of new toys he'd bought with a grin. A ball gag, a new pair of handcuffs, and something Jimmy had invented, a collapsible spreader bar. "Oh lord, Jimmy," the fox whispered as he fingered the spreader bar through the bag. "What will you come up with next?" The fox chuckled and wandered his way through the mall. As he walked, guys would smile and wave, the adventurous and brave ones whistling or brushing up against him for a quick grope. Wildfire just grinned as he shopped, not looking for anything in particular, just wasting time. Eventually, he found himself near the little hallway that led to the restrooms near the Billiards' department store on the ground floor. The fox grinned and swished his tail, heading down the hallway.

Wildfire peered around the restroom as he opened the door. The stalls all stood empty and the only other guy there was a wolf washing his paws. The gray-furred wolf looked up at him, and Wildfire flashed him a grin as he headed for the last stall. The wolf was tall, fairly buff, and quite cute. The fox chuckled a little to himself, setting the bag from Yiff R Us on the ground and unbuckling his belt. The stall was like every other stall in malls across the world, except for the fact that it had a real lid on the toilet. Wildfire suspected that was Jimmy's handiwork. The dog had once complained that public restrooms didn't have any proper place to get bent over. The fox grinned and turned his ears backwards to listen as the wolf finished drying his paws and took a few steps toward him, away from the door. Wildfire grinned and swished his tail from side to side, unbuckling his pants and letting them slide down the curve of his rump as he pretended to use the restroom. Wildfire grinned as the wolf growled softly and moved closer. That move always worked on the big canines. You swished your tail and flashed a little rump, and then they always wanted a piece. The wolf padded up behind the fox, a paw reaching out and rubbing the back of the fox's jeans, pushing them down even more as the wolf said in a gruff voice, "Hey fox, you looking for a good time?"

Wildfire licked his lips and grinned, "Oh, and what if I am, huh?" The fox flashed a grin over his shoulder, his tail flicking back and forth, the tip across the wolf's chest.

The wolf grinned and squeezed Wildfire rump. "Well then, fox, I'm gonna give you one." Wildfire grinned and let go of his pants, letting them fall down around his feet. The wolf shoved a paw in his pocket, pulling out some lube as he unbuckled his pants and pulled out his cock, which was already hard as a rock. Wildfire growled softly when he saw the wolf's cock. He was well hung, nearly eight inches long, and thick. Wildfire grinned wide and gripped the railings of the stall tight as the wolf rubbed the tip of his lubed cock under his tail, his paws gripping Wildfire's hips as he kicked the stall door closed behind him. This was going to be a great ride.

The wolf and fox moaned together as the wolf's cock pushed into Wildfire, stretching his hole open slowly. The wolf growled into the fox's fur as he pushed forward, and Wildfire kept groaning in pleasure as the fat wolf cock sunk into him. "Oooh wolfie..." Wildfire's tail flicked back and forth against the wolf's leg and he arched his back, squeezing down on the wolf's cock as it slid out. "You're a real big bad wolf..."

The wolf chuckled and put an arm around the fox's chest. "Oh, am I? You like my big cock inside you fox, don't you?" Wildfire growled in pleasure, his eyes closed as the wolf thrust into him. He hadn't had a male like this inside him in ages. The wolf's cock was thick and long, stretching him open wide and making his whole body tingle as the stranger humped him hard and fast. The wolf's well-lubed cock pounded into the fox's hole as Wildfire growled loudly and moaned in pleasure, his tail hole clenching and flexing around the wolf's cock. The wolf damn sure knew what he was doing. He thrust in hard and quick, pulled out slow, making sure his cock rubbed against all the fox's sweet spots, the fat tip banging into Wildfire's prostate with each hard thrust.

Wildfire bit his lip and whimpered as the wolf's paw wrapped around his hard cock and gave it a stroke. "Oh yeah, you like this don't you fox? You're a good little faggot..." The wolf trailed off as he nibbled the back of Wildfire's neck, his paw stroking the fox's cock. "You're just like every other fox; you just can't resist having a cock shoved up in you." Wildfire's eyes opened a bit and he glared at the wall in front of him. He let the comment slide because he didn't want things to end now. The wolf was just too hot and too good at fucking. Wildfire closed his eyes and let his thoughts drift back into the pleasure of the wolf's thrusts. The wolf kept a steady hard rhythm, varying the way his paw stroked at the fox's cock as his cock thrust deep inside him. The wolf nibbled Wildfire's ear as he said, "All you foxes are the same. A real guy like me comes along, and you flick your tails and drop your pants without ever even being asked. But you're especially good, faggot." The wolf growled and thrust his cock in hard to emphasize his words, "You've got the sweetest ass I've ever had, faggot..."

The fox gave the wolf humping him an absolutely evil glare, "You know, you're just as much a 'faggot' as I am...and stop calling me that or get out of me." The fox's words dripped with ire. Wildfire didn't like the way the wolf was acting. Humping a guy is all fine and dandy, but you don't trash them while you do it.

"Oh ho," the wolf chuckled, "no, I'm not fox." The big wolf's arms squeezed Wildfire's waist as he thrust faster, his growing knot teasing the fox's entrance. "You're the one with a cock in your ass; you're the faggot. But it's cool. I like faggot foxes like you; you'll let me fuck you anytime I want," the wolf chuckled softly, his paws rubbing Wildfire's chest. "You faggot foxes are the best cock warmers." The wolf laughed, and Wildfire set his jaw and spread his legs a bit.

Wildfire's ears flattened against his head. That was it. This wolf needed a serious lesson in humility. Wildfire eyed the pipes that connected the toilet to the wall and then his bag from Yiff R Us. An evil grin spread across the fox's face as the wolf kept humping him harder, pushing himself closer and closer to climax. Thanks to Jimmy, the fox was perfectly prepared to give the wolf his lesson right now.

Wildfire moaned loudly, pushing back against the wolf as he leaned over and slipped his paw into the bag. The wolf, concerned now only with how far he could get his cock into him, didn't even notice. Wildfire smirked as he leaned back up and twisted in the wolf's grip, an arm wrapping around his muscular neck as the fox brought him into a deep kiss. The wolf smiled a bit into the kiss, closing his eyes and thrusting hard. Wildfire acted in one fluid motion. He bent his knees, pulled the wolf forward and flipped him over his shoulder in one smooth motion, the wolf's cock roughly pulling out of his tail. Wildfire grinned with satisfaction as the wolf landed on the toilet spread-eagle, his legs straddling the bowl.

The wolf let out a mighty howl of pain, stunned by the fox's sudden attack, and that moment was all the time Wildfire needed. He grabbed the wolf's right paw and slapped the handcuffs he'd pulled from his bag around it. The wolf growled in sudden anger, but Wildfire's knee found a tender spot in his back as the fox grabbed his other paw. He pushed the wolf paws together, threading the handcuffs behind the metal pipes for the toilet and forcing the wolf's other wrist into the cuff. Wildfire grinned and let go of the wolf's paws, and the wolf howled in anger as he struggled with them, but he was securely handcuffed to the back of the toilet.

"Fuck you, you little faggot! I'm gonna…mmph!" The wolf's words ended in a muffled howl of anger as Wildfire rammed his new ball gag into his open muzzle, pulling the elastic band back behind his head.

"Oh, I doubt you'll be doing much of anything, Mister Real Man." Wildfire flashed the wolf an evil grin as he took a step back from him and held a small metal tube in both paws. "Except finding out the hard way what it's like to be a faggot." Wildfire pulled the ends of Jimmy's collapsing spreader bar apart, the metal rod lengthening with a menacing series of clicks as it expended. The wolf's eyes widened in horror, and he started to struggle hard, lashing out at Wildfire with his legs as the fox grabbed for his ankles. But Wildfire was stronger than he looked, and he pulled the wolf's pants and underwear off him and forced the wolf's hind paws into the leather straps on the ends of the spreader bar, forcing his legs open wide. Wildfire took a step back a bit to admire his handy work.

The gray wolf was handcuffed to the wall, bent over at the waist because of the toilet and his feet were held about four feet apart; making his tail hole easy to see despite his attempts to cover it with his tail, which was now firmly tucked between his legs. Wildfire grinned evilly, grabbed the wolf's lube out of his pants and stepped over the bar holding the struggling wolf's legs open. He leaned over the big wolf as his rubbed his hard cock between the wolf's furry cheeks. "Do you still think you're such hot stuff now, Mister Real Man? Huh?" The wolf's eyes stared at him, round as saucers as the wolf tried to pull away from him.

"Let me let you in on a little secret wolfie..." The fox rumbled as he rubbed the lube over his cock, his nose rubbing against the back of the wolf's neck as he struggled and growled, his muffled howls of anger making Wildfire only grin wider. "Being a man doesn't have anything to do with whether you let another guy fuck you. It's in how you act that makes you a man." The fox nipped the back of the wolf's neck, and the wolf's eyes widened, and he whimpered as Wildfire pressed his cock tip against the wolf's hole. "Now take this like a man, wolf..."

Wildfire's paws gripped the wolf's hips, and he ground his cock into him, pushing hard against the wolf's obviously virgin tail hole. The wolf howled in pain, but even muffed by the gag, it was loud. He clenched down, but Wildfire didn't pull back. "Relax, wolf, or it'll hurt even more," the fox whispered in his ear, and the wolf howled again. Wildfire gripped the scruff of his neck in a paw and growled, "Relax now, wolf!" The wolf froze up in fright, and he relaxed his tail hole, and the fox pushed in hard. Wildfire's dick stretched the wolf's sphincter open slowly, his cock sinking into the hot and very tight passage. The wolf moaned through the gag, half in pain and half in pleasure. Wildfire just growled in pleasure, sinking his cock deep into the wolf's ultra-tight ass and biting the back of the wolf's neck. The wolf howled and twisted in his bonds, shaking in pain and pleasure as the fox sunk his entire cock into his virgin tail hole, pulled back out and slammed back in again. The wolf whined loudly, trying to pull away from Wildfire as the fox huffed in pleasure. The wolf's ass was so tight he couldn't believe it. This big bad wolf was definitely a virgin; there was no other way his ass could be so tight.

"What's wrong, wolf? Not enjoying your first fuck?" Wildfire grinned as he pushed the wolf down and held him still, pounding his cock deep into the wolf's ass, his hips banging into the wolf's rump. The gray wolf howled through the gag, jerking at the handcuffs and throwing his head back as one of Wildfire's paws slipped around his waist and wrapped around his hard cock, eliciting a moan from the wolf. "Oh, I guess you are enjoying this, aren't you, wolf?" The wolf's eyes closed, and Wildfire just grinned and thrust faster, plowing his cock deep into the pinned wolf.

Wildfire settled into a steady, hard rhythm as he buggered the wolf, whose ears were pressed flat against his head. The wolf's eyes were shut tight, and his breathing was shallow as Wildfire mounted him hard, the wolf pressing himself flat against the toilet, trying to keep Wildfire's paws away from his cock, which was dripping pre as the fox fucked him. Wildfire smiled as he pulled the wolf's head back and began to nibble on his neck, making the wolf moan even louder, his tailhole flexing around the fox's invading cock. "Oooh yeah wolf...that's it, squeeze my cock..." Wildfire pinched the wolf's left nipple and nipped at his neck. "Squeeze my cock, and I'll make you cum, wolf." The wolf whined through the gag, pushing his hips back against the fox's thrusts. Wildfire grinned as the wolf opened his eyes and whined in pleasure, hanging his head in shame. Wildfire's paw ran across the wolf chest and up under his chin, lifting his muzzle up as Wildfire kept thrusting into his tailhole hard. "Come on wolf, take this like a real man, and admit you're enjoying yourself..."

Wildfire chuckled loudly as the wolf growled at him and tried to push him up off his back, but Wildfire wrapped an arm around the wolf's chest, his paw squeezing the wolf's cock hard. Holding the wolf's body tightly, he put all his strength into his thrusts. Wildfire grinned, feeling his growing knot barely pop out of the wolf's tail hole. He was so close to climax he could taste it. He gave the wolf's ass a few quick, hard thrusts with the full length of his cock and slammed his knot deep inside the wolf, locking them tighter. Wildfire grinned as the wolf's body twisted in his grasp as his growing knot popped in and back out of the wolf's tail hole. The wolf thrashed back and forth and howled as the fox's knot popped in and out of him with every thrust of his cock. His cock jumped in Wildfire's paw, and the fox grabbed the back of his neck in his muzzle as the wolf came hard. The wolf howled through his gag, his body shaking as his cum shot across the stall. Wildfire's back arched as his cock pulsed inside the wolf, pumping his fox cum deep inside the shaking wolf's body. Wildfire yipped in pleasure as the wolf continued to howl behind the gag, his body convulsing as the fox's seed flooded into his ass. The fox and wolf convulsed together for several long minutes, the fox's arms holding the wolf's chest, Wildfire's cock trapped deep inside the wolf's no longer virgin tail hole.

Wildfire panted hard, leaning onto the wolf's back. "Oooh lord..." he whispered softly, swiveling his hips and moving his cock inside the wolf's guts. The gray wolf whimpered and growled something, but the gag muffled his words. Wildfire pushed himself up onto his toes, his knot pulling at the wolf's tail hole, forcing him to raise his rump into the air. Wildfire grinned as he put his arms around the wolf and forced him to stand up. The wolf whimpered as Wildfire pulled him upright, the new position forcing his tail hole to tighten down even harder on the fox's hard cock. The fox's paws stroked the wolf's chest from behind, and Wildfire laid his paw on the ball gag. "Now I'm gonna pull this outta your muzzle wolf, but if you scream, I pull this—" the fox gave a little tug on his firmly tied knot, "out as well, and then you'll really have reason to scream. Got it?" The wolf's eyes widened in, and he nodded weakly. Wildfire pulled the ball gag out of the wolf mouth.

The wolf worked his jaw painfully and whispered, "Fucking fox...I'm gonna kill you for this." Wildfire grinned and put his arm around the wolf's neck and his other around his waist and gave him a good, hard squeeze. The wolf gasped and would have doubled over in pain if he'd been able to move. The fox was much stronger than he was, and his hug felt like a vise.

"I'd like to see you try it, wolf," Wildfire sneered. "I'd beat you so senseless you'd be begging me to fuck you. Now, what's your name, wolf?"

The wolf gasped for air as the fox released his grip slightly, "Kevin. Kevin James."

"Well, Kevin, I don't see what you're so upset about. You came in this stall all by yourself."

The wolf glared back at him, "Yeah, to fuck you!"

Wildfire grinned and ran his fingers across the wolf's still slightly hard cock. "And turnabout's fair play wolf." Kevin growled and tried to snap at Wildfire, but the wolf stopped the moment Wildfire's paw cupped his balls, his short claws touching the base of his cock. "Do play nice, wolfie. After all, we're gonna be here a few minutes." Wildfire moved his hips back and pulled on his trapped cock. Kevin moaned, and his tail tightened down around the fox's cock, and Wildfire chuckled.

Kevin glared back at him, "What are you laughing at, faggot?"

"You, wolf. You still don't get it, do you? You try and act all tough, like you're a real man because you don't let guys fuck you, when you enjoyed it just as much as any cock slut would."

Kevin growled and jerked on the handcuffs, "I'm not a cock slut! Now let me out of here so I can kick your fucking ass, you faggot fox!" The wolf thrashed back and forth for a minute, trying to bite the fox and jerking on the knot trapped inside of him, and Wildfire glared at him.

"That's it, wolf. I guess you haven't learned you're lesson quite yet." Wildfire grinned a he checked all the restraints holding the wolf in place. He tightened up the straps on the spreader bar a bit, and grinned. "Well now, wolfie, since it seems you haven't learned any humility yet, I guess I'm just gonna have to leave you here till you do."

Kevin's next words never left his muzzle. He just howled in pain and pleasure as Wildfire grabbed his waist in both paws and slowly pulled his knot out of the wolf's ass. The wolf's ring stretched open wide, and his body shook as the fox's knot popped out of him wetly, cum flooding out his ass and down his leg. Kevin panted as Wildfire took a step back, his hard cock bobbing up and down a bit, covered in white cum that he could feel sliding down his leg. "How does that sound, wolf? Say I leave you here a few hours, bound and gagged in the hottest anonymous sex spot in town, tailhole open for all to see, and come back when you've had some time to think and half the town has fucked you, hmmm?" Kevin's eyes went big as Wildfire's paw came up holding the gag. "How does that sound?"

Kevin tried to turn and bite the fox as he stepped forward, but Wildfire's other paw grabbed the back of his neck, and his fingers dug into the pressure point of the wolf's neck, making him gasp, muzzle open, as he went ridged with pain. Wildfire shoved the gag into his muzzle and pulled the band back around his head, making sure it was in just the right spot not to hurt the wolf's teeth any and so that the band wouldn't slip off. When he released the wolf neck, Kevin slumped forward and whimpered, mouthing the ball gag desperately. Kevin growled softly when it didn't budge at all, but the growl died when he heard the sound of a marker being uncapped. He looked back at the fox behind him, who was writing something on the stall door, which he propped open. Kevin's stomach turned into knots as he read what he'd written. "I hope you enjoy your afternoon wolf, cause believe me, I know a lot of the guys will enjoy you being here." Kevin swallowed nervously as the fox shoved the wolf's pants and shoes into the bag he had, pulled his own pants back up and set the bottle of lube on the toilet paper dispenser and gave him a big kiss on the lip, right over the ball gag. Kevin growled and rattled his binding, but the handcuffs and straps held, and the gag ensured nothing he said made sense.

Wildfire chuckled as he turned his back on the wolf, swishing his hips and flicking his tail back and forth, an evil grin on his face as he left the restroom, the wolf's growls and muffled howls following him out.

Galen padded his way into the restroom of the Haden View mall. The raccoon knew what kind of reputation the restroom had, and he always used it because a couple times, he'd been able to see a couple of guys fucking in the stalls. He'd never been brave enough to do anything, but he still liked to watch for just a little while. Galen watched as a particularly buff tiger came out of the last stall, tucking his still dripping cock back into his pants and grinning down at the smaller raccoon. Galen swallowed as the tiger passed him. The last stall door was propped open with the words, "This Slave is here for Punishment. Fuck as much as desired, but do not release. I will be back to collect him later. Thank you, His Master." Galen walked to the back of the restroom and peered in the stall.

In the stall was a dark gray wolf on his knees, handcuffed to the toilet with his legs spread open by a spreader bar. Trails of sticky cum ran down his legs, and he was panting for air, a big blue ball gag stuffed into his muzzle. The wolf's eyes met Galen's, and the raccoon just stood there for a long moment, wondering what he should do. But as the haze of pleasure left the wolf's eyes, he smiled despite the gag, and the wolf hauled himself back up across the toilet seat and lifted his tail, waiting. Galen licked his lips and glanced back at the door. Then, he undid his belt buckle and took a few steps toward the wolf that was grinning at him.

INTERLUDE

"Alright," the German shepherd said, "I get it. Let's just move on."

Zinc grinned at his partner's nakedness and licked the edge of his snout teasingly. "Oh, come on, I didn't think you were the bashful type."

Barba added, "I certainly don't mind seeing you like this either."

Derek thrust his paws firmly between his legs, hiding his firm erection and glaring at the other two. "That last story wasn't even sexy. It was just *wrong*."

Scooting his chair closer to Derek, Zinc pressed his paw under Derek's and squeezed the tip of the canid's cock, making him yelp in surprise. "Well, your dick disagrees, dear." Before the dog could force the tiger's paws away, Zinc bent at the waist and lowered his head onto Derek's cock until the tip pressed at the back of his throat. Derek tilted his head back and moaned in both ecstasy and embarrassment.

Barba chuckled. "I would typically tell you two to go get a room, but I'm kinda enjoying the view myself." The horse felt his own erection press against the back of the podium, but he did not touch himself. He had done that plenty during everyone's stories. Now, he just stared at the trimmed brown chest of the German shepherd, a horny tiger bobbing his head up and down on the bulging red cock. "The cards got this one right, for sure. Zinc is Lust all over."

Tail twitching, Zinc sat up again, wiping his snout on the back of a paw. "Ok, I'm not *that* bad. I've never cheated or anything like that."

"No," Derek agreed, as he lowered his head, his body shivering from the sudden cold air on his heat, "but even in a relationship, you're more...open sexually than I'm used to."

Zinc folded his arms and nodded toward Derek's wet cock. "I don't see you complaining."

With a lascivious grin, Derek growled, "And I'm not."

"Heh," Barba smirked, "shall we move on to the next card, or should we have an orgy first?"

Seeing Zinc open his mouth, Derek preempted him, "Let's move on to the next card!"

Barba chuckled again, a deep, hearty laugh. "Alright, the next card is supposed to represent *your* essence. This one will be your element and the best representation of your soul..."

As Barba went on, making the interpretation seem super dramatic and life-changing, Derek looked past him at the stained glass windows. They were starting to lose their glow, and he knew the sun's light must be all but gone. He had hoped they would be home by now, but they were still only getting started. He had shit to do. He interrupted, "Barba, seriously, is this going to take all night?"

Zinc lightly punched Derek's arm. "Hey, no worries. Barba smokes: he has a lighter. We could just light some of these old ass candles. It's a Friday night. You and I had no other plans tonight, right?"

Derek growled back, "I just don't want to be here all night, okay?"

"Get the knot out of your hole, D," Zinc said as he leaned back. "It's just seven cards. Let's have some fun. Just this once. Play along."

Crossing his arms over his chest, Derek no longer cared if Barba saw his cock. "Fine, whatever."

"Whiiiich," Barba said, "brings us to our second card!"

As he flipped it over, Derek stared at it with wide eyes. On its face was a massive bear. The bear's eyes glowed with the same white fire that was in the fox's eyes, and thin tendrils of black smoke poured from his maw. Its expression was purely evil, as if it wanted to inflict pain on the three.

"Derek, your essence is Wrath."

Shaking his head, Derek protested, "That's not even—"

Zinc smirked. "Yeah, that's pretty accurate." Derek opened his mouth in shock as he turned accusingly toward Zinc. The tiger raised his paws defensively and said, "Hey, look, I'm just calling them as I see them. Part of what attracted me to you was how you blazed on the football field back in high school. I've seen you beat up kids half your size just because you could, and—"

"That doesn't mean I'm *angry* though. That just means I'm strong."

Barba interrupted, "No, Zinc has a point. You've always been intimidating. If it weren't for Zinc, I probably wouldn't have approached you one-on-one myself. Everyone knows not to get on your bad side."

Zinc continued, "Yeah, and the few times we've fought, you've...well, you get really loud." He lowered a paw instinctively toward his ribs where he felt the bruises from two nights ago, and the pain made him wince.

Derek regarded him with a cold stare but just said, "Fine. Whatever. Let's keep playing this damn game then. More stories. But this time, the person who can tell the most wrathful story gets to decide if we can quit this game early or not."

Zinc and Barba exchanged a look, and then, smiling, Barba nodded. "Deal, and I'll go first."

"Fine."

BONES
SEARSKA GREY RAVEN

The shovel was empty, so he filled it.

It had taken time to get into the rhythm, but now the motion was second nature. The moon hung like a silver dinar above him, framed by the rim of his rectangular hole. A few fireflies flickered like vagrant stars against the backdrop of the blackened city sky, searching for their celestial counterparts. (It was all in vain, of course. The stars don't shine in the city.) The digger paused and picked at his teeth. Something stringy was stuck between his molars, and he absently pried it loose with a grime-crusted nail. Grave dirt coated his tongue, and he spat it out in disgust. The ground was so dry that the dirt crumbled back into the hole almost as fast as he dug it, and yet it seemed determined to worm under his claws, between his toes, and now, between his teeth.

The shovel was empty, so he filled it.

His spade rose and fell, steel flashing through the streaks of rust-colored dirt. With each motion, it became more apparent that this was no ordinary digger. His back was bowed at an odd angle; his knees bent digitigrade. And what could be mistaken for the tails of a coat were, in fact, a single tail of the canine variety. He paused for a moment and ran the blistered pads of his paw-like hand through the thicker fur behind his neck. He had the manual dexterity of a human—it was what made using the shovel possible—but he had the fur, the tail, and the face of a…well, his Lady called him a husky. It was she who had rescued him from the Bad Place With Bars, she who fed him

Tasty Crunchy Things, and she who scratched him *just so* behind his ears. And it was she who had bade him to drink from her own footprint by the light of the full moon, triggering the first Change. And as he became more like her, she became more like him. Her teeth grew long, and her ears became pointed, and together they howled with joy at the darkened sky. They ran through the night together—dancing through the urban jungle, darting from streetlamp to streetlamp, and he marveled at this world of steel and glass. She taught him how to live again! She had but to ask for the moon, and he would leap until he caught it for her.

This wasn't the moon, just a hole. A simple thing. It was just one night; the Change would come again. But, she said, only if he did *exactly* as she said. He looked up. The moon was as bright and round as his first Change all those months ago. Could he bear never seeing it again? He gritted his teeth. He had to keep going until it was done. If he faltered, if he was caught, he would lose both the moon and his Lady.

She handed him a canvas bag that fell heavily into his arms, told him to be quiet and careful, the knife in her other hand still dripping darkly in the dim light of the bedroom, the scent of copper thick and heavy in his nose—

The shovel was empty, so he filled it.

The pile of dirt forming above him grew taller, a mountain of soil, obscuring the gleaming moon from view. With a grunt, he shoved the point of the shovel as deep as he could and came up with a chunk of pale clay. *Almost there,* he thought, launching the chunk out of the hole. It hit the side of his new-born mountain with a dull thud and rolled into the dew-covered grass. He had to pause again. He stabbed the spade into the ground and leaned heavily against the side of the hole, but he refused to take more than a few gasping breaths as a break. His tongue lolled from the side of his muzzle and he was sore from the tip of his nose to the tip of his tail, but he was almost done. Just a little more. He reached for the spade, but the capricious soil shifted, and the handle fell loose, smacking into his side with a dull crack. He bit back a yelp and knocked the shovel aside.

It wasn't the shovel that hurt him—very little actually *hurt* him anymore—but the memory of crunching bone was still fresh in his mind, and his side still bore the remains of a boot-shaped bruise. All the trouble began with the Bad Man. His Lady stopped smiling when the Bad Man came into her life. Something was *wrong* with him, but he couldn't put it into words. It was an animal feeling, a warning, and his Lady couldn't feel it. (Or, if she did, she ignored it. It was a common flaw among them, he'd seen.) Because he loved her with all his heart, he retreated from his instincts and tried to do what would make her happy. But as the months passed, she *wasn't* getting happier. The light slowly went out of her eyes, and it was like watching his own transformation in reverse. And then the unexplained bruises began to appear; the lilt slowly went out of her voice. He became protective of his Lady, and would growl at the Bad Man every time he came near her. The Bad Man would frown, and back off for a time, but he had that *look*, like he was contemplating something awful.

As it turned out, the Bad Man had something in mind. A cage appeared, and every time the Bad Man was present, he forced him into it. There was nothing he could do. He threw himself at the bars, mad with rage, but could not break free. It was then that he learned the meaning of hate. But he still had one secret, one ace in the hole. *Wait, patiently wait. Your time will come,* she whispered to him. The moon rose, spilling its pale light across his cage, and he grinned. The bars shuddering as he shifted, the feeling of the lock snapping between his paws. He remembered bursting through the cage, snarling, the Bad Man losing his balance, his neck falling between his canine jaws like ripe fruit—

The Bad Man shouldn't have touched his Lady.

Shouldn't have kicked him.

Shouldn't have—

The shovel was empty, so he filled it.

Slowly, the pain in his side faded as the dull burn of flexing muscle overwhelmed it. His back was stiff, his fur caked with dirt, but at long last, it was done. He peeked his nose over the rim of the hole and sniffed the air. There was still a lingering trace of humanity on the wind, but it was old and fading. He pushed the shovel out of the hole before pulling himself the rest of the way out. His red tongue hung from between his black lips as he panted, and for a moment he simply lay in the cool grass and let his aching body take a much-needed rest. His ears twitched at the sound of an owl crying out, but it was a half-hearted motion. *Just need to bury the bones, and I can go Home.*

Home. It wasn't a new concept to him, but it was strange to hang a human word on it. It was a place-feeling-memory before it was a word. Home was his Lady's dwelling place, soft grass, red bricks, and a tall fence. It was where, after his first Change, she had embraced him, told him she loved him, and promised to protect him. His ribs, once pressed against his hide, had slowly filled in. His fur was smooth and sleek, and even the ragged ends of his ears had slowly healed with each Change until they were as good as new. And as he healed, her smile grew broader, her eyes became brighter, and the nights sweeter.

At least, until the Bad Man came. He didn't know how or why his Lady ended up with him. From the look on her face when the Man first appeared on her doorstep, she knew him and had been waiting for him to return. She was Pack—more than Pack—and he would die before he let her down. With a muffled grunt, he picked himself up, determined to finish his task.

Tombstones stood out all around him, pale moonlight illuminating their faces. Even the gravestones were ghosts tonight. He hoped the ghosts would keep their silence, and not tell where he was burying his Bones. It wasn't his idea to come here. His Lady gave him the idea, and his sore body thanked her for it. He hadn't dug the *whole* hole. (He shuddered at the thought. If his body ached this much after digging half the hole, he wasn't sure he would have been able to dig the whole hole.) Another human was meant to be laid to rest here.

Another human, who had died of natural causes, or cancer, or over-indulgence. It didn't matter. All that mattered was that there was a ready-dug hole that only needed a little bit of deepening to be of use to him. He rubbed his neck again, wishing for the familiar jangle of his dog tags to soothe him.

"Why do you keep that damned dog around? I hate that damned dog."

He shuddered, glancing at the bag. He knew that voice. It was the Bad Man's voice.

"I mean it, get rid of that damned dog. I can't stand those freakish eyes. He's always looking at me with that green eye. Something's wrong *with that damned dog."*

He snarled and kicked the bag, his foot connecting with a hollow thump. "Shut. Up." He growled, his voice as rough as gravel. "Bones don't talk. Bones get *buried*."

He shoved the bag with his foot, hard, and it tumbled to the bottom of the hole. A wet thump echoed from the hole's rim. At the bottom, he could see the bag curled in a fetal position, and the sight of it made his lips curl into a feral grin. As a final farewell, he lifted his leg and gave the hole a good watering.

The shovel was empty, so he filled it.

Behind him, the moon began to set.

The sound of birdsong woke him, but he wasn't outside; he was lying on something soft. Her bed, and he was surrounded by her blankets. He was smaller, his hands once again paws. His Lady must have found him outside and brought him indoors to sleep off the Change. He whined and snuggled into the blankets, his nose filled with her scent, and fell back asleep.

He didn't nap for long. An unfamiliar sound caused his ears to twitch again. Strange car, approaching his Lady's home. He roused, shaking his neck and making his dog tags jingle. He sat on her bed for a long moment, listening to the sound of a strange engine. The car's engine thrummed up to the house and cut off in the driveway. Alarmed, he shook off the last of his sleep and trotted to the front door. A pair of Strange Men in dark clothes approached his Lady's front door. He huffed, and barked once to get her attention. She was at his side a moment later, holding a coffee mug, a concerned look on her face. He whined, and she dropped her hand behind his ears. Her left eye was half-closed, a pool of dark, puffy flesh preventing her from opening it fully.

"You be a Good Dog, okay?" She said, trying to smile.

He whined again, promising.

She didn't even give the Strange Men a chance to ring the bell. "Tell me you found him," she said, sounding anxious.

One of the dark-clothed men shook his head. "Sorry ma'am. He seems to have vanished. It may be a good idea to cancel any credit cards he might have gotten a hold of, and you may want to consider getting a home security system. Though," he glanced down, "with a dog like that, you may not need one. Is that…a husky, ma'am? When we got the call last night, no one mentioned that you had a dog."

"Really? It's no surprise. I think he spent the night hiding under the bed. Between the fight and all the strange people, I bet he got spooked. There's a little German Shepherd in him. His tail isn't curled quite like a husky." She replied, her nails working magic behind his ears. "Stewert…wasn't very fond of him. He kicked him awfully hard last night, and I was afraid I'd have to take him in to the vet today. But he seems alright now." She smiled and bent down to kiss his nose. "Such a brave boy."

"He looks like a wolf. What do you call him? Fluffy?" The second man asked, chuckling.

"He's a shelter dog," she replied. "I got him four years ago. The shelter people had no idea what he really was. Animal control found him in an alley, trying to dig scraps out of a dumpster. They said he didn't even put up a fight, he was so weak." She scratched him behind the ears, and he wagged his tail happily. "Looks like life in suburbia agrees with him. And his name is Luther." His ears perked up at the sound of his name, but he was quickly distracted once her fingers went back to scratching.

"Some guard dog!" the first Strange Man said. "May I?" She nodded, and the Strange Man scratched him behind his ear. He decided these men were no threat, and he relaxed. He rolled onto his back and looked at the man expectantly. The Strange Man laughed and rubbed his belly.

"Luther doesn't have a mean bone in his body. He just looks scary. But you're just a fluffy teddy bear, aren't you?" She said, rubbing his chin.

He made a tolerant grumble as his tongue darted out to lick her cheek.

The Stranger smiled, still looking at Luther. "Strange eyes. I've never seen eyes like that on a husky before, but I've heard of it."

She nodded. "It was partially why I got him. Such a unique pair of eyes."

The second Strange Man snorted. "Not really a pair. Looks like he couldn't decide, and got one of each!"

They laughed, and the Stranger spoke to his Lady for a little longer, took a few more notes, and handed her a small, white card with dark writing on it. "Be careful, ma'am. And if he shows up, don't hesitate to give us a call." The Strange Man left, and his Lady quietly shut the door. She hugged Luther close, her slender frame shaking. He whined and nuzzled her shoulder, but she winced away. He caught a flash of darkened skin through the V of her blouse—a fist-shaped bruise splayed across her collarbone.

"It'll heal, boy. He didn't manage to break it. Luther, did you do exactly what I said?"

He yipped, nodded, and licked her face, his tongue brushing gently across her black eye.

She wrapped her arms around him and squeezed tight. "*Such* a good dog! I'm sorry you had to spend your full moon digging in the dirt. But you did a Good Thing, for both of us. I have something for you." She got up and opened her star-covered canvas bag and drew out a slender, tan object that had a broad knot at both ends.

He barked and jumped up and down with anticipation. His tail was wagging so hard that his whole backside wiggled.

"*Such* a good dog!" She said, giving him the bone. "Now don't go burying that one with your other ones. Or *they* will find them. And we don't want them to find your bones, do we?"

No, he didn't want anyone to find the Bad Bones. Bad Bones needed to *stay* buried.

Those Three Letters
Rayah James

"I...It's...HIV," he said as a fresh wave of emotion and tears washed over him. He realized that it was the first time he had said it aloud to anyone including himself. Those three syllables stung worse than anything he'd ever endured as a soldier. A pamphlet from the military processing station sat beside him with those three letters plastered across the front of it in a bold font.

Within a few minutes, Rhea pulled up. It only took her a few minutes longer than him to get there. She had no trouble finding him though. The large white wolf looked small. He had collapsed on the front steps, sitting bent over with his head buried in his paws...

Words were not needed. Rhea sat on the step beside him and put her chestnut brown paw on his large lupine leg and gave him a loving squeeze. Orion let his massive frame fall onto the much smaller bunny, and she held him as the tears fell.

"I need you to go to the doctor with me." He finally managed to sit up. "It's got to be a mistake." He was still holding onto that shred of hope. Right now, that was the only thing he could do.

"Okay," Rhea said and nodded through tears of her own now.

Rhea was always so good to him. Orion knew that she was the one he wanted by his side through this. He often told her that she was the one that kept him grounded, and he knew he would need that quality now more than ever. He couldn't help but feel that he had let even her down now, and he couldn't imagine what he would do without her.

"Can you drive?"

She nodded, and he handed her the keys.

The doctor's office with its bare walls and sterile surfaces felt like an inescapable prison to Orion.

Mistake, mistake, mistake...It's all just a mistake. Orion chanted these words in his head. He was innocent, and he didn't want a life of doctor's visits and tests. While he'd never truly enjoyed his military career, it was all he knew, and he'd rather be under fire right now than sitting on this cold table.

The doctor carefully swabbed the Orion's gums. When he was finished, Orion nervously licked his snout. He looked over at Rhea. Her ears drooped, and he could tell as he looked into her wide eyes that he was letting her, himself, and everyone in his life down. He couldn't live life with this virus.

After sliding the swab into the testing liquid, the doctor explained to them how the test would indicate the results and what would happen either way. He explained the intricacy of the virus itself and how it was treated. Orion sat with a blank stare. It was hard to absorb the information even though it was the second time he had heard it that day. The doctor then excused himself, and said not to worry and that he would be back in a moment to check the results with them.

The test was sitting on the counter at the far side of the exam room. The indicator for the test was facing away from them. Rhea tried to start some friendly conversation. She desperately wanted to distract him, if she could, for just a few minutes longer from the pain she knew he was about to feel.

He had to know though. It had to be now. It couldn't wait for any doctor. He leaped up from the table and took one of the two long strides it would take it to get across the small room. Before he could take the second step, he felt the familiar small chestnut paw on his arm. Usually it was a comfort, but right now it was a hindrance.

"Are you sure this is what you want to do? It might be better coming from the doctor."

He hesitated. "I need to see it. I won't believe it until I do."

"Okay. Remember he said it's one line for negative...two for positive." She held onto his arm for support, and he did everything in his power not to flinch away from her. He knew she was trying to comfort him, but nothing she could do would help now. One line held his fate now, and he hoped it was missing.

His paws carefully turned the tray holding the test around, and he closed his eyes. He wasn't ready for this. His held onto the edge of the counter, and his claws dug into the formica. A good soldier is never put into a position like this. He's alert and doesn't let things sneak up on him. He's careful and precise. People don't take advantage of him because he doesn't allow it. His stomach churned, and his chest tightened.

Rhea looked up at her friend, who had yet to open his eyes. He was crying again, this time silently. She glanced at the results.

"I..." he opened his eyes, but instead of looking at the test, he looked at Rhea. "Did you...see?"

She nodded somberly, as a tear rolled down the already dampened fur on her cheek.

He shifted his focus to what was in front of him. There they were. Two clear lines. There was no mistake. There was no more confusion. He knew what happened, and his paws slammed the counter, causing the test to topple over and Rhea to jump back.

Orion let out a low growl.

He did this to me.

"You know you are going to have to tell him," finally breaking the silence as she pulled his car into the driveway.

"Tell him what? He already knows. He has to know!" Orion's paws slammed the dashboard in front of him this time.

Rhea jumped again. "Are you sure that there is no other way?"

Orion's hurt-filled eyes met Rhea's.

"Of course there's not. I'm sorry. That wasn't a good question." Rhea, like Orion, had always wanted to see the best in everyone even if there wasn't much good to see.

"I should have seen it coming" he said. "I was so stupid. I thought he was so nice. I thought I was going to *marry* him."

"You couldn't have known. You loved Byron. Nobody would have guessed. You are not to blame." She reached out to hold his paw.

He recoiled at her touch this time. "No, I could have prevented this. If I could go back..."

"You can't though, Orion...and this is not your fault."

Muttering under his breath. "...that bastard hyena..."

"Orion..."

"No, you don't understand, Rhea. He's going to pay for what he did to me. I don't know how yet, but he's got to pay for this."

"Shouldn't we take care of you first? Please don't do anything that you are going to regret." Rhea pleaded.

"We aren't doing anything." Orion got out of the car, walked around to the driver's side, and opened the door. "Get out, Rhea." He could see the tears welling up in her eyes. He never talked to her this way. He'd ordered soldiers and asserted authority in other areas of his life, but he'd always been on equal footing with Rhea since their friendship had begun. He hated to order her out now, and he hated to disappoint her. This bunny was the one true friend he had in the world. There had been many moments in his life where she had been the driving factor in his making the right decisions, but not today. Today, he experienced a more primal urge than he'd ever experienced before, and he was not the docile wolf that Rhea knew and loved. His tears were spent, and something else welled up inside him now.

She eased out of the car and brushed her paw against his arm. Her eyes implored him to rethink what he was about to do.

He looked down at her and only hesitated for a moment. Another wave of despair hit him, but it quickly turned back into anger as he slid into the driver's seat, slammed the door, and revved the engine. He needed Byron to hurt as much as he did right now, and he was determined that was going to happen tonight.

Leaning against his car, he looked up at Byron's apartment. He hadn't talked to him for a couple months now. Things hadn't ended well between them. He'd broken his heart, his faith that good remained in the world, and now as he'd come to find out…even turned his own immune system against him. He felt like Byron had not only wasted the last year of his life, but he had ruined the rest of it, too. The more Orion stood and thought about all of it, the more he seethed. As much as he wanted to though, he couldn't face Byron himself right now.

He needed time.

Many empty, dark landscapes appeared and disappeared through his car windows that night. He drove to get away, away from the trouble that he might find himself in, away from Byron, away from his problems…He tried to get away from the anger that kept coming to the surface.

He watched the sunrise from the parking lot of a small country hardware store in a town that he didn't even know the name of. He didn't know how many miles from home he was, but he was definitely too tired to go any further. He dozed off for a moment, and when he awoke, the sun was high in the sky. He wondered if it had all been a nightmare.

His eyes darted to the seat beside him. Those three letters on the pamphlet still stared up at him, asking him what he was going to do now.

Stretching and exiting the car, he walked around the parking lot and entered the store. A gruff, old lion behind the old fashioned register asked, "Need help finding anything, son?"

Orion shook his head and wandered to the back of the store where a display of knives sat on the shelf. Orion took in the knives, each one glimmering despite how dimly lit the musty old store was. It reminded him of a store that he'd visited with Byron. Byron had asked him to pick out a ring that he might want someday, all while texting another wolf and making other plans. Byron always did that to him.

One knife stood out. It was a long Bowie knife with a double-edged point. It came with a sheath and holster-like belt that could be easily hidden underneath clothing.

Maybe he *would* let Byron seduce him one last time.

Orion picked up the knife with one paw, and ran his other over the shiny blade, and he let out a small gasp at its beauty.

He felt someone behind him almost breathing down his neck. The feeling again reminded him of a time with Byron. Orion recalled times that Byron had come home unbeknownst to him and surprised him from behind by wrapping his arms around him and kissing his neck tenderly. Then Byron would take him back to the same bed where the hyena had cheated on him so many times before. That wasn't what was happening here though. Byron would never do that again. Orion had chickened out before, and he knew it.

A large paw patted him on the back. "That one's a mighty fine one. Really sharp. Be careful, it could do a lot of damage to ya, son."

Orion nodded. He wanted to do damage though, a lot of damage, but not to himself. The damage had already been done to him through those tender kisses and lies. The thought of the knife repaying Byron for those nights of deceit were enough to give Orion a sick sense of excitement. His heart pounded as he thought about just where he would like to put the shimmering blade. He put the knife in the sheath next to it, and followed the lion to the front of the store.

"Will that be all for ya?"

Orion nodded obligingly again.

The lion gave the almost crazed wolf a look of concern, but rang up the purchase anyway.

Orion was out the door shortly after that, weapon in hand. He placed the knife in the seat on top of the pamphlet, and turned the key in the ignition. It didn't end here. Byron had it coming.

For the Sins of the Father
Sisco Polaris

Anger, rage, wrath, and vengeance. They aren't really healthy, are they? Of course, that really isn't something we care about, certainly not while we are pissed off. There have been studies conducted that show when we are angry, rational decision-making flies out of the window. Even the most cautious and gentle person can turn violent. In legal terms, I believe this is what is known as temporary insanity.

Of course, I know all about that, not because I have even pleaded it, but because of my former job: corrections officer. Twelve years' service, wolf and pup. I saw many types, from career criminals, cold and calculating to the meekest accountant who finally snapped and smashed his bowling league trophy over his wife's head. Poor Reggie, if only he'd been a worse bowler maybe he'd still be stuck in that loveless marriage, instead of serving twenty years.

That is the real hook of anger: you don't think of the consequences. You just give in to that id, that beast inside you. It cares nothing for the future, for others; it just wants to be heard. I must admit I have been bitten by that beast a couple of times in my life. Like the third time I was passed over for sergeant, that was the end of my career as a corrections officer. It is hard to come back from punching your boss. Still on the plus side, he didn't press charges, after he came to, that is.

Afterwards, I spent a few years "finding myself." Turns out I was right where I left me, in the shits and needing to do some hard work to get out of them. Mind you, I never was a wolf afraid of hard work. Long hours, overtime, weekends, you need it, I'm your lupine. I think my work ethic is what got me back on track. Filling in applications left and right, being willing to start at the bottom. Eventually, it paid off, and I got a position. It was office work, not exactly thrilling stuff, but it paid the bills.

Of course after being with the company for three years, I was hoping for a promotion. When a space opened up, I put myself forward. I was never shy about going for what I wanted. The company gave me an interview, and I was feeling pretty confident. I had been there longer than most, put in more than my fair share of unpaid nights and weekends. Through hard work and diligence, I had netted a few new big customers, and I certainly felt like my star was in ascendancy.

Then one Friday, a few weeks after my interview, my boss called me into his office. The skunk (that is not an insult: he was a skunk) was looking a little ill when I came in. Poor guy, I can be a bit intimidating when I'm on a rant. What can I say I'm almost six feet tall, and I work out a lot. My dark gray fur really highlights my blue eyes; it makes me look intense and brooding. Weird thing is I can be one of the lightest fun guys, when I'm in the mood. Smooth and charming too, I've talked my way into many a guy's pants.

Still, that day, he knew he had some bad news, and he was a stick-thin twig of a man. Not a bad manager though. I have to say paw on my heart I don't think he was out to screw me over. He looked up from his desk and gave a nervous smile, "Hello For, please have a seat." Yes, that's my name; well actually, that's short for Forrin (yeah I'm from out of town; believe me I've heard all the Forrin-Foreign jokes). Everyone calls me For, for I like it. See, I can joke about my name too.

"Thanks Neil, cool tie." It wasn't. It was a rather nerdy Star Wars tie. But classy, it looked just like a pattern only if you looked close; the pattern was made of tiny green Empire symbols. Now true, I have exposed my own nerdy leanings by showing I could spot a subtle nerd, but hey, I am old enough to remember Luke and Darth on Cloud City before everyone knew they were father and son. Now that, my friend, leaves an impression.

"Th...thanks," he replied, a little flustered. Poor guy, he was your typical good guy heterosexual. He didn't have any gay friends, and thus he wasn't really comfortable when I complimented him. You know the type, right? You can see their minds whirling as they work the compliment over in their heads, just in case you were hitting on them. I don't flirt in the workplace...well not usually. There was this one time in jail, you know what they say about bunny boys and how they will do anything too...actually I probably shouldn't tell that story. I think a good part of what happened was illegal.

Anyway, the compliment fully analyzed, and the flirt content identified as a mere ten percent (otherwise known as background flirtation; some of us studs can't help it you know), he gave me his serious look—the one he always gives when he has bad news for the team and he doesn't want back talk. You know the one; you've seen it from your boss: slightly uncomfortable, a little hint of sweat, and a short, yet deep, breath before they start to speak. "I know you are waiting to hear the results of the recent round of interviews and well...I wanted you to hear this from me first."

He didn't need to say more: nobody says they want you to hear it from them first unless it's bad news. That line had preceded most of the worst events of my life. Some examples of "I wanted you to hear it from me first": "I got drunk with Steve and had unprotected sex...but only on six occasions it didn't mean anything," or, "I got a job in Europe, but we can still Skype all the time," or my favorite, "I had sex with your brother." That last one was really impressive...mostly because I don't have a brother; my boyfriend was stoned and nailed the pizza delivery guy. I wouldn't have been that mad, but the guy was a badger; he looked nothing fucking like me!

Ok, we are off track again. Your fault of course, keep trying to get me to talk about all my sexy fun encounters. I know your type, and it is a fun type especially when they squeal. You a sexy squealer? No, damn it...we are off topic again! Right, anyway,

Neil continued to say, "Unfortunately, the selection panel feels that Justin is a better match for the job requirements."

"Justin?!" I don't think I can convey just how shocked I was to hear that name. Justin was a leopard. He'd joined the company just six months prior. He never put in a single day's worth of overtime. His bungling had cost the company one account already. What was worse he was a ladies' man, or rather he thought he was. There wasn't a single female under the age of fifty in the company he hadn't tried to nail. He'd hit on several clients as well.

The thought of that horny moron getting a promotion above me was enough to make my blood boil. "He's useless at the job, and he's probably going to get the company sued for the way he treats the female employees. Last month when things went down with the Tyson account, he took off early 'to watch the game.' While I stayed behind and worked my ass off getting everything smoothed over!" I spat the words with far more bile than poor Neil deserved.

"I...I agree, that's why I recommended you for the job. However...there were some concerns on the panel about..." The skunk withered under my death stare. I wasn't giving him the eye; he was getting both eyes and teeth as well. "L..look, I...it's just that..."

"What, what did I do? I put in all the hours I could, and I've never had a day off sick...what is it?" I was leaning over his desk at this point, eclipsing the light, and I could see him shrinking back more.

"They didn't think you were right for management...I argued for you, but I was pretty much told to shut up." The skunk glanced up at me and then leaned forward and whispered, "I overheard Mr. Simons saying he wasn't going to have a queer as a manager."

"It's two-thousand and fucking sixteen!" I snorted and slammed my fist down on the desk. "That fucking fat feline shouldn't be able to do this."

"I agree, but there isn't anything we can do." the skunk said, giving me a sympathetic shrug.

"It's illegal. I could take them to court," I ranted at the top of my lungs, I knew everyone in the office would hear me, but I didn't care.

"You need evidence. I doubt one overheard comment, that might not have been about you, is enough," observed the skunk, and then he sighed. "Look, this isn't fair, but there's nothing I can do. Why don't you take off early and see if you can calm down?"

I opened my mouth to reply. I'm not even sure what I was going to say. It wasn't going to be nice, and I think it involved the word "fuck" several times. However, the door to the office opened, and in walked Mr. Simons; he was actually an inch or two bigger than me. The photos on his office wall showed that he used to play football in college. His broad shoulders were the last holdouts of his former physique. Now, his stomach was far broader than his shoulders; his belt was like Atlas, destined to forever hold a planet-sized bulk in place. Being a successful businessman, husband and father to two kids, had allowed the old lion to let himself really go.

"Ah, Mr Jackson. I am sorry about your recent application. There was an applicant who gave a better performance on the day. Better luck next time," The old lion didn't even blink as the lies rolled off his tongue, positively dripping with sincerity. "Neil, we need to go over a few things." And that was me dismissed, like the undervalued underling I was.

My fists clenched, and I felt the red mist descending. I began to count to ten slowly in my head. When I reached seven, I was just calm enough to get out of my chair and leave the office. Neil had been right about one thing: I didn't want to be there any longer than I had to. Going back to my desk was an assault course of co-workers, all of whom wanted to know what I had been yelling about.

What was worse was the one who clearly knew what I was yelling about, Justin. He knew who had got the promotion. Ok, maybe it's clichéd for dogs to hate cats, but oh god, his smug smiling face was too much for me to bear. He was standing by my desk as I returned. With a mocking tone, he said, "Hey, buddy. How's it going?"

I spoke not one word of a reply, just grabbed my coat and slammed my shoulder into him as I left. Ok, it was childish, but it felt oh so good just to nudge him. I mean I wanted to do so much more than that. Especially when I heard him say, "Typical gay guy, all strung out on his emotions."

Ok, technically, he wasn't wrong, and as I stood in the office elevator, I imagined stalking, killing, and skinning two annoying big cats. By the time I reached the lobby, I was in a full-on rage and stormed out of the building. The problem with this sort of issue is that I tend to roll it around in my mind over and over. Each time, I do or say something different, punching the fat lion, headbutting him. A million other ideas, but each one only served to make me more and more furious.

So, I did the one thing that would definitely not help and had a great chance of making things worse. I went to a gay club called Bottom's Up, not exactly a subtle name, but they did a surprisingly good range of craft beers. Plus, a bunch of my friends tended to hang out there. I had a good chance of running into someone who would offer me a sympathetic ear, shoulder to cry on, and cock to suck.

The place was mostly empty when I arrived. It was only three on a Friday afternoon, so that wasn't surprising. The bartender defied all bar staff conventions by not asking me what was bothering me and just getting me the drink I ordered. Then a few minutes later, he brought me another, still with the stoic silence.

Drinking alone in a gay club, I know what you are thinking, and you are so right. I do get laid by the end of the story, but there is a bit of a twist. The next few hours, I drank a few more beers, enough that I had a healthy buzz on. Though all that cool frothy liquid could not calm the burning fire in my stomach. For once it wasn't indigestion; it was pure anger. Despite a few hours, my blood still boiled when I thought of the large lion, or that smug, spotted bastard.

The place had started to get more and more packed. I finally started looking around, hoping to see a familiar face, or maybe an unfamiliar one looking for a good hard screw. Beer makes me horny and stupid; it's one of the best things about the glorious malty liquid. Then, my eyes fell on a face, one that was familiar and yet I couldn't quite place it.

It belonged to a young lion; he was almost hidden in one of the darker corners of the club. A wallflower, not that unusual for a first-timer. They tended to hang back, clinging on to the wall, too scared to actually go forward, worried that if they speak to some hot stranger, they will burst into flames. His mane was dark brown, but his fur had that classic golden wheat color lions are known for. Interestingly, he had a little permadye tattoo on his arm, just a little Zen symbol with some tribal swirls.

I do like ink on males; it kinda works for me, I don't know why. Not that I have ever gotten any. I could never settle on something I could live with for life. Young cubs often get them, probably as a rebellion, though this young guy had it on his shoulder, high up. That would be easy to cover with a t-shirt. Something his parents would never see was my guess, a hidden rebellion.

His body was a little chubby, not that I minded that, chubby guys are often fun. Though there was a big difference between this shy flower and the chubby bears you normally find in Bottom's Up. He was only slightly chunky, and he wore some small glasses. Something about the look in his eyes said nerd, yet he was dressed in a tank top, to show off his tattoo. Down low, he had some skinny-fit jeans, that looked a little silly on him. I must admit my anger cooled for a moment; it was hard not to when you see a first-timer like that, dressing gay and trying to look like they belonged.

Then suddenly I made the connection in my mind, why I recognized his face. I had seen it before, in a photo, on Mr. Simon's wall. My homophobic boss's son...oh I know what you are thinking: "That's so cliché, nailing your boss's son for revenge." While you are right it is cliché, it is also a super fun way to get your revenge. It's not smart, especially when your boss clearly hates you and would look for any reason to get rid of "that damned homo." However, like I said when I started this little tale, anger messes up your decision-making abilities, alcohol doubly so.

So you can understand how when I recognized the little guy as my boss's son, my mind wasn't exactly running smooth. I didn't think that it might be wrong to seduce a young guy, clearly innocent and probably a virgin, just to get silent revenge on his dad. Nor did I think that he might be hurt if he found out. All I thought was the kid was a delicious present, wrapped in a tank top and skinny jeans. Revenge and a hot night of fucking in one, deliciously innocent boy half my age.

Now, right now you are probably thinking that I must be an arrogant ass to be so sure I could nail him. Truth be told, he was an easy mark, and if I am honest he wouldn't be the first wallflower I had talked into going home with me. Of course, I don't think any of them ever complained about it. I've been around the block a few times, and I know how to fuck. Specifically, I know how to fuck until your toes curl and you tear the bedsheets, before you are hit by an orgasm so powerful you can't breathe or think straight for five minutes. Now, you might think that I'm just bragging, but I am willing to prove it, if you want me to. Maybe after the rest of the story?

Well, I'm pretty sure it'll come as no surprise to you that I downed the remains of my beer and walked over to the cute trembling little wallflower. I caught his eye as I approached. He blushed and looked away and then back again. You could see the wheels turning in his mind, surely this big daddy wolf wasn't walking over to little old him. Well, I gave him a rather lascivious wink, and I got to watch him squirm delightfully. While inside, he was going into full panic mode, a guy was coming onto him, this is what he came for; at the same time, getting what you want is terrifying.

Damn he was just so cute, I could already feel myself straining down below. What a day to go commando, sure it would help later, but right then it just meant my cocktip was grinding along my zipper. Still, I was way too manly to let the discomfort show, and I may have swayed my hips just enough to draw his eye down to my crotch. It's a natural reaction: every guy does it straight or gay. Psychologists have noted we can't help but check out the crotch when we meet someone new. I got to watch the shock and desire in his eyes as he realized the guy coming over to him had a raging erection in his pants.

"Hello, you're new here," I rumbled my words giving my naturally deep voice some extra depth. I stared right into his eyes, and he glanced away, and I could sense the heat of his blush from where I stood. My place as dominant alpha, established in one line: that is how a real top takes control, no physicality just a look and a word.

"H...hi, yes...yes, how did you know?" His voice was a little high-pitched, mostly because he was so nervous. I swear, I could hear his heart it was beating so fast and so loud.

I gave him a toothy grin and a wink, leaning closer, partly due to the loud music but mostly so that he could get a whiff of manly musk. "Well, cause I've never seen you before. Believe me, if I'd seen you before we would have already...talked." I licked my lips before I whispered that last word, my muzzle right against his ear, so my hot breath flowed over his neck. The lion shivered and pushed himself further against the wall.

"I...I...thank you." The kitten was so cute, lost and helpless, my body blocking out most of the rest of the club, giving him a little privacy. While at the same time blocking any exit. Now, I know how that sounds; if he made a move to go, I wouldn't have stopped him. I'm not a monster. Everyone I have taken to bed has wanted to be there. However, you have to understand, sometimes a little manly dominant display is all you need.

"Nice ink. Can I get you a coke or something?" You probably have to be experienced to spot how wonderful that line is. A compliment on his hidden rebellion, with a reminder of his junior nature, along with the classic buying a bitch a drink: the start to many a good night.

"Thanks, it's a tribal Zen. I like the Celtic designs." The young guy was clearly feeling both proud and defensive of his little patch of black ink.

"Mmmm, I just think it looks sexy. Does it have a special meaning?" I reached out a paw and ran some fingers over the mark, tracing along the tribal swirls. He gasped at my touch, but didn't pull away, a good sign for me.

"It's...I just...wanted something, and this spoke to me," he muttered clearly embarrassed and yet enjoying the attention.

"It speaks to me too," I muttered, my fingers still tracing along the endless Zen. My sensitive nose picked up a new spicy scent in the air. Oh, what is it about cats and dogs, that makes us just love to fight or fuck with each other? I suspect it's our predatory ancestral nature, especially with lions and wolves, pack creatures where the alpha controls all. "Now, would you like a drink and to give me your name?"

"Colin...can I have a beer please?" he whispered looking around and gulping nervously. Of course, all he had done was given me an excuse. I reached down and took a gentle yet firm hold of his wrist. There a blue band was wrapped around his golden fur. It was given to him by the bouncer, upon checking his ID. It showed he was eighteen, old enough to be in there and totally legal to fuck, but not to buy a drink for.

"I assume you meant coke," I added, just a hint of growl to my voice, a little authority to put the young male in his place. Now, many guys I know would have bought him that drink and a few more. Drunk guys are easier to score. However, not me; as I said, I want my guys willing. Hell, not just willing, I want them desperate, eager for me. I don't want them too pissed to say no; I want them screaming yes as I make them happy: they consented.

"Y...yes, Sir." Oh fuck, did my cock throb when I heard him say "Sir." He adjusted his spectacles as he spoke, and I so wanted to kiss him in that moment. However, some things you gotta wait for: anticipation makes things sweeter. Like presents on Christmas morning, I couldn't wait to get his wrapping off and start playing with my new toy. "Don't move, I'll be right back." I gave the words a little extra growl right into his ear and got to watch as he squirmed even more.

It only took me a few minutes to get a new beer and a coke; he was standing exactly where I left him. His eyes had never left me the entire time I was away. I knew cause I glanced back every now and then to check on him. It was clear that the dominant daddy wolf thing was working for him. Hardly surprising given his homophobic father, daddy issues were a safe bet.

When I returned, he took the coke from me, his paw trembling just a little. I took a swig and leaned close to say, "My name's For."

For the first time, he looked a little confused. "For?"

"Yeah, like the number after three, short for Forrin," I replied, my slight joke getting a bit of a smile off him. I reached up and brushed some of his ragged mane out of his eyes. "You look good when you smile." That only made him smile more, until he had to try and hide it by drinking a sip of his coke.

"Y...you look good too," he mumbled into his drink and looked up nervously, as if I were going to bite his head off for complimenting me.

I gave him my best smile and reached out to stroke his tattooed arm again, "Why thank you For the compliment." It took him a second to spot the mild joke, and then he giggled: it was so cute. He might have been looking for a big strong alpha wolf, but I had to admit he was bringing out my protective urges. I wanted to put my arms around the young thing and make sure the world didn't hurt him.

"So, you have any more ink?" I asked as my thumb slowly stroked over his Zen marking.

"N...no, I want some more, just haven't been able to get a good artist booked," he replied and then lowered his voice to add, "Plus my dad really wouldn't approve, and he is gonna pay for me to go to college." I couldn't help but find him lowering his voice adorable, as if anyone around us would have cared that his father was paying for him to go to college.

"What are you going to study?" I asked, while my paw gave his biceps just a little squeeze, the little butterball had some muscle under the soft cuddly exterior. I have to admit I was liking him more and more, my cock certainly wanting to get to know him a lot better.

"Economics," something about the face he pulled as he spoke made me doubt that was his plan.

"Is that what you really want to study, or what your dad wants you to study?" I leaned in a little closer and sniffed his mane: his scent was sweet and yet earthy. When I exhaled, I gave a soft moan of delight, just loud enough for him to hear and know I was liking everything I was seeing, feeling, and smelling.

"No...I wanted to study art. I loved sculpture in school. I won a couple of awards," the last part sounded just a little bit defensive, I could almost see him using that when he lost the argument on what he was going to study with his father.

My free paw stroked down his arm and onto his paw, stroking over his fingers before lacing my fingers with his, while I whispered softly into his ear, "I love a guy who is good with his hands. Your father is wrong: you should study art. We need more artists in the world; we have plenty of boring accountants."

"Yeah, well he's the one who is paying..." he stopped as I leaned closer and sniffed his neck and then he whimpered as I took a very quick taste of his fur.

While he was shivering and panting into my ear, I added, "Fuck him. You can always try for a scholarship, or arts program. It's your life, not his." Encouraging him to rebel against his father. Maybe it was childish, maybe it wasn't. Truth be told, I have a feeling that any side of an argument that Mr. Simons was on was the wrong side. Besides, it was the kid's life to live. "College is about exploring and learning what you want to learn. Of course, there is the question: what do you want to learn about?" As I asked, I squeezed his paw and stepped a little closer, so our bodies were almost touching.

"I...want..." The young male couldn't even finish, or look me in the eye, so I took a chance and leaned forward. Just for a moment, our lips touched. I could feel him tense up and then relax as our lips gently caressed each other. He moaned softly, and I pushed just a little closer, letting my chest push up against his; the rapid beat of his heart could be felt through my shirt. His eyes were closed, and there was a cute dopey smile on his lips as I pulled back.

"Would you like to try a sip of beer?" I whispered mischievously. His eyes opened, and I could see the blush on his face. I doubted it would truly be his first sip of the malty gold, after all if he'd gotten some ink, he was likely to have rebelled a bit more. That wasn't the point of course. As he nodded, he reached out for my glass.

With a smirk, I pulled it away from his grabbing paw and took a drink myself. Then while he was giving me a slightly confused and indignant look, I pressed forward again, much harder this time, my lips conquering his. My tongue wormed against his lips until they parted, and then I let a river of beer flow into his maw. He gasped and struggled a little in shock, until my torso pressed to his, forcing him firmly back against the wall. This time, I didn't break the kiss quickly, my tongue inside his maw, plundering it hungrily, stroking against his own tongue.

My free paw stroked down his flanks, as I ground my hips lewdly to his, giving him no aspersions as to my desires. Our hard members ground into each other, separated by mere millimeters of fabric. I growled softly, and he moaned as our desires began to take hold. I kept the kiss for as long as I could, his glasses almost falling off his muzzle as our lips wrestled. He was unresisting in my paws; more than that he was eager. His free paw stroking over my chest, finding a pert nipple under my shirt, the cub squeezed. Sparks fired in my mind, my anger briefly forgotten through my desire.

Gasping loudly, I broke the kiss and growled into his ear, "I want to fuck you." Nothing classy, nothing smart. Just the raw, brutal truth of my desires and his. "How far to your place?"

You note there's no asking if he was coming back to my place. I may have been desperate to plow the young guy, but the thought of doing it under his homophobic father's roof, shit, that really seemed like fitting punishment. It also seemed like a fucking hot idea: forbidden lust is a huge turn on for me.

"My...my dad..." he stammered; of course I knew exactly where his dad would be. It was his monthly "business trip" for "networking." Which is code for he and some of the rest of the top brass go golfing and hire some prostitutes. Because they don't just want to portray the cliché; they want to live it too. So, I didn't let him finish. I bit down on the scruff of his neck, through his shaggy mane, and I let my paw slip down to grab his crotch. Let me tell you, junior was packing some full heavy weaponry; my fingers squeezed his cock through the denim.

"How far to your place?" I repeated as he ground his erection desperately against my groping paw.

"J...just a few minutes' walk," he replied this time, submitting to my wishes. The boy was a born bitch, not that I have any complaints about that. I downed my glass of beer, and he ditched his almost full coke on a random table as we rushed out. I was shameless, my arm slipping around him, my paw landing on his rump and squeezing. Firm feline mounds, they were burning to the touch, and his tail was thrashing with excitement. I couldn't wait to delve between those golden mounds and to take that sweet cherry. I hadn't asked if he was a virgin; I didn't need to.

People in the street gave us some looks, and who could blame them? A forty-year-old wolf, his paws all over a guy less than half his age. It made Colin blush and shrink against me, but I liked that. I stood tall and squeezed him close, stealing kisses from his cheek whenever someone gave us a look of disgust. All their outrage did was make me more determined.

A few blocks away, we reached a rather posh apartment block. I could see Colin eyeing the doorman nervously, and I took my arm off him before the doorman saw us. I may be a dominant ass, but I didn't want to get the kid into trouble. That and I had a feeling he might have bolted. The young lion nodded at the doorman, and I couldn't help but notice the feline trying to hide his ink by keeping his arm still at his side. We trotted past the desk quickly and up the stairs.

As soon as we were out of the lobby, my arm was back around him, my paw firmly resuming its exploration of those golden mounds. Colin led me as fast as his legs could take him to his home: inside was a rather nice neat and tidy apartment. Spacious, with some nice art on the wall and plush carpets. However, I didn't notice any of that: as soon as the door was closed, I had the kitty in my arms, and our lips reunited, like two long lost lovers meeting after decades apart. They wrestled and stroked as our tongues fenced happily. I pushed him against the door hard, and he began to purr.

My paws reached down and pulled his tank top off; underneath was his beautiful chest. He wasn't cut, he had slight chubby man breasts and a sexy pert round tummy. His dark brown mane ran down the center of his chest, all the way down to his jeans. I licked my lips at the thought of finding out just how far down that treasure trail led. Standing back, I admired him hungrily as my paws slowly unbuttoned my work shirt. His golden full frame, starkly contrasted by his huge shaggy mane. Behind his glasses, golden brown eyes looked at me with desire.

I cast my shirt off, and he got to see my white chest. I was a regular at my gym; it was a good place to work off steam after work, when you can't get your paws on sexy, young, willing bitches. So, his eyes got to enjoy my rather tight body.

He moaned as I reached out with both paws, slipping my fingers under his jeans waistband. Under his jeans was a furnace, and I couldn't wait to get inside and quench those flames. "Bedroom?" I asked, and he nodded pointing to a set of stairs. A two-floor apartment, in the heart of town no less. I could never dream of affording a place like this. With a smirk, I turned, keeping one paw in his pants. I pulled him with me up the stairs. He stopped me and opened one of the doors.

Posters on the wall, clothes all over the floor, books scattered, and the controllers from a Playstation 4. At the far wall was a single bed, the blankets all messy. I shook my head,

"Naw, not big enough for two." I didn't wait for a response. I opened the door opposite and found a far tidier room, a huge king-sized bed, walk-in wardrobe, and ensuite bathroom. "Much better."

"No...that...that's my Dad's room: he'd kill me," the lion whimpered, and for the first time I saw genuine concern in his eyes.

"When is he home?" I asked, knowing full well the answer was several days' time.

"He's away...for a couple of days," the young lion replied, a little hesitant, but I could see the seed of my idea had been planted.

"Then, we clean up afterwards, and he doesn't have to know anything," I growled into his ear, suddenly pushing myself close, my paw slipping down inside his jeans. He gasped as my fingers grasped around his sticky hot shaft. I licked slowly up his neck and nipped on his ear, whispering, "Come on, you can't let him rule your life forever." I didn't wait for a response. I went on the attack kissing and nipping on his neck, while my paw stroked up and down his swollen maleness. He moaned and panted in my ear, trembling under my paw.

There was no resistance as I pulled away, my paw still on his cock guiding him into his father's bedroom. I didn't give him time to think, turning him around and pushing him so he fell back onto his father's bed. Out of the corner of my eye, I spotted an oil painting of Mr Simons attempting to look regal. It takes a special kind of pompous ass to have an oil painting of themselves over their own bed. Normally, it would be a turnoff, but today looking up at his smug face while my paws were removing his son's pants, my cock was positively aching in my pants.

His jeans, shoes, and socks were pulled off in a matter of seconds. I knelt down between his legs, kissing his lips softly while my paws stroked over his maleness. The feline was certainly packing, a good pawful or two of throbbing lion meat and thick too. Certainly more than enough to make any daddy proud.

While our lips parted and my head dipped lower, my eyes flicked to the image of his father, and I couldn't help but wink. Then, my lips kissed his son's cock; the young feline cried out, and a jet of pre coated my lips. I knew he would have a hair trigger; after all, most young guys did. It takes time to learn to hold off. Of course that just made my job much easier, to suck the first load out of him, so he would last longer once my cock was inside him.

Pushing my head forward, my lips devoured his meat, my lupine tongue lapping hungrily over the thick meat. His moans were music to my ears, and my paws reached up to stroke his nuts. They were huge and sweaty in my paws. While my lips kissed his crotch, I tugged very gently on his nuts. Suddenly, his cock was throbbing, and my mouth was flooding with feline cream. His voice was lifted in ragged, panting cries of bliss.

I sucked softly as his cock throbbed, milking it of every drop and drinking it with relish. The fluid was watery and yet with a hint of cinnamon. I relished every drop until the flow slowed. I pulled off his cock, the meat slipping out of my mouth with a slurping pop, a drool of cum dripping down onto the duvet. My eyes glanced up at the oil painting, and I licked my lips.

"I'm...sorry...You were..."

My paw shot up to his lips, "Sshhhhh, you get a pass your first time: everyone knows it. Besides, a shot in the mouth makes the fuck last much longer." As I spoke, I stood up, my fingers unfastening my pants, and suddenly the stench of wolf musk filled the room. I pulled out my glory. I had the length to beat the lion cub, though I think his might have been a bit thicker. Not that it mattered, it was a cock, a real cock right before him.

The boy didn't need any encouragement: his head was leaning toward my maleness before I finished kicking off my pants. He paused and looked up at me. I gave him a nod and said, "Go ahead and explore. I'll tell you if you do anything wrong." I could see his glasses steaming up on his face.

Reaching down, I pulled them off and said, "Let's keep these safe and out of the way."

He didn't resist. I suspect because he was close enough to see all he wanted to. His trembling paws took hold of my hips. He leaned close and sniffed the tip softly, his hot breath making me moan. A few drops of my pre leaked out, landing on the plush carpet. "Go on, have a taste." I encouraged, and that was all he needed.

His tongue was rough as it lapped over my leaking tip, my hips thrust forward slightly. The young male paused for a moment to savor the experience and then placed his lips fully around my cock, closing his eyes and suckling firmly. I looked back to his father's eyes, smirking as his son moaned loudly in pleasure sucking on my cock. That face brought back the anger, the hatred. But more importantly, it made me feel strong, powerful. He may have fucked me over, but I was going to have the last laugh. When I deflowered his son, on the man's own bed.

Feline paws stroked over my creamy orbs and then onto my shaft. The young male sliding his mouth further onto my aching length, his maw was like a sauna, warm and moist. I wanted to thrust more but bit my lip, holding back on that desire. His broad feline nose huffed warm air down my length. I knew my musk was all he could smell and taste. The boy was mine, and he knew it. I gave the picture another wink as my paws reached down to stroke his head encouragingly. "Mmmm, that feels good. Now use more tongue and suck a little harder. Shit! Yeah, just like that!" I cried out as his tongue lapped eagerly over my coronal ridge and glans, teasing my meat delightfully. Then, I felt him purr, the wonderful vibration running down my cock, my hips thrusting on their own. He moaned deeply, but didn't pull back, as I stuffed his muzzle full of thick wolf meat. My paws ran through his thick mane, enjoying the feel of the hair as it ran between my fingers. "There's a good boy. You like the taste of man?"

His response was muffled by the cock in his mouth, but the extra suction and how he thrust his head further onto my shaft left me in no doubts how much he loved it. I grinned heavily as I looked up at my nemesis, thrusting into the lion's hungry mouth and moaning deeply. The wonderful sensations running up my cock made me fill the room with grunts and moans of pleasure. "Oh fuck, that's it...ohhh damn."

My fingers took a grip on his mane, light at first, while my hips thrust faster and faster. His purring grew louder as he submitted to my whims, thrusting faster and faster. I locked eyes with the picture; the feeling of power and vindication was almost as intoxicating as the warm mouth around my cock. The feelings of his tongue squirming as I stuffed my cock deeper and deeper drove me wild. I could feel my nuts were churning as his inexperienced paws tried to caress them, "Mmm fuck...Just a gentle tug...that's it...good boy...just like that. Oh fuck...oh yes!" I bit back a howl as I felt myself nearing the point of no return. My blood was pounding through my veins, my heart beating faster than ever. My paws gripped his mane tighter, I heard a soft whimper, but I couldn't stop myself thrusting faster and faster. "You are so hot...gonna cum," I cried out, the words echoing around the room as I drove my thick maleness deep into his maw.

He didn't struggle; he just let me take his maw, his eyes looking up, a heady mixture of fear of desire in his gaze. Then, I tilted my head back and howled. I couldn't help myself. I wanted the world to know I was claiming a new bitch. My cock was throbbing in his hungry muzzle as a flood of spunk filled his maw, the flow far too much for him to contain. Looking down, I could see my seed spilling out of his lips, dribbling down his chin and neck.

My eyes flicked to the painting, I smirked and decided to do a little painting of my own. Pulling my cocktip out of the lion's mouth, the last few jets of my stream landed over Colin's upturned face, pearls of white getting caught in fields of gold. My paws ruffled his mane lovingly as I whispered, "There's a good little cock sucker." I wondered how many times his father had used that as an insult, or what his father would think if he saw how the name made his son purr with pride.

I picked up the slight slurping sounds of a paw on drooling cock and looked further down. There I could see an eager paw rapidly stroking an erect cock. "Now, now son, don't get ahead of yourself." I must admit I relished the word "son," especially knowing where we were.

Lions of course are well known for their virility, as well as their hair triggers; however, I didn't want him blowing until I had made him earn it. "On the bed, all fours." I barked it like a command and was delighted to see the young man jump and quickly get into position. Now that he'd had a taste (literally and figuratively), he was desperate for more. Of course, he wasn't the only one to be all giddy and eager. There was a wonderful thrill of deflowering him in his homophobic father's bed. However, more than that, I liked him: he was sweet and innocent in a way I had forgotten guys can sometimes be. If there was anything I felt bad about, it was taking that from him.

At the time though, I was ravenous, and there was a full lion peach just pointing at me. Much like Adam and the apple, I just had to have a taste. He squealed when he first felt my tongue and cold nose under his tail. My long lupine tongue lapped hungrily on his pucker, and his squeals turned to moans, to gasps of pure bliss. I showed him no mercy, feasting like a starving dog, and my tongue wormed its way past his defenses. His hips bucked, but my paws held him firm and in position, while my lips kissed his pucker, my tongue swirling around in his tight, hot hole.

My cock was back to full attention at the taste of a young male; the sound of his squeals had woken it from its temporary slumber, and it stood to full desperate attention. My thick tongue wormed and squirmed in circles as the boy gasped and cried out, clutching at the pillows and blankets for dear life. He asked for no quarter, and I sure as hell was going to show him none.

With the scent of lion in my lungs and the taste of his ass in my mouth, I felt bestial animal urges rising inside me. I pulled back and grabbed my jeans, pulling something from the pockets, a packet of lube. Then smeared it over my thick shaft.

The red flesh mirrored in the wide open eyes of the lion, his tongue hanging out as he panted, lost in his own animal lusts.

He squealed as I shoved a lubed finger into his tight ass. I knew I was being rough, but my mind was filled with the need to take him. A second slick digit forced its way inside, swirling as I finger-fucked him none too gently. To his credit, he took it well, even pushing back for more. One thing I knew for certain: this wasn't the first thing he'd had up there: I guessed he would have a draw full of toys in his room.

That was all of the preparation I could give him, my lusts in control of me. "Onto your side, cub. It makes it easier, for your first." He flipped onto his side so fast there was nothing but a blur of gold and the thud of him hitting the bed. I spooned up behind him, my thick meat sliding over his taint until I felt the moist entrance.

I nipped on his neck gently and then whispered, "Okay cub, I want you to clench down as hard as you can, keep it clenched for as long as you can. When you can't hold it anymore, squeeze my paw." Hey, I told you I was a pro: I know how to get myself into a virgin the painless way. He nodded his head in understanding, and for a few seconds we lay together, the anticipation building. The heat of his pucker seemed to grow moment by moment, and my instincts howled at me to rail this bitch.

Then a firm squeeze, and I was away, my hips thrusting forward hard, his exhausted ring stretching easily around me, his warm depths almost pulling me in, like warm molasses. He whimpered, and I gasped as within a second I was hilt deep inside his tight ass. I licked his neck and shoulder, giving him a few seconds to adjust to my size, while above us, his father glared down with disapproving eyes. I gave the old git another smirk and a wink as I started to fuck his son.

My hips moved slowly at first, just using an inch to slid in and out, slowly stretching the cub. My eyes locked with the old lion. I remembered that afternoon, the smug look on his face as he denied me my promotion. A growl erupted from my throat, and Colin squealed as I thrust forward with extra strength. My paws gripped the young male tightly, holding him in place like an alpha holds its bitch down.

I remembered the feeling, the anger, the rage, and the need for vengeance. My hips became a blur as my thick cock reamed harder and harder, using the full length. It slammed inside the young male, stuffing his ass again and again. Colin mewled like a bitch, and I bit down on his scruff. This was my moment, my turn for revenge and satisfaction. Turn me down for being gay, fuck you! Fuck your little faggot son!

With animalistic growls and snarls I rutted the young male like a bitch in heat. His paw reached down, and I could hear the young guy stroking himself furiously; while his voice was never quiet, he moaned and cried out again and again. While I fucked him desperately, there were no more concerns about his pleasure: this wasn't about him. This was about his father. I kept my eyes fixed on that damn painting, while I fucked him with everything I had. In my mind, I was laughing, betting that fat hetero had never fucked a bitch as hard as I was nailing his son.

The rush of pleasure flooding me was far too much for me to hold off. I could feel my swollen knot slapping against his ass. Normally, I would never tie a virgin hole, but this wasn't just a virgin. This was the son of that fat fucker, and he was going to take my knot. My teeth bit down harder, and he whimpered; suddenly, I felt his ass clamping down, and the room flooded with the scent of lion spunk as he sprayed.

His ass clamping down so tightly it almost forced me out, my instincts felt the bitch challenging me. I would not be challenged by this bitch, not in that room. With a deep growl, I thrust forward with everything I had, my huge knot battering against his tight hole. I used every ounce of strength, bashing that tight hole while the cub squealed. I showed no mercy until I felt his ring give, and he squealed like a stuck pig, while I stuck him with every inch of my maleness, fucking my knot deep into him, spilling my seed into the guts of my enemy's son. I howled in pleasure, letting go of his shoulder, my hips continuing to buck as I pumped jet after jet of hot wolf spunk into his ass.

Exhausted, we both lay panting desperately for breath. I could feel his tight ass around me. I felt guilty, especially when I looked down to see traces of blood staining the sheets. I stroked his large stomach tenderly and covered his neck with kisses. "Are you okay?"

"Yeah...a bit sore," he whispered back, and the guilt burned a little deeper.

"Sorry, you were just...I couldn't stop myself," I confessed and kissed his shoulders gently. "It'll go down soon."

"It's ok...I...I just wasn't expecting it," the lion uttered, wriggling back against me. "This is nice though. Can...can I see you again?"

The question cut right into my heart. I hadn't really expected it. I'd seduced him for the wrong reasons, but I had to admit I had fun, and a second round would not be unwelcome. "Sure, pass me your phone, and I'll put my number in it. You can come over for coffee, and sex on the coffee table, then dinner and sex on the dining room table. Then, maybe I'll show you my bedroom."

"Then sex in your bed?" He chuckled.

"What, on a first date, do you think I'm that easy?" It was an old joke, but it got him laughing, and as he laughed I slipped my deflating knot free. I turned around and grabbed my pants. He passed me his phone, and I entered my number. The bed was a mess, a mixture of wolf and lion cum, with a few traces of blood. It would not be easy to clean, but the young male had all weekend to fix it up.

The slam of the front door broke us both out of any post-coital bliss. The roar of an angry male shouting, "Can you fucking believe they canceled my flight...Colin, why are your clothes in the hall?"

Like a true hero, I got out of there as fast as I could. Mr. Simons gave me a death stare and confirmed my employment status, or lack thereof, as I left. He didn't even wait for the door to close before he started to bellow at his son.

Anger, wrath, rage, and vengeance. They do stupid things to your mind. Logic flies out the window. It can lead a guy to fuck someone they really shouldn't. It can lead a father to batter his son for being a dirty faggot; he forgets the years of love and devotion.

I have never felt lower than I did that night when I got Colin's call. He was whimpering and not making a lot of sense. With a growing pit of guilt in my stomach, I agreed to meet him. He was dressed in the same clothes he had been wearing in the club, only the shirt was stained brown with dried blood. His glasses were gone, and one of his eyes was so swollen he couldn't open it. A fang was missing from his jaw.

The weird thing was, I didn't feel angry. I felt ashamed, I knew I had more than a paw in what happened. He looked so pathetic and lost, I knew what I had to do. I took him in, and I never looked back. His father ended up doing time, after I convinced Colin to file assault charges. The young guy's in college now, studying art, like he wanted. However, we always have fun when he comes back home.

My job was actually safe, but I quit anyway. I was never cut out for office work; instead I went back to my old passion. With help from some old friends, I got into police training and passed. I've seen a lot of stuff on the job that pisses me off, even more than what happened to Colin. However, I've also found that a studly wolf in uniform is a big hit down at Bottom's Up. So I always know where I can go to blow off a bad mood, or have it blown out of me anyway.

I BURNED THE BRIDGES TO HEAVEN
WEASEL

The room was filled with the smell of cakes and pastries, as well as coffee. Plates and silverware clanked together voraciously as the people around them ate their sweets and discussed the normal politics of the day. "Bachman said what? Still they protest? We should be thankful for what?" The bakery was practically a historical monument of its own sitting through all the historical changes that have happened in its tiny block. It has seen marches and influential people plow through; People protested then, much like they protest right now. Of course, it was never New York, but each state "must be occupied" as they said on the news and internet podcasts. Nevertheless, The Modern Day Delilah has lived, and it continues to breathe as much life into the cracks of that corner as the influential gods of television.

Social politics grew and changed over the years; some people never did but there are always a few who never return. Her tables never empty, and her customers rarely denied her the grace of attention. There were her regulars, the lovers in a turbulent world, the spiteful in a lovesick world—they rarely mingled amongst each other. Special tables were set up for special customers, and the bakery loved its modern regulars such as the singer. Her voice never left the walls of her favorite morning delight. So remembered by the staff, they gave her a special on the menu. The Modern Day Delilah will be hushed the day she never returns. But her voice will never leave, as much as her elegance which always matched the words she sang daily.

How it lavished in the lines she sang as they graced the walls and the ears of the people. Such a world would never be the same without them—without her! Such is the life, and somehow the bakery knew its old regulars would return in some way. It would just have to be a surprise, much like the special of the day, which was never a standard delight.

Delilah knew her share of love. From the first timers, the know-it-alls, the "together forever, but tomorrow forever ends" groups all loved the bakery, and frankly Delilah loved them. They were her own soap opera, only a better deal than the sleazy television nonsense she had to make her customers sit through sometimes. She has heard and seen everything there is to world of love and then watched it create a new world in a rapture it has not yet experienced.

"Larry was nothing more than an invalid, dear. He had no style, no sense in this world at all. He was nothing like you, Derrick" the words rolled viciously from the squirrel's tongue. Jay carried a black shine to his coat of fur, and from his chin to the neck of his shirt, one could tell he had a blue underbelly. His hazel eyes grew into the usual dreamy "I love you more than the world" look as his hands wrapped around the black hands of the raccoon sitting across from him. They slid up to Derrick's auburn arms for a moment, and he let out a faint smile.

Jay was never the one. In fact, to Derrick, Jay presented himself to be sort of creepy. He was the kind of clingy guy who would follow your every footstep like a ninja at night, waiting for you to come home and becoming jealous of any single person who looked their way. He attached himself to the raccoon as he rubbed Derrick's arm for a moment. Derrick's body began to tense up as he realized the situation could get much worse, maybe not at that moment, but progressively worse if given the time. He could just imagine the squirrel's lovesick eyes darting at every scrap of fur he left behind, and here at this coffee table, it needed to end.

Jay was like all the rest he had met, and Derrick still holds the scars from a couple of mistakes. He inched back a little bit and diverted his eyes to the tabletop thinking of how Jay was going to react when he gave him the message to go away. His hands had never been touched so gently before. Derrick could almost feel the love pouring through Jay's fingers as they rocked back and forth. It took him back to Andre, a wolf who had left so many bruises on the raccoon's past that Derrick had forgotten that the sun also rises. Jay's touch brought back the smell of sterilized hospital rooms. The beeping of the monitors synchronized with the clanking of the silverware. He could hear the machine now, making sucking noises as it pumped air. Derrick closed his eyes, and he was back in the bed, waking up to find a silver and white wolf staring at him. It held nothing; Andre's eyes were empty as they watched Derrick slowly wake. "Thought I had lost you," the wolf said as he laid his hands on the raccoon's, the same loving touch as the squirrel.

"Derrick?" his name echoed in the room, but no one was speaking. The wolf was silent. "Derrick? Are you okay?" The raccoon blinked once, and he was back at The Modern Day Delilah, Jay sitting in front of him though only holding a small card. "Listen, I have to leave now, but maybe we can do this again sometime. Here's my number," the squirrel said nervously as he dropped it on the table. From his pocket Jay's phone began to ring, and he flung it out while walking toward the door. Derrick sat back in his chair and watched the squirrel jump out into the winter weather falling from the sky. From outside, you could hear people singing Silent Night, their notes sweeping across the sidewalk as they heaved their voices through the cold.

The Christmas month had begun. The carolers were out, on time as usual on the first of December. The raccoon's coffee was getting cold now. He left some money on the table and slid on his gray hooded sweatshirt, walking out into the snow. He looked up at the sky for a moment, and then began walking up the street. Away from Andre, he had hoped.

This was New Jerusalem for the raccoon. His freedom, his escape—everything he could hope for all bunched into one small rubber ball, bouncing up and down. And still the ever-growing need to look behind him, over his shoulder in fear of the past, which had vanished years ago, would be standing right there as if to say, "How's the patient today?"

That was all the past now, a photograph he could look back at and smile, or weep as he put it back in a box closest to his heart because one day Derrick will open it, and everything he saw then, sees now, and may see soon will have changed. But the spirits will twist in his stomach until then. They will sing and dance as he moans to forget that he was never born until he left the cage of a thirst. Spirits are never a matter of forgetting, nor are they a matter of remembrance. They've no memory in this life, or even the next. It is only the ones they haunt that the remembrance of the past is given to.

Derrick shuffled into his apartment, escaping the awkward date if one was to call it that. He leaned his back against the door, laying his head on its surface, as if he were catching his breath, but he felt no fatigue. The cold was forced to retreat as the warmth of his home pushed it back; heating up his body he had to throw off his sweatshirt. The lights were all off, and he sat there in the solemnity of the passing.

His legs felt damp for a moment. They were cold and swishing around as if he were in a pool. His body quivered as he stood there in the darkness, legs cold and wet. His hands dropped down to feel what it was that covered him, and as if his hand was lashed by the cold force, he snapped it back and waited for the pain to numb away. It was liquid he felt, as if it were an ice cube melting in his hands, the water swishing in his palms, and he was immersed in it.

Derrick placed his hand along his front pocket. The raccoon rubbed his thumb along the outline of what was a small tin box. The box was everything to him. He carried it wherever he went, taking in life with it, only taking what he needed—never indulging in any more than necessary. He stole a bit of life every day, and felt that maybe he'd learn that it was more precious tomorrow than it was the moment he picked it up. He rubbed his thumb along the outline as the liquid around him began to rise, slowly starting to drown his waist and soon the box in his hands. Derrick pulled it out, stared at it, and opened it up. When he looked up from the box he saw he was standing in water, a cold stream sloshing around his legs. There was a mild confusion inside him, but it was subsided by the box as he looked at it again. As if he were holding his own child, he cradled it in the palms of his hands. He didn't move in the water, just stood still and faced its current. He took his fingers and reached inside the box, lifting something out. It was thin like a sheet of paper, folded neatly and slightly faded yellow. He began to open it, seeing a small bit of ink. A smile trudged across the raccoon's face as he began to remember what the ink was.

"Where've you been?" a voice interrupted him. His body began to tense up, afraid of the voice. It held in it a small piece of spite, its tongue lashing out with chains. "I asked you a question: where have you been?" Derrick flashed his head around the area, the water no longer surrounding him. It was his apartment that held him captive as he stood there silently watching a speck of fur appear. It was Andre. The past stood right there in front, and there was no angel to save him in this cage. The raccoon could not move; only stand in the quiet of the room, fearful of what Andre would do to him.

There was a wildness in his eyes. A look of frenzy that demanded blood; that demanded the raccoon be punished for leaving, for not answering—for existing. Derrick's heart went crooked as he stared the demon in the eyes, not able to return an answer. He wanted to shout out an apology; anything to prevent the wolf's anger from pummeling down into him, but in the darkest parts of him, he knew there was nothing to prevent the pain. There was no god between them, no heaven, nothing more than the tense atmosphere and Andre staring his down to his fragile bones. Derrick was patience—an embodiment of how many bruises you can have and pretend they don't exist. Patience never had to know god to keep the bruises from hurting. He only had to think of how empty he could make his heart each time the wolf's eyes turned to him.

"I'm..." The wolf jumped at Derrick, pinning him up against the wall. The raccoon's voice grunted as his back was slammed against posters and thumbtacks, his legs dangling above the ground. He sealed his voice and closed his eyes. He could take it if he didn't have to see it. He wouldn't have to fall apart. Andre drove his fist into the raccoon's stomach, his limber body arching forward, blood escaping his mouth. The wolf drove another, and another until Derrick's grunts became dull screams of pain. He never opened his eyes. He wanted to vomit as the blood came back down. Whatever remained from his spit pooled around his teeth and he swallowed it without recoil.

The wolf dropped his toy to the ground, driving a hard kick to the boy's face. "I ought to burn you. But I keep you alive even though you continue to fuck up. You're just a miserable mistake that I have to clean up after." His words dripped into Derrick's ears. He told himself it'd be over soon. The wolf would get tired of the beating and go out for a drink. He just had to endure a little longer—but that's the lie he'd be telling himself for all the years he carried his bruises. It was always just a little longer, just a few more scratches. On bad nights he would reach out to God but get no answer. He was alone in this universe; trapped with a man who hated him, yet loved him. But what love is there when you do nothing but drive your cock into the thing you hate?

Derrick lay there on the ground, waiting for another kick, another mark, anything—there was only silence. Andre was gone. Slowly, the pain he held in his stomach whilst his attacker stood before him washed away, going back into the waters whence it came. The marks that should have been there never appeared, only the old remained. The raccoon picked himself up, still wanting to feel the pain as he cradled upward like an elderly man in the snow. His feet rushed toward the bathroom;

he felt sick, nearly deathly in the darkness. Tearing off his shirt he saw the scars, pulled his fingers along the branches of his back, how they sprawled out and consumed his fur! It was his curse, carrying the weight from seeds he never wanted planted in him, but was forced on him. A dreamer can only bear so much pain before they collapse.

    Derrick walked away as the pain lingered among him. He entered the solemnity of his home once again, hoping it would stay as such. Peace is a gift he had always longed for, but it was too pricey for him to hold, even for a small time. Andre was gone now, he told himself. He was gone, and he could never plant another seed in him. Derrick cradled his box again, held it close to his chest as he poured himself onto the couch, laying his head backward and closing his eyes. "I burned the bridges to Heaven," he murmured softy as he drifted away.

Interlude

Everyone was silent at the end of Zinc's story. Barba looked down at the podium awkwardly, shuffling his hooves. Derek looked away from the other two, fuming. Zinc's tail twined around his leg in embarrassment.

With a nervous grin, the tiger broke the silence, "Well, do I win?"

Derek grunted and replied, "Sure, Zinc. Let's play this damn game all night. See if I give a fuck."

Zinc's ears flattened, but Barba spoke up, "Hey, let's keep going then. That was the deal."

Derek stood up suddenly, pulling his phone out of a pocket of his jeans that were still in a heap on the floor. "I'm going to light some of these damn candles." Zinc and Barba watched him turn on the light to his phone, grab a lighter from his other pocket, and start going around the room lighting candles.

Nodding toward Zinc, Barba muttered, "Hey, are you okay?"

Zinc winked back. "Yeah, he gets like this, and that's okay. Usually, he takes his anger out with sex, and you don't see me complaining about that one."

Barba smiled, but Zinc could see the concern still gleaming in his eyes. Zinc thought about how he had met the horse. It had been at a poker game after school. Although Zinc had already been dating Derek at that time, he had loved the way Barba flirted with him throughout the game. At that point, the silver ink was still shiny and wet, and Barba was entranced. However, Zinc had no real interest in the horse apart from the occasional flirt and being good friends now.

Stretching his arms high over his head so the purple sleeves fell back to his shoulders, Barba said a little more loudly, "Well, we're two cards in, and we've got five more to go. Do we want to keep doing the stories, or do we want to just read the cards? We can do the latter if you guys want. I don't want to keep you guys out all night if you have other plans."

Derek finally came back and slumped into his seat. With a grin, he replied, "Let's do the damn stories. I think at this point we might as well. Surely, it can't get worse." Although Barba was skeptical of whether Derek was being sarcastic or not, Zinc *knew* he was being facetious.

"Well, what is the next card supposed to be, Barbie?"

Barba placed a tentative hoof over the edge of the next card. "Well, the next one is supposed to be the Connection card. It should show how you guys connect."

"Like our common interests?" Derek asked.

"No, not quite. This is more of a depiction of your relationship."

Zinc placed a paw on Derek's bare lap. "Kind of like a card that would describe our relationship."

"Oh," Derek said. "I getcha." He leaned forward, grabbed a pack of smokes from his jeans, and lit up a cig. Its smoke immediately tendriled around his snout, and the red glow of the cigarette cast shadows across his face.

Barba waved a hoof in front of his own face, clearing away the smoke that drifted in his direction. "Alright, let's see what the spirits say."

As Derek rolled his eyes, all the candlelight went out, flooding the chapel in darkness.

They heard chairs falling, and then one of them released a high scream. Derek was heard shouting in his baritone, "Holy fuck!"

Suddenly, the lights went back up, the candles' flames even higher than they were when Derek had lit them. Barba, who had been crouched on the floor behind the podium, stood up and said, "Hey, are you guys okay?"

Both Derek's and Zinc's chairs had gone out from under them somehow. Derek pushed himself up into a sitting position amid the splinters of his chair, and he groaned, "Yeah, I'm alright. What the hell happened though?"

When both Derek and Barba looked to Zinc, their eyes widened. The tiger was covered in a series of bloody lines.

"Holy shit! Zinc, are you alright?" Derek cried as he crawled over to his boyfriend.

Moaning, Zinc forced himself up. "Y-yeah…" Derek and Barba crouched over him. He was covered from head to hindpaw in claw marks. Zinc looked himself over, wincing as he pressed a paw to one of the marks. "I just suddenly felt claws rake across me when the lights went out."

Barba eyed the cuts. "None of them look deep…Should we take you to the doctor?"

Zinc waved a paw dismissively. "No, I'm fine. They just all sting like hell."

Standing, Barba said, "Hold on. I'll go check in the priest's office. Maybe there will be a first aid kit or something?"

At first, Derek was inclined to argue, but he shut his mouth, realizing the effort couldn't hurt. He turned back to Zinc as Barba went off in search of bandages. "Hey, are you sure you're alright? You look bad."

Zinc started to stand and winced as his skin stretched in places. "Yeah, I'll be okay. With all this blood though, maybe I should change my nickname to Red, huh?"

Derek glared hard at him.

"Let me just go to the bathroom, and I'll clean up."

Derek raised a brow. "Are we sure they even have running water here?"

The tiger shrugged and went looking, leaving Derek alone by the podium. Derek's eyes scanned the area. Was there someone hiding there with them? Or had it just been the wood splinters that had sliced Zinc up? How had the lights went out and then back up? He found himself wondering if this was a prank Barba and Zinc were pulling on him. Fuming at the possibility, he turned around to face the entrance, and that's when he saw it.

When Zinc heard screams from the main room, he turned off the sink and ran toward the central area. "Derek? Derek, are you okay?"

As he entered, he saw Barba come in from a door on the opposite end of the room. They both saw Derek at the same time. He was pointing toward the front door. Barba and Zinc turned to look at what he was pointing to.

Zinc felt his jaw drop.

Written in his own blood on the massive door to the chapel was a message.

"BEWARE THE DEMON AMONGST YOU!"

Derek yelled at the two of them, "Did you guys do this? If you did, it's not fucking funny. The game's over."

Barba and Zinc started walking toward Derek, but kept glancing back at the door, the flickering candlelight making the blood glisten. Barba spoke, "I don't know what you're talking about, Derek. I was at the podium the whole time the lights were out. Besides, it happened over a few seconds. I couldn't have attacked Zinc, ran over to the door, written that in the dark, cleaned my hooves, and then ran back. Besides, my hooves don't even *have* claws."

Zinc nodded. "He's right. Besides, I didn't *feel* anyone next to me. I didn't smell anyone or hear anyone come up to me."

Derek shook his head in disbelief. "What the fuck are you even trying to say? That *ghosts* did this? You've got to be shitting me."

Zinc and Barba exchanged worried looks.

Derek bent down to pick up his clothes. "That's it. We're out of here."

Zinc was the first one to the door, eager to get out himself now. As he pulled on the doorknob, he froze. "No," Zinc said softly. "We can't leave."

Derek turned toward Zinc. "Why the hell not?"

Zinc stared at the bloodied door. "The door is either locked or bolted from the other side. It won't budge."

Derek strode over to Zinc, and the tiger moved out of the way, sensing the dog's anger. He grasped the two doorknobs violently and shook the doors on their hinges. "*Fuck!*" he cried. "Well then, I'll just break the damn doors down."

Barba called back from near the podium. "What if you're the demon?"

Both Zinc and Derek slowly turned to look at the horse. "What?" Derek hissed.

Barba visibly shook. "The message says that one of us is a demon. Maybe you're only wanting to get out of here so bad because you're the demon."

Derek laughed. "You don't believe that horseshit, do you?" At Barba's silence, Derek looked to Zinc. "You don't, right?" Zinc only lowered his head. Feeling his anger rising, Derek clinched his fists. "Well, while we figure out who we can trust, why don't we pass around another fucking kum ba yah ass stories? Get to know each other." Still laughing, Derek walked toward the horse, and Barba took a step backward. "Oh, don't get your saddle in a twist. Let's just play the fucking game." He grabbed a candelabra, brought it near the podium, and sat down. He looked over his shoulder and called, "Get over here, Zinc."

The tiger hesitantly walked toward the dog and horse, his tail twitching with fright between his legs.

Derek growled, "So, what will we wager this time?"

Barba tested the waters. "Let's see what the card is first?"

The German shepherd nodded and lit another smoke, his cigarette lost in the mayhem of the past ten minutes.

Barba flipped over the card. "Your connection…is Greed."

All three stared at the card's face. On it sat a colossal frog. On its arms and shoulders, more frog faces protruded, and a final frog rested in the central frog's gaping mouth. Dark splotches of ink across its body denoted either blood or grime. The disgusting image gave Zinc shivers, but he smiled despite himself. "I know a few stories about greed."

"As do I," Barba said softly.

Derek held out his paws to show he had nothing in mind. "I'm sitting this one out. My nerves are too bad anyway."

"So, what's the wager?" Zinc said with a smile.

Derek offered, "I'm tired of being the only one naked here. The person with the best story gets to keep their clothes, and the one with the worse one takes theirs off."

Barba snickered, half whinnying. "Deal."

"Deal," Zinc replied.

THE COLLECTION
T. THOMAS ABERNATHY

My old car was pushing 90 as I maneuvered it down the interstate. I glanced nervously at the small glowing display of the dashboard clock. 11:18. I had thirty miles to go, and only twelve minutes to do it in. I let my paw press more heavily on the accelerator.

It was my own fault I was late. I was reorganizing my collection, and completely lost track of time. 11:19. I hoped that they would wait for me. Pieces for my collection weren't exactly the easiest to come by, and I didn't want to miss out on this one for being just a few minutes late. Since my earlier reorganization, I had a prime spot, right up front. I didn't want to go another night without filling it. I don't think I could have gone another night. It sounds silly, I know, but that's the way collections have always been for me.

Have you ever gone grocery shopping on an empty stomach? It doesn't matter if your cabinets at home are full of the best food imaginable, or if you only stopped by the store to get one or two things. You'll always leave with more than you intended to. There's a drive there. A need. A hunger. That's the feeling I've always felt, ever since I was a cub. A hunger. A drive to collect more and more things, to obtain perfection.

I don't know when it started for me, but when I tell people that I am a collector, one particular memory comes to mind. I was very young. First grade, to be specific. It was a show-and-tell day in class. I remember being extremely nervous, because I didn't bring anything to share. It wasn't because I didn't have anything, no. My family was very well off. I just didn't want anyone to see my stuff. What if they had stolen it? So I was empty-handed, and it was recess. It was hot, and everyone wanted to play kickball. Tigers vs Lions. My team, the tigers, was sent to the outfield first, and I couldn't have been more excited. Not because I wanted to play, of course. The other tiger cubs in my class had a tendency to either ignore me, or insult me. Most of the time, I remained silent to avoid the insults, and was content to be ignored. That day, I was able to use it to my advantage. I had slowly backed away from the field, pretending to be absorbed in the game. Then, I reached the woods that bordered the playground, checked to make sure nobody had noticed, then slipped behind the trees.

Ah, the woods. It had been a gorgeous day, and the sunlight filtering down through the trees bathed everything in the woods with a golden glow. I had planned to spend the rest of the afternoon there, exploring, maybe reading a book. But then, I saw it. A spider, almost as big as my paw. It was on a gigantic web that spanned itself between two trees. I moved closer, and the sun hit the web at exactly the right angle, turning it into a dazzling display of golden spun glass. This was it. My show-and-tell. I quickly pulled my lunchbox out of my small knapsack, and dumped the banana sandwich my mother had so carefully made that morning onto the ground. I snapped the lunchbox closed over the spider, taking a decently sized chunk of webbing with me. I carefully packed the box into my bag, and sprinted back the direction I had come. I couldn't wait to show this treasure off to everyone in the class. Maybe then they would stop treating me like I didn't belong. Maybe then they'd—

At that moment, My paw caught itself on a root. I fell forward, flailing my arms to try to regain my balance. All I managed to do was fall backward. Directly onto my backpack. I cried out in pain, and heard a small pop. My lunchbox! I scrambled to untangle myself from my bag, and opened it, tears in my eyes. My plastic lunchbox had shattered into pieces at the bottom of the bag, and the spider...where was it? I reached my hand into the bag, and felt around. Nothing but broken pieces of lunchbox, and then, pain. I yanked my paw out of the bag, and stared at it disbelievingly. There were two small puncture marks where the spider had bitten me. I remember the pain, and I remember feeling betrayed by my new friend, and then the world went dark.

    11:21 now. The highway was completely deserted. I looked down at my paw. I couldn't see it now, of course, but somewhere under the fur the spider had left its mark on me. It took them three hours to find me, and then I spent another week in the hospital. My parents had said that I was lucky to be alive. I didn't care about that. I cared about the spider. I wanted to know more about it. I was a tiger, one of the strongest species I knew of. If something that tiny could bring me down...that was absolutely fascinating. Insects had become my first real interest. My first collection. As soon as I had gotten out of the hospital, I read as much about spiders as I could. I would catch every single one that I saw. My bag, which normally only carried my lunch and school supplies, was now starting to be filled with glass jars. The jars would be filled, then labeled, then moved to the ever-growing shelves in my bedroom. I even managed to find him: *Phoneutria*. Common name: The Wandering Spider. The one that started it all. I remember taking so much care to capture that one, and feeling so happy that it was finally mine. Soon, I branched out from spiders to all of the local insects, but not even that could sate my hunger. I began sending letters to my family in other locations, asking them to send me whatever they could get their hands on. As I grew through school, and then college, so did the collection. At least once a week, I would get another package from somewhere with a new species for me to study. Learning, growing. Collecting. It was a constant in my life. Something I could set my watch by. Or, at least, it was, right up until the accident.

    11:25. My phone vibrated. I glanced at the screen, and saw one unread text message. My heart skipped a beat. I was terrified. This was it. They were calling off the deal. My hand started shaking, and I opened the message. They were running late as well. I breathed a sigh of relief as I swerved into the left lane to pass an 18-wheeler that was slowly climbing up a hill. At least that bought me a little bit more time. It wasn't all that unusual for me to be out this late. Once I found a piece I wanted, I'd drive all night if I had to. Especially now, after the accident.

My father had a saying. Whenever things would get tough, he would look at me with his amber eyes, and flash me a smile. "Don't worry about it, Coop," he would say. "Even if everything around us was burning down. It would be okay. You can always rebuild."

I thought back to that night. I remembered the heat of the flames stinging my nose, and singing the fur on my arms. I fought my way into my parent's bedroom. They lay in their bed, unmoving. Their unseeing eyes reflected the flames creeping up the walls just like glass. Glass jars. At that moment, my stomach dropped. My collection. My life. I barely felt the pain as I broke through the smoldering door of my bedroom. The glass vials that had adorned the shelves since childhood seemed to scream at me in anger as the heat exploded them one by one. I screamed back as I tried to salvage what I could. The fire was overtaking everything. It pushed me back down the hallway, past my parents' room, and back outside. All that I had left was what was in my backpack. One jar. One empty jar with a faded label. I sat on the lawn, turning it in my hands blankly, watching the remnants of my life and my family go up in smoke.

"Don't worry about it Coop. You can always rebuild." I kept hearing my father's words. And I tried. After my parent's life insurance policy came through, I was able to get the house repaired. I moved back in. But it was so empty. Everything that I had worked for had evaporated in a single night. The idea of trying to rebuild what I had lost was so daunting. I tried collecting other things. Trading cards, antique furniture, but nothing fulfilled me. I ached for the feeling I had in my youth:

that soul-satisfying gratification whenever I'd place another jar on the shelf. I was miserable.

11:35. I finally saw the sign for my exit. I took it, and entered a small suburban shopping center. I pulled into the parking lot of a little diner, and turned off the car. Other than the employees' cars in the back, I was the only one there. I was early. I began to feel excited.

I'd only started collecting again recently. I was browsing the local classifieds online a few months ago, just looking at what was available. Then, it hit me like a punch in the face. The craving. The need. I looked at the ad, copied down the number, and called immediately. I was thrilled just to have the feeling again. When I got it home, it was perfect. It had been so long since I'd felt that joy. The same joy I had on that day for show and tell. I carefully selected a container, and put my new treasure inside. I dutifully labeled it, as I used to: scientific name first, then common name. I made up my mind then and there. I was going to have the biggest, and best collection, more than anyone in the world. My bedroom was going to be too small for this. I remember making so many plans as I lugged my new treasure down the stairs to the basement. My father's tools, untouched by the fire, seemed to beckon to me. I had crafted a shelf that night, and placed the container on it prominently. Things picked up from there. Soon, I was back to adding new containers to my shelves at least once a week. I was so thrilled. I loved getting that feeling, and I would take it every chance i could get.

I typed a quick message on my phone. "I'm here. Out front. Blue Buick," and sent it. I was happy, and I basked in that feeling. Even though I had been delayed, I was still getting what I wanted. And if I'm being honest, the delay had been worth it. I had always kept my collection in perfect order, but tonight, I had to reorganize. I had run out of space in the basement, and I knew I wasn't going to have room for this piece. So I expanded. I had built shelves in my parents' old room, and had lovingly moved each container to its new home. It was tiresome work, but the thrill of studying each piece as I moved it, combined with the excitement for tonight, gave me energy. Like I said, I had completely lost track of time. When I finished, I stood back and admired it. My collection. "I have to go," I whispered softly. There was no response. The darkened shapes never gave a response, but that's what made them special. They always listened. "I'll be back soon, and you'll be getting another piece!" The light from the streetlight outside danced on the smooth glass surfaces. There was no response, but even the air in the room seemed to echo my excitement. I softly closed the door, and made my way to the car.

My phone buzzed again. I opened the message. "Pulling in." A grin crept over my face. A car pulled into the lot, and idled next to mine for a moment before turning off. The door opened, and a large bull got out, and began walking around toward me. The feeling grew stronger. The want. The absolute need. I reached into my satchel in the passenger seat, and pulled out the empty jar from the night of the accident. I gently caressed the faded label for luck, as I did every time I was meeting someone. I looked down. It had faded over the last year, but I could still make out the name. *Phoneutria.* The wandering spider. Even though it had died in the fire, I had grown to not regret releasing my prize into my parents' bed that night. "Even if things are burning down, Coop." My father's words again. I silently thanked him for the idea. I gently placed the jar back into my bag, letting my fingers gently graze over the serrated edge of a small hacksaw. I checked my reflection in the rearview mirror. I straightened my shirt, and opened the car door. The awkward cub had grown into quite the handsome tiger, and the tiger was hungry. I gave the bull my most winning smile, showing off my sharp teeth. *I'm going to need a bigger jar for this one*, I laughed silently to myself. I extended my hand to the bull. *Bos taurus.* Common Name: Austin.

"Hi. I'm Coop."

STAY
HYPETAPH

"Breakfast is ready!"

On the dot every morning, 7:38 a.m., the table would be marked with four plates, on which two of them would be an average meal: eggs, some hash, a few pieces of sausage. Cecil took pride in her cooking, and though Kal was always late coming to it, his lack of punctuality did not dampen her mood while she sat by her plate and waited. A stressed hinge sounded from the upper floor, leading Cecil's ears to perk as she listened for, and soon saw, her son walking downstairs.

His fur, though messy, caught the filtered sunlight with splendor, a contrast to his fading black tank and lounge pants. His gold fur was one of the more astounding features he and his family had, a characteristic of "true, pure, Himalayan wolves," his mother would say (though Kal wasn't certain that was true.) His sleepy footsteps had to avoid a few misplaced boxes along the way, in which were collected books, electronics, and various other things.

He seated himself across the table, and then the two began to eat. Between bites, they exchanged pleasantries:

"How did you sleep?"

"Hrmm."

"Did you dream of anything?"

"No."

"Did you want to go to that new café in town?"

"Mom, I alrea—"

"They have some of the *best* soups, I've been told. Marissa—you know Marissa—Marcus's mom, she told me—"

"Wait, mom, I ca—"

"*She* told me that they even offer discounts on Saturdays, so today is perfect if we—"

"You know I can't, I have to pa—"

"And," Cecil raised her voice, "Don't interrupt—and I would be willing to pay since I know you're not in the best of finances right now."

Here it goes, Kal thought, "Mom you know I'm moving out on Sun—tomorrow, actually—, I have to stay home and pack."

"Nonsense, you have plenty of time."

Kal folded his ears back. He was done arguing. He just wouldn't go. She would make the plans regardless of his opinions (as she always did), and he would just have to disappoint her (as she always said he did.) He finished his food in silence—his mother did not. Rather, Cecil kept talking about arbitrary subjects in an effort to lighten the mood, discussing food, and school, and Kal's girlfriend, and "if your brother were here," and—

Kal stopped listening.

Having finished his meal, the wakened wolf scraped his plate clean before setting the dish in the sink, and retreated back to his room upstairs. His walls were bare; much lighter squares decorated the areas where posters and pictures had been hung before being rolled up and (difficultly) organized into boxes.

"...if your brother were here."

The words resonated within him, stirring uncomfortably. Kal was accepting of the reality, honestly: his brother had left them about six years ago—for college, Kal knew—but he had not told them what day he was leaving. Kal had not expected much else, for their mom had been acting just the same way: overbearing, refusing to listen, in some ways hindering—it made sense that Eric had left without wanting another household scene to instigate. That ultimately did not bother him…what did was that his older brother had never contacted him again afterward, as if he hadn't just been avoiding the scene, but distancing himself from the family entirely. That was what hurt the most. Even weirder was that some of his things had not been taken, as though he were in more of a hurry than any of them had thought. These boxes had been put in the crawlspace by Cecil. No one was allowed to touch them.

But as the previous days had permitted, Kal understood more and more why that may have been the case. Every day there was something new to stop Kal from preparing for the move: a garden to be built, a trip to town to be made, a goddamn café to visit. Cecil was exhausting in her attempts to persuade Kal to stay—or if not stay, just to "stay a little longer." The wolf picked at his teeth.

Downstairs, Cecil was cleaning the table. The food was delicious as it always was, and following her own she collected the two unused plates and stacked them in the cupboard with the others. So...her little Kal was growing up. The nest would be empty, and the idea terrified her. Since the disappearance of Eric, the idea of her second son vanishing left her with knots in her stomach, and she could not help but fear what she would fill her time with in his absence. As she paced, she cleaned countertops and cabinet handles in a shaking attempt to distract herself from the reality that soon, ever so soon, she would be alone. Unsure of what else to do, she began to cook: little cookies, a gift to Kal.

There was a knock at the door.

"Kal!" Cecil shouted, "Kal, be kind and grab the door for me?"

Her son traversed steps and boxes again, this time in a pair of jeans and a color-blocked Henley, before opening their home to their guest, a black panther with eyes of golden amber, almost enough to match Kal's fur. "Oh, hey Claire!" he greeted his girlfriend.

She let herself in with a hug, and the two of them laughed. Cecil stopped stirring the batter, "Oh, hello Claire. I didn't realize you were visiting."

The panther stepped back and smiled, "Sorry! I thought Kal had told you." Kal looked down, his ears folded; he had not. Claire continued, "I'm here to help him pack, I hope that's okay. I mean…if now isn't a great time, I can just—"

"No, of course it's fine! I can't just turn away a guest! Stay, help; I'm making cookies actually, so you came at a fantastic time!"

Claire was thankful, for she had taken a bus, and having to leave would have been an incredible inconvenience; with "thanks" from the two of them—Kal's more apprehensive than hers—the couple stole upstairs, the final remark being Claire's: "Your mom is always cooking; she is so cute."

Back to cooking Cecil went, though now she stirred the mixture with a little more force in her wrist. Her eyes were glaring to the yard outside her window, rather than the bowl. Her thoughts wandered about as she struggled ever more to come to terms with the fact that her son was leaving. *And that bitch*, she thought, *He invited her over just to annoy me. Don't call me 'cute.' I am your elder.* She doubted they were even packing, *probably looking to desecrate my house. It's bad enough that he couldn't have found another Himalayan, or at LEAST a wolf, heavens.*

She rummaged through her shelves, searching for vanilla, some sugar, a few other things; "Damn, I thought I had more." She threw a bottle to the trash. She'd already started making the cookies—no point wasting them just because Claire had come over.

There were tons of things still needing to be put up, but most of the big things had been cleared. Kal's desktop had been wrapped and stored, but his laptop sat alone on his desk. The television was no longer on the wall, and now Kal and Claire were packing up (or throwing away) the smaller things in the room. Pictures, souvenirs, binders and books—honestly, Kal knew he was capable of finishing the task himself, but it was less upsetting to do it with Claire.

"I'm so proud of you hon: you're heading off to college!" She sung the last two words, and Kal smiled. Claire had been going to the local state school for a year now; without her insistence, Kal knew, he may not have even applied anywhere else. But here he was, moving a city and an hour over to go to an incredible university for programming.

The wolf responded with a teeth-baring smile, and the two shared a kiss, "Seriously Claire, thank you. This is crazy. I never thought I'd even leave this house, really." It felt weird to say, but he and Claire had had this conversation before.

She cupped his chin in her paw, "Look at me. Look. You cannot—you can't always stay here. I know your mom will miss you. I know what you're feeling, but *you* shouldn't feel like you have to sacrifice your future to make her happy. It isn't your fault your brother left, and you don't have to stay here for her because of it."

It was even weirder to hear, but Kal had been thinking the same for days, weeks. It was tough for both him and his mom when Eric left. For a while, Kal was mad at Eric just as well, but the more he was the sole subject to his mother's lamentations, the more he understood why Eric avoided her when leaving. Sure, it was tough to grow used to: the now-uninhabited room adjacent to his, the second empty plate at the table, the nightmares that follow abandonment.

Oh, the nightmares: they always involved pipes, or vents, or some reverberating metal sound which would startle the poor soul into waking in a cold sweat. He and Eric, when they were much younger, would talk quietly through the vent between their rooms, whispering about whatever came to mind: games, school, and girls, anything they could. They mostly did it just because their mother told them not to.

Eventually, however, the nightmares stopped reminding him his brother had gone. Now it was only his mother doing so.

"Kal," Claire said again, stronger. The wolf shook his head—he had not heard her the first time, "Kal, this is great. This is *great!* You have no idea how much you will love living on your own."

The bedroom doorknob struggled, "Kal, what have I said about locking your room?"

The two sighed, and Cecil's son opened the door for her, "Sorry mom."

She brushed the topic aside, not wanting to argue in front of Claire, "Just don't do it again—oh, gosh, you won't even be able to soon, will you?" Kal did not reply. "Oh! But enough with that! I finished the cookies for the two of you!"

The three talked about nothing for a while as Kal attempted to make awkward suggestions to her to leave, and after about thirty minutes and a plethora of topics she finally swung the door inward and left—Kal had to finish shutting it, "She never closes my door."

"You want any?" Claire asked, taking a treat from the tray Cecil left.

"No thanks. I just ate. Maybe later."

Claire and Kal continued packing and talking, occasionally kissing and laughing, and Cecil sat downstairs with a book and some coffee. *There wasn't much left to box up. Claire won't need to stay any longer, thank God. Then Kal and I can eat and talk and maybe he'll abandon this notion that he has to move for college. I don't know why he cannot stay here—an hour drive is barely anything when compared to the cost of living. Oh, he's young; he doesn't know what's best for him yet. But he is my son, so of course I need to look out for him. I've always had to.*

She had been reading the same page over and over, not really focusing on the contents. The book had been suggested to her, and she'd read things by the author before. His work was always well-written, and while Cecil was not a fan of his rather queer characters, she read them so that she could discuss the books with her friends. Yet, she simply could not focus, and ultimately had to sit the book down. *It's been at least half an hour; when is she leaving?*

A door slammed, and Cecil jumped; her coffee spilled slightly from her cup and accosted her paw: *Goddammit.*

"Kal! Kal, is everything alright?"

She was answered by retching and splashing water, but no voices: "Kal?"

"Mom, hold on!" A door slammed again.

I do not fucking think so. She marched up the stairs, and one of the boxes collapsed down them as she deliberately made no attempt to avoid it. Something shattered. *Oops.*

The coughing came from the bathroom, and without announcement Cecil let herself in, "Oh, my!"

Claire was huddled over the toilet, Kal resting a paw on her back. She lurched forward and with one paw grabbed the rim of the bowl while the contents of her stomach forced themselves out of her. The panther cried lightly, to which Kal responded with soft a "Shh, shh; you're okay." Cecil grabbed some water and medicine before rushing back, "Oh honey; here, here, take these if you can."

A few minutes passed, and the vomiting ultimately subsided. Graciously, Claire accepted the medicine and swallowed it without hesitation. "Claire, sweetheart, I think you need to go home."

Kal looked at his mother in disbelief. *Offer her a place here!* he thought, but he knew arguing would be useless. Instead, "She didn't drive here: she took a bus. I can't make her wait that long."

"Oh, in that case," Cecil retaliated, "I'll drive her home"

Claire was in no position to argue, and Kal knew it would be worthless. Cecil continued, "Claire, do you have any roommates that would be able to let you in if I brought you home?"

The panther coughed, "I live on my own—I have keys though. It's not a problem."

Kal and his mother helped the sick panther downstairs and into Cecil's car. "No, no," Cecil said, "Lay in the back Claire, get some rest. You shouldn't be sitting up if you feel sick. Kal, will you please grab my bag for me?"

"Yeah, yeah, no problem," Kal darted back inside. After searching longer than comfortable, he found it beside the living room recliner. As he left the house with the bag in his grip, he paused. His mom's car was not in the driveway—she had left. *Are you fucking serious?*

Nearly an hour later, Cecil returned home, humming as she entered the house. She locked up behind her, and as the front door *clicked* in place. Kal demanded, "Mom, what the hell? Why di—"

"Don't you curse in my house!"

"Mom, fuck that," Kal ignored her, his voice rising, his tail swaying angrily, "Why didn't you wait for me? I cannot believe you would do that while my girlfriend is literally throwing up!"

"That's exactly why," Cecil responded, her voice softer now, "She started heaving again, I knew I had to get her home, I just couldn't wait any longer; I didn't want her throwing up in the car."

"Why could she not have just stayed here?" Kal retorted, "What made you think driving for half an hour was the better decision?"

"I don't know!" she yelled back, tears began forming in the corners of her eyes, "I was just trying to help, okay? All I know was I saw someone important to my baby feeling terrible and I just wanted to help and now, now—"

Oh no.

"—and now I'm being yelled at for trying to do something right!" Cecil concluded, tears flowing much more freely. Kal could do nothing but awkwardly comfort his mom, for there was no arguing through tears. An uncomfortable hug led the two in silence for ten or so minutes before the crying eventually stopped, and without another word, Kal went upstairs.

He had texted Claire to message him when she was feeling better. While he was still mad, he was nonetheless happy that his mother had taken her home—Kal would rather she be safe and comfortable, regardless of whether or not he got to see her to it. The sun had since descended, which was a good indicator for Kal to go to bed. He had finished most of his packing, and the movers didn't come for another day anyway, so following a stressful day he figured he would call it quits early.

He pushed the door in with a *click*, pulled his shirt off, and climbed into bed, flicking the lights off on his way. The room was an eerie sort of quiet, the usual comforts absent from the walls. His game posters typically provided a sense of familiarity; the letters from friends were hovering kindnesses. Now, his room felt more along the lines of a cell. His phone was unusually inactive—Claire must have gone straight to bed, and Kal figured he ought to do the same. With agitated exhaustion, he rolled to the side and allowed himself to close his eyes.

The night settled softly, darkening the room and its inhabitant. Kal tossed lightly in his sleep, snoring lightly, grunting at other times, until suddenly he lurched upward with a sharp inhale of breath. The sounds of pipes rattling in his ears dampened his fur with sweat, and as he studied the room with frantic eyes he paused, before letting one soft breath slowly release: *just a nightmare*, he thought.

He groaned and lay back down, before shielding his eyes from the blinding light of his phone as he glanced at it: no new messages. Huh. That was incredibly unlike Claire, unless she had been super tired, Kal concluded. He sent her another message, one for her to wake up and smile at receiving: "Love you Claire. Hope you're feeling better <3"

A light shone at the other end of his room, sitting on his desk. *Are you serious?* The wolf forced himself up, and he stepped unevenly to the source. Claire had left her phone. How he had not noticed while cleaning, he was unsure, but he was sure that he had been stressed, and this at least alleviated the idea that she had not been texting him back. He looked at the screen and read his own message back to him, and a small snicker rumbled inside him; he couldn't believe he had actually thought Claire wouldn't text him ba—

A slam sounded from outside which drew Kal's eyes away from the phone and pulled him toward the window. His eyes were readjusting to the darkness, but they grew acclimated just in time to see his mother walking back inside from their backyard. Kal turned to leave—at one a.m., what could she possibly be doing outside?—and as he reached for the door and pulled it toward him, he realized he had not needed to turn the knob—he was certain he had shut it before going to sleep.

"Mom?" he asked as he descended toward the kitchen, "Mom, what's up? Something happening outside?"

Cecil was at the base of the stairs before he had reached them, "Kal, why are you up so late? I thought you had gone to sleep?"

"I woke up. What were you doing outside?"

She shifted, "Oh, just taking out the trash. Cooking earlier made a bigger mess than I thought, and there's always garbage lying around this house."

I'm not doing this now. "Okay, well, goodnight. I'll see you in the morning."

Kal returned to his room, and this time he was sure to lock his door.

Again, Cecil had cooked in the morning, but Kal was unable to eat much, for the movers were there earlier than he had anticipated.

He and they—two stallions—began to collect his things, and Cecil could find herself only silently fuming at the reality. Boxes upon boxes were loaded into the back of the truck, and soon the desk, his chair, bookshelves, among other things. He sent Claire an email before packing up his laptop, so she would not be worried about her phone.

"Mom, could you help with the smaller boxes?"

"No."

Oh my God.

"Where are you going to sleep tonight?"

"What do you mean?"

"Well, they're taking your bed, right? Where are you going to sleep?"

"Oh. Well, I figured I would just crash on the couch. They deliver the stuff to my apartment overnight and load it into the house for me. I'll be there either Monday or Tuesday after I collect the smaller things—dishes, cleaning supplies, stuff like that. I planned on buying those before I left."

"That's a convenient service," Cecil responded, unenthused. She did not look at Kal, "Well, you'll have to help them disassemble your bed. It won't come down the stairs in one piece."

She was right, Kal mused, and as their conversation concluded, he headed to his room: "Hey guys, would you mind helping me out with this?"

Cecil paced the kitchen. *This can't be happening. He can't leave, he can't, he's my baby.* She grabbed a rag and began compulsively scrubbing the countertops. There were crumbs from breakfast scattered about, a splash from the sink—*how can I make him stay? Not again, not like Eric.* She paced further, then paused—Kal had the right idea: cleaning supplies. She wasn't a scientist, but she had watched enough trashy day television to know about sabotage.

In a box of her own, she collected sponges, soap, trash bags, bleach—specifically bleach—and made her way to the van. The three boys were upstairs, more than likely fidgeting with the metalwork of his bedframe, and with a quick glance around to ensure no one was looking, she unscrewed the van's gas cap, uncapped the bleach, and poured half of the mixture into the tank. Ever as swiftly, she circled to the back and slid the box against the other packages. Cecil made her way back inside, just in time to meet them carrying the frame and mattress downstairs.

"Mom, why are you breathing so hard?" Kal asked, shifting the weight of the frame pieces beneath his arm.

"Oh, well," she paused, "I had thought about what you said, needing cleaning supplies, so I packed a box for you. It was just heavier than I thought it would be is all."

Kal was visibly surprised, "O-oh, well, thanks. I really appreciate that, mom."

She waved her paws, "Don't worry about it, baby. I know your financial situation isn't fantastic so I thought I'd help in even a small way."

Kal rolled his eyes—of course it had to be another jab, trying to make him feel guilty. He appreciated the bleach all the same; ultimately it was less money he would have to spend.

The frame and mattress were the final things to be stored away, and after a pawshake and three hundred dollars later, Kal sent the two workmen on their way, excited for his possessions to reach his new home. He relaxed at the base of the steps, sweaty and tired. His footpaws were a little sore, his arms even more so, and after resting for a bit he rewarded himself with a warm shower. Things were going well—his mom seemed to be more and more comfortable with the idea of him moving, even if she wouldn't admit it, and he could bring the phone to Claire tomorrow as an excuse to leave earlier and spend time with her before leaving for his new apartment. He would email her again, but his computers were all packed up and on their way.

"Kal!" his mother shouted from the living room, "Kal! Come quick!"

The Himalayan wolf groaned and rested his head against the shower wall. Why did she have to be doing this now? "Coming!" he shouted back, before leisurely stepping from the shower. He toweled off, his wet fur pointing every direction, and pulled on a tank and some gym shorts before, still wet and annoyed, following her voice.

She pointed at the television, "I was just watching the Game Show Network when this—this emergency traffic bulletin thing came on—that's...that isn't the same van, is it?"

Everything was silent. Kal could not hear anything anymore beyond the newscaster on in front of him. Even his mom, who was rattling on, emitted no sound that was not overshadowed by the otter with a microphone:

"I am standing on the roadside of a wreck before the I-68 exit where a large wreck has caused three lanes to come to an absolute standstill. It seems that the truck swung right—presumably due to the engine stalling, as police have told us—before side-swiping a sedan, and compensated by over-adjusting left, at which point a semi collided directly with the driver-side door. The van's driver was pronounced dead on the scene, and four others involved in the wreck have been rushed to the hospital, two in critical condition. Debris has been scattered across the roadway, and emergency crews are working diligently to clear the wreckage. Expect delays for at least the next two hours."

Kal did not know what to say. He felt absolutely defeated. That was...that was everything he had: how could he start school with no computer? No books? No fucking bed?

"Mom, what...what am I supposed to do?"

She did not hesitate, "We can replace your stuff—I'm just so glad you weren't in that car with them. You could stay here until then, sweetie."

"Mom!" Kal yelled. He turned to Cecil with fire in his eyes, "I am not, *not* staying here! Goddammit, my scholarships have already *paid* for tuition. You think they'll just refund that? I *have* to go; that isn't the question! It's about my goddamn stuff!"

Tears began forming in Cecil's eyes, and Kal stepped back with an exaggerated sigh, "No. No, you don't get to do this—this isn't *about* you, okay? This is about me, my stuff, *my* future, do you fucking get that?"

"No, it wouldn't be about me, would it?" Cecil retorted, "No, you're just like your brother, wanting to leave me—you probably won't talk to me again either, will you? No, I guess I didn't sacrifice my time for you, or my money, or my youth—no, this is all about you, isn't it?"

Kal was dumbfounded, "Yes! Yes, me going away *is* about me! What the fuck makes you think otherwise? Are you serious right now? How can you be so selfish—so fucking greedy—that you cannot understand the fact that this isn't about *your* future."

"Oh, so my son leaving doesn't affect my future? My plans?"

"I am not doing this. I'm not. Do not fucking talk to me right now. I'm catching a bus in the morning, and I am out of here."

Cecil argued, but Kal was having none of it. He stormed upstairs and slammed his door, locking it behind him and pacing the emptiness. He would sooner sleep on the floor than be subject to her tirade on the couch. For nearly twenty unanswered minutes, Cecil pounded at the door and pulled against the doorknob, but Kal was unrelenting in his silence and after so long, she understood the futility of her efforts and descended the stairs.

He went to bed angry, uncomfortable, and cold, his breath as heavy as the weight of his fears for the future.

Again, a loud sound erupted in the night, though this time it was much closer than outside, and much less isolated. Multiple *bangs!* and *thumps!* echoed in the hallway, and Kal, dazed and only half-awake, knew well enough the sound of his mother shouting, "Kal! Kal, help!"

He bolted up and the room spun around him. He staggered to the door, nearly tripping over the ends of his lounge pants, and pushed himself to the hallway. In the dim night light he could see a crumpled mass at the foot of the stairs and his heart skipped a beat, "Mom?"

There was no reply.

He inched down the first step and called again, "Mom?" Had she fallen down the stairs? Why was she up here anyway? "Mom, are you oka—"

A furious jolt of pain surged through Kal's back as something cold and forceful cracked against the base of his spine. A soundless breath emptied his lungs, and for a moment the wolf could not find air. His legs gave out and he toppled forward, grunting and groaning with every step until he collided with the garbage at the foot of the stairs. He was assaulted by the smell of old eggs and cleaning solution, and through his pain and dizziness and confusion he saw a figure walking toward him.

"Mom...?"

In Cecil's paw was a crowbar, which wavered menacingly with each slow, frightening move she made, "I told you. I told you I wanted you to stay here."

She took another step, and Kal flinched, "Mom, stop, I—"

"No, *you* stop." She pointed the tool at him, and he recoiled. "I told you, I told you this was about me. You only wanted to think about your future, and what it had for you; well I will be *damned* if you think you can leave me to die alone so easily." She moved forward.

Kal attempted to push himself back through the mess, "I promise, I wasn't leaving forever, I swear, I swear it."

The crowbar connected with Kal's shoulder, and he yelped in pain; his entire arm rung with uncontrollable shivers as he attempted to stifle sobs.

"No. None of that crying. Not now. You had your chance to stay," Cecil kneeled down and cupped his head in one palm, her voice a whisper, "You're my baby…you can't leave me alone."

His paw searched frantically for anything it could find, before wrapping itself around a bottle. His confusion was heightened by the words across its label—"Ipecac"—before he realized, too, that Cecil claimed to have taken out the trash the night before—why was the bag so full? He went to hurl the bottle at her with whatever strength he could collect, but before the bottle could escape his paw, the crowbar met his with a resounding, sickening, bone-shattering blow. He whimpered and cried out desperately, and his jaw too was met by the cold metal; a pain so striking and so sudden surged through his mouth and along his ear that it eclipsed the agony of his broken wrist as he attempted to comfort his face. Blood pooled in his mouth as he coughed, and escaped through his teeth like a grotesque waterfall of fear as his mother stood ahead of him.

"You're my baby."

The force of the swing against Kal's head was so excruciating that his falling unconscious was a kindness.

The night air was cool, and the cold, wet grass rubbing against Kal's back shook him from his slumber, but only for a moment. His next waking moment was in darkness, the scent of mildew and wood shavings filled his nostrils, and as he attempted to move he found his arms bound behind him. His wrist pulsed and flared, and Kal could only bury his face in the soft earth beneath him as tears rushed down his face. As he scanned his environment, there was nothing he could see beyond blackness.

A small prick of light sparked and held steady, held in the paw of a face only barely illuminated: Cecil. She waved the match lightly and crawled closer to her son, "You're my baby, you cannot leave, no, no."

The Himalayan wolf looked away. His once magnificent golden fur was stained red around the face, and every part of him ached with reverberation as he tucked his tail between his legs, "Please...please I will stay, I promise, please."

Cecil shuffled. Kal flinched.

"I told you...I told you—you were being selfish—you were being so, *so* selfish to leave your poor own mother to be alone. You think I don't know why you chose a college an hour away? Do you? There is a fantastic university just twenty minutes away—you should know, your whore girlfriend went to it—and you *still* chose to abandon me."

Kal pulled his legs closer to him and Cecil met his knee with the blunt crash of her weapon. He recoiled inward further, and through sobs stifled, "What do you...what do you mean Claire 'went?'"

Cecil breathed inward, "Poor word choice, but I digress. That bitch was helping you, I just know it. Helping you abandon me. So...so I had to rid you of the negative influence."

"The ipecac."

Cecil nodded, "Among other things."

Kal was visually confused, before his eyes widened in terrified realization, "Mom...mom you didn't."

She crawled back, the match flowing with her, and as she moved more to the opposite of the crawlspace, in the darkness Kal could see Claire's emotionless, statuesque face staring at nothing.

Kal began sobbing, and Cecil inched toward him again, grasping his face in her paws and pushing their foreheads together. The match fell to the cold dirt and its light dissipated into smoke, "No, no, baby, don't you see? This is good. This is good! I get to have you all to me—all to me—no school, no Claire—all to me."

"People...others will look for her," Kal argued through his searing mouth, "People will wonder where she went."

Through tears, Cecil shook her head, though Kal could not see it, "Oh, I'm sure, I'm sure. People will look for you too, sweetheart. But come now...two lovers? Vanishing together without a trace? At the start of a college career? Key word: *together*. Classic love story, sweetheart. You are a lovesick runaway, whose sad, lonely mother has no idea, no idea where you could have gone."

Kal's stomach churned, and the scent of weak smoke distracted him. He wanted to shuffle his weight, to move, to stop hurting, but he feared the crowbar: "How did you kill her?"

There was silence.

"How did you kill her?"

"...it is astounding...truly, how easy it is to suffocate one dizzied by ipecac."

Kal had nothing more to say, and though Cecil did, he was not listening to it. This could not be happening, this could not be happening—everything was supposed to be smooth sailing; he would leave and learn and live a life of his own, and he and Claire could have had fantastic times: dating, eating, reading, laughing, fighting, getting over it, loving—all the normal shit two people do when they love each other...but now—now they shared a tomb.

"Oh, being silent will not fool me. I've learned that lesson already. Eric taught me that. No, no. I thought he would be quiet too, and then he started screaming. At first I thought I was imagining it, and then you had your nightmares and I knew—I knew he was screaming."

The darkness was more impending than ever, and Kal was at a loss for words. Was this...she had done this before. Eric didn't leave. He had *wanted* to leave, and mom had done exactly what she was doing now.

"But oh, oh no, don't worry sweetheart, I'm not just going to leave you here—I love you, after all, you're mine—you're mine, and I love you."

Kal was crushed by the weight of the darkness.

"You'll get a box all of your own."

Interlude

Derek nodded to Barba at the end of his story. "Fuck, that made me uncomfortable."

The horse stretched his arms wide and snickered. "So, I guess that means I win?"

"Fine by me," Zinc said, pulling his shirt over his head and tossing it to the dust-coated floor. His pants soon followed, and both Derek and Barba marveled at his lack of underwear. They stared hard at his already erect spined cock. While Derek felt a loving desire for that cock, Barba smiled with a more primal hunger. The tiger purred as he noticed the two men staring at him. "Hey, Barbie, why don't you go on and strip, too? Might as well at this point, right?"

"Don't mind," Barba started, lifting his purple silk robe over his head, "if I do." He tossed the robe onto Zinc's pile of clothes, and Derek grimaced. As hot as the muscular horse was, Derek was not yet a hundred percent comfortable with multiple partners, even if it was just for a one-time thing. He lacked Zinc's openness. Still, he did not protest and merely growled softly in thought.

Derek pulled out his phone. "I'm gonna see if I can call someone to open the damn doors. This is fucking ridiculous."

Zinc reached a paw out to rub Derek's side. "Still in a hurry? Well, I guess it can't hurt. I'm really sore from these scratches anyway."

At the tiger's touch, Derek shivered. While he turned on his phone and pulled up his address book, he looked out of the corner of his eye and could have sworn he saw something, red stains on the tips of Zinc's claws. His eyes went back to his phone. His first thought was that maybe Zinc had scratched himself up after all, but then, he remembered that Zinc had went to the bathroom and cleaned up. He might not have focused on his paws too much. Besides, there was no way the tiger could have written the message during that short time in the dark.

"Fuck," the German shepherd said.

"What?" was Barba's reply.

"Can you believe it? No fucking service."

Barba snorted. "Mine is back in my car anyways, so it wouldn't do us any good."

"Same here," Zinc added.

"So," Derek said, "we have no communication with the outside world, and we are trapped here with some fucking ghosts, or spirits, or demons, or a crazy homeless guy who's probably watching us from some dark corner or something. And we're just stuck here playing a card game. Do I have that all correct?"

Although Zinc's ears flattened, he offered a sly smile. "Yeah, but you're also playing a fun card game with your sexy boyfriend and your best friend, both of whom are naked in a dimly lit cathedral ruin. How much sexier can you get?"

Snorting again, Barba said, "How much more sacrilegious can you get?"

Derek growled back, "I'll be blasphemous all damn day as long as I get out of here in one piece." Still, talk of blasphemy had him thinking about the message on the door, the message that claimed one of them was a demon in disguise. Despite himself and despite his love for his partner, Derek kept an eye on Zinc. The tiger was too relaxed, too comfortable. He wasn't sure if this was all Zinc's sick idea of a joke, or if maybe the message on the wall was pointing to Zinc. "What's the next fucking card supposed to be, Barba?"

The horse brightened at talking about the cards again. He, too, had had his eye on Zinc, and immediately questioned the tiger's religious beliefs. He had known Zinc for a while but had never known him to be so blatantly atheist. "Yeah, so the next card, our fourth one, is supposed to be you guys' common ground. *This* is the one that shows what you both bond over."

At the same time, Zinc said, "Knots," and Derek said, "Sports." The two looked at each other in almost angry disbelief.

Barba laughed as he flipped over the fourth card. Staring back at him was a wild-eyed wolf, snarling as black, writhing snakes ate their way through its skull. Raising a brow, he called, "Your common base is Envy..." As Derek and Zinc started talking, Barba zoned them out. "Wait a second..." He looked back over the past four cards. "These are all..."

Zinc finished his muttered sentence, "The seven deadly sins. What kind of deck do you have there anyway, Barbie? Satan's Tarot for Dummies?"

Barba shook his head. "The sin cards were just seven bonus cards for the deck. I kept them in more as a gimmick. They're pretty easy to read and interpret, so I added them. But I swear I shuffled them..."

Zinc winked at the horse, "Maybe it's your inner demon that picked the cards out, huh?"

Closing his mouth, Barba nodded slowly. "Sure, maybe that's it."

Derek folded his arms. "Alright, so what's the wager this time?"

"Well," Zinc said, "since we're all already naked, how about we just make it simple? The next winner gets to give a dare to the person who told the weakest story."

"How do we judge?" Derek replied.

"We will just decide after," Barba said, distracted.

"Fine," Zinc said. "I will start!" He sat back and waved his paws as he talked, his tail twitching with excitement.

Derek thought to himself, *How did the blood get so far into his claws?*

Barba looked to the side, spotting a splintered table leg, the splinter a sharp knifepoint. He eyed it as Zinc spoke, ready to leap for the weapon if the lights went out again.

THE BEAUTY REGIME
EVELYN PROCTOR

Tawny hands ran over the thickly-furred ruffs of speckled cheeks, combing through the white fur there. Slender fingers curled into the fur and tugged, but it refused to yield so easily. Recently manicured nails slid over a blunt muzzle and square jaw, feeling along their shapes. Perverse. Ugly. They had to go.

After long hours spent in quiet consultation with the magazines, the television, the bus-stop advertisements, and the Internet videos, she came to her decision at last. She selected and purchased the implements with care and only after poring over testimonial after recommendation, advertisement after guarantee. The brush, the comb, the scissors, the cosmetics, and the razor sat neatly by the mirror, each colored in sleek metallic hues or garish pastels. She felt a kind of kinship with them: they had been designed with the same attention to detail and the same meticulous scrutiny as she had employed in selecting them. "To be perfect, one simply *must* begin with perfection."

The lynx gathered up her long, thick hair, and swept the dark strands up into a black, elastic band. One, two, three twists to pull it into a long ponytail, away from her face. By drawing back the curtain of hair, she threw her stark ruffs into the light, and exposed their hideous perversions. After a single deep breath, she plucked up the rubber-handled scissors and raised them to her face. *Snip.* Her hands trembled upon the metallic-purple handle, as the blades ate through a few millimeters of fur. It crumbled like cigarette ash into her sink: a few loose strands of fur. "Three steps to a better you"; she had taken the first.

The next slices came more easily. The ravenous scissors devoured her wintry pelt, trimming the fur down almost to her cheeks. No longer ash, but snow, it descended in white clouds to the sink, only to be melted by a rush of hot water. The remaining stubble felt coarse and thick against her fingers, but she smiled. Already, she looked more like the girls at her university. But she had more to accomplish. "Beauty is a process, not a goal."

She dusted her cheeks with a white towel to clear off the remnants of trimmed fur, then returned to the mirror. Leaning in, she took hold of her right ear with her right hand; the left held aloft the scissors. Her hands still trembled as she aimed for the root of her tuft, despite their earlier practice with her ruffs. The blades slid up and down the black hairs in jerks and starts, until the lower blade rested just upon the top of her ear. The *shuck* of the blades dragging along one another frightened her; for a moment, she stopped. One strand of her tuft fell to the sink. Her ear twitched. Her resolve returned. She found the base of the tuft again, then sliced neatly through it, trimming it to the base.

Although she would have to touch it up every so often, her right ear looked better now. Her tufts were neither right nor natural: an anomaly passed through her family's hateful genes. They exaggerated her already freakish ears, lending a grotesque accent to those ill-proportioned spires. Smiling, she set the blade against her other ear, and sliced through the next tuft with confidence.

She yowled and spat as the scissors sliced through the tip of her ear, drawing a line of crimson blood. Panic briefly overtook her as she saw the mutilated cartilage in the mirror. Her ears swiveled and pinned back; she threw open the medicine cabinet's door and found a bandage to apply. A thin layer of bloody flesh had fallen upon the counter. If she acted quickly, she might be able to have the hospital reattach it. But without the money to pay for it, she stood to lose more than a bit of her ear. She bandaged her ear, plucked up the dripping scrap of flesh, and threw it into the wastebasket by the toilet.

Upon reflection, she found it not so bad: perhaps a good start, in fact. Were she to trim up around the edges of her ears, she could reduce them in size to the reasonable triangles of the women in the movies. But surgery required funds she didn't have, so she shelved that dream for the time being. Instead, she turned her attention to her whiskers: with her ruffs reduced, they now stuck past the limits of her cheeks, and made her look gaunt. She lined up the scissors and trimmed them on the left side, holding them taut by the ends. They snapped like violin strings afterward, springing forward into place again. "Good proportions make for good looks." Off came the right whiskers in the same style. How beautiful did she look?

Not at all beautiful—not yet. She opened the pink bag she had purchased from a beauty parlor, and drew out a tube of dye. Twisting open the cap revealed a blotting device. She drew up a few droplets of tawny dye, matched to her base fur color, and dripped it out upon the prominent marking in the middle of her forehead. Almost instantly, it disappeared: the blotch transformed before her eyes into an even field of color. She smiled, and continued her work.

Over the next several hours, she occupied herself with the methodical elimination of her speckled pattern, at least on her face: she would have a professional remove the markings on the rest of her body later. In the meantime, she could hide it with high-collared blouses and long stockings. She stared into the mirror until her eyes watered, shaking hands fighting to avoid misapplications. The afternoon sun descended from its zenith as she worked. By the time she finished, she had to turn on the bathroom light to admire her smooth, tawny pelt in the best lighting. A quick use of her blowdryer set the color.

When she finished, she regarded herself in the mirror, but the results dismayed her. She might have the pelt and general look of one of those gorgeous domestic felines, but her bone structure simply wouldn't do. If anything, removing her ruffs only revealed the disgusting squareness of her jawline. By narrowing her face's profile, she made her ears appear that much taller. Although she could hide her jaw with her hair, her ears were not so fortunate.

Filled with new resolve, she lifted the scissors high and placed them along the edge of her ear. She sliced through the skin and cartilage, remembering her days of cutting through the thick, black borders drawn on construction paper. She had made crude paper dolls then, but there would be nothing crude about her work today. Though tears sprang to her eyes and blood welled from the raw wounds, she hacked apart her ears until they bore the shapes in the magazines.

New panic struck her when she found that her bandages could not easily staunch the bleeding: her ears seemed to her to be splitting in two. She ran into her room, dripping lines of blood all the way, and grabbed a stapler from her desk. Blinded with pain and terror, she worked along the edge of each ear, screaming in pain as she forced her ears to hold together. New blood sprang up along the pinprick holes, but at least she no longer feared that her skin would split. It took the rest of her box of bandages to line her ears. With that, she spent the better part of an hour cleaning the blood from her sink, counter, floor, and fur. Afterward, she soaked in her tub and sobbed quietly, washing down the pain with ibuprofen and wine.

Disillusioned but not finished with her work, she moved again to the mirror once her fur had dried. She forced her thin lips back into a smile: how pretty her ears would look once they had healed! Yet once again, her improvements only paved the way for fresh horrors, and she nearly despaired of her work. Her narrow hips and flat ass would hardly fill a skirt. Her tiny breasts might sit loosely in an A-cup bra. Her waist was too thick, her feet were too big, her jaws were all wrong, her thighs were too slender. With an anguished cry, she struck the mirror with her bare hand, shattering it into jagged shards and slicing open her hand.

After cursing and spitting, pinning back her throbbing ears, she realized that she had presented herself with her answer: why stop at her ears? Men loved small, dainty feet; she had tremendous ones made for traversing snow. If hers didn't fit the slipper...a cleaver from the kitchen might do the trick. But she needed something to saw through the bones, and some way to staunch the bleeding, afterward. No, her feet would have to wait. Instead, she moved to her waist.

Perhaps a waist-training corset, tightened two inches below her current size, would do the trick. Two inches wouldn't do too much damage. Neither would it help her hips, however. As nature had not seen fit to gift her with curves, she could do little enough about them. Wrapping her hips in costuming foam might give her the shape, but she'd know her own lie. And yet without those hips, she'd never be pretty enough. "Men like big hips to have something to hold onto," said the lurid articles.

She collected her sewing kit and sat on the edge of her bathtub. To her left, a needle, thread, razor, and the kind of linen used in bandages. Her fur could probably grow right through that. To her right, the remainder of her bottle of wine. She guzzled it down, letting the fluid run down her chin. From there, she waited for the buzz to hit, then for the pleasant haze of drunkenness to overcome her. What more effective painkiller?

Having traded the tremble of her hands for a swimming stagger, she raked the shining razor down the fur of her hips. It bounced and skipped on occasion, leaving ragged furrows in her flesh, but the pills and alcohol dulled the sting. She ran hot water from the faucet and washed thick clumps of fur from beneath the blade, then resumed her task—she continued until the entire side of both hips had been stripped down to the white flesh beneath. It reminded her of raw chicken, bloody and pale.

Her stomach turned momentarily, and she felt herself retch, but she resolutely carried on. This next part would require delicacy. First, she laid a patch of linen on her bare hip. It absorbed some of the blood, immediately darkening. Digging the tip of her needle down through the linen and into the bare flesh, she tried to twist it and push it back through the other side. Even through her dulled senses, she screamed and cried, unable to finish her task. It had been a stupid idea to begin with, stuffing herself like a doll. Cursing and whimpering, she withdrew the needle from her flesh and clasped the linen over it. She ran a shallow bath and soaked her leg in the water to clean it, then crawled out of the tub and across the cold floor.

Her legs ached and throbbed: lacking both the resolve and the coordination to stand, she had to drag herself along the tile, then the hardwood, then once again to the tile of her kitchen. She managed to force herself upright long enough to grab a bottle of whiskey, which she poured over the hole in her thigh in order to sterilize it. It burned and brought fresh tears to her eyes; she collapsed to the ground. She held her stomach and sobbed, chest heaving and belly aching. Soft moans poured from her lips between choked gasps. Her stomach contracted, and hot bile rose from her throat, pouring over her chin. She convulsed and gagged, vomiting all over her chest and the kitchen floor.

The lynx woke with a headache an hour later. The room whirled about her head. The white fur of her chest now bore a thick crust of vomit. As she staggered to her knees, her short tail stuck to the floor for a moment. She stumbled past the sink full of filthy dishes, the empty cupboards; past her barren living room and the rotting food in her trash can. Twenty-thousand in debt, failing her classes, failing in life. No wonder her parents had abandoned her—what a worthless cunt.

She woke again on the floor of the bathroom, and crawled into the tub. Pouring more hot water into the tub, she rolled onto her front to let the water wash out the bits of that morning's greasy sausage and the evening's frozen meal. Temptation to dunk her muzzle into the water tickled at her mind. "A permanent solution to a temporary problem"—but what happened when the problem stopped being temporary? What happened when the problem was *her?*

What happened when it was ruffs and tufts that would never stop growing, mutilated ears that would remain lumpy and hideous for the rest of her life? Maybe she'd get an infection in her thigh: with her luck, it wouldn't kill her, but they'd amputate and leave her with another ten-thousand in hospital bills. She groaned miserably and rolled onto her back, reaching down to feel at the lumps between her thighs. No matter what she did, she'd never be a woman, much less one of the pretty ones. If she ever made it out of college, she'd be paying off student loans for the rest of her life. Insurance didn't cover the surgery she needed.

She turned up the water, but remained on her back. It poured over her hair and soaked her head, but her muzzle remained free of it for now. All she had to do was roll over. Already, fatigue threatened to conquer her—would death be any different? She could roll over right now, and simply fall asleep. She only had a moment left. Drunken exhaustion crept across her brain like fog shifting across a lake. She rocked sideways, trying to shift her weight enough to roll...

Water coated her bathroom floor. It had filled the tub to the brim, then spilled over. It must have been running for at least half an hour. She turned off the water and groaned, then crawled out again. Still drunk off the wine, but starting to sober up, she collected towels and soaked up the water on the floor. Releasing the stopper allowed the water to flow out of the bathtub; it had mixed with the blood from her wounds and assumed a pinkish hue. She shuddered at the sight of it, and crawled on all fours to her bed. The sun had not yet risen.

She woke with a dry mouth, thick tongue, and pounding head. In her pile of clothes, she found a clean blouse and skirt, and pulled them on. Afterward, she gathered up her magazines. She took the razor, the cosmetics, the scissors, the comb, and the brush, and she threw them away. She opened her half-functional laptop and deleted the bookmarks and the history. Then, at last, she swept up the shards of her mirror and put them in the trash. Tomorrow, she would check with her work's insurance policy to see if she could get coverage for a therapist.

Today, she would be beautiful.

RICHARD CORY
TRISTAN BLACK WOLF

He always smelled of sex, whether his own or someone else's mixed with his own. I guess he couldn't help it, if I'm being honest—how many maned, long-furred, melanistic tigers are there, much less one so perfectly lean and hard-muscled in all the right places? Look up "sleek" in the dictionary, and the words would pale before a picture of him. I ought to know, considering how many times I tried to describe him myself, in a story or (gods help me) a poem. I made sure that he never saw them. He was tolerant enough of me to be my dorm-mate, but I doubted that he'd like to know that I'd had a crush on him from the first moment, and damn me for enacting the cliché, but it's only true. Holy *gods*, he's beautiful. And he knows it.

Somewhere, the Great Brain of the university must have thought it amusing to pair up a senior with a sophomore, or a feline with a rodent, or a jock with a nerd. I've not yet determined if there really is a St. Turing to pray to, but I'd be on my knees 24/7 in supplication just to have five minutes of hacking the damned computer's guts, preferably with an axe. I'm a computer nerd, but not in a hacking sense; I just know how to find information faster online than I can in the library. If the reverse were true, I wouldn't be in that dorm room nearly as much as I was, but it was just easier to research online. I mean, Holy Ones save us from Lickipedia, "where everyone can get his licks in." You'd think it was a porn site, but what they did was just as obscene: A "compilation of facts" with almost no fact-checking behind it. I know how to get online references from books, papers, magazines, anything that's gone from print-to-media, so I can cite my sources just fine. That is, when I can concentrate well enough.

This is one of those modern dorms, where the school prepares you for life in a cubicle. The ceilings are high, the two beds are lofts, and the work areas are underneath. This leaves more floor space, and they tucked the wardrobes and built-in dressers at the far end. When my "roomie" was out doing whatever it was that he did (and with whom), all that saved me was that he was at least kind enough to stash his dirty clothes in the cupboard; the only thing that still smelled of him was his bedding, and as might be expected, it was quite saturated with his scent. And say whatever you wish about rats, but when it comes to the sense of smell, we're up there with bloodhounds and grizzlies. We've got cilia in our nostrils that can detect changes in *emotion,* and the vomeronasal organ that's sensitive to pheromones…

Yeah. I know. I can even cite the source. Who cares? I guess it's my way of coping, tucked under my bed in my "student workspace," as the uni brochures call it. Big whooping deal. The only thing that helps is that about two-thirds of it is closed off from the rest of the room, to provide wall space for notes, posters, whatever. Like I said, it's to train us to be tame little drones in the corporate cube-farms of our futures. Bullocks. I keep a can of coffee beans at my desk. I don't drink coffee; I'm wired enough as it is. It's so that I can sniff them and clear my nose of him as much as I can. I can barely think when he's actually here. He smells of… I may have to create a new word: sex-cess.

I heard a keycard swipe the door lock; the tumblers clicked, and my roomie shambled in without even the hint of grace that one might usually expect of him. With the differences in temperatures between the hall and the room, a burst of air permitted his scent to enter before him, and I caught every nuance, whether I wanted to or not. Dinner had included something with Italian sausage, or else whoever he was humping smelled of fennel. Dessert had been tiramisu and coffee. The artificial fragrance his date had worn was something in the Oriental portion of the scent sphere—a poor choice to go with garlic, since the scent was flowery and spicy. Much of it was on his mane, I suspected, although the female had no doubt had her scented muzzle elsewhere on his body as well. His own muzzle smelled of cervine, and as he walked, his well-fitting trousers billowed enough to carry the mixture of tiger and deer musk like a billboard advertisement for the nostrils. I struggled not to pay attention as he stripped, chucked his clothes in the general vicinity of his wardrobe, and climbed naked up to his bunk; he wrapped his bedsheet around himself and, within less than two minutes, was snoring with a soft, self-satisfied rumble that was almost a purr.

I tried very hard not to hate him.

Grabbing the tin of coffee beans none too quietly, I opened it and sniffed deeply. I capped the lid on it again before my few tears fell off my cheeks. Nothing disturbed his regular breathing, and I felt myself burn as I always did on nights like this. I shouldn't be comparing myself so much. I was only a damn sophomore; maybe when I was a senior, I'd know how to bed whatever I wanted, if ever I figured out exactly what that was. Maybe I'd get some fur-tats, something to break up the ridiculously solid white that covered me from tip to tail-base, with the exception of a dark brown patch that no one would ever know about, if things kept going as they were.

I rolled my chair back slowly, looking up at his bunk. He always slept stripped to the fur, no matter the temperature indoors or out, and he never covered himself with anything more than a sheet. Blankets would be redundant with that long, thick pelt. I had to wonder about his lineage, what genetics gave him such a damnably perfect blend of features. His fore- and hindpaws were large and agile, with substantial pads as black as pitch, and he could no more stomp like a jack-booted thug than he could fly (although the way he slam-dunked a basketball was enough to make you wonder if maybe, just maybe, he *could* fly). His fur, similar to that of a Turkish or Persian feline, had a glow like mahogany or the richest cocoa, striped with black except on his firm chest, belly, and inner thighs. (He wasn't modest, and I tried not to hate him for that, too.) His headfur was more like a close-cropped lion's mane, including the ruff down onto his chest, and almost paradoxically, it was a stunning, dark antique gold that could catch whatever light was in the room and convince you that it was actually a kind of halo-like aura around his face. His long tail, poking out from under the sheet, was still save for the tip which tapped softly against the bed, as if signaling a dream or some unspoken language that I couldn't learn no matter how many lit classes I took. And his scent...

He had it all, and he had it so easy. Rich family and private schools; picked for the college b-ball team in his freshman year, not a star, but a solid player; enough brains to get by, at the very least; a perfect body, perfect smile, perfect everything, and all the sex he could want. He just coasted by like the Queen Fekkin' Mary. And maybe he deserved it. I kept trying to remind myself of that idea, that maybe he had earned all this adoration and sexual conquest. It wasn't that I didn't want him to have it. It was just...why couldn't I...

I put the laptop into idle and turned off the desk lamp. If I had one more thought, I'd either explode or dissolve into a puddle of tears, and I'd be godsdamned if I let myself get there yet again. My clothes went onto my desk chair, and I climbed into my own bunk. It always felt too big, even though it was just a full-sized mattress. It felt empty and cold, with a big hollow place that nothing could fill. I covered myself with a sheet and blanket, curled up even smaller, and buried my nose in my pillow, hoping that the scent of the laundry soap would mask everything else, and hoping that the pillow wouldn't get too wet from my crying.

...found in the victim's room included hard copies of papers written for classes, electronic tablet (contents being analyzed, appears to be texts for classes consistent with his listed schedule), laptop computer (hard drive being analyzed, may have been wiped),

clothing (inventoried, identified by parents), jewelry (inventoried, identified by roommate). No note found.

(from Walker County Sheriff's Office report)

"I'll never know how you can do that."

I took the printout from our shared printer and looked at the tiger, clad only in shorts, seated in the desk chair under his loft bed. "Do what?"

"Knock out a class paper so fast."

Shrugging, trying not to show any particular concern, I put the papers into the side pocket of my courier bag, a last gift from my parents before I went to live in the dark world of student loan debt for the rest of my life. "Always been able to string words together," I said. "Not like a foreign language or something."

"Speak for yourself." His grin, that damned endearing smile, still had its effect on me. He leaned forward, his elbows on his knees. "Maybe you could help me sometime."

"Sure," I said. I'd heard this line before, but he'd never actually gone ahead and asked for my help. He turned in his papers, one way or another, but maybe that was just one more thing he got out of his conquests. Some of the sorority females were actually students as well as easy conquests. Or maybe he did well enough on his own; he wasn't stupid, which was just one more feather in a cap already resembling a damned peacock tail. I put on my rings, put the ear cuff on my right ear, gathered up my tablet and other papers. "Time to turn it in."

"Matty?"

My name is Matheson, but it was futile to try to correct him. I still couldn't quite look at him. "Yeah?"

"It's almost March."

"Yeah."

"B-ball finals coming up. Might even be on the road a little. You'll have the place to yourself sometimes."

"So?"

"Just sayin'." He shifted a little in his chair. "I'll try not to leave a mess behind."

"Thanks." I shifted the courier bag on my shoulder a little. "Class."

"Yeah."

I grabbed my coat, figuring I'd put it on before I left the dorm. Fact is, I felt so pissed that I was halfway to my classroom building before I remembered that I was carrying it instead of wearing it. It doesn't snow this far south, at least not usually, but the wind chill can chew your tail and ears off. I picked up the pace, managing at least to sling the coat around my shoulders. It helped a little.

The Language Arts building housed everything from foreign languages to lit classes. My major was shortened to "English," since anything worth reading was written in, or at least translated into, English, right? No one got a B.A. in "Literature" anymore, unless it was lumped into a generalized "Liberal Arts" degree, and that one sounded even more useless to cube-life than my declared major. The four-story building had an elevator, but most of us never used it. The universal joke was that one might get stuck between floors with Dr. Biedermeier and die of being lectured beyond endurance. I actually liked the old red-eyed Norwegian (perhaps rodents stick together after all), but I could understand the fear residing in those students who had not come to college to think.

I padded up the wide staircase to the top floor. My class this morning was in Room 415, "Literary Forms and Substance," with Dr. Donald Stalling. It was a junior level class, and as a sophomore, I had to petition and interview for entry. Lucky for me, Dr. Stalling had been roped into teaching one section of second-semester freshman English (usually the last English class most students ever take), so he had taken my measure already. I'd taken his as well, and in neither case do I mean anything that would concern the moral turpitude clause of his teaching contract. If I had my way, I'd have him teach all my classes and be my thesis advisor for a doctorate, if I ever got that far.

Most of the class was already seated when Dr. Stalling padded in. I'm not quite sure why I always think of him as having the quintessential "regal bearing." Being feline was enough, I suppose; being such a perfect example of the king cheetah species was another. Fastidious to the point of being called "finicky" by his detractors, Stalling was the perfect mix of professor and mentor; anyone in his class smart enough to realize it would learn a lot from him.

"Good morning, all," he began. "Let us use today to take a dip into the realm of the seven deadly sins—metaphorically, of course. Can we name them all?"

He stepped up to the whiteboard, dry marker in paw, ready to write. I thought I'd let my classmates founder for a bit. At last, one voice managed to squeak out, "Greed." Stalling wrote it on the board. "Pride," said another. Frankly, I was impressed, given the caliber of the average student here; maybe that old movie had some benefit after all. "Lust" and "Gluttony" managed to make themselves known. One female voice offered, "Jealousy?"

"Almost," the professor acknowledged. "Try again."

A good half-minute passed as the assemblage tried to tap out the question on their tablets. Dr. Stalling waited patiently, one eyebrow raised high, thick tail starting to twitch, before I volunteered, "Wrath, sloth, and envy."

"Well done, Mr. Knox," he said, writing the remainder on the whiteboard. He turned back to the female who had suggested "jealousy" as an answer. "You were close, Ms. Stuyvesant, but there is a distinction between jealousy and envy, albeit a fine one. Jealousy, as Shakespeare put it, is 'the green-eyed monster that doth mock the meat it feeds on.' Someone who is envious of another may admire a trait or feature about them, and he may wish it for himself, but he does not accuse the admired of not being worthy of having it. On the other paw, jealousy claims not only that one deserves having that trait, but also that the other party does *not* deserve it. The distinction is the difference between wishing one had a thing and wanting actively to deprive another of having that thing."

"Wouldn't that make jealousy more deadly than envy?" she asked.

"In many ways, yes," Stalling admitted the point. "But notice that, on the surface, the seven deadly sins affect the person who sins, more often than they do the person sinned against. It's a toss-up, I admit—wrath, for example, is exacted upon another, thus it's potentially deadly to both parties. Gluttony affects the sinner most, unless it deprives another of food. The reason that they are called 'deadly' sins is because they are considered mortal to the soul; he that thus sins is in peril of losing his soul, either for the destruction wrought upon himself, upon others, or both. Mr. Knox," the cheetah smiled at me. "In another class, you impressed me by knowing both a song from the 1960s and the even older poem on which it is based. Do you recall it?"

"E. A. Robinson's 'Richard Cory'," I said, recalling the paper well. "Paul Simon wrote the song about it."

"Would you say that it was about jealousy or envy?"

I thought about it, ignoring the hard stares of a few in the class who clearly thought that I was being Teacher's Pet. "There's a feeling of wanting to be like Richard Cory, but there's not a sense of wanting to take away what's his. The chorus of the song says that the speaker wishes he could be like Cory, but despite a certain derision in describing Cory's life, there's nothing about him not deserving what he had. So I'd have to say envy."

"And what of Mr. Cory's fate?" the regal cheetah asked, a glimmer in his eye. He knew that this was what would get the students' attention.

"The song is more explicit, more angry, saying that Cory should be satisfied with all his wealth. Robinson's poem is almost reverential; even so, the last two lines are: 'And Richard Cory, one calm summer night, / Went home and put a bullet through his head.'"

There's no need to create a Zen koan about the sound of several jaws dropping; the whole class heard it.

...whereabouts the night before are believed to have been at the Steak and Spirits restaurant with a female companion, after which he accompanied her home and left, presumably to return to his dormitory room (see accompanying statements). When asked, neither she nor friends nor the victim's roommate can recall any unbalanced behavior prior...

(from Walker County Sheriff's Office report)

The weekend of his first away game was going to be like a vacation for me. I held out hope that he'd make good on his promise not to leave the room a complete mess. Maybe I wouldn't have to use the coffee beans as much. I gave myself reasons to be out of the room until later Friday evening, when I could be certain he'd already be gone. I unlocked the door and braced myself for the onslaught of tiger musk, with or without any side-dish of his latest dish. I was surprised when what I smelled first was the remains of a modestly-scented laundry soap. My whiskers danced as I tried to find more traces of him. When I looked over to his bunk and study space, it was all astonishingly neat; his laptop was powered down and closed, the chair was parked up against the desk, and the bed above looked smooth and freshly-made. I wondered for a moment if I had somehow gotten into someone else's room by mistake.

It was the right room; it was just clean. Apparently, he had even washed everything that was in his wardrobe as well. I was, like the firefly who flew through the lawnmower, de-lighted, no end. I imagined the possibility of nearly forty-eight hours, distractionless, limitless, tigerless. I set up my rarely-used speakers, putting my headphones aside while I let my favorite music stream unfettered. I gave myself the luxury of playing one of my games for a full half-hour before turning my attention back to the reading I had to do for the next week. I camped out on my bed, free to move in any direction without having to worry about the headphone cord being tangled. I forced myself through a chapter in the biology text first, to get it out of the way. Eventually, I discovered that it was a reasonable time to get to sleep, and I didn't have to worry about my roommate waking me by returning at some unconscionable hour of the morning. I shut down the music, climbed happily into my bunk, and settled in for a comfortable night's sleep.

It didn't happen quite like that. It took some time for me to get relaxed enough to fall asleep, and when I woke, I felt uneasy. It wasn't the first time I'd slept in the room alone; it may have been the first time that my nose was alone. That Saturday morning held a feeling unlike any that I'd had before. Something about it scared me, but I couldn't tell what it was. I dressed quickly, took my tablet, went to a café for a cheap breakfast, read through the various posts and such on my websites, and then realized that I didn't know what to do with myself for the day. I had plenty of options, from reading for classes to playing some games, or going for a long walk, watching a movie online, browsing through what's left of downtown shops in this college burg...but I couldn't focus.

I got back to the room eventually, and I made myself settle down with a textbook. The streaming music helped, along with a few tricks I'd learned in high school to get myself to work when I didn't want to. Eventually, I managed to get most of my required reading taken care of. I could even remember some of it.

The new distraction, for me, was now the emptiness of the workspace and loft bed across from me. I kept expecting him to walk in early, for some reason. The game was far enough away that, even though it happened that Saturday afternoon, the team wouldn't be headed back until Sunday. (Okay, so I checked the details. Freakin' sue me.) Why should I care that he wasn't there?

It was early evening but still light out when I finally climbed down from my loft and violated his workspace. I'd already known how cleaned-up it was, from when I had first walked in last night and glanced in. Actually being in the space, though, it felt almost as if it had never been used, and that idea spooked the hell out of me. He was away at a basketball game, I knew that, and there was no news of anything happening to the transport, or the team losing a player to injuries, nothing like that. He was okay, doing what he did best (out of bed, at least). It just felt so empty.

I jostled his desk chair as I leaned against it, and I heard something like crinkling plastic, and the scent hit me moment later. Pulling out the desk chair, I found a plastic grocery bag with some clothing in it. One of his sweatshirts. It must have escaped the laundry somehow, and he'd stashed it here, maybe hoping I wouldn't have to smell it. I did, though. I don't mean that the scent simply rose from the bag; I opened the bag and stuffed my muzzle into it. I didn't even think. Then the scent took over, and I couldn't think if I'd wanted to. I inhaled him (it was only him, no other scents, just him) for a full minute before something in me finally snapped awake. I thrust the bag into his desk chair, pushed the chair back, and scrambled into my loft, shivering. Even wrapping up in the blanket didn't make the shaking stop; I quivered like a plucked harp string, teeth chattering, tail lashing, my ears flat back against my head, as if I'd been attacked. Feelings of shame, embarrassment, and something horribly desperate ripped me apart from the inside out.

I don't know how long it went on. My thoughts were so jumbled that it was actually a surprise when I realized that I'd stopped shaking. It was full dark, and something felt very late, even though the digital alarm clock on the protected shelf at the head of my bed told me that it couldn't have been. The only light in the room was below me, from my workspace. I could see well enough. I could see just inside his own workspace, and I knew what lay there. I climbed down slowly to the floor, reached into my space to turn out the light. I took off my clothes and put them onto my own desk chair. I crossed to his, took out the plastic grocery bag, tossed it up onto my loft. I climbed up, my heart beating hard but slowly, excitement and comfort, a heady thudding like a giant metronome, *largo espressivo*. Slowly, I took the sweatshirt out of the bag, held it up in the dark as if imagining him wearing it. The feeling wasn't sexual; I had no intention of using the shirt the way other males used socks, jocks, and catcher's mitts. I held it against me, larger than any of my own clothes, but it seemed somehow fitting. As I lay down on the bed, my head to my pillow, the sweatshirt against my chest, I felt myself relax again, my body heat helping to release the scent in the cloth more fully. In the quiet, I realized that only his quiet, purring snore was missing. I didn't mind that so much; my ears were, for the moment at least, secondary to my nose. I fell into a deep sleep almost on the instant.

Some mention has been made regarding the victim having a firearm in his possession, but no records have been found for the purchase of any firearm or ammunition in this or adjacent counties. Gun shows are prevalent and frequent in several cities within 100 miles, so an unregistered purchase is possible; the victim does have a car, although it has not been found within the county thus far. According to the victim's family, the victim has never shown any interest in guns of any kind, nor any reason ever mentioned for getting one...
(from Walker County Sheriff's Office report)

I'd put everything back where it was, showered twice, tried not to look suspicious or guilty when he came back early Sunday evening. I made sure that I was in my own workspace when he walked in.

"Hey, Matty."
"Hey. Saw you won."
"Yep. Another step up the ladder."
"Congrats."
"It was all teamwork."
"I'm sure you did your part."
"They could have done it without me."

I didn't react to that statement then; I was too self-conscious about the whole thing with the sweatshirt. It wasn't until later that I realized how it would sound, if I'd known what he was really thinking.

He opened up his duffle, and in moments, the room was filled with his scent, just as it usually was. He put the dirty clothes into the bottom of his wardrobe to tend to later, put his tablet on top of his laptop in the workspace. I began sweating, hoping that he wouldn't notice anything had been disturbed. He didn't seem to. He took the sweatshirt, plastic bag and all, and tossed it into his wardrobe. He stripped off his jeans and shirt, and they followed the bag. From his dresser, fresh athletic pants and sweatshirt were donned quickly. "Gonna go for a run," he said.

"Okay."

He paused at the door, looked back over at me, seemed about to say something, stopped. "Back soon."

After the door closed behind him, I couldn't concentrate anymore. He was going to say something about the sweatshirt in the bag, I was certain. I felt my face burning. He knew. However it was he knew it, he *knew*. I had no idea what to do. It wasn't even full dark yet, but I thought maybe I could climb up to my loft and pretend to be asleep when he got back. It would only postpone things, and then only if he really thought that I was asleep. Did I snore when I slept? I had no way of knowing; no one had ever been with me long enough to tell me, and I wasn't sure I could manufacture a convincing snore even if I wanted to. I'd have to just hope that he wouldn't try to wake me.

I turned out the light in my workspace, put my clothes on the chair, got into bed, sheet and blanket both. I knew I wouldn't be able to get to sleep. I could never tell how long his runs would take—twenty minutes to an hour, depending on distance and how hard he pushed himself. I tried to make myself not look at the clock at the head of the bed, but after a long time, I couldn't help myself. Time stretched, and the clock silently registered nearly 90 minutes before I finally heard the tumblers in the door click into place. He padded in quietly, the dark room signaling—I hoped—that I'd gone to sleep. My back was turned to the center of the room, but I kept my eyes closed anyway; the tiger's eyes were even better at seeing in the dark than mine were.

I heard the rustling of clothes, and of course the smell of him filled the room, damp, warm. I sensed more than heard him step up near the head of the bed.

"Matty?" he whispered. "Maybe you're asleep and can't hear me. Maybe you'll hear me and think it's a dream. I'll get the nerve to say something when you're awake. Better be soon. Meanwhile..."

I felt something cover me softly, something warm, damp, soft in touch, strong in scent. The sweatshirt he'd been wearing on his run. I didn't dare move, speak, even breathe.

"Sleep well, Matheson."

His body whispered up to his own bunk, and he lay down, adjusting the sheet over himself. I listened, but I didn't hear the purring snore for a very long time. It took longer than that for me to get to sleep.

I woke to the sound of rain and sleet tapping against the window—exactly the sort of fatalistic harbinger that Monday mornings usually feel like. My alarm wouldn't go off for another few minutes, and tired as I was, I didn't feel that I wanted to be jangled by that raucous buzz. I shut it off and sat up, realizing only then that I still had the sweatshirt covering me. I looked up sharply and saw the tiger, sitting on his bed, naked, looking at me with eyes that I couldn't read.

"Rain woke me," he said softly.

"Uh-huh," I agreed with him.

"Good day to play hooky."

"I should get ready for class."

"Screw class." He leaned forward, his deep hazel eyes pleading. "Matheson. I need to talk to you."

"I shouldn't—"

"Because he moves like one of the gods, that's why," he quoted from a source that I knew all too well. "Because his scent hypnotizes me into thoughts that scare me, but that I want so much. Can he, does he, know what he does to me? How much I wish I could be like him?"

I could barely breathe.

"Yes, Matheson. I read them. All of them. More than once. I didn't mean to, I swear that I didn't. You'd left your laptop on when you left for class one morning, and I got to it before the screensaver locked me out. I swear to you, I was only wanting to see what search engines you were using for your papers. That, and yeah, maybe get a copy of your citations and sources." He paused, something like a smile on his muzzle, but one that was more shy than any I'd ever seen there before. Shy, and with more than a little pain.

"You don't want to be like me, Matheson. You don't, I promise you. 'Me' is not a very nice someone to be. I want to be different. Truth is, I want to be like you."

My jaw fell open, and I felt my eyes bulge outward.

"You're studying what you want to study. You work at your classes because you want to. You don't apologize for who you are, and you never pretend to be what you're not. By the gods, Matheson Knox, I wish that I could be like you."

"I don't understand."

"You know the difference between you and George Washington? He said that he could not tell a lie. You *can* tell lies, but you won't. That makes you stronger. So much stronger."

"What are you...I don't understand..."

"No, I guess you wouldn't. You have no idea how much I hate myself. How much I hate what I'm becoming. You never met my father." He shook his head, his short mane dancing, glowing gently even in just the gray light of the rain-filled morning. "He loves to brag about all that he'd done in school, all that he'd accomplished. Oh, a decent GPA in business courses, but he was talking about his athletics, about his track record with females, with how he could drink other males under the table and still bang sorority twins, and then not have a hangover in the morning, so he'd bang them again." The tiger winced. "That's the word he used. I don't think he ever 'made love' in all his life. Not even to my mother. I was the result of him 'banging' her one night, about 23 years ago."

Something inside me broke, and I found myself clutching his sweatshirt closer to me.

"Do your parents love each other, Matheson?"

"Yes."

"Do they love you?"

"Yes."

"Do you like yourself?"

I paused. "Usually, yes. Sometimes, I'm ashamed of something I do."

"Like sleeping with my sweatshirt Saturday night?"

He did know. I could only nod slowly.

"I left it for you." The tiger shifted on the bed, passing a forepaw over his muzzle (wiping away a tear? could it be?). "I cleaned absolutely everything. I sprayed fabric freshener on my bed, washed the sheets, my clothes, everything. I took my morning run first, put the sweatshirt into the bag, hoping you'd somehow find it. I showered, laundered, cleaned, wiped down, got rid of every trace of my scent, except for that sweatshirt."

After a long moment, I croaked out, "Why?"

"Because I didn't want you to be alone."

"Why would you—"

"Because I had read what you'd written, and because it made me realize that I wasn't just lying to myself. I was lying to you. Without ever saying a word. Matheson, did you never wonder why I would come back here after bedding those females, and not talk, not do anything but stumble into my own bed and pass out? Did you never wonder what I was thinking, what I was doing?"

Another pause. "Your father."

He nodded slowly. "I was trying to become my father, because that's what he wanted me to be. And you, Matheson...you bemoaned your plainness, your ordinariness, the idea that there was nothing special about you." He shook his head briefly. "That is so completely wrong. You're everything I wish I could be. I envy you down to my soul."

I could no longer speak. I managed to breathe, and I tried very hard to think, but I couldn't form words.

"May I..." the tiger began, and then I was sure he was crying, because I saw two huge tears running down his furry cheeks before he could wipe them away with a sniff. "Matheson, I want...I want to know who you are, while I still have some 'me' left. I want to face the truth, for once in my artificial life. If I truly make you feel that way, then I want to do something I've never done in my life. I want to know what making love feels like."

The rain and sleet nickered, nature's susurration of urging him, urging me, to dare. I raised my arm slowly, extending my forepaw to him. He came down from his loft quickly, up the ladder of mine, pausing there, a silent question on his lips. I nodded, reaching for him, setting aside the sweatshirt in favor of the source of the scent that had so captivated me. I took him into my arms, feeling him tremble, uncertain, needful, all the things that I could never have imagined him to be, never once. I reached up and stroked his mane softly, took his chin in my forepaw and, trembling myself, let my lips meet his in a kiss so tender that it was as if neither of us had ever kissed anyone before. Perhaps, until that moment, we hadn't.

He wrapped his arms around me and let himself go, tears so long in the making that it was a wonder he'd not drowned himself in them. "Gods," he rasped in my ear, "Matheson, I want to be you."

"Don't. I want you to be *you*, not me. I want you to know who *you* are. To be who *you* are."

"Not that strong."

"First steps." I pet his mane again, nuzzled his neck, inhaled his scent, for the first time tasting the fear that he had suppressed for so long. "Just hold me. I won't let you go. I swear to you, Richard, I won't let you go."

...no further information was available from our interviews and investigations. Because of the nature of the crime and the jurisdictional

issues involved, we hereby close this case locally, setting all information and jurisdiction into the paws of the FBI for further inquiry, as requested by the victim's parents.

(from Walker County Sheriff's Office report)

We spent the rest of our semester secretly sharing our bed every night, except when he had a game on the road. On those nights, I would sleep in his well-worn sweatshirt, making the blanket superfluous. He made excuses to the various females, and he never came back to me smelling of someone else's sex, only his own musk; if the female got her perfume on his clothes, they ended up in the wardrobe even faster than usual.

The sexual exploration happened gradually, waiting as it did on his slowly rising confidence in himself and what he wanted. The only promise we made to each other was to be there, to support each other. We were quite active in our lovemaking by the time the semester was over, and his graduation day loomed closer. He had performed well enough in his classes, and the college team had played well, just missing the Final Four; his degree would be in business, like his father, so even if some pro b-ball team didn't pick him up, his future would have looked bright enough, save for one problem: me.

That was what finally decided it, you see. That's what finally made him do it. If you want to say it that way, it was my fault. He planned most of it, but he included me. He wouldn't leave without making sure that I would be okay. I knew I'd miss him, but that couldn't be helped. The night before, he had one last dinner date with a female who, had he followed his father's pawsteps more precisely, could have been the one he would have "banged" to pass along his father's self-sainted name. That was something that he just couldn't live with. Instead, that night we made the sweetest, most passionate, most unifying love we'd ever experienced, and the next day, May 7th, Richard was gone.

Word spread quickly enough when his parents arrived on May 8th, what would have been his graduation day, and he was still missing. It's usually a 48-hour wait before the police could start a missing person's case, but money always speaks louder than the law. The local sheriff was "persuaded" to look into things, and after another 24 hours, they brought in the FBI, his father fearing that it was a kidnapping, his mother carefully avoiding thinking that he had killed himself. There was a rumor about a gun, but I told the authorities truthfully that I'd never seen one. I was asked if I thought that Richard would kill himself; I replied truthfully that Richard was too much like his father and left it at that.

There was quite an uproar when Richard's car was found in Houston's gay district. Circulating photos at the various bars yielded some hits, as did some surveillance cameras outside of some of the clubs, but that didn't matter: his parents quickly shut down the investigation to stanch rumors about the business mogul's only child being a homosexual. The case was officially handed off to the FBI, considered a possible kidnapping, until they too were informed of the location of Richard's car. Although the father tried to claim that he had received a ransom demand, the FBI surveillance and investigation turned up no such activity. Richard's father was warned against wasting the time of the police and federal officers, and ultimately, all trails ran cold.

I had long since moved out of the dorm, partly for police reasons, partly because the dorms would close up until the summer courses. I wasn't too worried about that. I'd talked to Dr. Stalling often after that March Monday morning; it was he who had helped me get into another program at a very good university far away from that one. I wouldn't be able to start classes until the fall, but after a brief stay with my parents, I convinced them that I could afford an apartment in the town, perhaps find a part-time job that I could keep through the school year if I needed it. They weren't sure about it until I explained to them that the new college had offered a very special fellowship, not a student loan but a scholarship award that would give me something just short of a free ride. They'd never heard of the grant, and I told them that Dr. Stalling had helped me to find it.

It was true. Dr. Stalling had a great knowledge of how such grant-making institutions were created, how they worked, and what paperwork would be necessary. Of course, it wasn't necessary for anyone but my parents to know about it; the university I was to attend was perfectly happy to take the cash that I used to pay for tuition, books, etc. And naturally, I'd have a roommate to help me with rent and such. It only made sense. Happily, I had the perfect roommate. He had stashed away far more of his allowance from his rich parents than even they were fully aware, so we would be comfortable while he provided for the rest of my schooling, and he continued discovering who he really was. Richard's father tried to make him into another one of himself. Richard could not, and did not, survive. Neither of us wanted that. Richard was, so far as the world was concerned, gone forever. My beautiful tiger, however, was newly born.

I'd missed him terribly for the brief time that I was with my parents, but by early June, we were together again. When first I saw him, I almost didn't recognize him; his magnificent mane had been dyed a discreet ash blond, and his right ear boasted a trio of piercings—copper, silver, and gold—that Richard would never have dared to wear. With the FBI and other searches canceled, changing his name lawfully was a simple, ridiculously inexpensive, and quiet affair handled in the local court of our new hometown. It caused not a blip on any radar, despite the Internet trying so hard to deprive us of our privacy these days.

His new self is recognized only for who he is, not who he was. He volunteers at the local gym, coaching a community league in basketball. It allowed him to accept and be glad that he wasn't a "star player" who was always in the limelight. I may get teaching credentials, to get us started; his volunteer work might get him recommendations for coaching at the local high school, and he could take the teaching classes with me for what they call "emergency certification." Our options are open now, and both of us intend to take full advantage to make a happy life together. One day, my parents will be stunned and pleased by the handsome young tiger who has proposed marriage to me. You might get an invitation to the wedding of Matheson Carver Knox to Daniel Jedediah Hawkins. It's going to be splendid. Guests, please leave your envy at the door.

Lucy
Dax

Long shadows painted the cement as the sun set behind the horizon, making it almost appear as though Lucy were being led along her path. The gray-striped feline shouldn't have been walking along this route. Instead, she should have been back in her small but cozy apartment, working on the paper that would be due in just a few short days. Yet here she was, strolling along the sidewalk that would lead her downtown, to the small family-owned café. She had never personally entered the restaurant, but she knew they would be there. It's where they went to dinner every Friday night. Lucy's pace quickened along with her heartbeat as she thought about seeing them, no, about seeing him again. The small one-and two-story buildings became merely a blur in her peripheral vision, her only focus getting to her destination.

Her pace slowed as she drew nearer, with its odd green roof and brick walls setting it apart. A small sign out front advertised that it hosted a family-friendly atmosphere and displayed the daily special, which they claimed to be the best soup in town. A stiff breeze blew down the street, chilling the evening air even more, but giving Lucy the perfect excuse to lift the hood of her jacket, taking a brief moment to get her ears situated. Across the street from the café was a small coffee shop, small metal tables and wrought iron chairs carefully placed along the storefront even though the cool weather sent most patrons to the interior seating. Not Lucy, though; those tables gave her the perfect view. Cautiously, she crossed over to the coffee shop entrance, her tail beginning to flick from side to side behind her in anticipation. Her mind was elsewhere as she walked up to the counter, a young and cheery looking deer standing behind the register. "Welcome!" the buck greeted. "How may I help you today?"

Lucy flashed a smile and politely ordered, her anticipation building. This was always her least favorite part. She hated waiting for the drink, with her back to the café, always afraid they would move and she would miss it, and lose her chance to see them. The moment the cup was in her hand, she hurried out of the shop, quickly sitting at the table that was closest to the corner of the café. It was that little corner booth, the one that looked so comfortable and warm despite being next to the window, that they always claimed. A couple and their two young boys always seemed to find their way to that booth every Friday night. When she used to frequent the coffee shop, it was for a much more innocent purpose. She was rarely bothered by anyone when she sat outside, so it gave her a quiet place away from home to focus on her school assignments. One night she'd looked up, into that fateful café, and that's when she'd seen him. His orange fur seemed to glow even in the dim light of the restaurant, black stripes accentuating that aura by contrast. Her heart had beat hard in her chest, and she'd frozen as she was unable to do anything other than watch him gracefully glide toward the corner booth. That's when her heart had broken, as waiting for him at the table had been a white tigress and two cubs, one with orange fur, and the other white. She saw how happy they were, the perfect family, and that was when envy took over. She had to have what they had, no matter the cost. She began to follow them every Friday night, watching them closely, but careful to keep her distance.

Soon after taking her normal seat, she saw the family heading toward their table, cubs bouncing along with huge grins on their little faces. The white tigress was wearing a light purple blouse, and Lucy took great pride when she looked down at her own body, to the almost identical garment that was hidden under her jacket. She was becoming successful, copying his wife's clothes, getting closer to her end goal. Tonight was going to be a special night; she could feel the electricity in the air as the wind continued to swirl around the street, causing her to shiver and wrap her jacket more tightly around her, concealing the purple shirt. Reaching into the bag that had been slung over her shoulder, Lucy retrieved her laptop and set it out on the table in front of her. While her mind had become clouded by envy for the unaware family, she realized that it would look suspicious for her to just sit there, staring at them. Her cover for this was to half-heartedly browse through the internet, keeping herself positioned so that she could still see them while appearing to be looking at her screen. The first website she visited was some generic news page, the same one she always pulled up, but this time the image on the screen nearly stopped her heart. Right in front of her were those piercing green eyes, that beautiful white smile accented by fangs. He was on the front page of the news. After weeks and weeks of having no idea how to find out who he was, something as simple as opening the news at the right time was going to give her the answer. Her blue eyes stayed locked on those green ones, that gaze pushing her into a fantasy world where those were the eyes that she woke up to every morning. She imagined sitting by his side, mother of his cubs, in that corner booth. Snapping out of her daze, she began to scan the article, desperately looking for information about him. His name almost immediately popped out at her: Axel Sterling. Now that she had a name, it would be easy to find out more about him, but she forced herself to continue reading the article, to find out what had put him on the front page of the news. Skimming through the article, another name jumped out at her: Lucy Sterling. Once again, her envy went into overdrive. How *dare* that bitch take her name? She was the only Lucy who should be married to that beautiful tiger. A little farther down, she finally got the answer to why the article had been written. Axel—no, her future husband—was being featured for the charity work he had done alongside his family to help the local hospitals, raising millions of dollars in just a few short weeks.

Sighing happily, Lucy silently praised her soon-to-be husband for the amazing work he had done, looking over into the café with love written plainly in her expression. Then her gaze shifted, the white fur of his false wife becoming visible. That tigress was undeserving of his love; she had no right to claim his name, sit across from him, much less look at him. Something had to be done about her. I, the rightful Lucy, needed to be by his side, helping those cute little cubs into their clothes every morning, cooking, and cleaning for Axel and their family. As she sat there, a plan began to formulate. She knew what she would do, but it would have to wait until next week. Excitement surged through her veins as she realized how close her goal was. So consumed in her plan, she didn't even bother sticking around to watch them leave; she merely headed back to her apartment to prepare for next Friday night.

By the time Friday rolled around again, Lucy was ecstatic. She hummed to herself as she danced around her apartment in the white dress she had bought just for tonight. It was almost floor length, and it made her feel like she was wearing a wedding dress. The top was strapless, baring her shoulders in a way that she hoped he would think was sexy. She needed to impress her new husband, even if it meant braving the cold for a few hours. Everything she needed was stashed inside of her bag, so she hefted it up, sliding the strap over her shoulder as she walked toward the door.

The coffee shop was pleasantly warm after walking through the chilly fall air, Lucy's dress keeping her just warm enough to stop her from shivering. Behind the counter was the same buck from the week before, and his eyes raised as he saw the feline in the dress walking toward him. Lucy, lost in her fantasy, didn't even notice as she walked up to him and ordered a random drink off of the menu, too distracted to order her regular drink. This time, after receiving her drink, Lucy chose to sit inside, wanting to stay warm and presentable for Axel. Concealed by the slightly tinted windows of the coffee shop, Lucy was able to stare directly at the Sterlings, waiting for them to finish their meal. The buck noticed her strange behavior, sitting in the corner, staring out of the window, and not even touching her drink, so he walked over to check on her. "Um, excuse me miss? Are you alright?" he asked timidly, concerned but still hesitant to disturb her.

A sweet sounding laugh fell from her muzzle as she replied, "Everything is completely fine, but thank you for your concern. I'm just waiting for my husband."

He glanced down at her hands and didn't see a ring, causing his concern to grow even more, but he decided to not push the issue and leave her alone. Lucy was able to sit undisturbed for the rest of the time, just watching and waiting for the family to stand up. Her heart started to race as she saw the check arrive at the table. She watched closely, waiting for them to stand up and leave. They seemed to talk among themselves for a few more minutes, and a smile broke out on her face as she watched Axel laugh from something that one of his sons had said. As soon as they walked out of the café, Lucy was on her feet and moving toward the coffee shop's exit, leaving her forgotten cup of coffee on the table. The buck watched her leave, concern plainly written on his face, but he again stayed silent as he saw her head down the sidewalk, not noticing the fact that she was following a family.

Lucy could barely contain herself to stay back from the Sterlings, not wanting to alert them to her presence. Her dress alone would have been enough to cause questions, but the family was completely wrapped up in themselves, oblivious to all around them. Fantasy began to creep into Lucy's mind, making her realize she was walking home with Axel and the two cubs. She was starting to live out her dream, and that tigress was the only thing in her way, the last obstacle. After a quick glance around, realizing they were on an empty street, she decided to move forward. Taking longer and faster steps, she rapidly closed the gap between herself and the Sterlings, her grip tight on her bag. She fell in step behind the white furred tigress before speaking. "Excuse me, what are you doing with my husband?"

All four members of the family turned, startled by the voice behind them. Axel straightened up as he turned around, placing a protective arm around his wife. He looked at the feline in front of him, clad in the white dress, noting the frenzied look in her eyes. "Can we help you? Are you lost?" he tried asking calmly, assuming she must have him confused with someone else.

"Of course you can help me," she replied smoothly. "You're my husband. And she's in the way." Lucy's voice stayed eerily cheerful even with the laced threat.

Axel's eyes widened in surprise. "You must be mistaken. This is my wife. And I would appreciate it if you would back away from my family."

Rather than stepping back, Lucy moved closer to the tigress, her hand sliding into the bag still slung over her shoulder. "No. No, she has to go. This is my family," Lucy was whispering to herself, although the family could still hear her.

With another step forward, Lucy withdrew her hand from the bag. Clutched tightly in her grasp was a kitchen knife, which she promptly raised to about shoulder height as she continued to advance on the white tigress. Shock flooded through the targeted feline, causing her eyes to widen and her body to freeze. "Lucy!" Axel shouted, pulling his wife out of the path of the knife.

The gray feline paused, ear swiveling, as she heard Axel uttering her name, mistakenly thinking that it was directed at her. Maybe he was going to confess his love for her, to say that he would leave that stupid tigress for her. Her head turned to face the lean tiger, adoration pouring from her gaze. Expecting to see the affection reflected in his eyes, she was startled to find his arms wrapped around the white feline, pushing her behind him and attempting to shield her. His green eyes hardened when he saw the knife-wielding feline still staring at them. "Leave now." There was a dangerous undertone in his voice. "Leave now and never come near us again. I want nothing to do with you. If you leave now, I will not press charges, as long as you leave us alone and never cross paths with me or my family again."

Lucy shook her head, trying to clear it. How could he say that? Didn't he know that they were to be married? They were meant to be; no one could deny it. That tigress must be clouding his mind, so she must be eliminated. These thoughts raced through Lucy's head as she committed to her decision. This time she did not walk forward; instead she ran full force toward the tigress and the tiger guarding her, completely ignoring the two cubs fearfully huddling together along the fringes of her vision. Axel held up both of his hands, grasping Lucy's wrist and stopping the frantic charge. She slashed out with the knife as much as she could with her limited range of motion, not caring about the shallow cuts appearing on Axel's wrist. All she could think about was trying to get past him and to her target. Axel shifted his grip, releasing one of his hands from her wrist to wrestle the knife out of her hold. The much stronger tiger was able to retrieve the weapon easily, but Lucy was relentless, as her envy completely clouded all rational thought. As Axel began to lower the knife, his grip slipped on Lucy's wrist, allowing her to fall forward against him, the weight that she'd been using to push against him in an attempt to get to the tigress now propelling her forward. Time seemed to slow as Lucy's torso fell forward, and directly against the knife that Axel had been lowering. The point of the knife, which had been directed toward the ground, became angled, and found itself being driven deep into the sensitive flesh of a belly.

The cubs and their mother began to scream as they saw the knife entering Axel, the blood spilling rapidly from the wound. Lucy glanced down, failing to comprehend what was going on. She watched the tiger crumple to the ground, blood beginning to trickle from his mouth, which was stuck open in a gasp. His hands moved to his stomach, trying to hold off the inevitable, but he was losing blood too rapidly and the knife had pierced the edge of his stomach, allowing those deadly acids to run rampant through his body. Lucy took a few steps back as she began to process the scene in front of her. She watched as Axel's struggles lessened, and the light faded from his eyes before his entire body became eerily still. Tears began to well up in her eyes as she realized she had killed her intended husband. It was an accident, but still she had killed him. It was then she became aware of the tigress screaming and moving toward her. "You stupid bitch! You killed my husband. I'm going to make you pay for that," she growled threateningly.

Lucy shook her head as she fell to her knees, whispering to herself, "No, he was my husband. I killed my husband."

Even as she watched the tigress pull the knife from Axel's lifeless body, Lucy made no attempt to move. She stayed completely stationary as the knife was raised high above her, and plunged down into her heart. The pain was intense, and she knew she was going to die. Somehow she found comfort in this thought while the white dress rapidly turned red as the tigress twisted the knife before yanking it back out. The tigress spat on her as she fell over, then turned back to her husband. She turned too soon to see the smile forming on Lucy's face. Her last words died on her lips with her. "I can finally be with him."

DEVIL'S SNARE
FAOLAN

"I hate you," the black she-wolf said while looking at her reflection in the black obsidian mirror in front of her. The only light in the cluttered room came from a few scattered candles and a window in the ceiling that allowed moonlight to rain down onto the naked young canine. The attic of her modest home was the only room in the house she would never allow any outsiders to step into. Here was where she practiced her art, one which was supposed to remain hidden from the eyes of common folk. The witch hunts may have ended decades ago, but that did not mean that people welcomed practitioners of witchcraft, especially those that focused on the darker aspects of it, like Savani.

Spell books, various herbs, and other instruments of her art were spread all over the room, but few were as important as her black mirror. Polished to perfection, it showed her exactly what she wanted to see, except when it showed the woman her own reflection. Savani had a body that many females would kill for: fur as black as night and as soft as a summer breeze, eyes that blazed like a bonfire, and curves in all the right places. There was only one thing the young wolf was not particularly happy with.

She had inherited her old father's awful genes for her hair, which sat on top of her head like a bird's nest. She had tried growing it out, hoping that the weight would allow her hair to become straighter, but it was no use. The nest only got bigger. She raked her claws through her hair in frustration and stomped over to her comb. The process of combing her hair was always a tedious one, and after she had broken off at least three teeth of the bone comb, she threw it out of the window with a frustrated snarl. Ignoring the pained sound coming from some unlucky sod outside, the wolf forcefully braided her hair and tied a thin silver ribbon in it to keep it in place. There had to be a way to fix this problem. She just hadn't looked deep enough yet. Savani's amber eyes darted through the room, resting on every book in her view. Nothing. None of her ancestors or any of the other witches she had books from had ever encountered this problem before. The girl knew this, because she had read every single one of these tomes and grimoires at least a dozen times before, and she couldn't recall any one of them mentioning a solution for her current problem. If only she had been adept at illusion magic, this wouldn't have been such a problem, but alas, she was not. No, she would just have to come up with something herself. Tonight was not the time for creating and wielding such difficult magic, though. It was already late, and Savani was tired, so after making sure every window and door was locked, she retired for the night.

☽○☾

Her dreams were anything but peaceful, as she kept finding herself walking through shadow and mist, the sound of thousands of giant insects moving around her, never to be seen. She could feel them watching her from out of the darkness, never getting close enough for her to see them, until one eventually ventured closer. What appeared before her was a most grotesque creature with an exoskeleton of the purest black, save for a huge pile of what looked like skulls both of species she was familiar with, and those she had never come across before. Her blood ran cold upon spotting some skulls that definitely once belonged to those of her kind.

"What are you?" Savani demanded as she stood her ground and gathered her magic around her, only to find that nothing happened. Where her energy would normally circle her as a barrier, there was only still air, and nothing more.

"I am what I am, and I take what I desire," the creature spoke with a voice that was neither male nor female, yet both at once, while its body barely moved. Only the antennae kept moving around, scanning the misty air for any changes.

She let her eyes move over the creature, resting them on the skulls on the creature's back. Even though they obviously didn't belong to it, they seemed to be part of the insect regardless. What was this monstrosity that had appeared before her in this dream land? "What is it that you desire?" she asked.

"I desire the power to subdue any and all enemies, to become the greatest of all," the bug answered before tilting its head slightly and looking at the black she-wolf with its faceted eyes. "And what, little wolf, do you desire?" it asked as it took a small step forward, looming over her like a tidal wave that was about to strike down.

The young woman thought about that for a few seconds, trying to come up with a way to fully express what she wanted. She knew it was a dream; however, it was all so vivid that it had to have had a special meaning in one way or another. She'd had lifelike dreams before, and even a vision or two, but it was never as clear as this. She had also never seen a creature like the one before her, so why would it appear like this otherwise, especially after she had been so desperate for a solution to her problem? Savani shook her head, the little nest on top wobbling comically, before turning her eyes on the giant insect again. "I desire beauty unparalleled. I desire beauty that will make any man fall onto his knees before me. I desire beauty that will leave any other woman far behind me," she stated loudly and boldly while puffing up her chest, to make herself seem bigger.

The insect's antennae moved around like the whips mostly used to keep animals in check, and she had the strange feeling that it was grinning, even though no emotion could be read off its face. "Then do as I do, and just take it," it said before it tapped the skulls on his back with an antenna. "Take whatever it is you desire, and make it yours."

She stared at the creature before her and looked at the monstrous collection of skeletons gathered on its back. "Make it...mine?" she asked softly while thinking about it. That might not even be such a crazy idea. Well, of course it was crazy, but it wasn't impossible. She just needed to get the right ingredients and would have to come up with a ritual for it, but it was certainly something that could be done. The wolf turned to the being again and bowed her head slightly. "Thank you."

The creature nodded its head, and both it and the surroundings started to fade away, the lines of the insect becoming blurry, until darkness once again ruled supreme. "I will see you soon, Savani," it spoke before the dream ended.

☽ O ☾

The beautiful thing about magic is that there is pretty much nothing it can't do, as long as the needed materials and rituals are combined with a witch powerful enough to work the spell. It is possible to come up with a completely new spell yourself, but it is often easier to rework an old one into a spell that suited your needs. This was exactly the reason why Savani dove back into her ancestors' grimoires. Coming from a long line of witches, there was more than enough material to go over. Spells for levitation, invisibility, and love didn't interest her at that time, but she knew that there was a transformation or transmutation spell somewhere in the tomes around her. She just needed to find it, and rework the spell so that it suited her needs.

After at least a few hours of going through dusty pages, the black she-wolf eventually found grandmother Enna's transmutation spell, which was used to bind different types of plants together into one. Savani remembered her mother telling her that Enna used to have a tree in the garden that produced apples, pears, and plums! Savani was in no need for a tree like that, but she could definitely rework the spell into something more suitable. After having done that, the only thing left on her list was finding the needed materials for the spell to work.

After doing some research on herbs and plants in one of her favorite and most-used tomes, she headed out to the market, wearing a green-hooded robe that would cover the ugly blemish on top of her head. She looked around at the beautiful hair most of the other women sported, and it just filled her with a jealous rage. Why did life have to curse her? Her hair had already chased away two possible suitors, and, while some might say that that was just superficial and they were not worth her time and love, she wouldn't have married herself either for the exact same reason. Looks were not everything, of course, but it would be nice to wake up next to someone she found perfectly attractive for the rest of her life. It was not as if she could just cut off her hair either, as that was supposedly unbecoming for females, and was reserved for males, who could pretty much wear their hair any way they wanted. Savani clenched her fists and ground her teeth together in frustration. The world was a very unfair place.

While buying various plants from a florist, she stumbled upon Amber, a most gorgeous vixen with luxurious long hair of a color that could best be described as sunlight hitting a river of molten gold. The female fox almost literally bumped into her while browsing the same shop.

"Oh, I'm sorry, Savani, I didn't see you there," she said with a voice that was both sarcastic and sickeningly friendly.

"Good morning to you too, Amber," the black wolf said begrudgingly, as she really hadn't wanted to meet this particular person, mostly because she made her feel weird, tingly, and insecure. She was known as the Queen of Gossip, and Savani always seemed to be her favorite subject for some reason.

"Have you had any suitors over at your place, lately? I swear I have to beat them away with a stick nowadays, haha!" the vixen giggled while looking sideways at the wolf, the corners of her muzzle turning up a little to reveal somewhat of a smirk.

Savani's claws were digging into her thighs as she tried to keep herself calm to no avail. At least she could appear calm on the outside. This question was entirely unfair, as Amber knew bloody well that no man had been interested in the she-wolf for quite some time. The vixen just seemed to love adding salt to injury. "You know as well as I do that it's been remarkably quiet," she said before reaching her paw out for a rose, which was quickly snatched away by the gold-haired woman.

"Whoops! Sorry, sugar, but that one is mine," she said while grinning one of those typical fox grins, one of those that Savani would just love to claw off of her face. "Also, it really is to be expected. I mean, even I would look unattractive with a crow nest on my head," she said before laughing and walking off, her hips swaying with a natural grace as she disappeared into the crowd after paying the florist.

Savani stamped her foot on the cobblestones beneath her and snarled as a hint of her energy started swirling around her. She took a few deep breaths and calmed herself down, biting her lower lip, before anyone could really notice. She managed to control her magic, but not her anger. That bitch was going down someday! Her eyes shot open and a maniacal grin spread over her face as a brilliant idea unfolded in her mind. She looked at the florist and grabbed a beautiful pink rose before holding it up to him. "I would like this one!" she said, handing it to the mildly shocked ferret.

)O(

After having visited the herbalist for the more common herbs and roots, the dark she-wolf returned to her home in the second of the city's three rings. The inner circle was mostly for rich folk, and it was also where the palace was located. The further out you went, the smaller the houses got. Savani lived in an area that could be called middle-class, which she owed to her heritage. Her family had started out as farmers, before the interest in witchcraft took over, and they moved to the city under the guise of being healers. They had earned their place in the city, and, ever since then, generation after generation of Savani's family had lived in that same house.

Her family's knowledge was still present in the form of books and supplies of all kinds, which explained why the she-wolf could get her paws on some pretty rare ingredients for her spell. She stood in the kitchen and opened several cupboards to take out pots with all kinds of herbs and animal parts. "Now, where is it?" she muttered softly under her breath while slowly emptying the cabinet, putting a pot with snake vertebrae on the counter. She was looking for one of the last ingredients: mandrake. "Ah! There you are, you little sneak," she said and grinned as she reached into the cabinet, moving her paw past a pot with crow talons. She wrapped her fingers around her target and pulled it out. "It's no use trying to hide from me," Savani said while holding the pot of manlike roots up into the light that streamed in through the kitchen window. They were always a curious sight to behold, but that wasn't the reason she was checking. The girl opened the pot and fished out one of the several roots in there. This one was female, and therefore exactly what she needed. She put the pots back and closed the cupboard before taking the strange-looking root upstairs to the attic, where she'd assembled the rest of the ingredients.

The easiest part of getting the preparations done was over now, and the hardest part was about to begin. For this particular spell, she was going to need someone else's hair, and Savani was quite sure that no woman would voluntarily give up her hair for her. She didn't really have a lot of close friends, so she couldn't ask for a favor either. That only meant that she was left with one solution: procuring it from an unwilling donor. The woman waited until after sunset, before donning a black, hooded robe that would definitely keep her hidden in the shadows of night. It had been enchanted by a family member to muffle steps and breathing. It also took away the ability to communicate by the use of her voice once the hood was on, as the spell was designed in such a way that it blocked out all sound the wearer made, making it the obvious choice for that night's mission.

By the time she had finished getting ready for that night, the sun had said its goodbyes for the day, and Lady Moon had risen up into the sky. After stepping out of her home, the witch bowed respectfully, holding her right paw over her heart. "Greetings to you, Lady Moon. May you watch over me this night, and keep me safe," she whispered before throwing on the hood, which rendered her silent. Savani had never been particularly stealthy, to her mother's chagrin, but the she-wolf was trying her utmost best to stay out of sight of any guards or suspicious eyes, while also staying away from the street lanterns that lit up the corners of well-traversed streets. It was the first time in her life that she'd chosen to travel by means of the numerous alleyways instead. Those could be dangerous at night. Hell, they could be dangerous during the day as well, but Savani was well-armed, and this wasn't the harbor district or the slums.

The dark canine knew exactly who her target would be, and she was moving toward the upper-class district, where she could find her. The Queen of Gossip lived in a stately house close to the center of the city, and it took the witch almost twice as long to reach it as usual, because of her sneaking and having to avoid people, but the fewer people who saw her on the streets, the better. Amber's family was quite wealthy, and she would probably have to deal with a few servants first, unless she could figure out which window was the vixen's.

Fortunately, Savani didn't have to wait long before the beautiful Amber showed herself by standing in front of a window, wearing not much more than a see-through sleeping gown, which probably cost more than what Savani spent on food for a month. She was truly a sight to behold. It was such a shame it would change soon. The female fox closed the curtains and moved away, giving the she-wolf no more time admiring her target's appearance. Oh, how jealous she was.

The black witch gathered her power around her, which caused the air to crackle a little, before she uttered a spell that went unheard, but worked its magic regardless. "Licht als lucht..." She slowly moved up, feeling as light as a feather, until her feet were no longer touching the cold cobblestones. This was great-grandmother Rikana's favorite spell, which she used to fly through the sky for hours, until she was eventually spotted and trialed for witchcraft. It was a dark day for the family, as Rikana was actually one of the few witches who only used her powers for good. She was the last of Savani's family to be put on trial, but the resentment toward the church forever lingered in Rikana's offspring.

The wolf carefully flew over to the window Amber had just appeared at, and waited for the light in the room to dim, before she touched the window and silently muttered, "Open." The lock on the window unlocked itself, and the window was no longer an obstacle. Moving the curtain out of the way, the witch flew into the room and landed gracefully, before taking in her surroundings in the dim light of the silver moon. She'd flown over a small table that held various items a woman used to make herself look her best. There was a mirror on it as well, and when Savani looked at her own reflection, she thought herself positively scary. She grinned and slowly made her way over to the bed, her feet moving over a very expensive rug. She wouldn't have made a sound in this room even without her enchanted outfit. Some people really had it all.

Standing next to the luxurious four-poster bed, the she-wolf looked down at the beautiful woman sleeping in it. It was a natural sleep though, and Savani couldn't risk Amber waking up in the middle of this mission, so she grinned and moved closer, sinking down onto her haunches while reaching down into one of the pouches on her hidden belt. The black canine moved her muzzle to Ambers and very tenderly kissed her lips before whispering in her ear.

"Wake up, beautiful."

The vixen woke up almost immediately. Having been asleep for only a few minutes, it was to be expected. Her eyes shot open wide, but before she could even scream, Savani wrapped her paw around the girl's muzzle and blew the blue powder she was holding in her other paw into Amber's face.

"Sleep."

After struggling for not longer than a few seconds, the beautiful vixen went limp as she was sent straight into a very deep sleep, from which she definitely wouldn't wake for at least a few hours. Savani caressed the girl's cheek before running her claws through the perfect hair. "I like you a lot better when you sleep," she said silently before pulling away the covers, revealing the female fox's beautiful body. The wolf placed her paw on the girl's barely-clothed stomach, and gathered her power again. "Licht als lucht," she uttered, and Amber's body started to rise up from the bed. Savani pulled her aside and made the bed before flying up herself and taking the vixen with her. After closing the curtains and window, making sure it was locked again as well, the witch took off with the final ingredient of her spell.

☽○☾

"Lady's Mantle for change, catnip and rose for beauty, Myrrh resin and violet for transformation…" Savani spoke while stirring in her black kettle as she added the ingredients of her spell. She had a fire burning underneath the pot to get the water boiling, making the room rather warm. It had started raining outside, and the constant patter of it on the roof window combined with the sound of the crackling fire made the scene seem calmer than it actually was.

At the sound of someone groaning behind her, the black wolf turned to look at Amber, who was now naked and tied to the ceiling by her wrists, and to the ground by her ankles. "Well, well. It seems as if someone is finally awake. You'll have to wait your turn though. I'm not quite ready yet," she said before tearing her eyes away from the beautiful vixen, and back to her potion. "Magnolia for hair growth, dandelion and ginseng for wishes, orchid for desire…"

Amber groaned again and weakly struggled against her bindings as she was still sleep-drunk from the spell. "Wh…What is all of this?" she asked while blinking a few times and looking around. The girl gasped at the scene that was laid out before her. "W...WITCH! You're a witch! The rumors are true!"

The she-wolf sighed. "I guess they are. Not that you'll be there to confirm them," she said and grinned before adding some more ingredients to her potion. "You'll just have to wait your turn, dear. I'll be with you in a moment."

"Stay away from me, you monster! HELP! HEEELP!" she screamed as loudly as she could, while also struggling against the ropes that kept her in place.

"It's no use, Amber. The walls and windows have been enchanted not to let any sound escape from this house. Spare your lungs and vocal chords. Why don't you sing for me instead?" she suggested while stirring. She added the final ingredients to the potion and smiled. "Mandrake for power, and dragon's blood resin to amplify it by three!"

"Stop this nonsense and release me right now!" the young vixen demanded while pulling on the ropes and trying to bite her way through it. Unfortunately for her, she was tied in such a way that her sharp fangs would never reach the rope.

Savani chuckled and stirred the kettle a few more minutes, before walking over to a low table and picking up a bowl with a white substance in it. "I guess you have waited long enough, my dear. It is your turn now. Just stay still, and it will all be over soon," she said as she pulled a stool close and rested the bowl on top of it. The girl dipped her index and middle fingers in it and touched the naked vixen's body, starting from the neck and painting down to her belly button, before renewing the paint on her fingers.

"Stop it! What are you doing to me? Let me go!" Amber yelled while trying to struggle as much as she could. It was futile though, as her bindings didn't give way in the least.

The witch couldn't be deterred from her goal though, and she moved her fingers to the vixen's forehead, where she painted a dot, before painting over the girl's muzzle, up to her nose. She added some more lines, before having to renew the paint again. She slowly moved her fingers over the trembling fox's torso, drawing lines and circles here and there, before softly stroking the female's perfect breasts.

"Ah! St...stop that!" Amber protested while blushing furiously. "You can't do this!"

"I can, and I will. You cannot stop me, Amber. Not this time," she said as she painted over the nipples and circled outward with them as the starting points. "Aren't you grateful? I am making you even more beautiful," she cooed while grinning. "If you can be a good girl for me, I will show it to you once I'm done," she added softly.

The wolf kept on adding the markings to the russet and dark fur of the vixen's body, before placing two fingers on the belly button again. She started drawing a large spiral around it while looking up into Amber's beautiful wood-brown eyes. "Did you know that the belly button marks the middle of your energy center?" she asked.

"N...no? Does it?" Amber asked unsurely while looking up at her captor. The feeling of Savani's fingers on her body had felt strange, but, confusingly, not entirely unpleasant, even though she still had no idea what the she-wolf was up to. "What are you painting with?" she asked softly.

"Bone meal," came the witch's short answer as she moved closer to the vixen and softly nuzzled her neck, taking in her scent.

"M...made from what exactly?" she dared to asked.

"You don't really want to know. Trust me," Savani whispered as she slowly brought her lips to the vixen's and kissed her tenderly while sliding her fingers down from the energy center, toward the tender flower hiding beneath, cupping it gently as she spread the paint there.

Amber moaned into the kiss, but didn't break it. She was simply so entranced by what was happening to her, that she couldn't even think of escaping anymore. It was no use anyway. The way Savani touched her was very alien to her, as nobody else had ever touched her like that before. After all, she was supposed to save herself for her future husband. Liquid fire simmered beneath her skin wherever the dark wolf touched her, and it left her panting and squirming.

Savani ended the kiss and softly licked over the other girl's lips. "Good girl," she whispered before stepping away, smirking at the sound of the bound female's whimpering. She put the paint away and fetched a simple mirror, which she held up for Amber. "As promised," she said, only to move away again after about ten seconds, figuring it to have been long enough to get a good look. She sighed and looked a tad sad as she stepped up to the woman and looked into her eyes. "I have always admired you, you know. It's just a shame that you've always been unkind toward me, and that you happen to have something I need. I'm sorry, Amber," she said before slamming her palm into the woman's chest, causing the white markings to light up light blue, her own eyes doing the same thing. If there was anything the witch was good at, it was energy manipulation. She forced her own energy through the bone meal markings and forcefully extracted the vixen's life force, pumping it into the hair instead. Once the energy reached the top of Amber's head, the hair started to grow at an astonishing rate. What would normally take months, was now happening in seconds. The female fox screamed and tried to struggle in vain, until she no longer had the energy to do so. She grew weaker by the second, and her fur lost its shine. Her bones poked through the fur, and her eyes and cheeks were sunken in as her body's energy was being converted into hair.

Once the hair was at the point that it started pooling on the attic floor, the witch stopped and stepped back, panting a little as performing magic like that took a bit of a toll on her as well. She stepped around the exhausted vixen and ran her claws through the beautiful long hair. "Absolutely wonderful. Thank you, my dear," she said softly before moving over to her altar to get her athame, a ritual knife used for rituals. She moved back to the poor woman and gripped the black-handled knife tightly into her paw. "Thank you for your sacrifice," she whispered before cutting off the female's hair. She walked over to a stool and sat down on it, taking the long length of beautiful gold-colored hair with her.

It was truly a terrible shame to see the vixen like that, but she kind of had it coming with the years of mental abuse she'd tormented Savani with. It hadn't helped that the witch had always felt a strange attraction to the woman that often had her imagination run wild at night. The black she-wolf undid her own hair and tied hers and the vixen's tightly together with the silver ribbon, before she went over to the cauldron and filled a stone cup with her concoction. She blew over it and closed her eyes. "Here's to change," she whispered before drinking it all in one go, not caring about the bitterness of her brew as the warm liquid slid down her throat, warming her body from the inside. She immediately felt the potion's effect coursing through her veins, as her energy was quickly replenished, leaving her feeling invigorated and powerful.

After invoking the four spirits of the watch towers in front of her altar, she kneeled down in a ritual circle that had been burned into the wooden floor. She hung her hair over her shoulder, stroking it a bit longer than necessary, while looking at the blonde locks. Those would soon be hers. She took the bone meal again and drew the needed markings on her obsidian fur, before raising her paws up and closing her eyes as she started chanting.

"Spirits high and spirits low,
my desire you will know.
Aching void within my soul,
new hair acquired will make whole.
What once was yours belongs to me,
now and forever for all to see.
Energy flow and claim as mine,
These foreign locks so serpentine.
Golden sun to darkness turn,
two into one with shadow burn.
Power flow through markings white,
shed your darkness on the light.

Spirits, spirits, hear my plea,
As I will, so mote it be!"

The black she-wolf felt the air crackle with power around her as it circled her and engulfed her in a maelstrom of energy. She laughed loudly as she felt it enter her body through the markings, only to send it upward to her hair. A sizzling could be heard as the new hair and the old were united into one, the darkness of the pitch-black hair slowly seeping into its gold counterpart, turning it as black as her own. Savani felt truly beautiful in that moment and tears of happiness rolled down her cheeks after escaping her mirthful eyes. She felt truly happy and was so engaged with the feeling of finally having beautiful long hair, that she didn't feel the same hair slowly moving up and around her body, as if it had a life of its own, like a gorgon's venomous locks.

It wasn't until the hair suddenly wrapped itself around the witch's neck, that she realized that something had gone horribly wrong. The hair had fanned out behind her like the rays of the sun, and had started wrapping itself around her limbs, torso, and neck. She desperately tried to claw herself free, but the hair was too strong, and she was getting weaker by the second. The tears that welled up in her eyes were not of joy this time. Instead, her face was filled with dread at the realization that she would not survive this. She tried to scream, but only a faint guttural hissing managed to get out.

She heard a faint thud behind her, followed by the sound of footsteps. The hair pulled her head backward, revealing the sight of the vixen grinning down at her as she slowly moved closer. She looked a lot better than just moments before, which was absolutely impossible. There was just no way she could have recovered and gotten out of her restraints. Savani tried screaming and coughing, but couldn't even manage that anymore as her world slowly faded to black. The vixen brought her face close enough to the wolf's that her eyes could be seen

clearly. The ones that used to be a beautiful sky blue were now replaced by the black faceted eyes of a giant insect.
"I told you we would meet again soon."

BLACK FUR
GULLWULF

Once upon a time, I had everything.
 I was the most popular girl in high school. I joined the best sorority in college. Everyone wanted to BE me. And then it all fell apart. How did I end up here, stuck in some crappy minimum wage job at a fucking coffee shop? How DARE anyone assume that I would lower myself to listen to the commands of others! I hate these animals—and that's all they are compared to me. Disgusting, salivating animals.
 Until I saw her.

The jackal looked up from scrubbing the counter in the shop and stared at the vixen who had walked through the door. Red foxes around these parts were a dime a dozen—but this fox was no simple red fox. The blooming fire of her pelt was smothered in an ashen hue along her back, framing her back in soot and silver. The edges of her neck were aflame with red, but the mottled pattern continued down her delicate paws, down her hind legs and brushed the underside of her black, ribbon-like tail.
 She was the most beautiful creature the jackal had ever seen. Her scrubbing stopped as she found herself staring openly at the fox, chatting amicably with the weasel at the counter. Every movement of hers was liquid, grace, and beauty all wrapped into one. Even her laugh at the weasel's dumb joke sang like chimes. As she left, she left a physical ache behind her, and the entire café was dimmer for her presence.

The jackal ran up to the weasel, slamming her paw on the counter. "Who was that?"

"Woah, Cherize, let's calm down a bit there sweetheart, okay?" The weasel gave her the most patronizing smile that only a mustalid could give. "You're supposed to be scrubbing counters, not asking about pretty vixens!"

Cherize had to resist wiping that smug smile off the weasel's face. Of course he knew how she was looking at the fox. Who couldn't look at that fox that way? Either way, the weasel blustered on, "Anyways, that was Luciana. She's a real nice fox. Came from a small family and worked her way up. Good, honest labor, you know?"

What would a weasel know about that? Cherize bit her tongue to keep the words from slipping out. It would do her no good to get snippy at her boss; he already had a thing against jackals. Too low, too...*unrespectable* for this establishment, or whatever his reasoning was. He wanted to keep a good storefront to attract other customers, which was why the jackal had been shoved to the back and was given tasks that included cleaning, cleaning, and more cleaning. It wouldn't do to have a low-ranking mongrel of a canine up in the front.

"So can I work the counter tomorrow?" Cherize leaned against the table, watching as the weasel had already moved on, checking the cash register and counting up the bills.

The weasel lifted a brow, his whiskers twitching. "What's with this sudden burst of initiative?"

"You just said that you admire that fox because of her working all honest-like," Cherize said, smiling as wide as her muzzle could split. "So maybe you'd like if I was more like that vixen?"

"The day that you become like that vixen is the day that I actually start making money in this business," the weasel snorted. "Why don't you get back to what you're good at, sweetheart?"

A snarl built in Cherize's throat, her paw curling around the sponge until her knuckles ached, watching as the weasel hummed a merry tune under his breath with the smuggest expression on his stupid, little muzzle. How easy it was to control a jackal for him, after all?

But none of that mattered. All that mattered was *her*, the fox named Luciana.

It would be a week before the vixen showed her muzzle back in the coffee shop. Cherize had been waiting for her, hovering by the entrance and talking to her other co-workers about her. Everyone else only had tidbits about the fox, nothing to really satisfy the jackal's curiosity. She was nice, that much was a given. She left great tips. Her clothes always appeared to be finely made—not too fine as to be intimidating, just fine enough to indicate her class. She was good stock. Her family had lived in the area for some time, but she had gone away to college out of state and had only recently come back. Her boyfriend was nice too.

Every little bit of information only strengthened the jackal's lust. A lust to learn more, see more of her. And perhaps a little maleficent streak that the fox could not possibly be *that* good, not the way that everyone was claiming. No one was perfect (and she had tried. She was going to *be* perfect had it not all fallen apart). The fox, by the sheer definition of that fact, could *not* be perfect.

But when Luciana walked into the coffee shop after the fitful few weeks that Cherize had spent waiting for her, Cherize realized that this fox was the definition of perfect. One of her co-workers, a serval, was manning the front, and Cherize was quick to rush over to him, tapping him roughly on the shoulder and making up a half-baked excuse that there was something he needed to check in the back. The serval was quick to leave. Cherize had but a few moments to straighten her apron out, flicking her paws behind her (too tall) ears and smoothing the (awful, coarse) yellow fur that puffed at her collar.

"Oh!" The fox's ears perked, her delicate nose twitching at the scent of Cherize. "I haven't seen you up front before. Are you new here?" The question sounded so sweet, like a chime, even if something settled in Cherize's stomach. Had she become so unnoticed?

"No, but I usually work in the back," Cherize said with a smile, folding her long ears back. Normally that question would have wormed its way underneath her skin, but she felt the need to play it nice, to be submissive to the fox even.

"I see." The teeth of Luciana poked over her muzzle, her tail swishing behind her as she shifted her paws. The words stuck in the air, and Cherize felt desperate with trying to right the situation.

"What can I get started for you?" The jackal's tail had started wagging behind her. It was the only way she had to diffuse the awkwardness that was building in her mind. She had to keep the fox here, keep the fox interested in her. And she was stuck with a retail script. Fuck this entire job, even if the fox was making it worthwhile.

"A vanilla latte. Oh, nonfat, if that's okay," she said with a smile, the white tip of her tail flicking. "If you have it! I don't want to be a bother."

"Nonfat is one of our most common orders. I'll have it right up for you." Cherize put on her best smile as she skipped to the espresso machine, grabbing nonfat milk and pouring it into a pitcher before letting the steaming wand slam down into it. It had been a while since she had actually worked the front, but she resisted the temptation to look at the recipe cards lest she look like an ass in front of Luciana.

"Thank you, you're so sweet." The words that slipped from Luciana's muzzle rang like a chime, and Cherize half expected them to solidify and sparkle in the coffee shop, crystals hanging in the air. She found herself glancing up from the hissing machine, staring at the ceiling and imagining how it would be to have a voice that could elicit such wonderful responses when heat began to flow over her paw, and her ear flicked to a voice.

"Sweetie! Dear, oh no!" The fox's voice had grown with concern, and it was then Cherize looked down to see that the foam had bubbled up over the drink and onto her yellow paw.

The pain hit her moments later, the jackal jerking back instinctively, but the fox had pushed the pitcher away, spilling the foaming milk on the counter.

"Are you okay?" Luciana's ebony paws had taken Cherize's own, caressing them as her pawpads pushed the milk through her fur. "Those things get so hot, I—I didn't want you to burn yourself just making a drink for me!"

Cherize couldn't even bear to keep her ears up. She turned her gaze to the ground, feeling herself shrink underneath the fox's gaze. "I...I'm sorry." She swallowed, getting the lump down in her throat. "You just wanted a coffee, and I—"

"Honey, don't even worry," the fox said, her smile lighting up her muzzle. "You tried your best, and isn't that all we can ask for in this world?"

Cherize opened her muzzle to reply when the patter of claws clanking against the tile filled the room. She tilted her ears and saw the weasel dart from the back room, his tie askew and the fur on his neck fluffed while his tail shook in agitation.

"Cherize! What the hell are you doing?" the weasel snapped. "You are supposed to be in the *back*, and where the hell is Dan?"

"Dan decided to take a break," Cherize whispered under her breath, flinching as the weasel growled.

"Lies, lies, *lies*! That serval's break isn't for another half hour, and I found him scrubbing the goddamn whipped cream containers!"

"Sir," Luciana said, and all it took was that one simple word for all the tension to dissipate from the store. "Your worker, ah...Cherize you said her name was? Has had a very rough day, and I think she should have the day off."

Cherize stared at her, slack jawed. *Even the girls in the sorority didn't stick up for each other as much.* The thought just made Luciana that much brighter in the jackal's mind, though she was pulled back to reality as the weasel began spitting.

"With all due respect, Miss Luciana, this *jackal* has a job, and with the way her reputation is, she should be lucky that she is currently getting as much! Now if you do not mind, I promise I will have our more competent worker come out here and make you a drink—"

Luciana placed her hand on her hips, curled her tail behind her, and lifted an eyebrow. "Is this really the kind of community spirit that you want to be showing in front of me?"

The weasel stopped in his tracks, fumbling and scrambling for another word. He lifted a paw, stuttered out some syllables, and then finally clicked his tiny jaws shut. "Of course not. My apologies, miss."

"Now, given that she hurt herself on the job, I feel like she should earn the rest of the day off." Luciana turned to her with a sense of coolness that Cherize did not think was possible. "Isn't that right, dearie?"

Cherize nodded. She worried that any word might screw up the situation that was happening before her eyes. The weasel resisted a snort, though the look on his face indicated how not happy he was about this entire relationship. But he waved both of them off with a paw, and Luciana began to walk out of the store. Cherize hesitated before she stripped off her apron and followed her, her paws grabbing the collar of her polo shirt and attempting to straighten it as she followed the fox outside. She couldn't help but feel underdressed, especially outside of her work environment.

"Hey, uh," Cherize cleared her throat, catching up to Luciana in a few steps. The fox's tail gave a lazy wave to indicate Cherize's presence. "Thanks, for what you did back there. Not that many people would have stood up to Yellow."

"Yellow? Is that what you call him?" The flash of teeth from Luciana's muzzle made her far more fox-like than she had been since they had met. Now that they were outside of the cafe, Cherize saw the swish in her step and the arch of her bushy tail. "Doesn't seem very flattering."

"It's not meant to be," Cherize said too quickly. Luciana even gave her a look, raising an eyebrow, and the jackal turned her gaze away. "He's just...kind of a jerk. He has this whole thing about image despite being a weasel, so if you're a less popular species like…"

"Like a jackal." Luciana's paw linked through Cherize's arm, and she beamed at her. "Come on."

"O-okay." There was no way that Cherize could even say no to her, and she shortened her stride to stay with her. "To where?"

"My house!" The fox's tail began wagging. "I mean, not technically my *house*. It's more like an apartment, I guess."

"Oh." It had been a while since Cherize had been invited to anyone's house, and it wasn't like she lived in the best area of town either. No one trusted the jackal in anything nicer than a ground-dwelling shack tucked between gum-streaked alley walls, for their own biased reasons. She couldn't help but wonder where Luciana lived—apartments were fairly common, but there was nothing about this fox that was *common*.

Luciana turned a corner and began to walk into the heart of the city. Cherize's ears perked, recognizing as the dusty storefronts turned into clear, well-organized windows full of appealing items. The streets were clean, the cement on the sidewalk gleaming, the air here clean and faintly scented with baking goods and fresh roasted coffee. They continued to walk, and finally came across a building, one that reached into the clouds.

"See? More like an apartment." Luciana indicated the tall building before them before she coolly stepped through the glass doors. The inside was crisp, clean—it looked like an office, with a green granite counter and a cougar manning the front, a hat set smartly between her rounded ears. Gleaming silver elevators lined either side of the hallway, a wild dog standing prim and proper in his green suit. While considered a pack animal, their frailty and weakness rendered them in a lower status, as well as their comically big ears and blotched fur. Still better than the jackal and the coyote, however. The wild dog's tail gave a small wag, but Cherize pointedly ignored him, tilting her muzzle up as she followed in Luciana's pawsteps. She was not one of them: she was with a *fox*.

The elevator was chrome, the buttons shiny, and didn't stick at all like with Cherize's place. Luciana swept in, pressing the top button and humming along with the generic elevator music. Her voice added an allure to the song that the speakers couldn't even compare to.

Even though Cherize had been mentally preparing herself for what to expect, the sight of it still made her dizzy. The walk from the elevator to the doorway passed in a blur; it was the sight of the penthouse, of the green door opening to the space, that had Cherize spinning.

Modern, curving furniture in sleek grays and cool white fabrics accenting the living room. The carpet was lush, caressing Cherize's paws as she crossed the space. The kitchen was granite, marble counters accented with swirls of black, every appliance modern and gleaming.

But the view. Nothing could compare to the view. A window that stretched from floor to ceiling looked out over the skyline, the skyscrapers that stretched into the clear blue sky and the cars that milled about like ants beneath. Cherize walked up to the glass that was so clear that, were it not for the reflection of the curtains and the furniture in the room, she would have thought the space had simply opened to the sky. She pressed her paws to the window, the dark pads reflected, the tip of her claws resting on the glass.

"See, as I said, it's just an apartment," Luciana's voice was soft. "But the view sure is nice, isn't it?"

Cherize shook her head in wonder, looking at Luciana from the corner of her eye. The fox was standing in the center of her living room, tail swept around her legs, the orange undertones of her black fur all the more suiting in the space of the apartment. "This is more than I've ever had in my life," Cherize said, staring at the fox in her perfect penthouse.

"Really? A nice girl like you?" Luciana tilted her head. "That just doesn't seem possible. Where do you live now?"

Cherize felt her ears pin back against her skull, a wave of shame washing over her. "Not in a place like this."

Luciana's whiskers twitched, her tail swishing behind her before she walked smartly over to her kitchen, pulling out a platter of meat and cheese that was perfectly prepared. She indicated for Cherize to sit on the couch, and then sat next to her, the tip of her tail touching Cherize's waist. "Maybe you should tell me a little bit about you," Luciana smiled, and all of Cherize's worries seemed to melt away.

Of course, I couldn't tell her everything. How would she believe me? That I was once popular, once everything that anyone could have dreamed of? That I, and I alone, kept up that popularity throughout high school and college? No one would have believed that as a jackal I could achieve anything. So I didn't tell her. I gave her the sad story that she would have wanted, about how I was always kicked around. She listened with sympathy, she put her paw on my elbow, and I swear I was in love.

It was not the first time that the fox and the jackal would meet up. It became a regular occurrence after that first night, where Cherize had spent the night in Luciana's apartment once they had tired their jaws from talking. Luciana would meet with the jackal at the end of every shift, and walk her halfway home before the two of them split ways.

This was how Cherize learned more about Luciana than most of her co-workers did. She knew that Luciana's boyfriend was a wolf! Cherize was not sure how she felt about the cross-species romance, but Luciana talked about him with such fervor, and knowing how wolves felt about keeping to their own packs only made Cherize's opinion of her rise.

Luciana had also just graduated college from across the country, leaving many of her friends behind in order to come back to her home town. She had a degree in economics, something unusual for foxes who were known to become lawyers and politicians moreso than economy majors. "I didn't want to follow in the pawsteps of my parents," Luciana explained to Cherize one afternoon after work, sipping some leftover coffee while Yellow kept to himself, though Cherize could see his tiny ears flicking from across the cafe, hoping to hear part of the conversation. "My father was a senator and my mom was considered his, ugh...'Trophy Vixen.'"

"Was she?" Cherize asked, her golden muzzle splitting into a grin.

Luciana gave her a playful shove. "What she was isn't the point here. The point is, I want to be known as something other than being a fox. Everyone expects it, I mean—either I find my way into a powerful family, or I become powerful. A CEO of some Fortune 500 company. Maybe own a Casino or three in the middle of coyote territory." There was a pause before Luciana's eyes grew wide, and she reached across the table to pat at Cherize's paw. "Not that I mean anything by that! Just that—"

"Coyotes and jackals naturally prefer the desert," Cherize said mildly, waving the words aside, her ears perked and tuned toward the fox. "Now what was that about wanting to be known?"

"Oh, every pup has fanciful ideas growing up. I just…I wanted to do something that could help other people and not just myself," Luciana said. "You know?"

Cherize shrugged. Truthfully, she didn't. Everyone else seemed to have it better than her, after all.

"I thought economics might be good for that. Get people to see the inequality that others have. To see how well the rich are compared to the poor."

This caught the jackal's attention. "You want to address species inequality?"

"I think it's important." The fox blinked. "This popularity contest among species, since I guess we don't have to worry about food is a bit trite, don't you think?" She wagged her tail. "Wouldn't it be nice if no one cared what you were? I mean, they could let you work in the front! No more rumors about jackals being hard to work with, or insecure, or riding on the tails of others!"

Pangs of guilt filtered through Cherize's chest, her ears folding back. "So…do *you* think that about jackals?"

"Of course not!" Luciana's nose twitched, her whiskers following the movement. "Oh, honey…do you really think I…No! You're one of my closest friends here! In fact, besides my boyfriend, you're my *only* friend here."

"Your...only friend?" Cherize blinked; she didn't really believe it.

"I mean, when I moved back to my hometown...it wasn't like any of my friends from college followed me." Luciana shrugged. "There was my boyfriend, but we were childhood friends and he still lives here. Everyone else is still busy with sorority life. So I kind of had to readjust." Luciana's smile spread across her muzzle as she clasped her paws with Cherize's. "And then I met you at the coffee shop! See, things have a habit of working out! And after I saw the treatment you received at the hands of that weasel..." Luciana shook her head, folding her ears back. "It's not right."

A smile flitted across Cherize's muzzle. "You are a very kind fox," she said. "A lot nicer than the girls in college."

"You didn't have a good time in college?" Luciana tilted her head, her ears perked as the ebony and umber fur around her neck fluffed.

"Oh...kind of. I mean, as well as it could be expected when you're a jackal going into Computer Science. Everyone has you pegged as the loner who's eventually going to become a hacker." Cherize shrugged. "The sorority kind of just...treated me as being there."

Luciana's eyes went wide, the pupils even expanding in the amber of her irises. "You poor thing," she said. "Didn't you have any friends before that?"

Cherize looked away. "What friends? Jackals are pegged as loners...who would want to make friends with a loner?"

Before Cherize could react, the fox had wrapped her arms around Cherize's chest, pressing her thin muzzle to the crook of the jackal's neck and wagging her white tipped tail. "That isn't right," Luciana spoke into her fur, her breath warm and brushing across Cherize's skin. She pulled away after a few too short moments, leaving Cherize feeling cooler and leaning into the space where Luciana once was. "I promise we're going to be friends, okay?" Luciana smiled.

Cherize felt the warmth that lingered on her skin bubble down into her chest, and a smile lifted her muzzle. "You really mean that?"

"Of course I do!" Luciana patted her shoulder, and kept her hand there, squeezing it lightly. "You've inspired me. You're a great person. And I think together we're going to be able to do good things for each other."

"For each other." Cherize nodded. "Yes. I like the sound of that."

Luciana was very inspired by her new friend. So inspired, in fact, that she decided to go straight to the source.

The jackal's story had intrigued the fox, and while she didn't go to school for journalism, she knew that the only way to prove her case for species relations was by heading to Cherize's sorority house and getting a look at these fellow friends of hers. Even if most of them had graduated, surely a few in the house would still know of the jackal. How could they not?

The sorority house of Chi Omega was quaint, sitting ten miles outside of the city in a residential neighborhood. A white picket fence surrounded the yard that was semi-kept—the best that could be taken for a sorority house, at any rate. At least they tried to grow petunias. Luciana gingerly opened the gate, mindful of the rusted lock, lifting her tail as she approached the front door and knocked. The house was strangely quiet for a sorority—Luciana double-checked the paper in her paw a few times, straining her ears for any amount of noise.

Soft pawsteps echoed, making the fox look up. The door opened, a slender, gray muzzle and twitching black nose poking out. A gray fox stepped into view, a head shorter than Luciana herself with whiskers that constantly twitched and a black skirt that hid her hind paws from view.

"Hi!" Luciana smiled warmly, her tail giving a relaxed wag behind her. "Are you one of the girls for Chi Omega?"

"Y-yes." The gray fox's ears perked, a bright spark entering her eye. "You here for pledge week?"

"Oh, no, I'm sorry," Luciana said, keeping her tone soft. "I was wondering if you knew anything about a golden jackal named Cherize?"

The demeanor of the gray fox changed in an instant. Her ears pinned back against her skull, her tail slipped between her legs, catching her skirt in the process, and she hunkered back behind the door. "The jackal isn't here anymore," the fox spoke quickly. "Please leave."

"What?" Luciana's tail flicked, her hackles itching to lift on her shoulders. "Were you not her sorority sisters? I only wanted to do something nice for her." The gray fox tried to shut the door, but Luciana stuck her hind paw in before the door could fully close.

"The jackal isn't here!" the gray fox yipped. "And I don't know where she went, and we aren't going to talk about her!" She kept glancing over her shoulder, eyes wide. "Please, just go—"

"What's going on?" The deep voice belonged to a caracal who pushed the door completely open, towering over the gray fox from behind and meeting Luciana's gaze evenly with mint green eyes, her black tipped ears standing forward. A nose-ring gleamed from her black nose, and the tank top she wore said something about fighting like a feline. Luciana dismissed the fashion in favor of the scowl that twisted the caracal's muzzle as the feline began to glower. "Who the hell are you?"

Luciana kept her smile on, fighting the snarl that twitched in her whiskers. Memories of her friend's words were worming their way to the front of her mind. *Keep civil*, she reminded herself, forcing her ears to go back ever-so slightly. "Hi," she said, "I'm a friend of Cherize's—"

The caracal hissed, loud and low. "You can turn that bushy tail of yours right the hell out of here in that case."

"Uh..." Luciana blinked. "I'm sorry?"

"We don't want anything to do with that goddamn jackal. Crazy son of a bitch," the caracal hissed. "And if you're associated with her, we want *nothing* to do with you."

"Because she's a jackal?" Luciana's tail stood straight behind her, and she couldn't keep her ears from folding back. "That's all that stands out about her to you guys, apparently. What is it about her species that you all so *twisted*—"

"You're talking to a caracal," she spat. "What the fuck do you think I have against her species? Everyone calls me a bobcat or a lynx for fuck's sake! No, *she* was the one who had a problem with being a jackal!"

"You're kind of just proving my point," Luciana said.

The caracal crossed her arms over her chest, glancing the cross fox up and down while the gray fox still kept to herself. When the caracal grinned, her fangs gleamed. "Oh, man," she said. "She really has you wrapped around her claw, doesn't she?"

"Excuse me?" Luciana growled.

"It's probably too late for you by now." The caracal rested a paw on the gray fox's shoulder, turning her aside and back into the house. "Shit, good luck. You're a red fox. There's no way she's going to let you go."

"Wait!" The door slammed shut in Luciana's muzzle, an inch from her nose. A growl tore out of her throat, and she found herself banging on the door, all of her fur bristling. She heard some muffled snarls, and eventually silence greeted her. She was forced to go back home, ruminating over everything that had been said.

The gray fox had reacted with fear, and apprehension when it came to the mention of Cherize. The caracal was pissed. No one liked her, but they all had laughed over the notion of a species bias.

Luciana was lost in thought as she went back to her apartment, tapping notes on her phone. The familiar tunes of the elevator music helped to quell her emotions; she still had yet to have her fur flatten. When she drew to the entrance of her apartment, her ears perked, and she stopped in her tracks.

Someone was in her apartment. She tilted her head up, catching a scent. Cherize. And…her boyfriend?

Luciana slammed the front door open, seeing her wolf boyfriend and Cherize talking amicably in the living room. He was watching the jackal curiously, a bouquet of flowers in his gray paws, tail wagging in a lazy beat behind him. Cherize had her ears up, staring at him like he was...

A good friend. They had noticed her entrance, and the wolf looked at her first, ears up and tail wagging furiously. Cherize's tail just about matched...exactly matched, for that matter. "Honey!" He ran up to her, embraced her, and kissed her muzzle. "I was just talking to your friend, Cherize. I'm so happy that you met someone in the city!"

Luciana felt her spirits lift, leaning into the warm fur of her boyfriend, nuzzling her snout into his neck ruff. "Oh, she's been a great friend," Luciana spoke into his fur. "Best I could ask for."

"She was telling me all about you too," the wolf said, pulling back with a bit of a smirk. "You never told me about your coffee addiction, or the new thing you do with your nose."

"New...thing?" Luciana blinked, shooting a glance over at Cherize. She was studying a picture on a desk, though one ear was tuned to the conversation.

"Yeah! Oh, Cherize, go ahead and show her!"

The jackal turned toward the couple, flicking her ears back, but then she twitched her nose, her fingers curling around her whiskers. They were never that long before.

Her wolf's deep, rumbling laugh echoed. "See? It's *just* like you! I swear, sometimes she reminds me of you so perfectly..." As Luciana continued to stare, the wolf licked the top of her head, handing the flowers to her. "I have to head to work, but I wanted to drop these off. See you for our anniversary tomorrow, yeah?"

"Mmhm." She absently hugged the wolf before he left, her gaze locked on Cherize. Cherize still had her fingers wrapped in her whiskers, never once looking away from Luciana. She waited until the door had shut behind them before she started moving around the perimeter of the penthouse.

"I really don't understand why you would ever leave this place honestly," Cherize spoke, trailing a claw along the golden edge of a vase. "Everything here is perfect. Even your choice of decor is impeccable."

Luciana watched the jackal's pawsteps weave through the carpet. By the pattern worn into the shag, Cherize had been here for a bit. She took a deep breath, quelling the mass of worms withering in her stomach. There were so many explanations for the behavior of the others and she was jumping to conclusions. "I talked to your old sorority house," Luciana began, and clicked her jaws shut as Cherize jumped.

Cherize's ears folded back, her tail stiffening behind her. Did her lip try to curl up over her teeth? She traced her claws along the armrest of the couch, taking a few moments to speak. "And what did they have to say?"

"Not much," Luciana admitted. She took a step closer to Cherize, discarding her jacket to keep her arms free. "But they didn't seem very happy with you. Actually, when I dropped your name, they—"

"Drove you away?" Cherize snapped, swiping her paw across the armrest. Rents in the fabric were left behind. "The moment you said that you were friends with me, they wouldn't talk to you, right?"

"Well...yes," Luciana admitted, taking the opportunity to stride closer.

"Because you're friends with a *fucking* jackal!" Cherize snarled, running her paws over her face, pulling at the yellow fur of her muzzle. "I told you—it didn't matter what I did, they hated me! Even the lowest fox had something above me. I was never going to be the picture perfect *sister* they wanted—"

"Cherize." Luciana grabbed her shoulders, spun the jackal to face her. She felt tension in the jackal's shoulders, saw how her gaze darted every which way. "They didn't hate you because you were a jackal."

Teeth flashed from the yellow muzzle, the jackal's amber eyes starting to blaze. Her voice grew cold. "Is that what they said?"

"Yes, but..." Cherize tried to squirm away, but Luciana clamped down hard, and wrapped her arms around Cherize's waist, pressing her muzzle into Cherize's chest, breathing in the scent of her fur. "Cherize, you don't have to lie to me," Luciana mumbled, feeling the tension bleed from the jackal. "I think something happened to you, something happened in that house, and I want to know. I want to help you. *You*. I would do anything for you."

"Anything?" Cherize's voice was smooth; her paw trailed down Luciana's neck, claws slipping through the scruff of black and red fur.

"Yes," Luciana whispered. "You're my best friend."

Luciana felt the paw's rhythm on her neck and relaxed. She knew it; the others had been wrong. The things they were implying were simply not something her sweet jackal was capable of. The paws drifted to her collarbone, and Luciana felt her tail start to wag. Things were right. It was going to be fine—

She couldn't breathe.

Paws closed around her throat. The jackal's teeth flashed, her amber eyes blazed with something that Luciana realized she had always seen, she had seen in the hungry glances of her apartment, her boyfriend, her own *body*. She swiped, she thrashed and flailed and tried to suck in a breath, but a hind foot pressed down on her paw and the grip tightened. Spots began to dance in her vision, her lungs burned, and yellow claws pushed her chin up.

"I want you," Cherize whispered. "Sleep, my dear friend."

She struggled. She tried to scream. Her weakened voice could not penetrate the walls of the penthouse.

Her vision faded.

The jackal's grin embedded in her vision as the last breath was strangled from her body. The last words lingered on her ear, just before the comforting blackness took her away: "Thank you."

I had to decide if I was going to skin her fur or dye my own. In the end, I went with a combination of both—the smell of a dead pelt was going to be hard to hide, even with the perfumes that the former Luciana had in abundance. It was hard to get the bright fire undercoat with the deep ebony, but having the corpse to study endlessly with no fear of retribution gave me the perfect canvas.

She looked so peaceful in death. I think, in the end, she knew that the best gift she could give me was herself. Herself, and everything about her life. That was why she died with a smile on her muzzle.

I don't know what to do with her boyfriend. I am a head taller than the former Luciana, though I now wear her fur, I am working on changing my eyes to her color, and I can imitate her perfectly. But he might get suspicious. He is an adorable wolf; it would be such a shame to get rid of him. I wanted everything about Luciana's life, and that included him.

Something happened that day. As I was studying her teeth and debating about ripping them out one by one and strapping the delicate fangs to my jaws, someone knocked on the door. My fur dye and the scraps of her fur were not perfectly on my body, it was too soon to talk to anyone! I had to try. It would be against Luciana's schedule to be away from home. I shoved the body in the bathroom and answered the front door.

A snow leopard was standing, framed by the ebony doorframe, making her pure white fur stand out like a beacon. Her crystal blue eyes glanced at me curiously, that long, luxurious tail of hers poised like a picture.

"Luciana!" Her voice was like a choir, reaching to soaring heights. "I was so hoping you were here! I just moved into the city with my boyfriend, you remember him, right? We're engaged now! Oh, he's just the best snow leopard I could have asked for, I adore him."

I was rapt with attention. One of Luciana's friends from college—I would have to study, but this opportunity was beyond anything I could have imagined. "Where do you live?" I said, careful to pitch my voice to the chime of Luciana's. Compared to the snow leopard, it felt grating, off-key.

"In the mansion on top of the hill!" She said gleefully, clasping her beautiful paws together. "Oh you would love it, I promise—it looks just like the summer house on the beach! You will visit, right? Promise me you'll visit!"

"*Of course I will,*" I said with a smile. The snow leopard's cheerful demeanor froze for a second, a crack in her facade as she looked at me, at Luciana. Her muzzle twitched into the smallest of smirks.

"*Good,*" she said. "*I do believe you deserve the life of felines, after all.*"

The snow leopard walked away, and I felt the sickness curl in my stomach. How dare, how dare that snow leopard think that she was better than me, a fox! After everything I had suffered through, after everything that Luciana and I had both suffered through...

I would find out everything about Luciana's friend. I would become her. I would consume her. No feline deserved their place in society; but I? I did.

INTERLUDE

The three sat in silence at the conclusion of the story.

After a few moments, Derek spoke, "Well, I actually think Zinc's story at the beginning was the best. It creeped me the fuck out."

Barba nodded. "Yeah…" He eyed the tiger again with concern. "It was certainly the most sinister of the set."

Zinc beamed, his head held high. "Hells yeah! So, whose was the weakest?" The horse and the German shepherd looked at each other.

Derek sighed and said, "I guess my first one was probably the weakest. I'm a sap for emotional romance stories, but I admit it wasn't the darkest."

The horse smiled. "It was still a good story. I loved it anyway."

Zinc jumped to his feet. "Alright, dog, time for a dare!"

Derek groaned and placed a paw on the bridge of his snout, covering his eyes. "Oh, c'mon, do I have to?"

"I double dog dare you!" Zinc replied.

The German shepherd's paw didn't move, and he just shook his head. "Fine, what's the dare, Zinc?"

"I dare you to let me brand your ass!"

Derek's eyes widened. "Holy fuck!"—"Derek!" Barba scolded—"Why would you want to do that for?" He spread his arms wide pleadingly. "I thought you were going to dare something like, 'Pat your head and rub your tummy at the same time.' What the fuck?"

Zinc folded his arms and walked over to the pulpit. "Oh, c'mon. It won't hurt that bad. Don't be a baby."

Growling, Derek said, "What are you going to brand me with?"

Derek and Barba watched Zinc lean down and pick up something from the ground. When he stood, they saw he was holding a metallic cross about three inches tall. "How about this?"

"Fuck, Zinc!" Derek stood from his spot and took a step backward. "You can't leave a mark like that on me."

Even Barba was smiling by now though. "Zinc's right, Derek. You a chicken?"

Derek glared daggers at the horse. "What the fuck is wrong with both of you?"

The ire on the canine's tongue made even Zinc widen his eyes. It was just a little brand, after all. Why was the canine so angry about it? As Zinc drew closer, slowly, Derek growled, "Fine. I will do it. But don't make it a deep brand. I want the fur to be able to grow back. Alright?"

Zinc offered his most innocent smile and replied, "Deal." He went back to his pile of clothes, grabbed a shirt, and held the very tip of the cross through the fabric. Then, he walked over and held the metal shape over a candleflame. He heard Derek's low growl as the metal heated and glowed. Once Zinc was content with it, he walked over to Derek. "Alright, bend over, baby."

"Fuck you," Derek snarled as he leaned over a broken pew. His legs spread, and Barba felt his cock stir at the German shepherd's exposed tailhole. "Get it over with."

Zinc could not help but grin as he pushed the cross into the brown fur on Derek's right buttcheek.

Derek reared his head back and howled. The earsplitting cry seemed to shake the chapel, and the stench of burning fur immediately filled the room. Both Zinc and Barba's jaws gaped at the deep cry of the dog. It sounded…unearthly. "GET THAT FUCKING THING OFF ME!" Derek roared.

Dropping the red-hot cross onto the ground, Zinc took a few steps back, and when Derek turned to face his boyfriend, the canine's eyes seemed to glow in the burning light of the twenty candles of the hall. "I'm sorry, babe," Zinc muttered, his ears flattening.

Derek's paw clenched his ass. "I told you not to press so damn hard!"

Heart thumping in his chest, Zinc watched his boyfriend in horror. Derek seemed to have transformed before his eyes: his jaw was clenched, baring his glistening teeth; his ears were pinned back like triangular horns, and his eyes burned with such hatred in them.

"I...I said I'm sorry. I didn't mean to."

Suddenly, the candles flickered and then went out, flooding the room once more in darkness. They each heard the sounds of someone tripping over wood. When the lights went back up, all three of them had moved. Barba was crouched on the ground, holding up a broken table leg. Zinc stood against the side wall of the cathedral, paws planted flat against the chipping paint. And Derek was trying desperately to open the door, but to no avail. He looked up, froze, and then yelled, "Fuck!" as he stepped away from the door. "Look at this shit!"

All eyes went to the door where a new message, still in blood, dripped down the wood: "THE DEMON KEEPS US HERE! FREE US!"

Derek retreated toward the others. "Oh, great. So, now the lost souls of this damned cathedral are trying to help us. Do any of you have any abilities in exorcism?"

Both Barba and Zinc were frozen in fright though, not believing that Derek was joking about this.

Snarling, Derek pressed on, "What is the next fucking card, Barba? I'll read it myself. Just tell me what it is."

Barba's lower jaw quivered. "It's the b-b-b-background card. Tells you Zinc's h-h-history."

"Alright," the dog said with a sneer. As he reached the podium, a few feet from the shaking horse, he flipped the fifth card. A goat grinned back at Barba, half its face melting with black herpes. "Sloth...another of the seven deadly sins." He turned to Zinc. "Let's start telling more fucking stories and see how angry we can make the angels in the room, huh? I'll go first. This time, winner gets to ask the other two for three truths, alright?"

When neither responded, he started the first story.

REPOSITORY
HYPETAPH

Through the window, the pallid orange light of a setting sun crept onto the bedroom's hardwood floor, though with much difficulty—it first had to climb beyond the piled bowls and askew silverware, small mounds of precariously balanced porcelain and plastic hindering the ray's path from pane to paneled floor...if it could reach even that. Instead, such light outlined the misshapen, scattered pieces of clothing from...yesterday—no, a few days—maybe?—since Parks had last crawled from the mattress in the far corner of the room.

Atop his figure rested a sepia quilt, a shade only marginally lighter than the deep brown of the German Shepherd's fur. It matched the exposed brick walls of the repurposed apartment (it had once been a factory, Parks had been told) which were all the rage in the modern inner-city scene, Parks had also been told, and—by whom? he was not wholly certain; names ran into other names like the nights did to days to nights again until they all conglomerated into an omniscient "someone told me" by whom Parks had been told of most subjects.

Parks shifted his leg beneath the covers, pressing his knee faintly against the back of his lover's leg, whose skin was familiar, soft, and cool. Parks's arm was limp across the coyote's torso; his fingers lightly massaged the fur at the base of his neck, and a small laugh gurgled up his throat, "Baby...c'mon Simon—you've got to get up. The day is almost over." His statement went unanswered and settled into the air like dust. Simon had not spoken for a while—for what reason, the German Shepherd was not able to understand. However, his affection for the coyote forgave such stubborn reticence.

He'd always enjoyed that quality of Simon—his steadfast, mildly aloof demeanor. Parks remembered specifically—oh, how he remembered—the night the two of them spent at Simon's grandmother's place: a cute house—a townhouse?—no, a duplex; but like a lone house (no one had rented the other half)—in which they were gifted a handmade quilt. It was inarguably their favorite possession, beneath which they often warmed one another. Of gorgeous white, the piece had been given to Simon. Said to both of them afterward was the off-color commentary, "I expect many sweet women to share it with you."

Given to Parks by Grandmother was a glare; to Simon by Parks, a look of disbelief; to Grandmother by Simon, some choice words; and later, by Simon to Parks, one of the most rewarding orgasms he had ever had—beneath her quilt, beneath her roof, and above her condemnation.

Parks loved that quilt. He loved Simon.

Fur floated softly in the crepuscule atmosphere as a small gust of outside air found its way through the unrepaired seal of the room's window. Through the same fracture breached a thin but active line of ants who for hours had been exploring the environment, absorbing the smells and stealing crumbs of last week's meals. Their tiny legs traversed with great effort the inconsistent platforms, the growing green on lazily discarded plates, and—with less effort—the matted brown of Parks's hind paw.

He kicked, lightly, without much dedication; the tiny, itching pricks were more of an inconvenience than something he found himself willing to remedy, and instead pulled himself closer to Simon, nuzzling his nose into the crest of fur running along the spine of Simon's neck, inhaling the strong scent. The coyote's smell was that of warmth and sweat and saliva: the two had been curled together for...for quite some time—oh, quite a while, and the German Shepherd adored every minute that passed pressed against his still lover.

"I love you, Simon—you know that, yeah?" Parks whispered into Simon's shoulder, his teeth wrapping around the Coyote's skin in a soft, playful, affectionate bite. His tail wagged beneath the quilt, like an excited but struggling worm beneath taut flesh, and again his voice uttered, "I love you, Simon."

Simon gave no indication he had been listening, but Parks knew he had heard him, sleeping or otherwise. The sun had since set and with it all the warmth it had to offer. In its place settled the chilling, dank air of a late fall evening, and the two lay together on the mattress. Parks wriggled his paw under Simon's heavy arm and pulled his chest inward, the two fitting together like a dark, sentient puzzle piece into the other—Parks liked the comparison—"as one," he would insist. Further combatting the cold, the German Shepherd threw his leg over Simon's thigh and—oh!—Simon!—god, he was so cold. Parks thought, *I wouldn't get up either, poor baby*. His chills must be a consequence of the fever he'd caught the other day, Parks reasoned: poor thing—it was the season for it.

Parks ran his paws through the fur of his lover's breast, raising his leg and tightening it around Simon's hip. The German Shepherd allowed himself to push his body ever so slightly atop his boyfriend, but not before pulling the quilt over them first. In the frigid air of the autumnal room, the blanket was a house of captured breath that insulated the two as Parks gripped between his teeth the cool flesh of Simon's shoulder while he thrust up and down, up and down his growing member against the soft fabric of Simon's boxers, gasping between bouts of outcries like "Simon, Simon, fuck me," and "Remember?" and "Like before," and "Tomorrow," and—and—and—

Parks paused. His cock ached, but in a sudden moment of clarity he realized—well, he always knew—but truly *realized*—that Simon had not said yes. He had not said anything. And while his body strained for the sweet eruption of release, Parks pulled his mouth loose of the soaked fur of Simon's collar bone, and pressed his forehead softly to the Coyote's. The quilt was damp with sweat, and the captured air smelled of musk and ammonia, of sea salt, of copper.

"Baby, I'm sorry, I—"

Simon fell to the side before Parks could finish his sentence. The German Shepherd could feel the deadweight movement of rejection, and though Simon could not be seen beneath the darkness of their favorite quilt, Parks knew he was facing away from him.

Soft *tap-tap-tapping* sounds rapped at the window, a force clicking softly against brick and glass. The morning sunlight provided just enough illumination to vaguely outline the creature—a deep black bird—whose beak assaulted the scavenging ants as they scrambled frantically to escape the fantastic terror. Parks inched his head from underneath the covers to glare at the bird, who was enjoying her desperate meal. He had not slept; instead, he spent the night staring at the shadowed space where he knew his sleeping partner lay.

"Simon, I'm sorry."

"Simon, I'm sorry."

"Simon, I'm sorry," he whispered, over and over and over again until the words faded into a dreary-eyed hymnal plea to hear his voice say softly back, "It's okay, sweetheart."

Parks's stomach rumbled, which he quickly dismissed—he did not want to eat, not unless Simon were eating with him. Not that it served him much good: there was little food in the house anyway. He rolled to his side and blindly permitted his paw to scan the hardwood, claws scraping through dust and ridges until, eventually, it made its way to an ornate teacup, filled halfway with tea made four—right?—no, seven—ish?—days ago. He dismissed any concerns and pulled the cup obliquely toward him, spilling some onto his bed, but most into his mouth, some of which ran down his chin and softened in the fur of his breast. The drink had an almost...grimy texture to it, but Parks had no interest—*it's old tea*, of course it had coagulated. He took another sip; the rim caused his nose to itch.

He and Simon had shared the drink together, he recalled; Parks had made it to aid his boyfriend's worsening cough. The coyote had come home from work that night—he'd actually come home early—having felt increasingly fatigued for a few days. His body had been shivering, and Parks greeted this by assisting him undress, settle into bed, and heating the drink.

"Parks, please, I—"

"Yes?"

Simon inhaled sharply, clutching the side of his ribs, and stifled a rough, searing cough that burned his throat like fading embers.

"I'll go tomorrow, promise," Parks said, "They're closed now. Tomorrow. Okay?" Simon fell into an uneasy sleep following; Parks massaged his partner's neck and temples to help with his headache until his hoarse breathing grew steady, consistent, soft, and let Parks know that everything would be a—

Tap, tap, tap, tap, sounded the indifferent bird, collecting the pieces of her meal, alive or no. The room was silent otherwise until the teacup crashed against the panel. The bird shrieked and vanished in a panicked scramble, and the shards of both window and ceramic came toppling down atop the mountains of dishware, sending them collapsing to the floor in a thunderous cacophony. The porcelain shrapnel spread everywhere: the sill, the floor, the clothes, the mattress—Parks shielded his eyes. The clamor settled almost as quickly as it had begun; a soft reverberation pulsed through the aggressor's head, and he buried his face under the sepia quilt.

His head began pounding harder that night. Parks pushed his palm against the bridge of his nose; his claws scraped along his forehead in distracted discomfort, which allowed him brief if ineffective alleviation from the growing ache behind his eyes. His paws shook as the headache forced him awake. In a desperate attempt for amenity and relief, Parks pulled himself to Simon, under whose arm he found himself wrapped in familiar comfort. There, he felt safe—and while the pain pounding in his temples did not subside, Simon's chin resting on his head almost made the agony disappear.

"Hon, time to get up…"

Almost.

"Get up!"

"Get up, Simon!" Parks demanded, his voice shaking nearly as much as his body. Again he had not slept, and the exhaustion was taking its toll upon his demeanor: "Get the fuck up; you have been lying in bed for days! You, you have been missing work! Do you even give a shit about your job anymore? Do you? Do you even give a shit about *me* anymore? Here I am trying to keep you company—keep you feeling well—hold you—love you—and you don't even say *thank you*, oh my god, I—I cannot fucking believe how—" his rage continued, in this internal monologue, as he faced away from his partner; he was fuming. He felt his forehead growing hot with rage, and his chest grew tighter, his breathing heavier. He wanted to blame Simon for this—for how he felt—if only the asshole would *talk* to him!

Hours had passed, but the sun had yet to rise. Beneath the quilt, Simon faced away from Parks, though Parks could not tell in the darkness. Shivers of increasing tiredness sent his body in light convulsions of cold sweat, and he leaned down to lick Simon on his nose, the dry skin rough against the German Shepherd's rugged tongue. He closed his eyes, but the room spun around him, as though he were the center of an orb that could not decide which way to travel. His empty stomach churned equally, and as his anger turned to mild fear, creeping up his throat he felt—oh no—the sensation of clawing bile, which escaped his mouth in a caustic heave, the strong corrosive collecting in Simon's unkempt hair.

"Oh, no, no, no, no, no," Parks ran his fingers through Simon's headfur, crudely combing the vomit out and onto the pillow behind him, "No, no, no, no—I am so sorry—I'm so sorry." Parks stifled sobs as he continued—Simon looked absolutely disgusted, Parks imagined, but permitted him to continue in sheer shock—reasonable, Parks thought—what else could be done?—there was, there was no—"Simon please, I am so sorry, I'll—I'll clean you right up."

He thrust his paw from beneath the covers until within reach he grabbed hold of the first cloth he could find (a shirt) and with it he wrapped Simon's head, applying pressure here, there, trying to clean the mess he had made. His grip was unsteady, his paws were lined with ants attracted to the scent, and his torso shook with cries and cold. He was safe, safe under their quilt, though he knew the shattered window was permitting no warmness to stay.

As Simon's hair dried, Parks pressed himself against his lover, who took him with no hate for what had happened. Beneath the covers, the two were engulfed by the scents of chemical and mint, and Parks buried his spinning head into the fur of Simon's chin. He wrapped his arms behind the coyote's back, feeling the wetness of the mattress beneath them. His body was a heavy house in which Parks found sanctuary in the knowledge that Simon could not have been angry at him.

"It is alright," Parks heard, he thought; he was sure.

He stiffened, and as he lay in the shell of his body he quietly, slowly murmured, "Simon...I am...please, I messed up."

Minutes passed without answer, and again Parks closed his eyes. *I'd be mad at me, too,* he thought. His nostrils burned as he inhaled the invasive, acidic air. His ears lightly rang in reminder of his exhaustion, yet as the room spun in slow circles he was almost certain he heard the ever-so-quiet whisper of his partner's voice reaffirm to him that "Everything is fine, sweetheart. I still love you, no matter what."

Parks moved faster than he had in days, situating himself on the coyote's belly, his hindpaws framing either hip. Tears trickled from his eyes onto the darkened shape of his partner, and though the room spun and his head pounded and his eyes burned, he felt the anchor of his lover keeping him grounded in the soaked bedding shallow around his shins. The German Shepherd—whose throat was dry and whose limbs convulsed—felt the intimacy of Simon's touch caress his fur as he guided his lover's paw gently to the space between his waistband and his hip. In the other, Parks wrapped Simon's paw and placed it lightly against the pillow, upon which Simon's head rested, which was met by Parks's mouth in a prolonged kiss.

Parks's tongue danced with Simon's in a torrid waltz, and his paw cupped the back of Simon's accommodating neck. The springs of the mattress were a choir of indecipherable pleasure as Parks felt the stiffness of Simon beneath him, and moved his own erect cock up, down, up, down, falling steady into motion against the base of his ribcage. Parks heaved and stifled the pain in his lungs as the heat continued to build between the two of them; the scent of Simon's maw was an aphrodisiac, the moaning a psalm, and the rapturous feeling of warmth throbbing within him a salvation as the world fell to spinning nothingness around him.

His head pulsed, and his chest pounded both internally and against Simon's ribs, a violent friction of fur and fury as Parks pulled his mouth loose of Simon's and instead enclosed it around his throat. His teeth pushed deeper, deeper; deeper as an insatiable despondence burned inside him, which ached for a means of—"Tomorrow, Simon"—he could taste iron—his legs itched—his tail quivered—a spasm of ecstasy sent shivers coursing through his body, which seized his ability to think. He shifted his hips and pressed his shaft harder against Simon's torso, and as the supple light of dawn began to saunter over the horizon, so too did the air echo Parks's elated moans into the dying night.

Fragments of glass embedded in the mattress dug into the flesh of Parks's knees—he winced in pain—a groan of euphoria followed—though the wounds were fresh and burned in wet fire, the—oh, *God*—the surging exhilaration that writhed from his ankles, through his hips, sent shuddering wordlessness up his spine. The bliss manifested in the form of erratic exclamations—"Fuck!"—"I—!"—"Simon!"—"I'm going to—" until with one final, aching convulsion, each cry and contraction coalesced in an ivory climax, which collected in the fur of his lover's collarbone. The German Shepherd panted, his breath struggled, and his lover lay peacefully still following the climax.

Parks slowly, with weak arms, lowered himself to lay flat atop his partner's figure, and buried his nose in the drenched fur. He absorbed the air, the salt, the chlorine, the rust, the sex—he ran his paws through the clay that was Simon's headfur. Parks raised the quilt and a gust of frigid morning crept across his shaking fur. His headache had been dispelled with his orgasm, and through sharp, pained breaths he continued to pant in contrite satisfaction.

Between their chests traveled the deep carmine scavengers, and glass rested in the joint of Parks's leg. His body felt dull, and all sunlight seemed even more so—his vision spun still—in ecstasy, surely—surely—and in the first moment of happiness he had felt since he had laid down with Simon those...those however-many days ago, he looked at him through a lens other than darkness.

Parks was lost. Lost in the blur and panic and—I can't move—and—"Simon, Simon help"—all Parks could see, through the dust and the ants and the fading hope, were the two gray epitaphs in Simon's bloodless eyes that screamed, "I should have gone."

No, no, no; I can't move, baby, please, everything hurts, I—
Tap, tap, tap, tap.

As the sun rose, the raven clambered from the windowsill to the hardwood, her talons sounding soft *ding, dings* as she shifted glass and enamel on her amble toward the mattress. The ants sought sanctuary in Simon's matted fur, and Parks could watch only in horror as the bird reached not for the insects, but for the weak flesh of Simon's cheek. Higher still, the indifferent sun rose. The subtle incandescence blanketed Parks—and as the light grew more vibrant in the morning sky, so too did fade the desperate glow in his once-vibrant eyes.

The Bear Necessities
Bill Kieffer

The afterglow was finally loosening its grip on him. Sladek rolled over into the sunbeam. The last, torn bedsheet fell off his chest. If he hadn't been starving, the skinny tiger might have slept longer. He deserved it. They both deserved it after the weekend's sexcapades.

His huge orange-and-white hand moved across the bed, searching for Prince. With the right amount of subtle whining, he knew he could get breakfast in bed from his master. That side of the bed was cold: the muscular raccoon wasn't there. Sladek's ears slid toward the kitchen, but he only heard the soft sounds of an infomercial coming from the living room.

It wasn't too often that Sladek got to have Prince to himself. Mostly, he had to share him with Prince's husband, a large black bear named Ferdinand. Ferdy was a switch and a powerful Tantric wizard, so there were plenty of benefits to being under the both of them. Still, outside of a scene or a ritual, Ferdy was an incredibly selfish lover...and from Sladek, that was saying something.

Sladek smiled and stopped thinking about his masters and his role as a sexual familiar for the bear. He luxuriated in his own slow awakening, stealing himself for the effort to climb out of bed. Images from the last few days played randomly in his mind. His loins stirred, but he was tapped out.

And hungry. He was so hungry, his soul ached. He barely made it out of bed.

Sladek felt a curious, nagging sensation. It was as if he might have left the stove on or had forgotten a shopping list. He checked the time; but his watch was dead, run down. Well, it was always time for more coffee. There was plenty of time for Sladek to recall whatever it was he had overlooked.

The cat wondered where the bear was and when he might be coming home as he got the coffee going.

The old coffee grounds missed the garbage can as the naked tiger suddenly recalled that Ferdinand had never left the apartment. He cursed and ran the ten steps into the living room, not at all sure what he'd find.

Ferdinand was right where they'd left him, right in front of the fireplace, spread eagle on his stomach. His black fur was mussed and clotted with their fluids. Except for his eyes, the mage was motionless. No, his eyes weren't moving. It was merely the reflection of the television screen on the glass orbs that made them seem to be moving.

Except for his head, the black bear had been crushed flat. Ferdinand was no longer among the living.

Sladek was on his knees before he knew it. It had all started Friday afternoon, after the mage's last appointment. The client had been there to research alternate dimensions; especially this one world that was very Earth-like. The people there were descended from naked monkeys and only came in three or four colors. It seemed very boring to the tiger, but to each his own.

Ferdy had taken care of the customer's inquiries, but he hadn't closed the link when the client left. It was a bust for the client, but for the wizard, there was great promise. This other world was saturated with untapped sexual energy. The Tantric field over there was, no pun intended, virgin territory. The bears of this world were unevolved, Ferdy explained, so he could not harvest any of it, directly. The same could be said for tigers, so the mage could not use Sladek as a tap.

The raccoons of that world were almost evolved enough, they seemed to have something like thumbs, but it made Prince sick when he allowed his husband to try to use him as a bridge.

Still, Ferdinand couldn't allow all this free energy to just sit there, wasted. He discovered that he could reach the hairless monkeys if they used a bear icon of some sort. There was one male in a bear costume on the other side and that provided a trickle of power; barely enough to keep the portal open.

He was ready to give up. Then suddenly, Ferdy discovered that the feral bears where sometimes killed and made into rugs in this odd world. These rugs were apparently used by some monkeys during sex or for nude photography. It was something somehow iconic over there.

It was rare for Ferdinand to use magic on himself. To transform into something else was even rarer. Changing species required more years of study than the mage had been willing to give. Still, he and Prince had been able to transform each other into inanimate objects before Sladek had come along. Objectification was a kink many mages of their caliber enjoyed.

The very thought of Inanimation was such a buzzkill to Sladek that they'd never tried it once he moved in and they became a triad.

Until Friday.

"Ferdinand?" Sladek inched forward. "Ferdy?"

The monkeys were civilized enough to have brothels. More than one of these had bear skin rugs in them. Because the portal had been open for so long, it was easy for Prince to get a fix on a suitable item to copy. The two magic users made a rotisserie out of the tiger, creating a conduit that allowed them to copy and connect with the dead thing on the other-side. Even as the bear came into his mouth and triggered the spell, Sladek could feel the bear flattening.

It had worked well.

Perhaps, too well.

Before Prince had even finished on his end, the magical energies had come roaring through the connection to the bear in an overpowering onslaught. They'd not only tapped into any sex on a bear skin rug on the other side; but they'd connected with a tidal wave of power. It was all Prince could do to set up a barrier to keep the energy inside the apartment. Ferdinand's soul nearly shattered right there, but he instinctively created barriers within his chakra to shunt the energies in without fear of burning himself out.

The bear was a switch and his years of opening himself up and just taking whatever Prince had given to him while in this role was paying off. As flat as he'd become in the real world, Ferdinand was ballooning on the astral plane. He stretched painfully and rather than allowing himself to pop and letting the energy go, he began releasing energy into Prince and Sladek.

They had quite a bit of sex on top of their new rug. Fluids splashed everywhere. Claws raked everything. Cuts healed instantly. Broken fingers repaired themselves in minutes. A thousand fantasies from alien bodies forced themselves down the men's throats. So much energy bled from them, changed by passing through them, sucked back into the bear, they'd felt like unlubricated cogs in a perpetual motion machine.

Sladek was incoherent when Prince was finally able to close the flow of the bridge between dimensions. Something that either the ursine mage had been unable or unwilling to do. It wasn't over, though: there was a bunch of energies and reactions that needed to be resolved.

Sladek remembered Prince trying to get them out of the apartment. Had he been dragged by his tail? The tiger wasn't sure. Either way, they'd instead ended up in the bedroom. Still, even that small distance from Ferdinand was enough to let them fall asleep. They violated each other in their sleep; he'd woken up for some of it. He didn't mind. The racoon's musk had been stronger than his own for a change. He treasured that.

He reached out to the inert form of the rug. Sladek's abused penis became engorged at the silky feel of the bear's hide.

Hello, lazybones.

The cat's fur stood on end. He tripped over his own tail trying to get up. He called out to the thing that used to be one of his lovers, but after a few seconds, he regrettably realized that he was going to have to touch the...to touch Ferdinand again in order to speak to him. A claw tip didn't do it. His finger pads had touch the coat of ursine fur and stroke it gently...if reluctantly.

I'm ok. Go make some coffee and come back.

"I can't leave you like this." But there was nothing Sladek could do. Ferdinand told him as much, and the only thing that kept the tiger from calling the raccoon in a panic was that Prince had already seen the bear in this state...and had left him on the floor where he was with only a few wards on the door to keep his husband safe.

Fortified with coffee, Sladek had brought two cups in the living room out of habit. Heavy with cream for his feline tastes and heavy with honey for the bear. He almost burst into tears as he realized that there was no way for Ferdinand to drink it in his current state.

Sit on me, we need to talk.

"This is very distracting," the cat said, meaning his raging hard-on. He trembled as he lowered himself down on to the mage's backside. The lush fur slipped around the brown and pink pads of his feet, almost tickling him. His claws pushed out, eager to sink into the rug, and Sladek gasped, as he leaped halfway back to his feet.

You can't hurt me, little kitty. I am made to be walked on.

"That's my line," Sladek said. A half-purr and a half-sniffle escaped his throat. He felt the bear's amusement radiate from his bottom. Then, to his surprise, he took a big gulp from Ferdinand's mug. The heat and the taste seemed to echo richly within him. He pressed the hot mug against his sheathe and licked his lips. He wanted to ask the wizard if he was controlling him somehow, but he took another sip and savored the awful sweetness before he could vocalize the thought. He hated the taste. He liked the taste.

I can't transform back yet. Not without losing all this power. I need to strengthen my walls and my wards...and I don't know how I can do that yet with my soul stretched so impossibly huge. I've never been so powerful, nor so helpless in my life.

"So, let it go." Sladek almost choked as the he brought the cup back to his lips. "Just let it go. We know how to go back and get more. We can be better prepared."

Although Ferdinand's head did not move, the tiger felt it give a shake of negation. Had it been his own?

I've already had this conversation with Prince. Don't be surprised that I know the two of you are in love. That's what I specialize in, after all. I love him, but I've been awful grateful to have you around to pick up the slack in the sheets. You've made everything easier for me and I'm grateful. And frankly, this will be easier for the three of us...With me like this, I don't have to eat or drink. You can eat for both of us, have sex for both of us...I won't have to do a blessed thing but think about magic.

Maybe I'll get bored in a few weeks, but I am not sure I will.

Sladek was terrified and thrilled at the same time. His fingers stoked at his furry crotch. "Am I to be your puppet?"

The feeling of kind laughter came up through the rug.

Only when you want to be. It'd be too hard to break you or to maintain that link when you aren't touching me...Waste of energy when I can feel that a part of you likes me using you. Still, before you get off me, I need you to promise to do me a favor.

Sladek nodded, feeling the blush of heat in his ears and nose. Ferdy was more attentive with the tiger's hands than the bear had ever been with his own. "What do you need, Master?"

The remote. Can you place it under my right hand? It's been out of reach all this time...and I'd really like to catch up with the news.

Sladek nodded and got the remote. He felt a silent bit of gratitude from the thing, like a satisfied sigh, when he picked up the thing-paw and dropped it on the remote.

He sat, terrified, on the floor a few feet away from it. The channel never changed. The cat sipped at his own coffee, barely registering that the cream had spoiled. Too many things were spoiled now for Sladek to notice.

Yet...yet...he could have Prince more to himself than ever before.

And his love must surely be okay with the new arrangement, for the raccoon to head off to his day job without waking him.

Yet, this whole thing smacked of necromancy. He hated that. He hated being a part of that. The cat had only agreed to help create a bridge because he hadn't believed it would work.

Almost two hours had gone by, when Sladek heard the key in the door. Prince came into the apartment, and the tiger felt his heart stutter as their eyes met. His master's green eyes set in their black mask looked haunted. They widened as the tiger ran to him...and Sladek didn't have time to brake when Prince flinched away from him.

Prince pulled him out of the apartment and the naked tiger didn't even think to resist until he was standing in the hallway. His neighbors had surely seen worse, so he was not overly bothered by the thought of embarrassment. It was the way Prince inspected him that frightened the skinny feline.

"You're okay." The raccoon didn't seem to believe it. He almost didn't seem to want to believe it.

"Yes," Sladek reassured him, feeling nothing like reassured himself. "I'm alive. I'm ok."

"When did you..." Prince's eyes darted and blinked as if he'd just had shock therapy. He gulped and grabbed Sladek by the shoulders. "When did you wake up?"

"Just now," Sladek said. "Maybe two or three hours ago."

The air seemed to leave Prince. He closed his eyes and took a deep breath. He grabbed his once luxurious tail and wrung it, sending a shower of shed hairs to the floor between his legs. Prince was a dom to his core. It hurt the cat to see his man so uncertain. Sladek noticed that his love was looking dirty and ancient. His huge orange and black hand touched the raccoon's gray and black head gently. Clumps of fur fell from Prince's head.

"What's wrong?" he asked, although he knew exactly what was wrong. Or, he believed he did. Prince had tried to pretend that he was alright with Ferdy's decision. Then he had gone to his office as if there was nothing wrong. Yet, obviously, he was not okay with the decision. That he had come home early to set things right and that he had hoped to fix everything before Sladek, their lazybones of a sub had even gotten out of bed.

Part of him might have wanted what Ferdinand had promised, but the dead and the living should not mingle. Ferdy was a bit of each in his current form.

Prince raised his head and slowly opened his eyes. He looked a million years old. The tiger instantly knew that his every assumption was wrong as their eyes shared a long look. There was an abyss in those green eyes that had never been there before.

"Get dressed," the raccoon said after a moment. "Don't touch Ferdinand. Don't talk to him. Just get dressed and come back out here. We'll go eat something."

"There's food inside..." Sladek began, but the raccoon began to sob and cut him off.

"There's nothing good inside," his procyon master said and waved him to get to it.

Frightened all over again, the striped cat quickly did as he was told, without even glancing at the thing that had made him touch himself and enjoy a bad cup of coffee without really trying at all.

At the corner diner, the raccoon and the tiger took their usual seats away from the window. They both recalled times when being with a male lover in public was considered indiscreet. But the truth was, they'd only ever hid from one person. And now, the raccoon's husband knew.

"That's not the important thing," Prince said, his eyes wide and wet. "Order something," he said when the waitress came to them.

Sladek blinked. His dom always ordered for him. It was just what he did. The skinny tiger hated decisions. The raccoon refused to meet his eyes, and finally the grumbling tiger stomach stirred Sladek into action. "Bacon cheeseburger, rare." Three forbidden foods on one plate. He stared at Prince as he nodded and pushed the menu at the waitress.

"I'll have that, too." The raccoon sighed. "Can you put salsa and sour cream on that, too?"

The waitress promised that it would be no problem as Sladek attempted to close his mouth. The jaw muscles stayed slack. Five forbidden foods...beef, pork, cheese, salsa, and dairy. Prince was obsessive about maintaining a fit and lean body. Not to mention, keeping the tiger even leaner, if less muscular.

Then the nod when the waitress suggested that they get fries with that.

Prince shrugged his gray and black shoulders. "Sure. Why not?" A puff of gray hairs flew up out of his suit in response.

Sladek stared at his lover, who now seemed as flat and two dimensional as Ferdinand was at the moment. If not his body, then his soul. "Master," he said, although this table had always been the one place he'd never used the title. "Master, what's wrong?"

That sparked something within Prince, but it was only a ghost of the surly look the tiger expected from such a stupid question. It was just that there were so many things wrong with the day Sladek had awoken into. The raccoon seemed about to snap out an answer when the waitress brought their water; a glass for the tiger, a pitcher and a dipping bowl for the mage. The eyes in the black mask closed as he thought over the words he was going to say.

The silence stretched on.

"We built the bridge," Sladek suggested, afraid of what thoughts were going on in that handsome black and gray head. "We can turn it off, burn it down...whatever it is that we are supposed to do to turn it off."

Solemn eyes met his. "You've been such a good sub...such a good familiar, too, but you've never understood what we do. You've never fully understood how our magic works."

That stung, but it was true. "A certain amount of ignorance is part of the job description for familiar."

"I've always been happy to do all the heavy lifting in our relationship," Prince said softly. "Balancing the needs of two men is hard."

Sladek wanted to protest, but he knew better. "I never had to worry about balancing the two of you. But neither did Ferdy."

Prince shook his head, but kept quiet as the waitress brought their burgers and fries. The smell caused the skinny tiger's stomach to rumble aloud. Sladek asked for a refill of their water and, with a half-hidden frown, she took the glass and pitcher.

When they had relative privacy again, Prince said, "I am a generalist mage, but Ferdinand was always specifically Tantric magic." Sladek nodded, waiting for the raccoon to take the first bite like a good sub. "What do you know about Tantric magic?"

"Sex," the tiger answered readily.

A short grin appeared briefly on his master's muzzle, only to vanish as if it had never existed. "We use it for sex, yes, but it's not about sex. That's only part of it. Tantric is...a system of...icons and how they relate. The sex part is terrific because...well, it's roleplay in part. Tantric sex treats partners like various gods...the sex acts become epic shadow dances of cosmic ideals. With Tantric magic, the partners touch the godhead...the spells take power from the gestalt by merging the microcosms with the macrocosm."

Sladek nodded as the trickle of fear and hope replaced the feeling of hunger. He'd heard Ferdinand discuss aspects of this before, but he never paid much attention. Mantra. Icons. Correspondences. He was at the wonderful mercy of his masters when it came to magic. Until today, he'd been content with his ignorance. "Tropes," he said, "His spells are cosmic tropes. Right?"

Prince gave him a pitying look.

Sladek started when the waitress suddenly appeared at their table. "Wow, I guess you liked your burgers, huh?" The tiger looked down at his clean, white plate. Prince's plate was also empty, devoid of even a single crumb.

"They were good," the raccoon agreed with a heavy, sad voice. Sladek wondered when exactly either of them had taken so much of a bite. Only a look from the black mask of his master stopped him from saying anything. The waitress grabbed their empty glassware and promised to return with more water and a dessert menu.

"I don't even remember eating..."

Prince sighed. Sladek stopped himself from talking over his master.

"I made it all the way to Georgia, Kitty. Georgia." Black hands rubbed at the black mask and gray cheek bones. Clumps of fur fell out and landed on his shirt.

Sladek waited for him to say more, but he did not. His master merely stared at his unused silverware. Eventually, he had to say something. "What did you do? Fly?"

The raccoon's eyes now bored into his. "I ran. Slay, I ran. I hitchhiked. I stole cars."

Sladek's stomach rumbled into the resulting silence as the room seemed to drop. "You took a day trip with your husband...dead? Or as good as dead?"

The waitress brought the water and two servings of pie ala mode without waiting for them to order it.

Prince barely waited for her get out of hearing range before he snarled, "I was gone three weeks, Sladek. Three weeks!"

The tiger shuddered and looked away. His mind whirled horribly, incapable of understanding what his master had just said or what it meant. His stomach growled again, and Sladek grasped at that desperately. Hunger was something he could understand. With a shaking hand, he picked up his fork. He had to concentrate on his grip to keep from dropping it as he moved it the few inches to his plate.

His small, empty dessert plate was so clean and shiny that he could see the fork reflected in it.

The fork clattered to the table from numb fingers. It was surprisingly loud in the near empty deli.

The bad taste in his coffee this morning came back to him.

The cream had spoiled.

"Three weeks," Sladek whispered. His ears began to ring. The table...the aisle...and then the cafe itself seemed to suddenly speed off with him trapped inside. He grabbed the edge of the table to hold himself upright.

"You were dead," Prince mentioned by way of apology. "I'd...I had...well, I had fucked you to death, Kitty. I'm sorry. I didn't mean to...but I did."

Sladek barely understood the words...he was concentrating on not becoming car sick. Only the ingrained, tight control of his gag reflex stopped him from vomiting onto the table. "Three weeks...you said there was nothing good inside the apartment..."

Prince nodded, unconcerned with the runaway building. "It was all spoiled by the time I woke up...I might have been dead, too."

Any second now, they'd be crashing into the East River. "How long...?"

The raccoon shrugged. His green eyes were dull and tired. "I think we were out...I was out a week. Like I said, you were dead by then." Prince blew his nose and dropped the wad to the table where it unfolded dryly, as if never used. "I begged him to save you, to bring you back...he had all this power at his command now, the power of a world with no wizards or mages to fight him for the right to it. And he said he would...he promised...but he never did."

"Not until I killed myself. Then he had to."

"I'm going to be sick," Sladek announced. He made retching noises until he was certain that he was going to turn himself inside out. But nothing came up.

Not even a hairball. His face and fingers tingled until he got himself under control. He reached for his glass...but it was empty again.

"There's nothing inside of you anymore but his power." Prince said softly. "We're connected to him...we joined in aligning his microcosm, and we touched the macrocosm of another world. Ferdinand doesn't just have the power of a god, he's become their god...the god they need. The god their world is prepared for."

Sladek staggered away from the table until he could see the street. The street that wasn't moving. The building was not moving. They were going nowhere.

"I don't understand," the tiger whined.

"I know," the raccoon said softly. "Neither does Ferdinand. Not really." Prince scratched his muzzle, releasing a little bit of fur into the air. "But that world evolved with no gods...none at all...that's why only one race evolved there. They never got past the spell of fire, they never learned to catch the spark of magic. They skipped right to electricity and medicine, to geometry and chemistry."

Sladek just sat on the floor, a hungry tiger lost in his own city. "I have to eat something."

"You don't have to eat." Prince said clearly now, with almost an apology in his tone. "You don't even have to shit. 'It's easier that way,' he told me."

"He told me that, too," Sladek said in a hollow tone. "But I have to eat. I have to."

"No," Prince said, "You don't have to...you, literally, can't be bothered to." The raccoon got up and then sat on the floor, next to the skinny feline with the big hands. "The lightest connection to his power now keeps us alive."

"I was able to drink coffee in our apartment... in our home."

"You were drinking for him." The raccoon shrugged. "I set up wards...The apartment's our Olympus. Outside of it...we barely exist except in certain contexts...people can leave us offerings and that's about it... get used to being hungry."

Sladek looked sharply at his master. "I don't understand."

Prince took his hand as the waitress walked over them like they weren't there. Like she couldn't be bothered to notice. "The world he tapped into never had gods. They have no need for them. No need for a god to do anything. Yet, there was a vacuum that sucked in our bear, and now he's the god of do-nothing. We're practically Angels of Sloth."

Sladek had thought his fur was already standing on end, but now it was as if a cold arctic wind had blown up his fur the wrong way. His bladder stirred for a brief instant, but then it realized that it was empty, too. "What are we going to do?"

"We have to kill him," Prince suggested. His voice was tired and a thousand years old. "Destroy the anchor holding our souls together. Cut him up, crush his skull, and burn the remains. That should do it."

Sladek closed his eyes and took a deep breath. If he got thick enough gloves so as not to hear Ferdinand's thoughts on contact, it might work. They were some vicious iron tools by the fireplace. He could dig out one of those huge vacuum pack cubes they used for the comforters. Maybe they could build a fire on the roof.

Maybe it might free them.

Maybe.

The skinny tiger opened his dull golden eyes and met the somber green eyes in the black mask. "I don't know, Prince...that seems like an awful lot of work."

RELATIONS
TJ MINDE

The mongoose took a deep breath before slamming his hips forward.

"Fuck!" the gray rabbit cried out in pleasure. His face pressed against the pillow, ears back and ass up against the mongoose's hips. "Again," he panted, lifting his head. He peeked over his shoulder. "Please, Aaron?"

The mongoose slid his hard shaft out of the rabbit, taking his time, squeezing his chestnut paws on his partner's hips.

"Please?" the rabbit begged again. "I need it."

"You *need* my cock, Justin?" The mongoose's voice dripped with sarcasm

"Yes. Please." Justin tried to push back on Aaron's shaft, but the mongoose pulled away, slipping out. "Oh don't tease me."

"Then don't over-exaggerate," Aaron said in a matter-of-fact tone.

"Oh, come on," Justin started, raising himself on his hands. "I'm just really horny." Justin shook his rump from side to side. "Come on," he whispered.

Aaron sighed. *So. Fucking. Demanding,* he thought as he lined his dick up with the rabbit's rear. Without a word, he pressed back in, trying not to think about his sister's comments.

The mongoose sighed and shut his eyes, pressing his paw to the bridge of his muzzle. "What do you mean 'you don't like him,' Shelly?"

"I mean there's someone better for you out there." The female mongoose put a paw on Aaron's shoulder.

"Is this why you invited me over for coffee?" he said, pointing to the cup and saucer in front of him. "To tell me you don't like my boyfriend?"

"Come on. I think you're just with him for sex, Aaron."

"You remember he's a rabbit, right? Lots of sex isn't a problem for him." Aaron wiggled his eyebrow.

The other mongoose sighed. "Don't be a smartass. Really, tell me one thing you and Justin have in common?" Shelly held her paw pad up expectant.

"We share a similar taste in movies." Aaron stared at his sister and crossed his arms.

"What was the last foreign film he watched?"

Aaron looked away. "He doesn't get them, so I don't ask him to watch them."

"Can you tell me the last book he read?" Shelly pressed.

"So what if he isn't a reader? I can talk to *you* about that, sis." Aaron paused. "I might complain about a lot of things. But all couples fight here and there. We have good times, too. Take Friday for example—we cooked a meal together. We made an elaborate salad, and I added some crab for myself."

Shelly huffed. "And this is the first meal in how many of the last five years?"

"He doesn't like to cook. And he is super selective about what he eats. Trying to watch his figure."

"He's a rabbit!" She slammed her paw on the table. "They're *bloody* herbivores! How does he need to watch his figure with nothing but vegetables?"

Aaron looked away. "Intake versus output," he mumbled.

"And didn't you two fight about him being overdramatic?"

"We weren't fighting, I told you." Aaron's paw returned to the bridge of his muzzle. "I was just telling him how I wish he wouldn't be so over the top." He dropped his arm back into his lap. "Besides, I had a bad day and was in a pissy mood. I made a bigger deal out of it than I should have."

"Sounds like you have an excuse for everything," Shelly said, looking away from her brother.

Aaron stood. "If all you're going to do this morning is berate me for my boyfriend, then I'll go." The mongoose stood and took a step toward the door.

"Aaron, wait." Shelly grabbed his shirt. "I didn't mean it like that." She stood to meet him eye to eye.

"Then what *did* you mean?"

She held his gaze for a moment before looking to the floor. "I don't think you're happy with him," she whispered.

Aaron scoffed. "I'm *more* than happy, Shell. I love him." He grabbed his jacket. "I'll see you next weekend," the mongoose said as he walked out the door.

Aaron squeezed Justin's leg as it rested over his shoulder. The rabbit's other leg wrapped around Aaron's hip as the mongoose thrust into the rabbit.

"Oh baby, yes. *Just* like that," Justin panted. The rabbit lay on his back, chin up and eyes closed as he squeaked out to the ceiling.

Aaron wrenched his eyes shut. *Could you cut the dramatics?* He let out a sigh as he continued the thrust into the rabbit. The mongoose opened his eyes, and Justin's met his. The rabbit started stroking his shaft. With each thrust of his hips, the rabbit moaned again.

"Oh, Aaron, you drive me *wild!*" Justin tightened his leg around Aaron's hip, pulling the mongoose deeper still and throwing him off balance.

"Woah!" Aaron cried out as he fell forward. His paw shot out and braced on the bed, stopping him from colliding with the rabbit. "Will you stop that? One of us is going to get hurt!"

"Sorry," Justin panted out. "You just," the rabbit closed his eyes and smiled. "You make me feel so good." The rabbit bit his lip again as he slid his paw up and down his cock. While Justin stroked himself, his gaze met Aaron's. "You like watching me?"

Aaron looked down where their bodies met. "I guess."

Justin stopped biting his lip and looked at the mongoose. "You guess?" He braced himself on his elbow. "What do you mean by that?"

The mongoose sighed. "I mean I'm trying to just focus on *my cock* in *your ass* right now, not your body or your words."

"Really?" The rabbit's long ears drooped.

Aaron pulled out. "I'm sorry." He closed his eyes and put a paw to the bridge of his muzzle. "Work has been distracting." The mongoose sighed. "And I'm being an ass." He tossed his legs over the bed and rested his elbows on his knees.

Justin crawled over and wrapped his arms around the mongoose, nestling his gray chin on Aaron's shoulder. "You want to talk about it, baby?"

"Not really," the mongoose said. He shrugged the rabbit off and stood. After putting on a pair of sweatpants, he walked out of the bedroom.

"So what did you two fight about last night?" the fox asked, looking over the cubicle wall.

Aaron glared at him before returning to his computer screen. "Is that how you ask everyone how their weekend was, Darren?"

The fox shook his head with a grin. "Nope. Just you." He crossed his arms on top of the short wall, and looked down at Aaron.

The mongoose continued to type away at his computer. He stole glances at Darren, feeling the fox's golden eyes waiting for an answer from him. "We didn't fight last night."

Darren chuckled. "Like I really believe that. I can see the tension behind your eyes. Let it out; you'll feel better."

"Really, dude?" Aaron balled a paw into a fist. "Does everyone think me and Justin *just* argue?" He slammed his fist on the desk.

Darren raised his paws, pads forward. "Woah, woah! Chill, man. I don't think it's just arguing. But that's usually the first thing you mention."

The mongoose closed his eyes and took a deep breath. "Fuck," he said under his breath.

"What's wrong?" Darren asked. "*Is* it Justin?"

"No," Aaron said. "My sister said some shitty stuff. How I'm not happy with Justin and shit like that."

"Are you?"

Aaron glared at the fox again, but Darren's features held no sign or mirth or judgement. The mongoose sighed and closed his eyes and put a paw to his temple. "I don't know."

"Well, you may want to think on that, then," the fox said as he put his headset on and sat down.

"When did you and Jessica know?" Aaron asked. "Know that you were in love?"

"I think we just knew." His voice traveled over the short wall. "Maybe you two need to work on your relationship more, like in other ways. See a counselor, or something. Or maybe you two aren't meant to be and should date other people. I mean, there are other guys out there."

Aaron stared at his computer screen for a moment. *Work on our relationship? Date other guys?* The mongoose sighed and put on his headset, pushing the thoughts away, as he readied himself for his first call.

The mongoose grabbed a book off the bookshelf at random, before plopping himself on the corner of the couch and opening it. After he curled up into the corner, Aaron turned to the first page, and his eyes danced across it, trying to lose himself in another world. Gray and pink caught his eye, pulling at his attention. He looked up as Justin sat in the opposite corner of the couch with his phone in paw. The rabbit wore a pair of tight pink briefs. The scent of sex was still on the rabbit; Justin had yet to clean himself up.

How do I actually feel about him? the mongoose thought. *Yeah, I told Shelly that I love him, but do I? And, if we do break up, how the hell does a guy my age meet someone new?* Aaron let out an audible breath as he tried to read on.

"What?" Justin asked.

Aaron looked up. "Huh?"

"You just sighed."

"I was just breathing, dear." The mongoose returned to his book. The couch creaked as the rabbit moved around beside him. *Let him be,* the mongoose thought.

"Okay," Justin said, typing away on his phone. "So, what happened at work?"

"Nothing," Aaron said, turning a page.

"But you said work has been distracting. Have you had rough calls?"

"No more than usual," Aaron said. *Must we talk now?*

Justin's phone clicked as it locked, and he dropped it on his chest. "So then were your coworkers being mean?"

Aaron slammed the book shut. "No, they weren't. And it wasn't metrics either. Long days have been making work more exhausting than usual. Don't worry about it."

"Oh, come on, Aaron. Why aren't you talking to me?"

The mongoose sat up and crossed his arms. "Okay, fine. Other than work, what do you want to talk about?"

"Well..." Justin put a finger to his chin. "What do you want to talk about?"

Aaron scoffed and rolled his eyes. "Any movies coming out you want to see?"

Justin thought. "Possibly. You?"

"Not right now," the mongoose answered.

Aaron crossed his arms as he kept his eyes on the rabbit, waiting for him to say something else.

Justin's eyes started to wander around the room. His expression drooped, and a pregnant silence filled the air.

"What else do you want to talk about?" Aaron asked.

The rabbit picked up his phone. "Nothing, I guess."

"Great talk," the mongoose said. He opened his book and returned to ignoring Justin.

Pages flew by, and Aaron became lost in the story, making everything else around him disappear.

Until three sharp notes broke the silence.

Aaron put his book down and looked at the rabbit. Justin rested his head against the arm of the couch with a paw behind his head and his eyes on his phone. His long, strong legs crossed under him, showing off the bulge in his briefs.

The mongoose brought his eyes back up to the rabbit's phone, cutting in though the silence. "Really, Justin?" Aaron asked.

"What did I do this time?" the rabbit responded, looking over his phone.

The mongoose held up his book. "Can't you see I'm trying to read?"

"I can."

"And you start watching a video?"

"Aren't you curious who Chelsea's dating right now?" Justin joked.

"No, I'm not." Aaron glared. "Could you at least use some earbuds?"

"Fine," Justin said as his shoulders slumped, and he walked back to the bedroom.

The mongoose returned to his book. He started to lose himself again when he felt the couch move. Aaron looked over and trailed his eyes from the rabbit's phone to his long ears. *At least he's quiet now.*

Justin snickered.

The mongoose looked to the rabbit again. Justin's eyes were still on his phone, and he chuckled a second time, a little louder.

He still has a cute laugh. And I've been with him for so long. I really don't miss dating, and the effort that goes into it…

Aaron let his eyes wander down the rabbit's lithe form.

Justin kept his fur trimmed short, letting him show off his abs. Swimmer's lines led right between the rabbit's strong thighs.

The mongoose sat up, holding his book in one paw and set the other on the rabbit's leg, causing Justin to let out a questioning tone. Aaron's eyes moved across the page again, and he started to pet the rabbit's leg, pressing down to feel the strong muscle there.

Justin squirmed under Aaron's paw but remained silent, otherwise.

As Aaron's stared at the open book, his paw would travel higher and higher, until his claws reached the hem of the spandex-based briefs. They stayed there, teasing the elastic and making them snap. *And he really is attractive. And the sex is good.*

"You know you can touch me, right?" Justin said.

"Huh?" Aaron looked to the rabbit. His red-brown paw teased under the hem of the pink fabric, and he ran his claws though the fur there.

"I didn't finish, and neither did you." Justin smiled at the mongoose as he raised his knee against the back of the couch, sliding Aaron's paw closer between his legs.

Aaron continued to stare. Justin's growing bulge stretched against the material. He set his paw at its peak, feeling the warmth there.

"And you already had me going, so I don't think I'll take long," Justin continued, pressing his hips against the pads between his legs.

Fuck if he doesn't know how to get my attention. Aaron leaned over and, using both paws, pulled the rabbit's briefs down from his hips without ceremony and slid them off, throwing them behind the couch. As one paw went to either hip, the mongoose ran his tongue across Justin's shaft. The taste of salty pre was still there.

"Hold on, baby," Justin said, pushing the mongoose back. "I don't want to cum in your muzzle. I want you to finish what you started."

"Do you need more lube?" Aaron said as he took off his sweats.

Justin shook his head. "Didn't clean up yet, hoping we'd finish."

Aaron crawled on his knees closer to the rabbit. "I thought so." His nose twitched as the scent of need and arousal filled the air. The mongoose ran his fingers along Justin's thigh and down under his sack. Leading with his short claws, he pressed into him. As Justin let out a moan, Aaron slid inside to his first knuckles, silicone lube easing the friction. He watched as Justin's cock became more firm, like his own.

"Oh, just take me," Justin cried out.

Aaron smiled. "You got it." He lifted the rabbit's leg over his shoulder as he lined his hard shaft up to his partner's entrance. With a push of his hips, he slid in.

"Ah!" Justin cried in surprise.

"You told me to," Aaron said. He moved his paw to the rabbit's hip while his arm wrapped around Justin's thigh, and he pressed in.

Justin let out a breathy pant. "No," he said, shaking his head. "I like the feeling."

The mongoose pulled his hips back, sliding out of the rabbit. One foot touched the floor, and his claws dug into the carpet as he slammed back in.

Hips met, and both men huffed in pleasure. As their eyes met, Justin nodded.

Aaron pulled back and shoved in again with more force, using his hips to thrust and pulling the rabbit's leg and hip down at the same time.

Justin reached down to his shaft and ran his paw up and down. "Oh Aaron," he said and bit his lip.

The mongoose only just heard his name as he pressed his hips against the rabbit, trying to get as deep as he could. "You like that?" he asked.

"Yeah." The rabbit nodded, eyes closed. "More," Justin moaned out.

With that, Aaron made shorter thrusts, sliding half of his cock out and pounding back in. Each time, the mongoose would try to press deeper, feeling resistance.

"Ahh, Aaron!" Justin called. His paw worked at a rapid pace on his shaft. "I'm getting close," he said. "Do you want me to wait?"

"No, I'm close too."

The rabbit reached up and pulled the mongoose into a kiss.

Aaron leaned forward with the rabbit's leg still on his shoulder. Hips continued to meet hips as their muzzles did the same.

Justin started moaning out in pleasure, in time with each of Aaron's thrusts, pitch rising squeak by squeak.

Hearing Justin, the mongoose started moaning as well. Each of the rabbit's tones pushed him closer to the edge. His pace became frantic, so close to the finish.

He broke the kiss. "Here it comes!" Aaron pulled himself as deep as he could get into the squirming rabbit below him. The first wave of the climax crashed over him as he peaked. Then with another thrust, the first rope of seed filled Justin. Then the second, then third. With each slam of his hips, his cock swelled, widening the rabbit's rear.

As Aaron continued to ride out his peak, Justin shouted, and his entrance tightened around Aaron's shaft as the rabbit's own climax hit. He stroked himself as the first rope of seed hit his chest, and subsequent shots of thick cum covered himself.

Aaron's entire body warmed, as he came down from his climax with a relaxed exhale.

"I love you, Aaron," the rabbit said.

The mongoose heard the earnest tone and deep truth in Justin's voice.

Do I want to rebuild that connection? Aaron lay there, resting against the rabbit in thought. He panted and lifted himself up to look Justin in the eyes. Such warmth and devotion in Justin's eyes laid there.

This is just easier. "Me too," Aaron said. And he slid out of the rabbit to go clean up.

A VOICE NOT SPOKEN
STEPHEN COGHLAN

NOVEMBER 9TH

The newspaper slapped loudly against the table. Across the top, in big bold letters, were the words "RATS WIN!"

If Chester had been expecting a reaction, he was sorrowfully disappointed as Smokey read the print, barely paused to wipe his eyes and tickle his whiskers, and continued to eat his morning kibble.

"Aren't you the least bit upset?" Chester asked his roommate.

"I didn't vote." Smokey murmured into his coffee. "So I can't complain."

"Typical." Chester hissed. The fur on his neck stood on end, and his tail fluffed out in obvious annoyance. "You couldn't get off your lazy ass to save your own life."

Smokey refused to argue so Chester wheeled on his legs and strode for the exit. He slammed the door so hard that plaster cracked and dusted down from the ceiling. Reaching for a napkin, the gray-furred Korat covered his breakfast and waited for the air to settle before he resumed his meal.

As he continued to eat, Smokey opened the paper and scanned the articles. The company that wrote the news was owned by cats, who published stories by cats, for cats. Usually the paper was thin, but today's edition was especially heavy, mostly thanks to the large comment section.

Dear Felines: one of the observations began.

We have allowed a great travesty to occur. For too long we sat, thinking that we, the predators of the past, would always stay on top, whether in the food chain or the great pyramid of politics or in the economic playground.

We deceived ourselves.

Yesterday, we were defeated in a landslide vote, thanks in part, to our belief in superiority. Our former enemies, our former prey, rose up in protest and made themselves heard. Record turnouts were noted all across the country as rodents, reptiles, and birds cast their votes.

As far as us felines, we only accounted for ten percent of the vote. The canines themselves, another fifteen.

We didn't have a chance.

Now that the change has happened, I implore you, take this as an opportunity to wake up and make a difference. Talk to your local member of parliament, make your voice heard, speak out against our indifferences or by Claw, we will suffer.

With a snort, Smokey set the paper back on the table. *So what*, he thought, *if the prey has won. The Supreme Court is mostly made up of old predators anyways. The prey can't touch us.*

Finished with his thoughts, he stood and stretched until his back cracked and all of his fur stood on end.

It was time to go to work.

NOVEMBER 30TH

It could have been the bad catnip he had used last night, or it may have been the fact that he had been fired yesterday, but either way, Smokey noticed that his coffee tasted exceptionally bitter.

He opened the paper that Chester had left on the table that morning.

WANTED
Prey species familiar with administration.
WANTED
Prey Species for management.
WANTED
Hard working, prompt individuals. Omni's and Herbi's only.

Smokey sighed as he finished the ads. There was nothing for him, and nothing that he was qualified for. It wasn't that he lacked skills, but ever since the election he had found the tension at the canning house unbearable.

He was almost grateful that he was fired.

It was amazing how fast things had changed. In less than a month, several of his friends and family had found themselves in similar situations. The Predators were being culled from the workforce.

Although he seemed to have a laissez-faire policy about most things in life, and he considered himself apathetic by nature, the loss of his employment concerned him. How else was he supposed to afford his catnip?

Fortunately, he had a backup plan. Chester had always said that his work needed delivery drivers, couriers and tough types for security. Although Smokey was not the most-fit feline in existence, he had a naturally large chest that made him look muscular and intimidating.

Satisfied, Smokey decided to take a nap.

JANUARY 1ˢᵀ

"Let's hope for a better year." Chester said as he and Smokey toasted the drop of the ball by touching their paper cups together. The two were on the nightshift, where they worked as "observe and report" security guards.

"Amen," Smokey agreed, and the two friends sipped their drinks. The warmth of the warm milk did wonders for their insides, but their extremities still froze.

Fireworks exploded in the distance. The bright colors seemed in contrast to their moods.

Chester changed the subject. "Did you hear what happened to Mr. Slithers?"

Smokey shook his head. Mr. Slithers ran the local convenience store. He was a nice, old, toothless king cobra who was known about town for his donations to charity.

"His store was smashed up really bad," Chester continued. "And someone sprayed everything down with canned musk. All of his merchandise is ruined."

"Poor guy," Smokey said. He actually felt bad for Mr. Slithers. He was nice, and had given Smokey his first job years ago.

"I wonder who did it," Chester thought out loud. "That old snake wouldn't even hurt a fly. Heck, he only eats unfertilized eggs."

"What are the cops saying?"

"Nothing yet." Chester sighed. "I was going to go down to the store first thing in the morning and help him clean up. Do you want to come along?"

Smokey thought about it, but he also thought about his bed, and getting enough sleep before his next shift. He and Chester had drawn the short straws for the holidays, and had both ended up working the night shifts. Twelve hours on, twelve hours off.

"I want to," Smokey lied. "But I want to be ready for tonight. We're on escort duty, and I'll need to be vigilant."

"Suit yourself." Chester shrugged. "Anything you want me to pass on?"

"Yeah." Smokey agreed. "Tell him I'm thinking about him."

Finished with his drink, the Korat handed his companion the empty cup. "It's time for my patrol," he stated, and then left the room.

FEBRUARY 14ᵀᴴ

"Why do I have to work tonight, again?" Chester groaned as he hung up his phone.

"Because we're lucky to have any job," Smokey reminded his friend. "Besides, you don't want to move too fast. Aren't you planning on taking Missy out on the weekend anyways?"

"Yes I am," Chester agreed. "But it is our first Valentines. . ."

"You only met her at Christmas," Smokey argued back. "Today belongs to the restaurants, markets, and consumers. Even if you did have the night off, anywhere you could go would be crowded, anywhere you would be allowed to go, at least."

Two weeks ago, Smokey had been kicked out of a local watering hole. The bartender had denied him a drink, and although Smokey had argued that he was allowed, he had given up trying to argue with the gerbil within minutes.

"I know," Chester lamented. "It was hard enough making reservations for Saturday. I had to fight with the owners, tooth, claw, and fang for permission to go there. Maybe if I had taken something less posh I'd be okay?" He checked the radio's batteries. "Bastards forgot to charge them." Chester hissed.

"Speaking of charged," Smokey said casually. "Any news from Mr. Slithers?"

If looks could kill, Smokey would have dropped dead instantly, but his back was turned so he did not see Chester's fur stand on end as he spoke through his fangs. "Didn't you hear?"

"No," Smokey said hesitantly.

The calico explained, "He went to the police station three days ago, on their request, but no one's seen him since."

"That's strange." Smokey said without thinking. "Something similar happened to Mr. and Mrs. Guana a week ago. They were on their way to argue against Mrs. Guana's speeding charge, when they vanished."

"I don't like it." Chester admitted. "There's been rumors that reptiles are vanishing everywhere. Did you hear about the incident at the mall last week?"

Smokey shook his head.

"The Naga's kid was beaten by a group of rodents, in broad daylight, and no arrests are being made."

"Was it the Rikki-Tikki gang again?"

"No. It wasn't the mongoose; it was a group of field mice." Chester shook his head. "And you know Jr. wouldn't lie about something like *that*. That does it," the calico said angrily. "I'm going to the station first thing in the morning, and I'm going to file a missing serpent report."

APRIL 3ᴿᴰ

"Our top story." The antelope's voice filled the apartment, disturbing Smokey from his nap. He sat up, his head groggy from a combination of sleep and catnip.

"The government has declared the Church of Fang to be dangerous."

Missy, who Smokey wasn't surprised to see in the apartment, as she had been spending quite a few nights with Chester, burst into tears and hid her face into her boyfriend's chest.

The announcer continued.

"Authorities will be visiting all known members of the organization over the next few days. All members are asked to answer questions honestly. Resistance of any sort will raise suspicion and alarm. Please, re—"

Chester hissed, and his hackles rose. The remote he had used to mute the television was flung onto the couch.

Pulling away from her lover, Missy reached for her phone as the Persian tried to smooth her facial hair. Chester guided his girlfriend into his room before he returned to Smokey's side and began to pace.

"What's her issue?" Smokey asked, his mind still fuzzy.

"Her parents belong to the Church of Fang, you idiot!" Chester snarled.

"Ouch." Smokey winced as he tried to straighten his whiskers. "Good thing you and Missy belong to the Church of Claw."

"That's not the point!" Chester barely suppressed a roar. "Don't you understand? This is both illegal and unethical."

"You heard the news!" Smokey shot back. "They're dangerous."

"You believe that everyone who worships Fang is a threat? Missy's mom is suffering from cancer and has lost all her hair. She's embarrassed to even go out to get groceries. Her dad works sixty hours a week to afford her care. They don't have time to be dangerous."

Chester's door opened, and Missy came out looking worse than she had moments ago. She ran to her boyfriend and grabbed his arm.

"C'mon," she mewled breathlessly. "They're already being detained. The police arrived while I was on the phone."

Chester didn't have to be told twice.

As soon as they were gone, Smokey turned up the volume and tried to sleep to the droning of the announcers.

JUNE 3ʳᴰ

Smokey didn't understand why they issued jackets when a simple vest would have done. He also did not understand why he, Chester, Missy and all predators were forced to wear the issued clothes. The material was cheap, the threading shoddy, and the only decorations on his jacket was a yellow-colored, clawed paw-print.

The wolf that handed over the clothing cast his eyes in shame. He was an Omega, and had willingly kowtowed to the cows that watched with their guns pointed in obvious threat.

"It's not that bad." Smokey said to himself. "The jacket's main color matches my fur."

Leaving his new clothing open, Smokey turned away from the line. He felt disgusted with himself for wearing the clothing with little argument.

Deciding on a shortcut, Smokey stepped into an alley.

The sounds of flesh being attacked reached his ears immediately. When his eyes adjusted to the gloom, Smokey saw a group of sheep beating on a weasel.

"That's right, you stupid Fang-loving bastard," one ram snarled as he laid into the mustelid.

"Eat this!" said another, as he brought a pipe down upon the weasel's shoulder.

"Ask Fang for some new ones," said a third as he kicked teeth out of the weasel's mouth.

Smokey felt like being sick. The weasel could not have been an adult yet; he still had some of his kit pelt. The mustelid cried out in pain.

Turning his jacket's collar up, Smokey turned away from the chaos.

"Where do you think you're going, Pred?" one of the sheep bleated.

"Home," Smokey answered more calmly than he felt.

"Tha-a-a-a-t's right." The one who had kicked out the weasel's teeth said. "Keep walking."

So he did.

AUGUST 20TH

"This isn't right!" Chester yelled to the crowd. He was up on the podium. His voice carried for all to hear.

Smokey admired Chester's courage. His roommate had begun speaking out against all the injustices that the predators were facing. Guilt, a powerful motivator, had finally encouraged Smokey to attend one of the rallies. For the longest time, he had hidden himself away in his room, chewing catnip and sleeping on his off hours.

Then, his boss had vanished, and the company had been dissolved.

As Chester's voice rose, Missy clasped paws with Smokey. The two were in the audience, where Chester thought Missy would be safer.

There had already been two attempts on Chester's life, and although he was worried for himself, he was worried for Missy more. She was pregnant with his kittens.

His thoughts soon became valid. As Chester's voice rose, so too did the crowd. Predators of all sorts began to chant and cheer. One by one they began to remove their jackets.

Keeping his grip tight, Smokey began to lead Missy away from the stage. He hadn't failed to notice the group of Cape buffaloes that had surrounded the masses.

All it would take was one act of violence from either side for a riot to ensue.

It happened just as the two made it to the very back of the crowd. A bottle, filled with fluid, stopped with a flaming rag, arched over the bovines, and smashed into the masses. Several raptors cried out in shock and pain as they were enveloped in the flames.

The silence was deafening. Then with a roar, the two sides charged each other, and the battle began.

"C'mon!" Smokey urged, and guided Missy into an alley. Behind them, a pride of lions fought a losing battle against the tough herbivores.

"What about Chester?" Missy asked in tears.

"I'm sure he's fine," Smokey lied. "But you won't be if we become involved."

She didn't make any further protests as they escaped back to the apartment. As they made their way, they were forced to duck into shadows and holes in order to avoid roving bands of police and prey alike.

The sun fell, the shadows lengthened, and it wasn't until darkness had swallowed the city that the two made it home. With shaking hands, Smokey fought to get the key into the lock.

As soon as they were inside, Smokey began barring the door with heavy furniture.

"What about Chester?" Missy asked.

Smokey didn't answer with words. Instead he turned on the television.

"*Our top story.*" A small vole began to squeak. "*Race riots break out downtown. The guilty parties have all been arrested, including well known speaker Cheste—*"

There was a heavy thump on the door, and only the heavy furniture stopped it from opening.

"Who is it?" Smokey snarled.

"Smokey? It's Tugs, open up," said a voice from the other side.

As he began to remove the furniture he had just put in place, Smokey hissed an order to Missy.

"There's a bag in your closet. Grab it and get over here."

"What's going on?" Missy asked, even as she hurried to follow Smokey's orders.

The table was at last moved, and the door was cracked to show a beagle, accompanied by a falcon and a Komodo dragon.

"Are you ready?" asked Tugs the dog, as his nose twitched and his tail swung in anxious circles.

Missy arrived with the bag slung over her shoulder.

"Good. Let's go," Tugs demanded, and the trio began to lead Missy and Smokey to the stairs. As they walked, Smokey explained the current situation to his roomie's mate.

"We're getting out of here. Chester set up an arrangement that if he was captured, you would be smuggled someplace saf—"

A crack interrupted his speech, and the falcon fell to the floor, dead from a bullet.

"Run!" Tugs yelled as he took off at a dead sprint. The Komodo turned to challenge the pursuers.

Out of shape, Smokey was winded when they made it to the parked car. The driver, a young ocelot, waited for the trio. Another crack rang out, and Tugs fell to the ground in pain.

The engine was started.

Smokey put two-and-two together, and, removing his jacket, he used it to conceal Missy as she crawled into the passenger's seat.

His left leg went numb, and Smokey fell to the pavement.

The car's tires squealed, and Missy disappeared from sight.

When the attackers approached Smokey, he put up no resistance.

NOVEMBER 8TH

He knew what the word "shower" meant. No one survived the shower, even though the prey went to great lengths to hide the fact that it was another way of saying execution.

As Smokey stood in line, he heard a familiar voice call his name.

"Chester?" Smokey said incredulously.

The calico stood behind him. His face was cracked and split and bruised. One eye was gone, and the opposing ear was missing.

The two friends embraced as brothers.

"So, here we are." Chester said, with fake levity in his tone.

"Yeah," Smokey agreed.

The line they were in began to move.

"I'll see you on the other side." Chester said grimly. Smokey nodded in reply.

As they approached the doors, the Korat made his final statement, "She and the twins made it."

Chester's smile was bittersweet. Then the door separated them.

Smokey was all alone in the metal room. Sighing, he reached into his pocket and produced the other reason why he had attended the rally turned riot.

It was a letter from Chester. It was a poem made famous decades past.

```
First they came for the birds, and I did not
              speak out—
    Because I was not a bird.
Then they came for the reptiles, and I did not
              speak out—
    Because I was not a reptile.
Then they came for the canines, and I did not
              speak out—
```

> Because I was not a canine.
> Then they came for me—and there was no one
> left to speak for me.

Licking the paper with his rough tongue, Smokey slapped it onto the wall in protest, as gas commenced hissing into the room.

Listmember Lost
Banwynn (Suta) Oakshadow

I was cleaning out my e-mail box today; a tangled mess of 200+ unread, unanswered e-mails I had been too lazy to categorize and archive. I guess that I am on too many lists. At least that is what I keep telling myself when I try to figure out why I missed this one. Would I have been able to do anything helpful? If I had been at my computer when this arrived, I would have ignored it until later if I was writing. That is what writers do. By the time I checked my mail, it was almost certainly too late to do anything about it. At least that is what I keep telling myself.

He and I did not correspond often. Months could go by without hearing from him and then a flurry of e-mails back and forth could take place over a matter of days or weeks. I have some fans like this and cannot be expected to notice when one of them stops writing, can I? He told me why he sent this to me. The fact that he did was important enough to write and send to me in spite of everything he was going through. I should have noticed. That it took this long for me to see how his good-bye shows how much I failed him.

But, my feelings, guilt, and shame aren't why I am sharing this with you now. I just wanted you folks to know that TSA lost a long-time member last January. I doubt that any of you would have recognized his name. He never posted here. I changed his name and address here to protect his family. But, he did read our stories and was a member of our community just the same. I know that there were a couple other writers that he corresponded with besides me. Since all of us know all about January, I'll just shut up now and share his e-mail with you.

Please read the e-mail before reading the attached story so that you will know why I wrote it.

I am sorry. I am so very sorry,
Justin Owleff

> From: Someone <someone@somewhere.net>
> To: <t-owleff@nowhere.com>
> Sent: Saturday, April 27, 2015 11:51 PM
> Subject: Shattered dreams
>
>
> Hi Justin,
>
> It's been a long time since we talked. I saw your posts under the other names you use, and know that you have been busy. (You didn't know that I knew about those did you?) I am really enjoying reading your stuff and watching as you change and grow...and stumble. I read both of your centaur stories. The short sad one made me cry. The big one, I wish that you had put most of the description of their adventures instead of every vein, every second play by play in furotica. I'm happy for you that publishers are paying something for your stuff now that you don't need it. That means you can go outside the genre without any risk other than a bruised ego, doesn't it? That's one of the reasons I'm writing you now. I wanted you to know that your stories have meant a lot to me. Even before I got up the guts to send you that first e-mail. The e-mails that we sent back and forth have meant a lot to me. I wanted you to know why this is the last e-mail you

will get from me so that you didn't think it had anything to do with you or your stories, or make you think that I wasn't your drooling fanboy anymore or anything. ;p~~

Things have been busy here as well. Fuck! You can't imagine what it's been like here the last few days. Or, maybe you can. I hope you can't though.

You have probably seen the news and seen some of the fucked up shit that happened last week. Unless you know one of the poor bastards that got changed you are probably as confused as everyone else. It's pretty doubtful that you know any of them though. Except one.

Don't believe me? That's okay. I don't want to believe it either. God, I wish that there was some way for me not to believe it! For years I have wanted nothing more in the whole world than to become Flare. (btw, you never did write a story about anthro tigers-like race on a planet in an expanding nebula like you said you would.) You know that the only reason I ever wrote to you in the first place is because of the lion stories you posted on the mail lists. I always wished I could write like you guys. But I just read the stories and jacked off a lot and wished that the stories could be real. At least for me. I just looked through all the posts trying to find tiger stories or at least big cat ones. And always, always wished I could be Flare.

Now I am.

Fuck! I hate saying that! I'm not me anymore! I'm not fucking me! I'm a big fucking tiger on two legs and not me anymore! No, that's not it. I am a big fucking tiger on two legs and I'm STILL me! That's even worse.

I always hated me. I never wanted to be me. Now I just want to be just me again. I would pray to God to be me again except that I hate God so fucking much now that I would try to rip his goddamn fucking throat out if I got the chance. You should see my claws. I think I could do it.

It just happened and I don't know why. All those fuckers on TV spout their shit and their expert opinions and they don't know fucking shit. I know more than them because it happened to me and I don't know fucking shit either. One minute I am clicking through a furry art website and the next thing I know is that I am covered in fur and am not me anymore.

I jumped up right away and fell on the floor. I couldn't figure out how to move! Everything worked wrong. It was the wrong shape and too big and when I fell I almost broke my tail. I think that is when it started to hit me. I had a fucking tail!

When I tried to get back up again I could see myself in the mirror on my door. I screamed and crawled between my desk and the bed and just curled up real tight and closed my eyes and tried as hard as I could to make it not be happening.

It's been a couple days now. I can't write this all at once. It is too much too fast. It keeps getting heavier and heavier.

Guess what? Tigers can't cry. I never thought about that when I dreamed of being Flare. I never thought about a lot of things. Now I couldn't even cry fucking tears. All I could do was lay there and shake. I didn't scream anymore because the sound that came out of me when I did scared the piss out of me. I can still smell it. I can smell everything now.

Back from another six hours of sobbing curled up in a ball.

It took me three days, but I finally stood in front of the mirror and looked at myself. I was kind of expecting it a little better when I saw the mirror this time. Btw, I am huge. I am probably almost 7 feet tall now. I got muscles on my muscles and everything. I looked in the mirror and saw Flare. I mean everything was just how I knew Flare looked. Only now he was there in my mirror looking at me and I was him.

Except for his eyes. Even though they had changed too, they were still my eyes looking out of his head! They were blue like I always knew they would be. They had round pupils like a human. But it was still me behind these fucking eyes! I could look and see that it was me trapped in there. I could see ME looking out of those eyes. I looked like Flare. But it was still me inside him!

I smashed the mirror. I am fucking way strong now. I just meant to break the glass but the whole fucking door came off and parts of it went all the way down the hall. I guess I'm still a geek way down inside cause I trashed everything in my room except my computer. I mean it looks like a bomb went off or something. I learned some things then. Claws are good for shredding mattresses. Chairs make a really weird sound when you crunch them in your hands. Bed frames have big flakes of gray paint come off when you bend them and then throw them through the wall. Never bite a clock radio while it is still plugged in...And that it was really happening.

It was kind of easier after that. When I was done trashing everything I could find, I felt kind of calm and numb. For a couple hours I just sat on the floor and touched myself. I had fur and it was just like I always thought it would feel like. It was not just soft to touch but I could feel each little hair when I touched it. I checked out shit like my teeth (huge and sharp), my claws (long and sharp and making them go in and out of my fingers is fucking trippy), and my ears (round and fuzzy and ticklish), my tail and all that stuff. Then I noticed that I could smell everything. I mean everything. I could smell what all the neighbors had cooked for dinner and what house it came from even. I could smell all the fucking animals in the neighborhood and even that there was a dog in heat on the next block.

My eyes are pretty fucked up. Everything looks like it is farther away or closer than it really is and there are almost no colors. I never even thought about that. I just assumed that a tiger's view of the world would be better than mine. I might as well be trapped in a black and white movie especially at night. I don't much think about it much now though.

I was just kind of numb inside and checked all this stuff out and it was like I was checking someone else out and that it was not me at all. That was kind of okay. I even discovered that I was not like a tiger in one way. I am pretty huge down there now. Before this happened to me I had kind of a tiny dick. I hated it.

In school in gym they called me pencil dick and bug fucker and shit. I hate them for that. If I thought I could get out of the house and move around without some feds catching me, and locking me in a cage in some lab somewhere, I would visit some of those mother fuckers and see what their fucking guts taste like.

Now that I don't need to be embarrassed about it anymore, it doesn't matter. I won't have to worry about gym class or school or anything else anymore. What would they do with me? Put me in an aquarium on the window sill next to the hamster and his fucking treadmill?

But I can't. I can't go anywhere. I can't do anything. Feds are just waiting to nab us as we pop up and make us disappear right away.

I'm not bothering with counting days. But it has been over a week now. I keep trying and trying to find something good in the real world about being the new me. So far, I haven't found one.

I kind of rolled back into a ball again after writing that and stayed there until I had to shit and got real hungry.

It was real.

It was me.

"Me" was only a lab animal now.

I can't even shit right! My tail got all wet because I forgot I had it when I sat down. Then when I was done I could not stop wiping. I used the whole roll and felt like I was rubbed raw down there and couldn't stop!

I know it is gross shit to talk about, but it really freaked me. It was like even though it was still kind of me inside here, I couldn't really control myself.

After some more time as a rolled up rug shaking on the floor I went downstairs. I could smell the stuff in the refrigerator and was like starving. There was a big thing of hamburger in there. Mom left it so I could make spaghetti and burgers and shit. I ate it all. Raw.

I probably got worms now or something. What am I supposed to do? Go to a fucking vet and get dewormed? I can't be like this. It was not supposed to be like this. Flare is supposed to be beautiful and strong and graceful and I guess I am now but he is not supposed to be a freak and be so scared that he almost pisses himself when he even thinks about someone finding out about him. I ate all the meat in the fridge too. And everything that I could find that had meat in it. Even canned chili. You haven't lived until you have smelled chili generated tiger farts. One more reason to hate this body. =@.@=

Fuck! No more food.

How long can tigers go without food?

How long until I had to walk out that door?

Doesn't matter.

I'm not going.

Don't care a whole lot like I will be losing all that much.

Justin, I know I am a loser. I know that I always have been. I never fit in anywhere. The only people who ever talked to me like I was even a person have all been online. If they ever got to know me for real they would probably laugh and ignore me too. But I guess that way down deep inside somewhere I knew that there was a chance that I could change and maybe fit in some way. I mean I could have like figured out how to dress better and maybe work out and hang out places and learn the shit they talk about or something. I don't know what. But there was a chance that I could to something to fit in.

Now I am a fucking tiger. I am ***NEVER GONNA FUCKING FIT IN ANYFUCKINGWHERE***. All I am now is a lab experiment or something for the freak show. I can't even go out of the fucking house cause I know that they are gonna take me away somewhere if they find out about me. Like that guy that changed into something on the news, and is in the hospital there and, no one is allowed to see him or talk to him or anything. They say that it is what he asked for but you know that it is just exactly what they would say if they wanted to keep him away so they could study him and shit.

I mean this is X Files for real here!

I'm sorry if I am kind of rambling all over the place. I am really tired now. Yawning my big furry striped fucking head off. But, I need to send this to you before I go to sleep. I won't be able to later. At least I hope not. The bottle was almost full when I took the pills.

Don't freak out. This is what I want to do. You couldn't stop me and I would just hate you for trying.

Anyways I spent the next couple days watching the news and the net for everything I could. I had to take the TV from downstairs cause I had seriously fucked up the one in my room. The one from downstairs was not even heavy to me now. Don't ask me why I didn't just watch it downstairs. I just feel kind of edgy and nervous when I am not in my room now. Btw, big fuzzy fingers make it a bitch to type. I can do it a little better if I keep the claws out but that makes my fingers hurt after just a little bit.

It looks like not many got changed and that they are all over but mostly in America. I watched as the news glommed onto to everyone that they could find and fucked with them and stalked their families and neighbors and everyfuckingone who ever knew them. It is a fucking circus and I don't want to be a circus animal. Look at the Tigerboy! Pet his tail for only one dollar!

Keep paying Old Scratch his dues for making a dream come true, and turn it into a nightmare.

I know that you are wondering about something. Every guy in the world would wonder about it. Yes. I tried it. Honestly, if I thought that I could spend the rest of my life in this house hiding so that no one ever found out about me, those feelings might even be enough to make it worthwhile. :p -:

Fuck. It has been a couple of hours now and I am just kind of tired and yawning a lot. I know that I am bigger now. Lots bigger. But come on! Most of a fucking bottle should still do the trick, shouldn't it?

Don't know how I could have forgotten the freezer. Tons of meat.

Well, a week ago, I saw that they arrested one really odd guy, and that the FBI took him away in under five minutes. That was it for me. I am not going out there. I am not going to be a freak for the world to gawk at. Mom and Dad are sure as fuck not going to let me stay here. They already want me gone so that they can get on with their lives without having to deal with a son that they would rather pretend that they never had. Dad even paid for admission to an out of state college for me even though going to the local one would be tons cheaper. They said it would expand my horizons. Ten minutes later I heard them talking about converting my room into a fucking music room.

Oh, and a third of the meat is gone.

Now I sit on the floor of my room, hidden under blankets and stay there until I need to shit or eat. I have the remote under the blankets so I can watch TV when I think I can handle it...which isn't now.

The parental pods have been at one of Dad's fucking conferences for almost a month. They are due back tomorrow night. Won't they be surprised? They will probably ground me for trashing my room and for having the nerve to change into an embarrassment to them without their permission. I guess maybe not. I have always been an embarrassment to them.

Fuck it. I am not going to face them either. That is why I got the bottle from their bathroom. The pharmacy only lets me get one week's worth of antidepressants at a time. They are careful not to give me enough to "do anything stupid" with. Bless you Mother for being such a bitch. She can't sleep if there is any noise at all in the house. I even had to switch to a membrane keyboard because she complained about the clicking sound my old one made even though their room is downstairs halfway across the house. I found a bottle of the Trazadone that she uses to sleep. It was mostly full. I guess she had more and took it with her or only grabbed some out of the bottle when she left. Dad will probably write a paper about me for those pompous journals. "The effects of spontaneous transformation on dysphoric adolescents" or something. At least then he will have found a use for me. I guess that I was supposed to be some perfect trophy for him to sit on the mantle as proof of his virility. Once he decided that I was not much of a trophy he mostly didn't have any use for me at all.

I hope coming home and finding a dead anthro tiger in the house fucks them up good. If it wasn't for them, I would never have had to dream of being Flare. All it would have taken is for them to love me and this wouldn't have happened. I just decided to trash the rest of the house before I fall asleep.

Over a month now since my "dream" came true. I haven't been outside yet. Whole communities are forming mobs to search each house room by room.

I'm back. The refrigerator went all the way through the wall into the dining room. It wasn't even that hard to pick the fucker up and throw it. I even took a dump in Mom's jewelry box. They never knew that I've known the combination to their safe for years! Merry Christmas Mom! Sorry your present was so late.

Justin, I am sorry that I wrote all that shit. I guess the pills are making me write almost everything that I think. I want you to do something for me. You are a good writer. One of my favorites even though you still have not written that tiger story. Whenever you sent me e-mails you made me feel like a person. Like

I mattered. You argued with some of my suggestions when I had the nerve to send you critiques. I liked that. It made me feel like I mattered or something. Like you respected me enough to disagree with some of the things I said. When I saw some of my suggestions in your rewritten posts I felt a lot of pride like I was partly responsible for the story. A tiny-tiny bit of a co-writer.

But then I would close the e-mail or finish the story and just be me again. I always thought that being Flare instead of me would make everything okay. I thought that I would be able to handle anything in my way if I was big and strong and beautiful. I never fit in anyways and so thought being so totally different would make it not matter.

I was wrong. On the outside I am Flare. Inside I am still me. I am still the freak. I am still the one on the outside looking in. Now that I am Flare, the only thing that has changed is that I can NEVER fit in. My outsideness shows now. It didn't solve anything! It only made more problems! At least before, I could step outside my own door without somebody wanting to lock me in a cage!

The month I spent on the psych ward last year after that bit with the car in the garage felt like a year. I was a prisoner there. Everything I said or did was written down by those fucking smugass nurses with their fake smiles. It was like I was this bug under a magnifying glass. Ban! That is what the rest of my fucking life is going to be like now! The rest of my life spent under a magnifying glass! I can't take that.

I want to thank you for letting me fit in at least in one place in my life. I want you, if you can, to please write a story about me and what happened to me. I don't want to live as a freak but I want people to know that they are making monsters like me every day that they shut people out.

The pills aren't working. I found an exacto knife and am going to go to my bathroom now. I remember one of the girls on the ward said that warm running water makes it not hurt as much. I am glad that I got the chance to know you. Now there will always be a tiger out there somewhere watching you, and hoping to inspire you when you write.

Thank you and goodbye,

<name removed>

Furry Confessions

Interlude

Zinc beamed as the other two lowered their hands, recognizing their own defeat. Standing with chest puffed out, Zinc started, "Alright, I'm going to ask Barba two truths, and Derek one."

"Fine," the two grumbled.

Zinc noticed Derek still grabbing his ass every few minutes, and he kept seeing Barba staring at Derek, too. Zinc, too, believed that whatever spirits were in this church were clearly communicating that one of them was a demon. He observed the hungry way that Barba kept watching Derek, as if he would kill him the next time the lights went out.

"Alright, Barba, you first."

The horse turned his head to face the tiger. Despite the seriousness of their situation, Zinc admired the tall, muscular build of the equine. Immediately, trailing his eyes back up to the horse's face, Zinc shifted his legs, trying to avoid getting hard on the spot. "What got you interested in Tarot reading?"

Barba looked down at the debris-covered floor. "Well, that's easy. I've just always enjoyed the mystic. It's as close as we can get to playing as God. It's not blasphemous like the Tower of Babel was; it's a very intentional pretense, an act. But it still makes you feel good, like you can read spirits."

Derek grunted, "Well, so far, you've been pretty spot on."

"Huh? Have I?"

Zinc nodded, his own eyes narrowing. "Yeah, you have. If there's one thing that characterizes my past, it's definitely being lazy."

Derek continued, "And you got it right that he's lust and I'm wrath. You got it right that we connected most over greed. We both are desperate for fame and fortune."

"And the one hobby we both have is being envious. While he envies other athletes, I'm always...well, I'm always envying their girlfriends." Derek gave Zinc a stern glare.

Barba shook his head. "It doesn't even make sense. I shouldn't even have pulled out that many of the sins from the start. I *swear* I shuffled them."

Glancing sideward to Derek to judge his reaction, Zinc felt sure Barba was the demon. Everything made sense except the claw marks though. Barba, who loved everything about display and extravagance, could easily have this whole place rigged. "Derek, the next question is for you." Derek's ears perked up, but the German shepherd did not turn to meet Zinc's eyes. "What are you most scared of right now?"

At that, the dog looked up finally into Zinc's eyes, and Zinc saw fear plenty in them. Derek looked away again and mumbled, "I'm not scared of anything."

That's my man, Zinc said with a smile.

"Dogshit," Barba snorted. Both Zinc and Derek turned to the horse in surprise. "You're quick to give these vague-ass answers that don't mean shit. How scared are you of us putting another cross to you?"

Derek clenched his teeth.

A wind moved in the chapel, and the candlelights wavered but did not go out.

All the same, the three looked around, expecting some shadowed intruder to appear. Zinc whispered, "How about we move to one of the other rooms, guys?"

The other two nodded. Zinc and Derek both grabbed a candelabra, and Barba grabbed the podium, which was light in his muscular grasp. With Zinc in the lead, they headed into the eastern part of the chapel. From here, Zinc knew where the bathroom was. He remembered passing a small study room off to the side. Once everyone was inside, he placed his candelabra in the center of the aged and dusty conference table before returning to the entrance to close the door. The three sat around the table, and Barba moved the cards, still keeping the remaining two cards face-down. He arranged the face-up cards beside the face-down cards.

As Barba moved to turn over the last card, Zinc grabbed his hoof, stopping him. "Not yet." When the horse gave him a quizzical look, Zinc responded, "One more truth for you." The horse reclined back, and the candlelight made his grin seem dark and haunting. "Do you believe in demons?"

The grin faded. The horse leaned over the table, his snout inches from one of the candle's flames, "Hell yes, I believe in demons! Boarzebub, Lucifur, Belfoxgur…there's tons of them!"

Zinc could not stop himself from asking, "Are you one of them?"

Barba gritted his teeth, "I believe in God. I trust in Him." Before Zinc could reply, he snorted, "You're out of questions anyway." He put his hoof back over the next card. "This one is supposed to show Derek's background—what made him the hound he is today." With a flourish, Barba flipped it over, revealing a tusked boar grinning at the three of them through the flickering candlelight. The horse smirked, "And it looks like another of the seven deadly sins: Gluttony."

Even Zinc fell back in his chair laughing. Derek merely stared at the card with anger, but he clenched his jaw. Finally, the German shepherd growled, "You two tell stories. The person who tells the least gluttonous of them will have to suffer a dare from me."

"From *you*?" Zinc asked in disbelief, knowing that if the tiger lost, Derek would dare him to do something terrible.

Derek merely glared at him. "Yes, from me. So, you'd better tell a story so fucking sinful that the goddamn pig on the card wants what you got. Got it?"

Zinc swallowed and eyed Barba, but the horse seemed to be studying Derek. Zinc's eyes trailed across the dusty chalkboards and shelves of rotting books along the walls. The shadows seemed to dance.

"I'll go first," Zinc breathed.

VICTUALS
DWALE

Salma was only halfway finished with supper when the knock came. She froze, triangular ears perked high on her feline head until the visitor rapped once again, startling her into motion. Her shift had been over for hours, so whoever this late visitor might be, their presence boded nothing good. Eyes darting in search of some hiding place, the Mau hastily settled on the drawer of her scuffed plastic desk and secreted her plate there, locking it in afterward.

She decided to spare a moment to compose herself before she opened the front door, afflicted with an overwhelming self-consciousness with regards to her tail, which lashed back and forth behind her with restless fervor. Getting it under control required deep breaths and concentration, through which she reflected on the irony of her own body's attempting to betray her.

It's probably nothing, she assured herself. *Just someone asking for directions.*

The scrapyard adjacent to her facility was a labyrinth of pathways twisting through the wreckage of times past. Walls made of little more than rust and sharp edges reached some five meters high in places. It was not unusual for new hires to become disoriented and end up at her shed. With that in mind, she steeled herself and slid back the bolt.

The sky had some light in it still, but the maze of ruined autos and industrial machinery threw a shadow over her residence. The effect was like her own personal darkness, a patch of night that arrived before all the rest. As a cat, this bothered her not at all. She would have been able to see this intruder in detail with no illumination but the stars.

"Are you 31559213, Salma?" the saluki asked. He wore baggy nylon coveralls with patches on the knees and elbows. His ears dangled from the sides of a narrow, white head, looking for all the world like he had shoulder-length hair. His mouth hung open as he panted in the quiet summer heat. His tail swept left and right in a lazy arc.

Her guts tied themselves up in knots at the sound of her name. She felt her ears begin to flatten in alarm and willed them erect. Every nerve in her body screamed at her to flee, but she could not. Not if she wanted to live.

"I am," she said, nothing more.

"Well," the saluki announced, offering his paw to shake, "I'm the new inspector for this district. I've been going around today, introducing myself. Though I think," he said, pausing to chuckle, "I would have put off meeting you until tomorrow if I'd known how long the drive was going to be. Name's Adam, nice to meet you."

She took his hand and gave it two stiff pumps before releasing it. A new inspector was not welcome news for her. Bribes were an essential part of doing business, but broaching the subject with a stranger was always a touchy proposition. What was more, she was not exactly overflowing with funds.

"So," he began. It occurred to her that she had been fixing him with a blank look for several seconds, and made to speak, but he beat her to it.

"That smell..." His nostrils quivered and glistened as he took measure of the air; his voice low and grave. "Did you burn your dinner?"

The words hit her like a punch to the solar plexus. She felt herself wince and knew that he must have seen it, but he let out a long peal of barking laughter; she realized he was only engaging in a little gallows' humor. Joining in, she tittered, though the sound was pinched and nervous. Once done, he resumed his smiling.

"So! I know it's late, but as long as I'm here, do you mind if we take a look at the main building?"

"No," she lied, straining to put on a pleasant expression and certain, in the depths of her paranoia, that she was failing. "I'll get the key."

The key was a digital one stored on her computer, which was already on her person. In the bedroom, she reached under a pillow and came up with a folding knife with a twenty-three centimeter blade. It was just short enough to slip into her pocket, and, at the instant of having done so, she became possessed of a most peculiar serenity. She had her words, her wiles, and these would be her first line of defense. If that wasn't enough…

When she returned, she found the inspector living up to his title by poking at a mobile she'd made from old tins and shards of glass.

"Ready?" he asked.

"Yes," she said, fingertips tracing the reassuring weight in her pocket. "I do believe I am."

Whoever had designed the facility had owned the good sense to build it far from the scrapyard, and to fell enough trees on the eastern side of the property to prevent their casting shadows over the lens array on the roof. The exterior of the main structure was unadorned concrete, smooth from weathering. It might even have been mistaken for a modest home were it not for the smokestack, which was darker in color than the rest, looming over it all with vague menace like a column displaced from the palace of some chthonic god. Adam kept looking up at it and sniffing as they walked over.

"The shape and placement of the array means the sun is on it from dawn to dusk," she explained. "The salt mixture is heated to almost six-hundred degrees Celsius. As it melts, it moves into an insulated storage tank underground. It's an inherently efficient set-up. Energy loss at that stage is less than one percent."

"I've never seen anything like it," Adam admitted, cooing approval at this rare technology. "But still, the chamber itself needs to be much hotter than that, if I recall?"

Salma nodded. "You're right, the salt mixture isn't enough by itself. We bring in water through the main and heat it over a metal plate. That drives a turbine in the back, which in turn powers coils below the chamber. Picture a space heater, but bigger; this thing tops eight-hundred degrees. And there's enough electricity left over for the lights and computer relay."

"I'm impressed. But what if it rains?"

"It hasn't been an issue," she said, shrugging her lithe, feline shoulders. "My understanding is that it retains several days' worth of energy. I've seen it go three in a row without any noticeable drop in output."

"Amazing." He stopped walking and so did she. They were a stone's throw from the entrance now. It was dusk. Stars crept in from the east like a swarm of torpid fireflies. His eyes flashed green with reflected light as he fixed her with a marked stare.

"And the coolers?"

Their visual worlds were monochrome, but if that hadn't been the case then he would have seen the color drain from the insides of her ears. The ease of their conversation up to this point had been enough to put her halfway off her guard.

"The coolers, too," she said, hand slipping into her pocket.

"I looked over your file," he said, not looking at her eyes, but at the end of her arm now engaged with the weapon he must have suspected she held. While she did not draw and attack, neither did she loosen her grip.

"You took a ration cut like everyone else in town," he continued. "But they also switched your formula to one with no taurine in it. Your nutritionist *does* know you're a cat, right?"

"There was a mix-up. I submitted some forms, but—"

She took a step toward him, then went rigid as a stone. His right hand had made its way into his own pocket, and there was something pointed at her through the fabric that might well have been his finger, but might just as easily have been a gun. Whichever the case, it was enough to stop her advance.

"Here's the thing that I don't understand," he mused, his smile gone from friendly to mocking in a blink. "In the middle of a famine, living on a formula supplement that's not nutritious enough for you, you still managed to gain five kilos in two months. So, would you rather confess, or shall I march you in there and have you open those coolers?"

Salma sighed and raised now-empty palms to him in resignation, in surrender. He knew. There was nothing to do now but consign herself to the truth and attempt some form of damage control.

"Tell me what you want."

All traces of humor vanished from his features, leaving only cold, animal logic in their wake.

"Simple," he said, not grinning, but showing teeth like a shark in the moment of striking. "I want in."

A quarter-hour later and she stood watching the inspector slink off through the darkness, a package wrapped in ebony plastic tucked in the crook of his arm. She'd gotten the best terms she could from the situation, which were poor enough, but reckoned the loss was an acceptable one compared to what would happen if he were to report her to the authorities.

Arrangements like the one she'd just made were not permanent affairs. If the saluki were to become too greedy, or sloppy, then odds were good she would end up giving him the "deluxe tour" of her solar-powered crematory.

The moon rose. Crickets sang in the grass. Somewhere far away, a dog bayed in the darkness. She waited until she was certain he had gone, then went back to unlock her desk and finish her victuals.

ANTHROPHAGY
ZARPAULUS

There are many predators who are content to subsist on ferals, and even a few misguided folks who try to derive nutrition from plants. But there are some rare individuals who can only be satisfied by that most taboo of meats: anthropomorphic flesh.

To most, we are nothing but stories, something that happened in the past or in distant places. On the rare occasion that one of us is caught, there's a brief story in the news, and then the masses forget within the month. I don't mind; it's easier to hunt when the prey don't know you're there.

Another perk of being thought of as myth: those paranoid enough to actually look for us end up expecting someone completely different. We're almost always thought of as either hulking half-feral brutes bloated with prey, or suave sexual predators who seduce you and devour you after making love. With those stereotypes, who would expect a petite little fennec?

Generally, I prefer to hunt in places where anthros traditionally go to meet one another: bars, nightclubs, sci-fi conventions. It's best not to hunt at the same place too often, and so this one night I was scoping out a bar I'd never visited previously. I was wearing a short red strapless dress and looking a bit out of place among the regular patrons. With the mix of truckers, frat boys, and listless middle-aged men I must have looked like either a prostitute or, ironically, easy prey. I wasn't afraid. The odds of running into another of my kind were unlikely, and meals who underestimated me were always the easiest to snatch.

Discretely, I scoped out the selection. What I could see wasn't promising to be honest. A pack of college boys, well marinated and fatty but a risk: if I separated one and he never came back his brothers might remember me. There were truckers, meaty but not lightweights and tough to digest. That left the older men, well matured and fattened, I just needed to figure out which ones wouldn't be missed. I passed over a bored looking horse in a workshirt and a small group of friends before spotting a mouse staring wistfully into his beer.

My prey in sight, I headed for a table not too far but not too close, and well within his sight. I sat displaying my profile to him, swirling my drink as I waited for the mouse to take notice. *Let them come to you*, I thought. After nearly ten minutes of waiting, and one rebuffed proposition by a random barfly, he took notice of me. I pretended to just take notice of his gaze then and returned it with a smile.

He became intrigued and perked up, starting to rise before hesitating, unsure. With one hand, I beckoned him over and his reluctance vanished as he walked over to me.

I didn't bother to remember what we talked about; it's always some variation of the same old script. "What brings you here?" Followed by an "Oh, that's too bad. Want to come back to my place?" After less than fifteen minutes of listening to his sordid tale, something about a wife wanting to leave him or something, we were leaving for my house.

Well, a condo really. Some think that an isolated cottage out in the country is best, but I find that regular visitors draw more attention from the neighbors where the population is sparse. In the city, you just need to make sure the walls are soundproofed.

After I made sure the front door was locked securely and all the windows were shut with the curtains drawn, I started to undo the zipper up my back, struggling visibly so that my prey would come in close to help. As soon as the hapless mouse had drawn my dress down over my breasts I shoved his face in between them, and then I led him into the kitchen. He did not protest as I bent him back over the sink. I spotted some disappointment in his eyes as I pushed his face back out of my cleavage but it turned to excitement as I reared back. Then, before he could react, I turned my jaws onto his neck and sank my teeth into his trachea.

His carotid spurted hot blood across the stainless steel counter as his windpipe crunched between my jaws. I relished his dying gasps almost as much as I savored his succulent flavor; I so enjoyed the taste of mouse meat, probably thanks to some primal urge. My head wrenched back, taking a chunk of his throat in my mouth, causing him to choke on his own blood while I swallowed.

As he died, I wriggled out of my dress and tossed it into the next room. Blood would not show on the red fabric but it would smell, and bodily fluids were a pain to clean off without bleach. Once his gasping had ceased, I set to work tearing the meat from his skull; there wasn't much but no point wasting it. The lips and cheeks ripped off easily, taking small strips of muscle with them. The eyes I scooped out with a spoon and popped in my mouth like grapes. I worked my way back to the thin little ears and set aside the worthless pieces of cartilage and gristle. I peeled off the scalp and scraped the flesh from it with my rough tongue; then I took an electric knife from a drawer and began to saw off the top of the cranium. As his skull was opened, the sink became littered with shards of cast-off bone and filled with blood and cerebrospinal fluid that spilled from the brainpan as the motorized blade sunk deeper. Finally, the knife sawed into empty air, and I deftly caught the severed top of the skull in my free hand then licked the fatty brains out. They're so sweet, but so quick to spoil.

After cleaning out the top of the skull, I wrenched the remaining half back up and plunged my muzzle in, greedily lapping up the gray matter. When I reached the thin membrane at the bottom of the brainpan, I set it aside and moved down to his pectorals, ripping away at them with my bare claws. I tore off strips of muscle and dropped them in my mouth, tearing and shredding the bloody flesh with no more concern for the mess, lost in the feeding frenzy. By now, my stomach was visibly bulging, one may have mistaken me for several months pregnant. I knew it would take days to digest this meal. My hunger sated for the time being, I decided that I would set aside the rest for later. I drained the remaining blood and other fluids into a pitcher; you would be surprised how many recipes include blood. I picked up another knife and began to carve away the rest of his meat. I pared away narrow steaks from his abdomen, deftly cut the biceps off his arms and the calves from his legs. His muscles and liver were saved in a series of large plastic bags, a rather large bag in the case of the liver in my opinion; then I began to crack open the ribcage so as to remove the heart. Most of the remaining internal organs were of little use to me, I'd probably just throw them in a lake for the fish later. I cut his hands off whole, the fingers would make good snacks. The large bones would have to be crushed and ground into powder once I'd sucked out the marrow, but that could wait, for now I just needed to rest and digest.

I wrapped the bones in foil and almost carelessly shoved them into the cupboard below the sink. That done, I slipped off to my bedroom to sleep off the meal.

Some time later, I was roused from my digestive coma by a loud banging on my door. Groggily, I lurched off of the mattress and absent-mindedly threw on a robe before going to the door.

"Where is he?!" an angry female voice demanded from the other side of the locked door. Instinctively, I identified the speaker as a mouse, in retrospect I would realize she was probably my dinner's wife or ex-wife, but at the time I was too tired to register that fact. Back then, I just thought of her as a weak prey species that I could easily scare off. I unlocked and opened the door a crack to tell her off and was greeted by the silenced barrel of a gun.

The sight of a middle-aged mousewife bearing an expression of abject rage and brandishing a handgun might have almost seemed comical, were it not for the fact that the gun was aimed straight at my forehead. I couldn't see anything else to do but back up and hope she gave me an opening to counterattack.

As I backed away and opened the door, I slowly straightened up, unintentionally emphasizing my still-distended gut. Her eyes darted to my stomach, her face fell, and she pulled the trigger.

A hammer blow to the belly, followed by another to the breast seconds later. I slumped back against the wall, bleeding from the two wounds as I felt bile rising in my throat. As I lay there heaving up the thick stew that remained of this crazy mouse's mate, I wondered briefly what made her react so violently before I blacked out.

There are a lot of legends concerning anthros who eat other anthros. For instance, they may believe that we shapeshift in order to blend in with our prey, or that we can enthrall our victims. A popular one is that we can live forever so long as we keep consuming anthros or something like that. Most social psychologists think that it's because anthro-kind has tamed all their natural predators but retain this instinctive fear of being eaten that requires an outlet. So they invent fictional monsters that Science hasn't yet managed to slay.

Too bad they're wrong on that count.

I regained consciousness as the bleeding stopped and the holes in my body started to close. I was sitting in a pool of red-tinted stinging fluid. Blood trailed from my stomach and my right breast; at least she had missed my heart: that would have been troublesome. I could feel the second bullet still embedded in my lung, but I could handle it until I could find a doctor who wouldn't ask questions. The first one was just barely visible among the bile and meat chunks on the floor; it had been stopped by the contents of my stomach and came up with it. After evaluating my own physical condition, I realized that the robe I'd been wearing was wet with blood and digestive juices. I'd have to burn it later.

A crash from the area of the bedroom told me that the mouse was in the process of tearing my home apart in search of her husband. She re-entered the kitchen, quite visibly frustrated at the lack of incriminating evidence. I decided to cut her off before she did too much damage. "Try the cupboard under the sink," I managed to croak out.

She brandished the gun at me again, I just sat there grinning like an idiot, but she cautiously opened the cupboard with her foot and then bent over to pick up the foil-wrapped bundle with her free hand. The package was too heavy for her, and she dropped it, sending brown bones tumbling out onto the floor.

The live mouse dropped down among the remains of the dead one, rummaging until she found the skull with its top sawed off. As she stared in shock and recognition I took the opportunity to cast off my soiled robe and get back on my feet. "You," she gasped, "you're a...a..."

"An anthrophage." I completed for her. A generic term, I know, but more accurate than "cannibal" and without the annoying romanticism of "vampire" or "werebeast," or "ghoul" as they called us back in my homeland. Really, the only difference is in hunting strategies. Those who called themselves vampires starved themselves on a bit of blood to just barely satisfy their need for anthro protein and minimize their chances of getting caught, while werebeasts prowled remote areas and gorged on lost hikers once a month; ghouls like most of my family were a bit somewhere in between.

She returned her gaze to my naked, bloodstained body, standing despite the wounds slowly knitting back together as she watched. I willed my claws to grow longer and my lips to curl back, prominently displaying my fangs. Looking in horror from her mate's monstrous killer to his remains, she became overwhelmed with despair. Slowly, she lifted the gun again and began to aim it at her own temple.

"No," I thought, this uppity little prey animal wasn't going to be escaping that easily. She had stolen my meal from me, after I had eaten it even! She had to be punished. Swiftly, I pounced on her, forcing the gun away and tossing it over to the far side of the room. My unnaturally long claws tore her blouse wide open, and she screamed as my teeth sank into her breast. The next slash ripped straight through the fat layer protecting her intestines. I tore away the mouthful of meat and swallowed, then began to dig into her guts and showed them to her as I ate. By the time I had hollowed out her lower abdominal cavity and moved up to the liver she had no breath left to scream. She simply stared off into space with her mouth hanging open until she bled to death.

When I was sure her chest had stopped moving and the light had faded from her eyes, I stood back and looked at the mess we'd made. The floor was covered in the bile and blood of two different species interspersed with mushy chunks of mouse meat. Out of curiosity I went back for the discarded gun and unloaded it, just the one bullet left, why had she only taken three? She'd spent two bullets on me and so far as I could tell she'd been planning to murder her husband and his lover, so what was the third one for? Was it simply a spare or had she been planning a double murder-suicide all along? But that still didn't explain why she'd wasted a bullet on my stomach.

It wasn't important now: I dismissed the idea, and went back to the kitchen. It would take all day to clean it all up, but I still had time before the smell became intolerable. For now, I could just sit back and appreciate my good fortune, it had been centuries since I'd managed to net two fat prey in as many days. I'd spent too much time being cautious; the prey had become numerous enough to gorge myself as much as I wanted. It was time to feast!

Interlude

Derek grinned as Barba finished his story. Zinc's ears drooped, and his tail curled around his legs. "Guess who gets a dare?" Derek said with a toothy grin.

Zinc sighed and said, "As you always say, let's get it over with."

The German shepherd ignored the jab. "Hm, what shall I have you do?" He looked around the room as if looking for inspiration, and then, he spotted it. Getting up from his chair, he approached the desk that was in the back corner of the room. He picked up something and returned to the table, still standing.

"What is that?" Zinc whispered.

Derek brought the object into a light. It was a pointing stick, the kind that teachers used to point at words on blackboards. "It's a pointer. Can you guess where this is going?"

Zinc swallowed. "Um…"

"Up your fucking ass."

Zinc's eyes widened. He nervously laughed. "That's not so bad, right? Let me go grab some soap from the bathroom to lube it up though."

Derek was lightning quick. He grabbed the scruff of Zinc's neck, causing him to gasp instantly as he was flung onto the table, knocking over a couple of the face-up cards and narrowly missing the candelabra.

Barba stood up and cried, "Whoa, Derek, what are you doing?"

"His turn for a dare, his turn for a dare," Derek chanted with a smile. He held the tiger down with one paw while he aimed the rod at Zinc's tail with his other. The tiger's tail was tight between Zinc's legs, and the pinned Zinc cried out,

"C'mon, Derek, you don't have to do this. I'm sorry about branding you."

"Yeah, well, you'll really be sorry in a second. Barba, pull his fucking tail up."

"Derek—"

"*I said to fucking do it!* Or you'll be next."

Barba swallowed but leaned forward, grabbing the tiger's tail as he muttered, "Sorry, Zinc." He did not trust the dog for a second, and now he was convinced that Derek was the demon, but he knew he could not stand up to the dog alone. It would have to wait until after this moment passed.

Zinc mumbled between tears, "Please," before the wooden rod was shoved sharply through his tight tailhole. "*Arrghh!*" he screamed, his whole body tensing, making the pain even worse.

"That's right," Derek hissed as he pulled the rod out and rammed it in again, ignoring the slick, red blood that coated the end of the stick. "Take it, you bitch. Where's your 'lust' at now?"

Three more pushes. Three more high-pitched screams.

"Derek, that's enough!" Barba cried, his eyes wild with fear.

Derek plunged it in one more time before tossing the bloody rod aside. "There. Now, that's enough."

The tiger's tail curled back between his legs, and Zinc sobbed into the table, his head lowered.

"Jesus..." Barba whispered.

Derek picked up the last card, saying, "I won't look, I promise. Let's just head back into the main room. This place reeks of blood and shit now."

As Derek left, Barba started to help Zinc up. "Hey, man...I'm...I'm so sorry."

But Zinc only glared daggers at the horse between his red, tear-rimmed eyes. "Get the fuck out of here."

Barba's ears pressed against the side of his head, and he nodded, heading back into the main room. He knew it was Derek now. It had to be. That bastard.

But even as Barba left, Zinc's eyes burned holes into the horse's back. "Fucking horse."

Derek laid the card face down on the floor in the center of the chapel room. "Fucking tiger got what he deserved," he muttered under his breath.

As the other two filtered into the room, Zinc said, "Alright, what's the last damn card supposed to be?"

"Goals. What you and Derek want out of life and your relationship."

"Should be easy enough," the German shepherd replied. "More sex. Isn't that right, Zinc?"

Zinc could not raise his eyes to look at either of them. He said, "Flip the card, Barba."

The horse snorted. "I bet I can guess the last one." He bent down to touch the card, and he flipped it. "Pride." A wild-maned lion growled up at him. A third eye sat in the center of its forehead, and its demeanor was indeed proud, although its fur looked matted and unkempt. "Foolish, foolish pride. No more games. Let's share a couple of stories, and then it should be dawn. Maybe someone will find us and get us out of here." The horse snickered to himself.

Both Derek and Zinc nodded, looking up at the stained glass windows that barely glimmered from the light of the candles. That's when they realized it. Somehow, all of the figures posed in the panels were all grinning. All the images were smiling at them. Posed behind Barba, they seemed to shadow him, laughing with him.

Seven Deadly Sins

THE MUSIC ON THE STREET
NIGHTEYES DAYSPRING

Shadow woke to the chill of damp, morning air. It was still dark out, but dawn's early light had started to appear in the east. He yawned, letting his tongue fall out of his muzzle, and he rolled onto his stomach in his thin sleeping bag.

The wolf let his ears pick up the sounds of the city waking up around him. He could hear the distant hum of early morning traffic, the high pitch squeal of brakes, and the low rumble of a diesel engine nearby. Sniffing deeply, he caught the faint smell of breakfast cooking. His stomach growled in protest since he hadn't eaten yesterday. The rain had made it impossible for him to work, and he was out of money.

He crawled out of the sleeping bag and stretched as best he could under the piece of tin roofing he had camped under. It was at least dry, he mused as he glanced around. Everything was where he had left it before going to bed, including the buckets that were his livelihood. He breathed easy and relaxed. Even though he tried to stay aware while he slept, you could never be too sure.

Quickly he pulled off the thin shirt he wore and reached for the dye and brush in his pack. He would have to hurry, if he was going to be ready for the morning commute. He also pulled out a small flashlight so he could see clearly as he got to work.

Shadow had adorned his jet-black fur with white markings. On each shoulder and arm, Shadow had painted a white spiral pattern. Around his neck, he had carefully painted lines up the side of his head toward his face. Gently, he dipped the brush into the dye and used a mirror to start touching up the markings. Carefully he refreshed the white lines in his fur that yesterday's rain had dulled.

It was annoying to have to touch up his markings every couple of days, but these were his power symbols. They protected him and helped set him apart from many of the other street ruffians. Without these marks, Shadow would be in danger in becoming the old him again. He didn't want to be the old him anymore. That was the part of himself he hated, that had driven him to this life.

After ten minutes, he was satisfied with his handiwork, and he put his supplies away and rolled up his sleeping bag. He slipped on a tank top to show off the markings, and he was ready to go. He wasn't sure exactly what time it was, but that didn't matter. He could hear the city coming to life around him. His stomach growled again, but he ignored it. There would be time enough for food after the morning session.

Shadow's favorite spot to perform was near the Seventh Street Subway Station. The people at the coffee shop nearby were kind enough to let him use the bathroom without harassing him for not buying. In addition, the cheetah who owned the newspaper and candy stand in front of the station's entrance tolerated him. Shadow waved to the cheetah as he started to set up for the day, but the cheetah only rolled his eyes. He didn't bother Shadow, but he wasn't friendly either.

Shadow laid out his buckets in a semicircle upside down against the wall of a nearby building. In front of his setup, he set one small bucket right side up for tips, and in the center of the semicircle, he set the largest bucket, placing his pack underneath it. Included with the buckets, he had two metal sheets for cymbals. When he was done, he seated himself in the center, a wooden drumstick held in each paw.

There were a few people milling about near the candy stand. The light of the rising sun had only begun to touch the street. The mobs of commuters that would climb out of the

Seventh Street Station like ants emerging from a disturbed ant hill were on their way. They would scatter like leaves before the wind to their office towers, taking their place as cogs in the machine to conduct the business that made this city turn. But before they reached their offices, in this small part of the street, they were his.

The wolf swiveled his perky ears and listened to the screech of a subway coming to a stop down below. He flipped one of the drumsticks in his hands and struck the first notes against one of the pails in front of him. Foot traffic was slow first thing in the morning, but it would pick up quickly as the morning progressed. Some would come from the station and head for their morning coffee. Then, emerging with warm curls of steam coming out of their paper cups, they would wander over for a few minutes to watch him and listen. A number of his regulars often dropped their change from the coffee shop into his pail before running off to their jobs.

The improvised drums echoed through the street with loud thunking sounds as he started to build up the music. The sound was unrefined, but it had its own unique tones to it. He closed his eyes for a brief moment to feel the growing music in his arms. The urgency of his music grew as the morning crowd on the street started to swell, and he layered rhythms and tweaked them. He needed to play. By playing, he could keep the urges down. He was himself but not himself at the same time.

He let the music roll off of him. Coins clinked into his pail. The wolf smiled and let the music take him away from the city. He didn't see the crowd. Instead, they were a silent shifting sea just beyond his perception where the current was always changing. Upon this sea, he was at peace.

On the edge of his vision, there stood a coyote watching him. He stood out like a rock in the shifting sea of people. A few people would pause for a while, but the coyote stayed and did not leave. At first, Shadow thought he was just a slow-moving lingerer, but the more he stayed still, the more he resolved himself to be a rock in the sea of people who moved before Shadow.

As Shadow brought a set of drumming to a close, the coyote was still there. Pausing to catch his breath, tongue rolling out, he gave the usual plea for tips before most of the people watching him dispersed.

"How long have you been drumming for?" asked the coyote. The coyote's accent was different from the locals, and Shadow could tell he was from out of town.

"A long time," replied the wolf.

"Why do you perform out here?" asked the yote.

Shadow reached for the tip jar. There were five dollars in singles and a few more dollars in change in the bucket. "It's a living," said the wolf somewhat distractedly as he took out the paper bills.

The coyote tilted his head and looked at the wolf carefully. "But why on the street with plastic buckets?"

The wolf looked at the other canine. He looked to be about Shadow's age. He wore business casual clothing over his neatly brushed fur. Instead of a look of disdain though, he had his ears focused on the black wolf.

"This is my temple," Shadow said grinning. "The crowd are my parishioners, and the music is my hymn. I come out here, tap out the beat of the city, and they reward me for a brief respite from their daily lives."

"It doesn't look like it pays well," the coyote remarked.

"This isn't twenty questions, you know. What is it you want?" asked the wolf, curling his tail against himself. He didn't like it when people asked too many questions. It was never a good sign when they did.

"Oh nothing," said the canine with a quick flash of his fangs and a bob of his head. "Just curious is all."

Shadow turned his attention back to the buckets. When he glanced up after he had started another set, the coyote was gone.

A few days later, as Shadow was finishing up his evening session during rush hour, he spotted the coyote in the crowd milling about listening to him. The buckets sang their throaty sound, as he poured his soul into the music. The skyscrapers were starting to cast deep shadows onto the street while the wolf beat out a rhythm to the setting sun.

The coyote watched him until Shadow reached the end of his set and let his aching arms drop to his sides. "That's all for tonight folks," he mumbled, tired from a long day of work. The crowd dispersed with a few more coins dropping into his pail. He reached for the bucket and started counting the money. The coyote lingered.

"Show's over. You can go home now."

"I'm waiting for you to go home first," laughed the coyote.

"What?" said the wolf, glancing at the grinning canine.

"Well, you are going to go home and not stay out here all night now, right?"

Shadow flicked his ears. "I am outdoors. The street is my home."

"Oh," said the coyote. "That's disappointing to hear."

Shadow laid his ears back. "I make do. Now, are you going to buzz off and leave me be?"

"I hear they call you Shadow. Is that what you go by?" said the coyote, ignoring Shadow's annoyed tone.

His ears fell. "Maybe," he said, trying to keep his tail from twitching. "What's it to you?"

"Nothing really. Just curious what you call yourself."

Shadow looked at the coyote. Was he someone who knew Shadow from before? He tried hard to keep people from figuring it out. "Do I know you?" he asked.

"No, but I know you," said the other canine.

Shadow felt a chill go through his back. An unease spread into his body. He turned to start stacking the buckets. He couldn't go back. He just couldn't.

"I've got a job for you."

The wolf shook his head. "No thanks," he said. "I've got enough problems already."

"It's easy," said the coyote softly. "This won't take you long."

"Look buddy, I don't know who you are, but I'm not interested. Now leave me alone," growled Shadow, turning back to look at the coyote.

"Oh come now," said the coyote. "It's no trouble at all. Less trouble than if you get caught performing out here without a license."

Shadow smiled. "I actually do have a license. Now, go away. I'm happy out here. I'm at peace."

"Oh you do? Is that registered to just 'Shadow', or do you use your real name for that?"

This coyote had to be someone he met in the past. Someone who remembered the wolf from before he'd run away from his old life. He reached down and picked up his buckets and slung his pack over his shoulder. Without saying anything, he turned and walked off.

"Hey now," the coyote barked, stepping after him, "Are you taking the job or not?"

"I told you. I'm not interested," said Shadow without turning around. He hurried down the street. As long as he got away, he would be okay. He didn't have to go back. He couldn't. There was no peace back there. Out here he was free.

He was worried the coyote was going to give chase, but he didn't. Shadow kept walking until he was sure he wasn't being followed. He ducked into an alley and dropped the bucket. It took almost thirty minutes before he could finally still his beating heart.

Whoever the coyote was, Shadow wanted nothing to do with him.

He didn't see the coyote again for over a month. At first, he had changed his routine to make sure he avoided a possible encounter with the coyote. The wolf performed at other locations in the city. After a few weeks, he returned to the Seventh Street Station to perform. He had almost forgotten about the curious canine when one day, going back to his spot after getting some lunch, he found the coyote waiting for him.

"Howdy," the coyote said as he approached.

"You're in my spot," said Shadow gruffly, putting down the buckets he was carrying.

"I don't see your name on it," said the coyote.

"No, I guess not," remarked Shadow, picking up his buckets. "I'll move down."

"Look, Trevor, I can call you Trevor, right? I really need you to take this job."

The wolf froze. "Who told you my real name?"

"Whoa, easy now. The cheetah at the newspaper stand over there told me."

Shadow knew the coyote had to be lying. He never used that name anymore. Trevor was dead. Trevor had been someone else. Someone Shadow couldn't be anymore. Trevor was the best at what he did. Shadow would always be a shade of Trevor, and he wanted it to stay that way.

"Who are you?" asked the wolf.

"The name's Rocco, but that's not important. What's important is that you do this job."

With a trembling voice, he spoke. "Please, I don't want any trouble with you or the law. Just let me be."

"Then listen and listen good, wolf," said the coyote, dropping his voice. "I've heard about you, and I know who are you are, Trevor Michaels. If you want to keep living on the street and painting swirly patterns on top of your fur, go ahead, I'm not going to stop you, but I know there are people out there who would love to find you. If you want me to keep this information to myself, you're going to do me a favor."

His tail curled defensively. "This is blackmail, you know."

"No, this is called work. The job is simple. You busk already anyway. I just need you to go down to the Copper District and busk. I'll even pay you to do it, and you get to keep the tips."

"The reason I stay out of the Copper District is because I think someone might recognize me."

The coyote smiled, flashing his fangs. "Nobody will recognize you. The paint changes your appearance. The only reason I was able to definitively know it was you was by consulting the records at city hall and going over the busker licenses."

That was the only clue Shadow knew of that led from his old life to his new life.

"What's this to you?" He could feel his fur curling. His pulse was hammering in his ears.

The coyote smirked. "That's not your business. Here's fifty dollars with instructions on when to show up," he said, pulling out an envelope and pressing it into Shadow's hands. "Oh and one more thing. Ditch the buckets." With that, the coyote started to walk off.

"Wait, what will I play then?" he called after the coyote.

"Open the envelope. The instructions will tell you."

With shaking paws, he opened the envelope and pulled out the letter. There was a street corner, a time, and below that a second address for a music shop. Below the address were instructions:

Go to the music shop in the morning. The owner will be expecting you and will give you a violin to perform with. You can return the violin at the end of the day or keep it. It's your choice.

The wolf shivered. Of course, if he had to perform with a specific musical instrument, it would be the violin. He had started playing at age six, so what better instrument was there than the violin for a virtuoso like Trevor to perform with?

Shadow had a few preferred places to sleep, but he made sure to always scout out new ones. For the past week, he had been sleeping in an alley behind a construction site that was currently sitting half-finished. They had left some assorted construction debris in the back, and he found it an ideal place to camp.

The previous night, he made the decision to go to the shelter, so he left the buckets at the construction site. He didn't want to be alone with his thoughts. This meant that the social workers at the shelter checked up on him. He had to answer questions and follow the strict shelter rules. Unlike other people, he didn't really mind the rules. They provided structure. The only reason he didn't go the shelter more often was that he wasn't trying to get off the street. He didn't want to take up space that could be used to help someone who wanted help.

Now, standing in front of the music shop, he sucked in his breath, and stepped inside. He had showered that morning and then spent a good bit of time restoring his faded markings. His clothes, while worn, were clean.

The music shop was big. In the front, they had drum sets and guitars. He walked back toward the counter, where an overweight weasel sat looking through some paperwork.

"Hi," he said to the weasel, not sure what else to say.

The weasel looked up at him and looked him over. "Are you Trevor?" he asked him.

The sound of that name made his skin crawl. "Y...Yes."

"One moment." The weasel hopped off the stool, went to the back, and returned carrying a worn violin case. He placed it on the counter between them. "This is for you," he said.

Shadow turned the case around so the latches were facing him and opened the case. Inside, there sat a beautiful instrument, oiled wood gleaming. He gingerly reached down and picked up the violin and then reached for the bow.

The weasel watched him curiously as he put the violin up to his chin, and he pulled the bow across the strings. Shadow frowned at the sound of the violin. The sound was pleasant but not right.

"I tuned it myself," said the weasel.

"An instrument like this needs to be tuned very carefully," said Shadow. He lowered the violin down and adjusted the strings, before he tested it again. This sound was better, but it wasn't till he adjusted it a second time and tested the instrument that it sang the way it should, clear and sweet.

"I play guitar myself," said the weasel, "so I did what I thought was right."

Shadow nodded and lowered the violin and looked over it. This wasn't a cheap student instrument but a concert piece. It wasn't the highest quality violin he had ever performed with, but it still had rich tonal qualities.

"I bring this back at the end of the day?" he asked the weasel.

"Rocco said you might, but it's yours to keep," the storekeeper said. "He's already paid for it."

Gently, Shadow put the instrument back in its case. He wanted to ask how much it had cost, but he was afraid to find out. A musical instrument like this easily ran a few thousand dollars. He had owned better instruments, back before he left it all behind, but that was then. This was now, and this was his, if he wanted it.

He shivered in fear as he thanked the weasel and left the music store. Deep down though, there was excitement. Finally, someone would see his true talents.

Trevor had always carried his tail high. He had always been sharp, prompt, and smartly dressed. When he took the stage, he owned it. When he entered a room, people would look at him in awe. He was proud of who he was.

Shadow, though, walked down the street like someone was hunting him. His tail twitched back and forth, and his ears flicked nervously. He felt compelled to throw the violin into the trash and cradle it against himself at the same time. He trashed one violin once, so why not another?

Yet even though he wanted to, he knew he couldn't. Could he still play it? Could he still make it sing like he used to? He was terrified he wouldn't be able to, but he couldn't let go of the instrument now until he at least tried. The part of himself that was once Trevor wouldn't let him.

The Copper District was the city's arts district. It had a bohemian feel with small studios and theaters interspersed with apartment buildings. Old brick buildings decorated with fire escapes dominated the district.

The intersection Rocco had instructed Shadow to go to bordered the district's park. Shadow was familiar with the modestly sized park. Back in his old life, he used to visit it often to relax when the pressure had gotten to him. The note had told him to play near the intersection from 10 am to 1 pm, but it hadn't specified what he should play. He chose the corner of the intersection bordering the park and went to sit down on a bench under a shady tree. Placing the violin case on his lap, he flipped the latches up and opened the case.

The violin was waiting for him. He took a deep breath and gently lifted it out of the case. He hadn't played since that fateful day so many years ago when he had run away, but two decades of practice had burned the music into his mind. He looked at the gentle flow of people passing by. He was nervous being here. What if one of them recognized him? If he walked away, Rocco might chase him down, but if he returned the money and the violin, what could the coyote really do besides let people know who he really was?

That threat hung in the back of his mind. One never really walks away from their old life completely without giving everything up. If he had abandoned performing music completely and taken to just panhandling, Rocco never would have found him. He had tried that at first, but it had never felt right. Music, even in its most basic form, had always called to Shadow. He knew that was why he went back to performing. It wasn't like what he did before, but it at least brought in some money. There were low expectations for a homeless bum with plastic buckets and bits of metal. That suited him fine.

Shadow glanced around to see if he could spot Rocco, but the coyote didn't seem to be here. If Rocco wasn't watching him, would he know if Shadow had actually performed? Even though he didn't see the coyote, he suspected that Rocco would be around somewhere, listening.

Even through his fear, he felt his fingers tingling. He hadn't touched a violin in over five years. Now that he had one in his paws, he had to play the instrument. He closed his eyes and tried to steady his breathing. It was just one performance. Nobody would recognize him. The wolf stood up slowly, holding the violin and bow in one hand. He stepped forward and bent down to place the violin case in front of the bench. Standing again, he stepped back.

Shadow gently pulled the bow across the violin as he put it up to his chin. The notes were crisp. Taking a deep breath, he launched into the music, starting with a solo violin sonata he had memorized years ago. He let the music carry him and take him away. He frowned, listening to the imperfections in his rendition. He was out of practice, but as he continued to play, it got better.

The violin was rich and beautiful. A few passersby paused to linger. Some dropped money into the case, but he didn't waste the effort to check the case. He put his heart and soul into the music. His hands knew the motions, his mind knew the notes, yet he felt surprised at how easily the music came out of him. Soon it was if he had last played yesterday.

After the sonata, he did a few traditional eastern European folks songs. Later, he performed another sonata he knew by heart. The music flowed, and the crowd came and went, but Shadow could have been alone for all he cared. The park and the people faded out, and it was only after he stopped to take a breather, and found two fives in the violin case, that he realized people stayed to watch him.

He played through the rest of the morning and over lunch. It wasn't till he was reaching the end of his three-hour job that Rocco appeared. Shadow had expected the coyote at some point; he just hadn't known when. Rocco watched Shadow finish a piece and lower the violin. As the crowd disappeared, he walked up to the wolf.

"You play well."

"Of course I do," he snapped, before he caught himself. Sheepishly, he added, "I'm out of practice though."

"Still you haven't lost it," the coyote said casually. "I can hear your talent."

Trevor had been talented. Shadow preferred to just feel the music now. "Who are you?"

"Is that important?" the coyote asked coyly.

Shadow traced his fingers gently across the smooth finish of the violin. "I know what one of these costs, you know. This isn't a cheap violin."

"$3,500: case, strings, and bow," said the coyote.

Shadow laid his ears back surprised. It was more than he expected it to be. "Why spend all that money?"

The coyote held out a hand. "To know that, you first should know who I am. My full name is Rocco Salazar. I'm music director for the New City Orchestra."

His heart jumped in joy and fear. He had to catch himself. "I'm not going back there," he said with a strangled voice.

The coyote titled his muzzle and smirked. "I took over the orchestra two years ago after Piretta retired. They still speak of you in an awed and almost frightened way."

Shadow closed his eyes and traced a hand across the instrument. "I'm not surprised."

"It was six months ago, while we were doing a fundraiser for a local hospital, that I was flagged down at the reception by an older wolf. She told me what we were doing was all well and good, but if we wanted to do some personal charity, we should look into what had happened to our star violinist. She felt that while we had component musicians, we were lacked a true virtuoso in the violin sections."

"Mrs. Soto always did have a special place in her heart for me," interjected Shadow.

The coyote arched his eyebrow and continued. "I knew you used to be part of the orchestra, but it wasn't until then that I started asking questions about what had happened to you."

With his eyes closed, Shadow spoke like he wasn't there. "Trevor Michaels was a gifted musician who played the violin from a very early age. He had a troubled childhood and used music as a means to escape. Eventually his escape became his prison. A perfectionist, he was obsessed with getting every note right and would work late into the night practicing alone. He was the youngest concertmaster ever in the New City Orchestra, but for all his success, he couldn't find solace in what he did."

Shadow opened his eyes. "He was haunted by his flaws, and the longer he practiced the worse his paranoia got. He needed to be better than he was. He kept practicing, kept tutoring aspiring musicians. Whatever Piretta wanted he would do. He did recitals and extra concerts in order to be the best."

"All of this took a toll on Trevor though. Eventually he had a mental breakdown, and after smashing his favorite violin in a fit of rage, he walked out of the New City Orchestra into a snowy winter's night. He was never seen again."

Shadow remembered that night well. Piretta had asked him to do another recital of a complex piece of music he didn't know on short notice. Piretta's comments when Shadow had said he didn't have time to learn the piece were burned into him. If Shadow couldn't fit practice for the recital in between practice for the season opener in two weeks and his teaching responsibilities, he should just stay later. They argued then, but it wasn't until Piretta left that Shadow had lost it. The boar always pushed his musicians hard, but he pushed Shadow, his concertmaster, the hardest. That night, the years of frustration had finally broken something inside of him.

Rocco nodded. "They say Trever committed suicide, but no body was ever found."

Shadow held out the violin to Rocco. "You can take this back. I'm not going back there. I haven't had a breakdown since I left, and I'm not going to put myself back in a situation like that."

Rocco shook his head. "The violin is yours to keep."

"I sleep on the street; I can't keep such an expensive instrument with me."

"Most people I asked about you thought if you weren't dead, you would still be performing out there somewhere. They said the music ran through your soul too deep for you to completely walk away. It took me months to find a lead on where you went, and even when I got lucky, I wasn't sure if it was really you. It wasn't until I went to city hall and looked at your busker license that I knew for sure."

"The license is the only way to get the cops to leave you alone," said Shadow.

"Why do you still perform?" asked Rocco, curious.

Shadow absently traced his finger pads across the edge of the violin again. He could feel himself starting to tear up. "The music is always there Rocco. I fall asleep, and I can still hear the notes floating through my sleep. I started drumming because to make it go away. Nobody is going to steal plastic buckets. They're not hard to replace if something does happen to them."

"You were born to play. You should be performing to an audience that deserves you."

Shadow flinched. "I don't want to be Trevor anymore. I just want to be me. Trevor was obsessed with being the best. Being Shadow, I get to focus on the mundane aspects of life. I set my own schedule and pace. Plastic buckets are imprecise things. They don't produce clear, crisp notes. Instead, they produce muddied tones. That's precisely why I started playing them. You have to work to get good sound from them. It's basic, yet it's still rewarding."

"I see," said the coyote. "If I tell people like Mrs. Soto you're out on the streets, they will come looking for you."

His ears flattened against his skull. "We had a deal. I'm happy out here. Can't you see that I can't go back? If I go back, it will begin again. I'm not doing that."

"You could be a star again. I'd have to start you in the back of the section, but you'd quickly get back to the first chair. Listening to you, I can see what Piretta saw in you."

"I told you; I'm not going back to that," Shadow hissed, feeling rising panic inside of himself. "I can't handle the pressure."

"You're still not putting down that violin either. You keep stroking it gently."

He had been stroking the violin, without even realizing it. He used to do that when he was thinking. He forced himself to walk over to the violin case and stooped down to get the money up out of it. "You told me if I did this job, you would keep my little secret." He gently laid the violin in the case and closed it.

"Today hasn't changed anything?"

Shadow stood and looked at the coyote. "Thank you, Rocco, for this opportunity, but I've had years to understand what I did." He held out the violin case to the coyote. "I know what I gave up and why."

Rocco's eyes widened in surprise. He looked down at the outstretched hand holding the violin case out to him and shook his head. "I see."

"Take this back, please."

The coyote scratched at an ear. "It's yours. If you don't want it, you can take it back yourself."

"I don't want it," pleaded Shadow.

Rocco shook his head. "Then take it back." He turned and started to walk away.

Shadow watched the coyote retreat across the street, ears down. His eyes followed Rocco, but he never turned to look back. He had expected Shadow would change his mind, that he would come back to the world he had left. He wasn't prepared for him to refuse.

Shadow lowered his arm and pressed his free hand up against his forehead. His head felt like it was going to split open. He held the violin case at his side, gently tugging on his arm. Quietly, he padded away from the park.

Shadow didn't count up the money he had earned until he returned back to his small campsite behind the construction site. His buckets, which he'd stashed under a ripped tarp, were still there. Laying out the money, he realized he made close to $100. Most days he made around $30, but today the wolf had done exceptionally well. Combined with the $50 Rocco had given him to do the job, he had plenty of money to put himself up in a hotel for the night with a bed and buy a good meal.

He still had the violin with him. It sat a few feet away on top of his buckets. He reached for it and pulled the case to himself. On days it rained, Shadow would huddle in whatever shelter he could find, trying to stay dry, praying for a break in the storm. He couldn't protect such an expensive instrument under those conditions.

The wolf opened the case and idly stared at the instrument for a few minutes before reaching down to pull the violin and the bow from the case. He brought it up to his chin and slowly ran the bow across the strings as lightly as he could. Soft, mournful notes floated out of its eloquent body as he idly tried to put his feelings to sound.

He could take the instrument back to the shop and return it. He could keep drumming, letting the sounds of the street be his accompaniment. He could even throw the instrument into a wall just to spite Rocco.

He closed his eyes, and kept playing softly. The mournful sounds coming to his ears became louder and louder as he felt himself start to cry while he played. When it became too much for him, he put the violin down and wept, tears staining his cheek fur. Suddenly, he threw back his head and howled. It was a feral sound, something he hadn't done since he was a kid.

He let himself go with the howl. He had given up his life for music and made it his passion. When that passion had become too demanding, he gave up that passion and ran away from it. Yet even at his lowest, he never had been able to give up music completely. He had made it his duty to play for the people on the street.

His long, pitiful howling emanated out from him like a death knell and slowly faded away. Afterward, Shadow felt childish and afraid someone would come looking for the source of the noise. Once, he had been a civilized person performing for the influential. Now, he was starting to act like a feral animal.

No matter how much he tried to deny it, no matter how much he pretended he didn't care, he missed playing the violin. The last five years, he had kept telling himself it was okay, that this is what he wanted. Today, he had stepped back into the sweet music of the violin and had tasted its intoxicating sound again. He could be first chair again. Trevor had been confident.

Trevor had been proud. Shadow could be all of those things again, if he would let that back into himself. The thrill of playing was still there.

Beyond that though was the darkness. The need to be better than everyone else. The drive to keep pushing that kept him playing alone at night. He kept the darkness at bay for five years, but the need was still there. The hunger was ready and waiting. All he needed to do was go back, and it would be like he'd never left.

In the gathering gloom of dusk, he picked up his pack and the violin case. There was no point in staying here. He could continue to wallow in his own self-pity or finally let the music carry him back. He glanced at the buckets and reached down to trace his hand against the lip of the stacked buckets.

The markings on his fur caught his eyes. He'd painted them on so he could be someone else. So he didn't have to be Trevor anymore. Trevor would destroy him if he let him come back. He took a deep breath and picked up the buckets. He walked away from the campsite.

Trevor Michaels played violin while Shadow was a street musician. He couldn't go back to the orchestra, but he could still indulge his passion. The people at the shelter could help him find a place he could afford on his tips. It wouldn't be easy, but he would figure it out somehow. The darkness inside of himself roared, but the music in his head played over it.

RUNAWAY
BANWYNN (SUTA) OAKSHADOW

An anorexic hobo with his ass on fire strolled down the shoulder of the interstate.

I was almost to Allentown when I saw the hitchhiker. I had meant to slow down and see what had triggered that odd image, not to stop. But there I sat on the shoulder, watching as a cross between a fox and a small man ran to the car. I figured that it was the red and white tail hanging out of the back of a shabby trench coat that made my mind say "fire." A red-furred hand tapped on the passenger window. I hit the button to unlock out of habit, and the first morph I'd seen in person climbed into my rental car.

I was low on gas, so refueling would provide a ready excuse to get rid of the kid in a couple minutes if I needed to.

Dammit! I hadn't even offered the kid my name, and was thinking of ways to ditch him. The guy was a kid no matter that he wasn't human; fifteen, maybe sixteen tops.

"Thanks, man. I've been walking for days. Seems that no one wants to give me a lift for some reason," a wry grin on the kid's mouth?—muzzle?

"So, where ya headed?"

The truth was the first thing that came to mind, and I said, "Atlanta."

"I'm not going anywhere in particular, so will go as far as you'll take me as long as it's away from New York."

I nodded and started the car moving again, "No worries, kid. Conversation on long drives is a valuable commodity."

"Does that mean that you should be paying me for providing conversation?" he asked with another of those yippy snickers.

"I guess it does. You're hired," I said. "The pay is food at whatever greasy spoon we end up at when I stop to refill. That okay with you?"

"Best offer that I've had in a long time." he said.

The kid shifted in his seat and looked like he was scratching his ass. I started worrying fleas and ticks when I realized that he was grabbing his tail. He eased it out from where it had been jammed between him and the seat. He draped it over his thigh. It was amazing. It looked soft, luxurious, and rich. The colors ran the gamut from bright orange to a muted umber, and the tip was a snow-blind white.

I realized that I was staring, and tried to watch the road. Despite my best efforts, I found myself trying to catch a look at the kid from the corner of my eye. I would jerk my attention back to the steering wheel when he glanced my way.

The fox started that odd yipping laugh again, and smiled at me, "It's okay Skin Man, you're going to give yourself a headache if you keep doing that. Go ahead and look. I don't mind. Let me guess, I'm the first morph you've ever seen for real, right?"

I blushed even deeper and met the kid's gaze, "Um, yeah. You are. I didn't want to be rude. Name's Drever."

"Ramble, good to meet you. I'm used to folks staring at me. I was born different, freakish. I happen to like how I look, so I'm not shy about it. Besides, I'd rather be getting curious stares than dodging rocks and bottles any day."

"Why 'Skin Man?' Is it the flip side of morph?"

"No, you got it wrong. It's a compliment but of the inside joke type. In *The Wizard of Oz*, the tin man wanted a heart and realized he had had one all along. It was his actions that showed it. The clock was just a symbol. Most humans treat us like dog turds on a paper plate. When we find one who actually seems to give a shit and treats us decent, we call them a Skin Man."

"Thank you for the compliment, Ramble. I'll do my best to keep earning it. Back to the subject at hand, you're not freakish. Yes, you're different, but I would say in an exotic kind of way. Even cute in a puppyish kind of way." *Damn!* "I'm sorry, Ramble. That sounded so condescending. I didn't mean that like it sounded."

"Easy, Drever. No offense taken. You meant it as a compliment, and that's how I took it. In fact, it's the first truly honest compliment that I have gotten since being tossed in the Zone."

"Thank you for understanding. I'm kind of in the deep end of the pool right now. I don't know what's insulting or tasteful or anything in between."

"How about we just talk, and if you are getting close to a 'fox paws,' I'll let you know."

I couldn't stop laughing for a bit. "Thanks, Ramble. I needed that." I decided to take the plunge since I was already in the deep end of the pool. "Ramble, your tail is magnificent. Would it be out of line or offensive if I asked to feel it?"

"Knock yourself out. I think it's my best feature. It stays beautiful, no matter what kind of filth it's dragged through."

I figured that there was a lot more hidden in that phrasing, but I let it go. He spread his thighs when I reached out to touch the tail. I refused to notice. I ran my hand under where it lay over his outer thigh and then lifted my hand up and away from him, causing the tail to flow between my fingers until it became a pool of fur on the seat cushion.

"I don't know how to describe it, but the feel of it pushes all of the other senses to the side. If it were much longer, we would be in a ditch or wrapped around something. Thank you for letting me touch it."

The kid's chuckle appeared a little confused. He shrugged it off and relaxed after re-draping it over his lap.

For the first few minutes after he got into the car, I noticed a distinct odor. It was like a mixture of urine and skunk musk, but not as powerful. Describing it makes it sound bad, but it wasn't. It wasn't a full-on, "in your face" kind of odor. It was rather more a scent than a smell; feral and right for the kid. I rarely noticed it after that.

What was served in the station's diner was bad, cheap, and plentiful. Ramble devoured everything in front of him. He appeared to be oblivious to the angry stares and mutterings. I noticed his ears pivoting, and his nostrils flaring and closing. He knew a hell of a lot more than I did about what the other diners thought of him...and how shitty the food was.

I was a bit pissed until I remembered my initial plan had been to ditch him right here. I had to swallow some of my own acidic anger at the others. I admitted to myself that I was a bigot and hypocrite when it came to morphs. Okay, I would let Ramble lead me down the paths to understanding morphs, their society, Zones, and things I didn't even know to ask about.

It would have been easy to drive away when Ramble ducked in to use the can. I had heard the desperate loneliness in the kid's voice. I had just seen his voracious appetite.

I was not a man who abandoned children. I knew perfectly well that Ramble had been forced into adulthood many years too soon. But I didn't. There was the child Ramble in his eyes. You do not abandon children. You did your very best to protect them; you die if you have to do it, if it will give them a chance. It is part of God's package deal when He gave us souls.

There was another very major reason. On her deathbed, the last thing my wife managed to whisper to me was, "Just stay the good man you are, and we can be with each other in Heaven."

"I'm sorry that I picked a place with such crappy food. I need gas and food to boot," I said.

"You kidding me? That was the first hot food I've tasted in a week. It's a whole lot better than what I ate back in the Zone. I shouldn't make you pay for everything. Except that I don't even have a credit," said Ramble. "Or did you stop here to let me off? If so, it's okay. You've been nicer to me than most, and I have a full belly of hot food."

"Ramble, if I wanted to ditch you, I would tell you that it was time to part ways, and would give you a few credits for food. So, if you are still tired of walking, get your butt in that seat so that we can get back on the road."

He hopped in and gave me a quizzical look.

As I grew more comfortable with my strange companion, I began to wonder just what it was about these people that most folks found threatening. Fur, muzzle, tail, and ears all said "animal"; but the fox's quick wit, sharp mind and infectious good humor all said that he was a person, and from what I had seen, a lot better one than many I've met.

The fox's conversation was constant and engaging, if a bit too crude for my taste. I figured that Ramble was not running away from a family, but from the streets that had been his home for some time. I wasn't about to pick him up like a stray, but decided that I could take the kid as far as Atlanta and see about hooking him up with Social Services there. I had heard that Corp Authority had special programs to help disadvantaged morphs.

Feeling a warm glow knowing that something could be done for the kid, I settled back and let the miles glide by under Ramble's constant, mostly fictitious, stream of stories. Many of his characters were actually from old TV programs such as the "Soup Nazi" from a particularly annoying one.

I countered with, "Where is Kermit's chef from?"

"Sweden. C'mon, that's the junior miss division. What was Samantha's mother's name in *Bewitched*?"

"I don't have a clue. One point to you. Who tended the door for the Addams Family?"

"Lurch! What was the name of Genie's Master's Co-pilot astronaut?"

"*Damn!* That's 2 for you, and I seriously doubt that this is your first time playing this game."

10 PM found us yawning over the remains of synthetic steaks in another cheap diner. This time, the glares and comments angered rather than embarrassed me, but Ramble didn't seem bothered. He lifted his head from the food long

enough to tell me that you get used to it, and it was a lot safer to let it go until it turned violent, in which case you ran like hell. I let it go as well. As I paid the check, I decided that I was done driving for the day. My expense account would cover a Radisson, but I decided to spring for two rooms in a less expensive motel instead. I didn't want the kid thinking I expected to be paid for giving him a lift. Not in the trade by which, I was pretty sure, was his only means of keeping starvation at bay and not quite freezing.

What could I do that would make him understand that I didn't want to fuck him to pay for the ride? That I didn't think that he owed me anything? That I just wanted to be allowed to help. Was he too scarred inside to ever believe such a thing?

I started, "Kid, we gotta talk. I promise that I am not going to ditch you. Like I said a minute ago, if that happens, it will be someplace safe, where you may be able to catch another ride, and with some money in your pocket. Do you understand what I'm saying?"

He looked at me and nodded. I could see that he didn't believe it. Everything was a lie until proven otherwise.

"Okay, let's try the flip side and see if you will believe me then. If you decide that you are tired of my company, I will drop you off with money for food. Open the glove compartment. Do you see a map in there?"

He nodded, but was trying to figure out what my angle was.

"Open the map twice. Now flip it upside down over your lap."

A CRN card fell into his lap.

"It's my emergency stash. It's only 50crn, but it's not account-registered. It is an open card that can be used by anyone. Put it in your pocket. It's yours."

Ramble had looked a little confused when I handed the fox the keycard to a room of his own, and had to argue a bit before he would accept it. Ramble told him that he didn't mind sharing a room with me...or a bed. I pretended to misunderstand and explained that my expense account covered a certain amount for lodging each day and that Accounting would not care whether it was spent on two cheap rooms or one more expensive one. Ramble gave in and entered the small room with its lumpy, queen-sized bed, rickety dresser, and small, plastic shower. I chuckled to myself as I went into my own cheap and dingy room. I felt like I was roughing it with these pitiful accommodations, but knew that the fox was finding his to be more luxurious and extravagant than he had seen in his life on the streets.

I hoped that Ramble believed he was free to make his own way any time he chose, and that I didn't expect to fuck him as part of the deal. Part of me also had to admit that I was not sure that I could trust even a good street kid not to make off with my money and watch in the middle of the night should they—*we*—share a room. Fuck! I had forgotten all about the 9mm I kept in the springs of the passenger seat. I had put it under the seat of so many rental cars that I didn't think about it.

I had to get that. I opened the door and headed for the stairs.

"You don't need to hide. Thanks for the ride, food, and company, Drever." He had been out, leaning on the rail, expecting me to ditch him.

"Back it up, kiddo! This crap has got to stop. I know some of the things that you've had to do back in the Zone and out here in exchange for rides. I know what you have offered me several times. I have struggled to be the kind of man that Macey would proud of. What would she say? 'Go ahead and molest a child. It doesn't count if they have fur.' I know that you are hurt and scarred inside, and have good reason for most of what you do, but I am damn tired of being insulted when you think I expect to screw you, or when you accuse me of dumping you. How many times could I have ditched you if that was what I wanted to do? I like your smell, even if it's not for everyone. Your coat is a different story. It smells like it was used to pick up road-killed opossums and store then under the sun until winter. I remembered that I have a warm jacket in the trunk with my samples and other traveling gear." I rooted around and pulled it from the mess, went up, and tossed it to him, "I was worried about a desperate street kid ripping me off and running. You were sure that you were going to be ditched. Are we okay?"

Ramble looked at the jacket in his hand and then back to me. I refused to notice a bit of moisture collecting there, "Yeah, we're good. Good dreams."

After shutting the door, I shuddered to think of the kind of dreams a kid like Ramble had.

It must have been sometime after midnight when I was jerked out of sleep by the frantic pounding at my door. I had jumped out of bed and flung open my door to find myself with an armful of hysterical foxmorph. I half-carried, half-pulled him inside and sat him on the bed. It was a long time before I got anything coherent, and it was almost dawn before I had the whole story from the young fox.

I had been right about Ramble and his life on the streets and of the things he had been forced to do to stay alive. Much of what I heard disgusted me, but my revulsion was reserved for the men that could use a child that way, not with Ramble himself. That was how the poor kid was used.

"Okay, I understand that much. You had a friend back in the Zone. And that he was too afraid to leave with you. Was he supposed to join you once you had gotten away? What has you so terrified right now?"

"I...I...I called Sabyl. I wanted him to know that I was okay. That I'd gotten away. I wanted him to know that I'd found someone who was helping me make it to someplace where he could come too."

"And what happened when you called him?"

"He...He...answered!" Ramble began wailing again, and it took several more minutes to calm him down enough to understand.

"What is wrong with that? Isn't that why you called him?"

"You don't understand! It wasn't Sabyl who answered the phone! It was Him!"

"Your manager?" In spite of knowing about his past and the overt sexual advances the young morph had made, I had a hard time even using words like "pimp" to a child. In spite of his outward toughness, I knew that the moaning fox in my arms was still a child.

"Yes! He said that he knew all about us. He said he had caught Sabyl packing to follow me. He caught him! And...and...he killed him! He said that I was next. That what is his, stays his...forever."

"Oh my God!" I wrapped my arms around Ramble and helped support him as the fox vomited and began to choke. When I reached for the phone to call the police, I was sure that Ramble's panicked wail would bring the police all by itself. I realized how it would look if anyone found me in a motel room in my underwear with a naked morph, for I had just realized that Ramble was wearing his fur and nothing else. If not for that realization, I would have argued harder when Ramble begged me not to.

"No, please! You...you can't. It won't help. He is too smart, and the Corp wouldn't care anyways. They don't give a fuck what happens to us in the Zone unless a skin is involved. Please, we have to get out of here. He is going to find me too! Oh God! Sabyl I'm sorry! I'm so sorry!"

"Sabyl wasn't just a friend was he?"

The head crying against his head shook.

"Your boyfriend?"

A sobbing nod.

"Oh, Ramble. I'm so sorry. I am so very sorry for both of you."

I just rocked the furry bundle of misery and stroked him while I let Ramble cry it out and begin to come to terms with his loss.

Much later, the fox just leaned against me, sniffling, but calmer. I suspected that horror and grief were being replaced by the numbness of denial. I could still see panic in the kid's eyes and tried to soothe him.

"You are alright, Ramble. You are safe. He can't find you here. He does not know where you are. You are safe."

"No, I'm not. Neither of us is. He can find me! He can trace the call or something. He is rich and powerful and won't let me get away! He's going to find me. Please! We have to leave. We have to leave now!"

I was not sure what was involved in tracing a phone call but suspected that it was more than some grungy street pimp could manage. To the kid's mind, some flashy gold chains and a string of call boys were symbols of power and wealth.

I continued to stroke and rock Ramble and convinced him that we needed sleep before I could drive anywhere. We were more than a day's drive from New York, and waiting a few hours couldn't hurt us.

We left before 10 AM, after I had made a trip to Ramble's room to collect his clothes. Ramble had made another invitation to share more than the bed. I refused, though I didn't stop stroking and rocking the child in desperate need to be held, whether he admitted it or not. The fox had fallen asleep on his bed while I drifted in and out of dozing while keeping watch over him from a chair beside the bed.

When he woke, he pulled back the cover to show a couple inches of moist, pink penis rising from his sheath. That did it.

"Cover yourself for fuck's sake! I feel like puking just thinking about anyone who could use you that way. Is this your way of testing what I meant when I gave you the jacket? You win. I'll be in the car when you're ready to go."

We didn't stop for breakfast, and lunch was a quick affair at McDonald's. Ramble didn't eat anything, fear overpowering appetite. I knew that the fox was safe, but saw how putting distance between us and the motel eased the distraught kid and so I made the best time I could without getting a ticket. Ramble was quiet throughout the drive, sunk in on himself, and speaking only when asked a question. I glanced over several times to see tears wetting the fur of his cheeks. I contented myself with being there when he realized that he needed to talk about it. Other than that, I gave the kid time and silent respect as he dealt with the death of his young lover. I wasn't gay, but I was no homophobe, and could see that the fox's loss was as real and unreal to him as I had been when breast cancer took Macey from me. Sometimes you just need solitude without being alone.

Dinner found us just on the far side of Petersburg, Virginia where 85 diverged from 95. We ate at yet another greasy spoon. I was getting sick of cheap diners, but the Olive Garden we had tried first refused to admit Ramble, pointing to a "We Reserve the Right to Refuse Service" sign on the wall, and a hand scrawled one under it that said "No Fur!" I thought about it as I paid the bill and headed back to the car.

Ramble had wanted to wait in the car, announcing that he was not hungry. I convinced him to try and eat something. He finished what I ordered for him, and then headed back out to the car as soon as he was done. I headed out not far behind him, but the fox was nowhere to be seen.

As I looked around the parking lot, I could not see him, and began worrying about what Ramble might do to himself in his current despair. I heard a frightened squeak coming from behind the dumpsters and saw the young morph waving to me, gesturing to go fast and stay slow. He kept pointing across the parking lot at a new, white Lexus Tyrant sitting under one of the lot's flickering yellow lights.

"It's him! I told you that he would find me! I told you! Oh God! We're going to die!"

I didn't believe for the slightest moment that the boogieman from the Zone was sitting in that car but could not help the chill that gripped my spine as I realized that Ramble believed he was. That not only was his life forfeit now, but that mine was too for having helped him to escape.

"Ramble! Ramble! Listen to me! That is not him. That can't be him. How could he have driven here so fast? He couldn't, now could he? Stop for a minute and think about it. That can't be him in that car." I glanced again at it and noticed something else. "Ramble, the plates are local. That car isn't even from New York. I don't know what made you think it was him in the car, but those flickering lights can play tricks with you. Now calm down. Try to breathe."

Ramble took several deep breaths but still trembled. I decided that the best course of action would be to get him in the car and put some distance between us and the diner before trying to reason with him.

"Ramble, listen to me. I am here with you, and I am not going to let anything happen to you. We are going to walk to the car now, and then we are going to get out of here. Nothing bad is going to happen to you. I won't let it."

I was able to get us moving toward my rental car while Ramble tried to hide behind me. Realizing that no matter how irrational the terror was, it was very real to the fox. I started the car and drove out of the lot. As I passed the Lexus, I couldn't help glancing in the open driver's side window. Staring back at me was a white- and silver-furred face pierced with two ice blue eyes. The tiger's muzzle wrinkled in a twisted smile in a way that said clearer than words, "Dead." I knew how the mouse must feel. My bowels threatened to cut loose as I jerked the wheel over, and slammed my foot down on the gas.

On the floor, Ramble buried his muzzle in his tail and continued to mutter, "We're going to die...we're going to die..."

I couldn't think of anything comforting to say.

I had intended to take I-95 down to I-20 and then over to Atlanta, but instead I jumped onto I-85, and then almost off of it onto Hwy 460. I had no idea where it would take us, but understood Ramble's terrified desire to put distance between us and the tiger. I had only heard "Zone" and "pimp" and pictured some mangy catmorph in a velvet suit and wide-brimmed hat standing on a street corner flashing gold chains as he hawked his wares. It took money to fly anywhere on no notice. It must have taken money and the power that Ramble had warned me about to track their location. Power that I didn't even want to think about, but realized that I had to if we were to survive. Hell, it had only taken one brief glance into those eyes to understand the true meaning of power. Those had been the eyes of a predator; and in them I had seen death.

How the hell was this happening? What the fuck was I supposed to do next? I was no big hero. I sold marble and granite floors to businesses and upscale apartments.

I tried to force myself to calm down, to think. The same things that I had urged to Ramble just minutes earlier. It wasn't working. I prayed for a city, a town anyplace that would have a Corp Authority station. Hell, even someplace that I could call Corp from. I should have headed north on 95 and back into Petersburg! I remembered my cell phone, and even as I dug it out of my pocket, it rang. The shrill beep made me drop it, and it rang several times before I could force my trembling fingers to pick it up. I thumbed the talk button and was greeted by a voice I had never heard, but did not need to be told.

"Nice evening for a drive, isn't it? You have something of mine, and I would appreciate it if you gave it back to me right now."

My throat was dry, and I realized that my lap was hot and wet. I forced myself to answer as piss pooled between my legs and ran down the seat.

"I have already called the Corp. They know where I am, and a cruiser is already on the way!"

The churfing sound from the other end sounded foreign, but unmistakable as anything other than an amused chuckle, "You are a bad liar, Mr. Arcturus Drever, 4593 Autumn Street, Newark, New Jersey. That pot bust when you were young must have crushed some dreams for you. My condolences for the loss of your wife. Are you so ready to be with her again that you are willing to die? I mean here, this day...knowing that it would be? Knowing that so many things will be left unfinished. You shouldn't lie to me. No one lies to me. I was just going to let you go, but now, you are going to have to be punished. If you stop right now, and give me what is mine, I am still willing to be generous with you. I am still willing to let you live."

The sound of my name coming from that mouth destroyed my ability to think. Panic was all I had left. I felt an overwhelming need to make the voice stop and flung the phone away from me. The device hit the steering wheel and was out the window before I realized my tragic mistake.

My eyes were drawn to the rearview mirror, and off in the distance, I saw headlights flashing. It was still too early for someone to need their headlights, and they were not the lights of rescuers. Twin bright beams flashed bright and then off then bright and off and bright...the lights went out for good.

He knew who I was. He knew where I was. I had something that the tiger wanted, and the bastard was not going to stop until he got it. Fingers gripping the steering wheel so hard that my knuckles popped, sitting in a cooling pool of my own piss, eyes staring at the road, I thundered down refusing to anything. On the floor, Ramble's reaction appeared to be just the opposite. Desperation seemed to wash away terror, and he was scanning the crumpled roadmap.

"Here! Here! Turn here, there's a road just ahead. He won't find us if we can get off the main roads! Turn here!"

I heard the words, but they didn't make sense until red-furred fingers grabbed the wheel and pulled it to the right. Tires screamed in protest as the car slid onto the graveled shoulder. I snapped back to myself and turned the wheel even further as I fought the fishtailing vehicle onto the exit at around ninety miles an hour. For an eternal second, the tires threatened to give up the fight. They grabbed the asphalt, and we were racing down a country road in the middle of nowhere, with the needle buried and no idea of where I was heading and praying for the sun to set and bring a welcome shroud of darkness in which to hide. Somehow all of that frightened me much less than the thought of looking up and seeing headlights flash in the rearview mirror.

Somewhere inside me, a voice kept repeating, "We're going to die...we're going to die."

I could have closed my eyes and not noticed much difference. The road, like the landscape around us was empty. I could look in any direction and not see a single building, just fields of something grassy and the occasional stand of trees. I was forced to slow down when potholes seemed more common than pavement and felt the crunch as the pavement disappeared altogether and gave way to dirt.

"Ramble, where are we? Is this the right road? Where are you taking us?"

"I don't know! The map says this is the right road. It says that there's a river ahead and that there's a town just on the other side."

"Okay. Great! We are okay now. We're going to be okay. Just hang in there. We're going to be okay." I could not have said who I was trying to convince.

A short time later Ramble's prediction proved correct, and we could see the river ahead. And there our luck ended. We were on a single graveled lane between hayfields. There was no welcoming bridge to salvation; instead the road turned to follow the much larger waterway. I moaned when the back end of the car spun around as I took the turn too fast. Dry dirt gave me no traction to work. I pumped the brake over and over as the car slid off of the road. Large rocks, cleared from the fields season after season scraped under the car. I thought that we might still make it back onto the road when a jerking crunch and a metallic scream announced the car's demise.

Ramble curled back into a ball on the floor wailing, "I'm sorry, I'm sorry! I'm sorry!"

I tried to comfort the fox, "It's okay, Ramble. It's not your fault. Ramble, it's not your fault. We need to get out of here. Now help me! We can run for the trees. We can swim the river. We can do something. But we need to get out of here now!"

On the floor Ramble continued his litany, "I'm sorry! I'm sorry!"

I threw open his door and reached down to drag the fox from the car. As I muscled Ramble out onto the grass, he looked over his shoulder.

In the distance headlights flashed. On...off... on...off...

Jerking Ramble upright, I grabbed his arm and pulled him behind as we fled toward the distant trees. We were halfway to the river when the crunch of tires on dirt and gravel announced the arrival of the tiger. There was nowhere left to run. With nowhere left to run, I discovered that I no longer needed one.

I turned to face the approaching tiger while screaming at Ramble to flee for the safety of the river. I knew that I was dead, but at least I might stop the beast long enough for the kid to get away. Somewhere inside myself I realized that I had known the child less than two days and was already closer to him than I had allowed himself to be with anyone since my wife died. Part of me died with her that day. Maybe the rest of me had stayed alive for this one thing. So that I could give someone else a chance to be free.

I heard Drever's urgent pleas. He saw the river right there, and the safety on the other side. He knew that I could make it. He could not stop Alexander, but he tried to slow him down...for a twisted, freak, rent boy from far over the wrong side of the tracks. He tried to give me time. Time to reach either freedom or a watery grave. I could make it. But I didn't run.

I could feel Drever's confusion as he turned to me.

I said, "I'm sorry. It wasn't supposed to be like this. I didn't know about people like you. No one has ever cared for just me, and not for what they wanted from me. No one has ever trusted me before. I'm so fucking sorry!" He took a step toward the towering feline and the man trotting behind him.

I didn't need to look back as I strode past him. I tossed Drever's 9mm in the grass, and continued to Alexander. The big tiger bent down to kiss me, and tell me that I had done a wonderful job. I didn't stop for the kiss or praise. I couldn't look back. I had seen pretty much the same looks on all of the previous fish. I didn't want to see his.

I didn't pause as I passed the well-dressed man carrying the holocam. He went running after Alexander and wailed about the fading light.

The passenger seat of the Lexus was soft leather that wrapped me in a luxurious embrace as I took my place and closed the door. The window had polarized, tinted but offered a clear view had I chosen to look out. Instead I stared at the small rectangle of plastic on the dashboard. It had my name on it. The digital display in the corner read 5,000crn. I wasn't going to get to use it, but grabbed it anyways.

As I sat, I thought about the hunt. Hooking the fish. It wasn't supposed to have been this way. I was supposed to get him to fuck me. Why hadn't Drever just fucked me? It was supposed to be that way. Some of the fish didn't even wait to be asked. He was supposed to have been like the others. But no, he had to be different. A savior. A rescuer. He had to care. That changed everything.

The car, designed to block out the annoying sounds of the road and traffic, did little to muffle the screams. They went on for a very long time.

I didn't look up when Alexander and Robert returned to the car. Robert, with his special itch. Robert, with the money to pay Alexander to scratch it. Robert, the voyeur with a taste for blood.

I had thought that he was like the others when I slipped the tracker onto the car, and called Alexander from the first diner to tell him that the hunt was on. The fish had the same guilty, furtive, longing look. He'd called me exotic and cute. He wanted to touch my tail. He was supposed to have been like the others. If he had gotten a single room it would have all been so much simpler. Once you had them in your mouth or up your ass, the rest came easy. Then it was just a gentle push to get them someplace remote enough for Robert to make them a star.

But not Drever. He refused to follow the script. He had forced the young angler to improvise, to find some other bait for his hook. I was proud of my little performance. The tears. Poor, dead Sabyl. The hysterical vomiting.

Only that wasn't really acting, was it? Realizing what kind of man I was leading to slaughter.

Sabyl. Safe and sound back in the pad that Alexander provided. Sabyl, the little bunny who was not too old to ignite the tiger's passions, and spent more nights with Alexander in a week than I did in a month. A regimen of growth hormone inhibitors starting in early puberty and a cub could be seventeen and still look twelve. I was twenty-three and looked sixteen. Too old to get the good tricks. Sabyl now filled that role.

I chuckled. I may not have been able to stop growing up for the tiger, but he knew that it was still me who held the tiger's heart. I was the angler. I was the one who could bring in the fish.

Those seconds before and after "Are we good?" at the hotel... Drever had never been a fish. The only thing he had done wrong was try to help the wrong kid.

I didn't know. Everyone played by the rules and I stacked the deck. But Drever didn't want to play cards. He wanted to give a bent and twisted kid a future.

Calling Alexander and begging him to drop the hunt, that I would find a better one. No answer. Just a "call ended" tone.

Seeing him reaching under the passenger seat before abandoning the dead car; the weapon already tucked into the back of my pants. Drever realizing that he was dead, pushing me behind him, yelling to me to make a run for it. Spending the last moments of his life trying to buy me a chance to escape. Would he have done the same if he knew what Alexander had planned for him? I didn't need to think about it. I knew. I knew that he would do what he had done all over again as long as he thought that it would buy me a chance to escape.

Drever had held me and rocked me, holding and stroking, not for any carnal reward, but because he cared about me. He had known me for two whole days, and had done all of this because he gave a shit...even when no one else did...not even me.

Now I know how being cared about feels. I know that it is the only time I will ever feel it.

Drever had been true, caring, giving, and sharing a thousand times. I fuck up my very first one.

I didn't know that I was going to do it, until I was bent over and puking on the floor. This time, it was no act.

I didn't look up as Robert's pants were ripped down around his knees. I didn't look, but could hear the grunts and moans as Alexander bit the photographer's shoulder and began thrusting into him. I didn't look at Robert's cock, squashed against the window, or at the two bloody paws pressed against the glass on either side of his hips. I knew that Alexander had chosen to fuck Robert just there, putting on a show for me as he finished his arrangement with his john. Telling me, showing me, that they are all just tricks...except Drever, who only wanted to give me a chance at happiness. This sure as fuck wasn't happiness.

In the end, they're all tricks. They all need something from you. He had needed me to need him. Always give the john what they want.

I don't want to feel this way.

I slid out the driver's door since mine was in use.

It wasn't supposed to be like that.

He didn't seem like he was the kind of man who would put a screwed-up kid back out on the streets. The only things he wanted from me was for me to be safe and have a chance to be happy. No muzzle or ass in return. What the fuck had I done?

I took off the jacket and left it in the field. I didn't deserve to wear it.

It wasn't supposed to feel like this.

Robert had been the one to foot the bill for this trick, but I had given Drever full measure all the same.

It wasn't supposed to be like that.

"Ramble."

Slipping the cell phone from him had been easy. Calling Alexander on it and slipping it back had been even easier.

It wasn't supposed to be like that. Tears made it hard to see. Who cares?

"Ramble?"

I almost laughed when I thought of our marvelous getaway, with the tiger listening on the other end the whole time.

It wasn't supposed to be like that! I tossed the 5,000crn card into whatever was growing in the field. The 50crn in my other hand was much more valuable.

"Ramble, goddammit! Where the fuck do you think you're going?"

I had to admire Alexander's timing. The bit with breaking the connection and calling right back as I grabbed his phone had been priceless.

"You forget that you belong to me, meat? You have about one second to turn your ass around and get back in the fucking car!"

I wasn't supposed to be empty like this.

I won't feel it, but I deserve to.

This is how it's gotta be.

Lights out.

Pride goeth before destruction, and a haughty spirit before a fall.
Proverbs 16:18 (KJV)

SHELTER
AVIN TELFER

"I knew I'd find you here."

Todd didn't have to look at his watch to know he must have missed the daily stand up in the common room. Why else would Sarah come to the observation deck?

"I have nothing to report," said the otter with a heavy sigh.

"You still have to make the meetings," Sarah replied with a sigh of her own. "How can I convince the crew to show up and report if I can't even get the captain to come?"

Todd had to admit, she was right. "Tell them I had an important task, and I apologize for my absence."

"What? An important meeting with the starfish? Writing a journal on what it was once like to be able to swim? Or were you just imagining all the different ways we could get rescued?"

In front of Todd was the largest window on the ship. The glass was at least 6" thick, Todd guessed. He couldn't quite remember the specs off the top of his head. They were lucky they were close enough to the surface to have some light. Both for the solar chargers floating above them, and so he could look out the window and still see wildlife without turning on the external spotlights.

Finally turning his attention to her, Todd asked, "When is the last time a system was abnormal, Sarah?"

Sarah looked at her tablet. "Well, the salt water purifier was showing unusually high levels of—"

"—All within normal parameters" Todd interrupted, waving his hand in a dismissive motion. "I mean really, when is the last time this vessel had a maintenance issue?"

Sarah thought for a moment, before answering. "If we don't keep an eye on the ship's systems, sir, the whole colony could die."

That made Todd laugh. "I still prefer the original title of 'Research Station' more than colony."

"Sir, if I may speak freely?"

Todd gave a nod.

"When is the last time any of us, besides you, did any work on our research?"

Todd couldn't recall. Months, for sure. Had it been more than a year already? "I don't know." He replied honestly.

"Do you think that is a problem?"

Todd had to think about this one.

When he didn't reply right away, Sarah continued, "Like it or not, the mission has changed. Since our lives are at stake, maybe you should put the same effort into our new mission you did the old one?"

Todd stared at her for a moment, and then turned back to look out the window.

She reached a paw out and touched Todd's shoulder. "I'm sorry."

"You're not wrong, Sarah." He imagined her stern pointed features slowly turning from something like anger into...sadness, possibly? He did not want to turn his head to find out. The truth was, he had no idea how she truly felt lately, and he did not want to ask. He hoped Sarah was understanding, his closest and possibly last living friend. He didn't want to know for sure if she was growing tired of him.

With no further reply, Sarah took her hand off his shoulder and climbed back down the access tube. Todd was once again alone.

The observation deck was designed to fit three researchers comfortably. Maybe only one or two, if some of them weren't otters. Then again, anyone besides an otter usually had a hard time getting through the crawl tubes in the first place.

Todd reached out and picked up one of his tablets from the other side of the room. There was still enough time left in the day to get a few more things done.

He decided to do another round of measurements. He pulled up the appropriate app on the tablet in his hand, and checked the size and location of all the coral he could see in front of him through the observation window. The data would not be ideal, as he had not been as vigilant as he should have been at taking measurements at a standard interval.

As he entered each measurement, he noted how long it had been since he last updated them. Six full months had passed since his last entry. He took this as good news, rather than bad. It was a lot less time than he feared. There was too much work to be done, and not enough hours in the day for one researcher to do it. It would be easy to slip up and make the data less useful.

He wished his team had the same drive he did. At least, Todd thought, he never had to fight for equipment time or extra hard drive space. As the captain, and the only one left doing research on the station, he could do as he pleased.

Before, he was always dealing with some bureaucratic task. Lobbying for more equipment time, filing reports to his higher ups, doing performance reviews for his staff. He wished he could go back to that life now. Go back to when everything was normal, where his worries were so trivial. Now, the things that distracted him were about survival.

He wanted to believe there were others out there in a better position. He wanted to believe that the world was not as bad as it seemed it might be from his position. He wanted to believe that his wife was out there, probably tending to her garden as he sat here and measured the growth of the coral reef.

Sarah's attempts to reason with him always had the opposite effect from what he suspected she intended. She had been pleading to him for months to finally stop his research. To take the scientist hat off, as the rest of the crew had. But every time she tried to convince him, it just made his conviction stronger. Why should he accept inevitable death, when he could build something greater than himself?

He fully believed they would die long before the research station would have maintenance issues. The station was top of the line when it was built; the designers seemed to have thought of everything. Their air was recycled, and their water passed through triple purification filters. They got energy from the sun, through a floating solar array connected by multiple long flexible pipes. The floating platform also had cameras and weather equipment, serving as their connection to the outside world.

Well, at least it did when there was an outside world to communicate to. Now, it served more as a reminder that there seemed to be no one living within hundreds if not thousands of miles from their location. You could still see the clouds from the mushroom blasts looming overhead.

The only technology that didn't work was their communication involving satellites, and there was no way of knowing if that was due to the radiation in the atmosphere, unknown damage to their systems, or…well, perhaps there were no more satellites left to communicate with.

This was the perfect self-sustaining underwater facility. Designed for zero environmental impact, and wound up becoming one of the most advanced "accidental fallout shelters" in the entire world.

Lucky them.

There had many discussions about trying to leave. Even in the most optimistic projections, it was determined they would die long before they could find another shelter or other possible survivors. They had neither seen a boat nor heard any radio communications since the first blast.

At their depth, between the water and the thick pressurized hauls, they were fully protected from the fallout. They had a small algae farm that was once Peterson's research, and now served as their primary food source that would have to last them for the rest of their lives.

In a way, it was almost perfect. A smart team of highly skilled otters who knew biology, mechanics, computer programming...Half of them had already been fucking each other even before they realized they might be stuck for the next ten or fifteen years. There was just one weakness in their survival plan...

Fresh water. Either through the algae farm, or by catching/raising fish, they needed to collect new water to survive. Purification filters and boiling only went so far. Eventually, they will find a fish specimen that has been tainted, and it will be over. By the time they could detect it in the fish, the water they'd been farming and drinking will have been contaminated for months.

At first, they wouldn't notice. Perhaps they'd only lose their appetite or experience minor pain. But it would be deadly, no doubt about it. From their position, there would be nothing they could do to survive the time needed for the radiation to subside.

It was only a matter of time. They probably have already been exposed, to an extent. Sarah and the others knew this they had to know this. It was the one variable they couldn't control for. The one part of their plan they couldn't fix, no matter what.

It made complete sense to Todd that they would simply chose to ignore it. In their mind, they had to act like they had a chance of surviving. That was most important to them, even if they likely would fail.

Not for Todd, though. His life was not that important. What value was the lives of a few otters trapped for years in a post-apocalyptic world? The entire world could be blown up, for all they knew. The battle hadn't started near them, and it likely wouldn't finish near them either.

What mattered now was his task. His profession. What he trained his whole life to do. To study. To research. To analyze.

His reports were more important than ever. Who would find them first? Would it be a rescue team? Explorers from a new culture hundreds of years from now? Or perhaps, even, aliens from another planet?

His audience was not his peers any longer. It was someone else. They would need to know how the ocean floor reacted. Did the coral still grow after the blast? What mutant creatures would emerge, if any? Science was more important than his life. Than anyone's life. Knowledge had to continue.

It shouldn't all be lost now.

In some future time when their bodies were discovered, this research could be the key to the study of long extinct species.

He finished taking down all the measurements he could, and decided it was time to sleep. As he climbed down from the observation deck, he could hear the sound of voices talking in various hallways of the ship. Whether the crew liked it that way or not, he seemed to be the only one on the ship that was regularly alone.

When he made his way to the heart of the ship, the conversations seemed to quiet down. They all went back to focus on their various tasks. Todd didn't even know who was in charge of what anymore; he had given Sarah full control over operations so he could spend more time with his research.

Despite not wanting to continue their conversations around him, no one seemed to pay any attention to him as he crawled past. They were distracted by planting algae on the walls of labs where it was not meant to grow, running pointless diagnostic checks on any and all equipment, or he imagined they'd be spending whatever free time they had left hooking up with whoever happened to be also off-shift.

Todd had given up his private room over a year ago to the survival effort. He couldn't even remember what it was currently being used for. He didn't care; he now only had his desk and what space he could take underneath it.

They would even take that away from him if they could, he thought. The research systems were the most advanced equipment on the ship. He plugged his tablets into his desktop and synced all the findings he had recorded today. They were automatically translated into as many languages as the computer could handle and duplicated onto every backup storage on the station. There was a long way to go before all the hard drives would fill up, and he intended to put as much as he could on them before they all died.

Already, it would take a team months to parse through all the data he had been able to collect so far. For all he knew, he could be in charge of the last remaining collection of scientific data in the world. Everything had to be archived like a historian, not just a researcher.

He pulled out his bedroll and settled in. There were no such thing as quiet hours on the ship anymore. At any hour of the day, the sound of someone or something echoed down to the main chamber. Otters would have to crawl over him to get from point A to B. He had grown used to it, he could sleep anywhere now. He never listened to them anymore.

Tonight, it was more quiet than usual. He put on a blindfold and ear plugs anyway, so his sleep wouldn't be disturbed when things picked up. He lay down on top of his bed roll, and thought again about the trouble of the crew abandoning their research. All those worries that he pushed to the back of his mind had been distracting him more as of late, and it made it hard for him sometimes to focus on his research.

Eventually, Sarah would be forced by the crew to make him choose between his duties as a captain and continuing his research. While he was in charge, he didn't think the crew would agree he was making the right choice. The last thing he needed was for the crew to start panicking.

With a sigh of relief, he finally made the mental choice to step down. Tomorrow, during the daily standup meeting, he'll announce Sarah will take over his duties as captain. At least in title, if that would make the crew happy.

He laughed as he imagined the scene she'll make when she finds out. Sure, she'll chew him out for not accepting his responsibility, but deep down inside he imagined she would be relieved more than anything. She'll appreciate having some control in her life again. Control, at least, over the rest of the crew.

Not him.

He hoped Sarah would be a good captain and not interfere with his research. Perhaps she'll surprise him, and with the promotion she'll reprioritize the original goal of this mission.

After all, what good is being captain, or even "president" of one of the last known living "colonies" if you wanted to call it that, if you couldn't be allowed to focus your time on your life's work?

Todd dreamed he was back home in his wife's garden, lying down on the soft dirt rather than his well-worn bed roll. He imagined his wife and family coming out to join him, surrounding him. There was so much he wanted to talk to them about, but at this point their voices had all faded from his memory. Now, even when he dreamed, he heard nothing but the low murmur of the crew's voices echoing down the corridors.

Tonight, his recurring dream was different. The voices seemed both louder, closer, and yet hushed like they were whispering. He couldn't make out what they were saying, but they seemed more real.

Suddenly, he felt trapped. The otters that surrounded him grabbed his limbs and held him down. He felt what he thought was a snake bite him in the arm, and someone pulled off his blindfold. His eyes flashed open for only a second before closing, blinded by the brightness of the light. He couldn't move his arms or legs, and as he struggled against the weight of a dozen hands holding him down. He felt his limbs growing cold and numb.

His mind wandered again, and he was back in the garden. He was aware there were others, but he only saw the beautiful face of his wife in front of him.

Was it his wife? The memories seemed to fade faster now. She touched him, but they were not the gentle fingers he remembered. She sounded like she was crying, but it was not her tears. He thought she seemed younger. Her face was narrower, more pointed in shape. Her fur a darker shade of brown than it should have been, like Sarah's.

The pain from the snake bite was gone now, and his body lay still. He could no longer feel anything. Had they let him go? If so, why couldn't he move? He imagined that the otter who in his mind was no longer his wife spoke to him, but it was not really her voice. He could not say exactly who she sounded like; the only voice he could remember now was Sarah's telling him that he should have stepped down weeks ago.

He felt his numb body being lifted now, plucked and carried away like the other vegetables in the garden. He tried to scream, but realized his mouth was gagged. The more he tried struggle, the more tired he grew.

Todd hoped that no matter what happened next, they would not erase any of the archives. They could take any of the equipment he had. All of it, if they wanted. They could take his life too if they demanded it. He wanted to have more time before he died, but he had done all that he could do. All that work had to have mattered.

He could no longer protect it. He hoped Sarah would understand. He didn't want her to stop them; he didn't want her to save him: he only cared if she preserved his research.

Right before Todd completely lost consciousness, he kept repeating the thought to himself that his research, not him, was the only thing that mattered.

It would be up to her now.

DROP TOWER
VARZEN

As urine trickled between his eyes, down his lean chest, around his erection, and onto the pink Alabama marble between his knees, bat Alexi Rosenbath thought of the teenage girls and their seasonal stampede. As shapely goat starlet Daani Asrighelli held her labia spread between two fingers and moaned above him, chanting out condescending entreaties as his "goat-mom," Alexi counted embossed designer blouses on his dry foot-hand, imagining mewling pubescents wearing this uniform as they foisted their phones in the air, their screens filled with her face, their headphone cords jiggling attached to earbuds stuffed in giant furry ears.

The pop sensation's piss hit him in his cupped vampire nose when she called his name and he raised his head. Snuffling the salty water as the stream subsided, Alexi asked her to repeat herself.

"I said everyone wants to be me but you!" she declared, pushing him over into the puddle. His rump hit the floor with a splash that echoed in the grand ballroom surrounding them. At the far end, a servant opened and then closed a tall embroidered wooden door.

"Why, yes, I'd sooner be *with* you," he answered, his ears turning as her hooves clacked away from him. Daani bent down low over a chest, her velvety succor splaying out as her tail went high, and retrieved a platinum-chromed strap-on.

Alexi remained splayed on the floor, nose pulsing in an acrid cloud of her musk, and slid a wing under himself, thumb rubbing at the ring between his cheeks. He sighed as she ratcheted her belt into place, her flat teeth shining as she let out a sardonic bleat.

"Oh, to *take* me?" she asked as she crawled in front of him, hooking a hand under his short knee. The goat slicked up her shaft and pressed it against his anus. "Then you'll *have* me."

Alexi grunted, feeling the inorganic organ spread his ring and then innards. "I don't already?" he grunted, precum burbling out his tip. He watched the slit, aimed at his face like the barrel of a gun.

Daani slid into rhythmic ministrations, thrusting the silver shaft inside him. One hand braced her over him, her breasts dangling over his chest, stomach rubbing against his cock. Her other hand pulled at his balls, rolling them.

"As much as you can, which isn't more than a few pieces of merchandise. You worship me."

Alexi hissed when the metal, warmed by his bowels, glanced against his prostate. Her thumb pumped his perineum. "Prostrated at a stone altar!" he gasped, a gossamer strand stretching down to his navel, his shaft bouncing with their hips. "A distant Goddess, not a woman of fur and blood!"

"Why would I be one of those?" she sneered, licking his muzzle, sucking the piss from it when she hilted him. He whined, bucking up against her. "Chipping my hooves on concrete, nose filled with the banal stink of rabble when I can reign above all in an ivory tower?"

The bat arched his back. "And rain down on them?" he parsed through gritted fangs, then let out an ultrasonic shriek as his cock erupted, spackling his flat chest and cupped vampire nose.

Daani pulled out of him with a lewd slurp, her platinum strap-on clanging on the wet pink marble. Alexi lay out flat on the floor, gasping and conspicuously empty. "It's lonely, high up," he said. "Even God came down to his people."

The goat bleated, clapping her hands as she clopped away. Her servant emerged with a tray of hot towels and crossed the room towards him. Daani called back to him, "And what'd his people do? They killed him!"

Alexi, Executive Accountant of Vertilaginous Projections, met her a week later in the recording studio, spinning a rare, gold-trimmed, zirconium-studded, mercury-autographed vinyl sleeve of her last album between his wings, his briefcase bouncing against his hip from a shoulder strap as his short legs and funny foot-hands toddled him through the illustrious Roman-themed building.

At a pair of double-doors, above which a "RECORDING" sign just recently flickered out, Alexi's ears craned to the sound of muffled screams as a security guard checked his badge at the end of a pink and green-marbled lanyard, and then let it drop against the bat's Italian five-piece suit.

Alexi took a deep breath and smiled at Daani's fabulous imprinted form on the front of the album, then waddled in. He had a pair of tear-drop spectacles on his face until a diamond-striped microphone, its handle shaped exactly like her muzzle, streaked across the room and smashed against the wall where his head would have been. His gold-rimmed spectacles flew skyward, and the bat snatched them in his mouth with a quick winged leap.

Daani saw him and smiled. "Sorry, didn't see you there."

"Just came in," he said, slipping his spitty glasses behind a silk pocket square. "You wanted your last album?"

"Just your copy," she said, extending a hand.

Alexi held the limited-release Zenith edition out between his wing thumbs, then pulled it back against his chest. "You're not going to smash it, are you?" he asked, twitching his head toward the broken microphone handle rolling on the floor.

Daani inclined her head. "And what if I am? Call it a tribute."

Alexi kept it pressed to his body, frowning. "Daani, any tithes beyond this one and you may as well strike me down."

The goat blew air through her lips, then tossed herself up on the equalizing board, knobs and sliders going way off course. "How much was that? Sixty-thousand retail?"

Alexi's muzzle creased. "It's not about the money; this one is mine. I love it, whether there's only sixty or sixty million copies."

"Yes, and I made it," she sneered. "And as I giveth..." she declared, thrusting her hand out.

He could feel the corners of the album poking the insides of his wings. As the seconds ticked by, the grin on her face fell, and her slitted eyes began to flare. A thousand futures rushed through Alexi's head, many of them ending in ruin—no, worse, apathy and Purgatory, a life away from her glory—and so with a knot in his throat that nearly brought acid, the bat sighed loudly, hoping to mask his whimper.

He knelt before her and held out the rare fetish. "...so you taketh away."

Daani giggled as she took it, holding it high for the room to see. Alexi finally noticed the others in the room, bereaved, tremulous technicians and exhausted understudies. In their best affected efforts, they looked reverently at the art-piece, squinting as its zirconia shattered the light into rainbow rays, at the embossed rendition of herself in the center riding a giant lizard's paw like Lady Godiva, her furry breasts covered by nothing but bands of flaxen hair.

Alexi raised his wings to the heavenly tablet.

"This album, *this edition of it*," she said, "is me. Made in my image for the enjoyment of my fans. In turn, my fans, through my merchandise, make themselves in the image of me. They are my children."

Holding the album out before her, she tapped its cover with her index finger.

"When they are restored to their glory, this is the form they will take."

Everyone in the room nodded in agreement. Some because they understood, some because of the threat if they didn't. She set the sacrament outside.

Alexi sighed, relieved. "Daani, or, My Asrighelli, if I may be so impertinent to ask?"

The goat grinned, her paw drifting along her thigh as a wisp. "Come, my child. Sit upon my knee."

The bat dared not address the obscene thump of livelihood that wriggled against the front of his polyester briefs, nor the fact that this perverted, denigrating form of pleasure was the only type she'd deign down to him. When he sat on her knee, she felt her warm, muscular thigh under him and a firm, confident arm wrap around his jacketed shoulders. His nose caught her perfume—a sharp, cloying mixture of cloves and spices, with the bitter balsam of myrrh—and his toetips tingled.

Daani gestured out to the recording booth, a jagged wasteland of shattered wooden instruments and an aluminum stool wrathfully bent into a pretzel.

"Please, let not the rigors of a fallen world frighten you," she said. "What is your question?"

The younger techs in the room gaped at the bat in the fine suit sitting on the starlet's knee. The older ones suppressed their frowns, aware of the cables and claws beneath her pelt.

"Daani," he said, counting on his footclaws the thousands of dollars pissed away in lost recording time, thousands more burned in the wrath of Daani's inferno. "Vertilaginous isn't going to force the release of your next album, not for your ego or to compromise its artistic integrity, but we are interested to know…Hell, Daani, what was all the yelling in here? Do you think the new album's that bad?"

A young tech, a rabbit in pink and green boyshorts, gasped at Alexi's sudden drop in formality. Daani scowled at him, then smiled down at Alexi, stroking the skin of his wing. "It's fantastic, actually. Better than my last one, combining polyrhythmics, tri-tonals, but still keeping with the same 3-4-5, 3-4-5 that will hypnotize a deaf person by vibrations alone, if you want the ugly objectivity of it."

An older tech fervently nodded. Alexi frowned.

"Then why the fury?"

"It's man's perfect structure."

"That's wonderful! A monument to your brilliance."

"To man's brilliance, to *our* brilliance, perhaps," she sighed, looping an arm under him and carrying the short, 40-pound, 36-year-old male against her hip. She exited the studio and caught an escalator up, riding alongside the great curved glass window that made the façade of Vertilaginous. They ascended several stories up the long shaft, curling around the building until they emerged to a balcony overlooking the Great Bay of Beatuice, their city. "To ours."

Daani set him on the railing to perch, then leaned on her elbows. The starlet's gold-star earrings swung in the wind, and when her ears twitched, clanging a few times against her horns. "The Tower of Babel was to be man's greatest achievement. A tower to Heaven, a bridge between us and the Almighty. But on the threshold of our epoch, the advent of our epitome, God struck us with a thousand different languages, robbing of us of our greatest virtue: that of communication, collaboration. Our ideas no longer reached each other, and thus severed they died alone; the Tower crumbled."

Daani's back straightened as she rose up from the railing, gripping it with both hands as she looked down on the Great Bay, watching motor-boats splash over the waves, a gaggle of furry beach revelers dotting the shore like sequins. "Even if my album is the link between God and man, a feat of immutable musical brilliance, I fear He will see reason to strike us down or worse, it won't reach Heaven at all. It'll just be…man's…great achievement. The work of a young goat maestro, the voice of an entire generation."

Alexi shifted his foot-hands on the rail, keeping his wings to his sides. "That's amazing, Daani; I don't see the…"

Daani glared at him. "Do you know what a generation of animal-men is to God?" she asked, holding her hand out before him, her middle finger bent as its tip pressed against her thumb.

Alexi lowered his head. Daani snapped. Moments passed, the wind roaring through their felt ears. Salty sea-breeze tickled their nostrils; cars far down below honked as traffic in Beatuice interwove.

"I thought you postured yourself as a Goddess," Alexi said. "Why worry of God?"

"It's figurative, Alexi," she sighed, parting from him for the far corner of the balcony, having him follow on balance-beam. "A Goddess does not face Her own mortality. In sixty-six years, I will die of natural causes, if not in sixty-six days from a starlet's drug overdose."

Behind his eyes, Alexi grew hot. He bared his vampire fangs, and stalked around Daani. "That's not the Goddess I know; that's talk of a lesser artist! Of a dilettante, a tyro!" he snarled. "You are a Goddess in mortal form, God's daughter descended from the Heavens to bring us His glory through your music...if you should even need God!"

Daani's head turned, her hair blew amidst her horns, ears and earrings as her slitted eyes studied him. "If not Him, then?"

"Who's to say He's our creator, and not a bored child slamming his toys together, ripping their arms off at His leisure?"

"It's flagrant blasphemy you're saying."

"We've built skyscrapers far higher than any presupposed adobe and wood tower to Heaven; and what is the incoherent power of a juvenile spirit against the laser-focus of Mecca's high Muse?" Alexi continued, the leather of his wings snapping as he spread them.

"God will damn you."

"I damn God!" he shrieked. A gust of wind caught his wings and blew him over the side. Alexi fell several stories, fluttering chaotically like a skydiver tangled in his own parachute. Daani screamed, hooves crashing across the steel flooring as she fled to the door, then to the stairs, then to the other side of the building where a mass of leather and bone shrieked across the glass horizon.

Her elbow cracked against a guard's muzzle as the cheetah tried to slow her, and others rushed past her, recognizing her, as he spun to the ground. A tour group of teenage girls, all bedecked in the rhinestone and gold fabric graphic tee of her last album squealed as she rounded the corner, and when the group didn't part, the goat slapped the first Daani-Pop sequined notebook and glitter pen out of the thirteen-year-old's paws and threw another one aside by the shoulders.

Their squeals turned to shrieks of horror as their Pop-Star Goddess stampeded through, trampling one that fell under. Daani emerged through the Vertilaginous gates to see a pile of Italian cotton, wing leather, and blood on the concrete. His face was bent, his muzzle half-flattened along the sidewalk, hanging open.

Daani fell to her knees, wrenching at her horns. Gravel dug into her shins; one of his teeth stuck into her fur. The police sirens came, then an ambulance, and Daani found herself done with the interview before she, herself, knew what had happened.

She walked back into the building, into the recording studio, where Alexi's zirconium-trimmed, gold-rimmed album sat on a disheveled control board. Her hand shaking, she picked it up. Her mercury-silver autograph gleamed in the light; she'd signed it on his back when once more, he'd stuttered out an earnest request, and she'd crushed it under her cloven hoof.

The young goat starlet, pop sensation and teenage demagogue, fell down in the recording chair and pressed the album against her forehead.

Daani wept.

MIGRATION SEASON
J. A. NOELLE

Again, she found herself staring down at the screen of her phone, reading those horrible words for the fifth time that hour.

"You have no messages."

Frustrated, she cast the phone aside with a sloppy flick of her wrist, sending the device hurtling through the air to collide with the edge of her dresser. Though the collision made a horrible thud, the phone appeared—from her vantage point on the bed—to be unbroken. That phone, after all, was a trooper. That was most definitely not its first flying attempt, and she doubted it would be the last.

On days like this, when the weather was pleasant and she had a rare respite from homework, the feelings of loneliness that lurked at the corners of her mind would come to the forefront. Unhindered by banal distractions, her negative feelings would slowly consume her every thought, leaving her paralyzed for the day as she stared listlessly at the ceiling. But she wasn't surprised. She had always considered herself forgettable, at best.

The previous week, she had gotten into a heated argument with her closest friend, and the two had both said many things that they would regret. Unfortunately, no matter how many times she reached out to Breezy, she had neglected to reply, leaving her alone with her thoughts.

Oh well, she thought to herself bitterly, hoisting herself up from her bed despite her lethargy. Her legs, as if feeding off of the pessimism oozing from her mind, screamed in protest and felt weak beneath her. *I guess she's no different. They're all the same.*

"Just another goodbye," she muttered aloud, pressing her long fur down around her cheeks with sloppy carelessness, and slipped out the door without glancing into the mirror. Going out for a walk while looking a mess seemed to be one of her new hobbies, and no one in the neighborhood gave her strange looks anymore. They had become accustomed to her restless wandering on the weekends, and had begun to turn a blind eye to her presence whenever she walked the streets after dark.

While disagreements between herself and Breezy were not entirely uncommon, this particular squabble had ended much more poorly than most. Breezy had cursed her for being so derivative, so unoriginal, and had sworn that she was putting their tumultuous friendship behind her.

"Honestly, everything you do is just a copy of me! You buy the same type of clothes, listen to the same type of music! No matter what I like, you suddenly have to like it too!" The feathers about her chest and shoulders were standing on end as she stamped away, her wings jittering restlessly at her sides with fury. She could hear the jingling of the necklace she had gifted her in seventh grade—a bell shaped like a hollow mushroom—with every furious step the sparrow took.

That necklace was likely in the garbage now, Sophie mused bitterly.

She walked along the sidewalks with an absent-minded familiarity, dodging pitfalls and rough spots in the concrete without so much as looking down. Her paws had trudged this same path so many times recently that the pink flesh had become hard and crackled about her toes. Her mother had warned her not to walk barepawed on such hard surfaces, since their delicate paws had been made for snow. But she frequently forgot her shoes by the door while in one of her moods, as her mind was too active in other directions to consider a trivial matter like padded shoes.

Though Sophie had always struggled to stand out in any way, she had—unfortunately—gained a reputation centered around those stupid shoes. It was uncommon for anyone to wear shoes in their city, since the weather was always so balmy and warm this time of year. However, being that she was one of the only Far North animals living in Berrymount, she had to protect her paws from the blistering heat of the asphalt during the day, and the remnants of its heat at night. While she had heard from previous friends that everyone started off with delicate feet in childhood, she had not met a single other resident that had retained that trait, as it seemed that young pups and kits purposefully exposed themselves to the boiling asphalt repeatedly. Did they do it just to prove who was toughest? Did they do it to make sure they wouldn't need shoes later on?

Sophia just didn't understand. But being that she did not want to expose her feet to such conditions on purpose, she had been wearing small slippers to and from school since she had moved to Berrymount...And unfortunately, that had drawn a lot of negative attention. Even her six-year-old sister, after being teased severely in class about her shoes, had tried to walk to school barepawed one morning. She managed to get there fine, but when the afternoon came, the pavement was so hot that Sophia had to go pick her up in the family car.

Being called "Tenderfoot" and "Glasspaw" had not suited little Clara either, apparently.

Her mind elsewhere, she soon found herself in the public park close to the elementary school where her sister was currently going to school. Though the sun was just above the horizon, there were still several small groups of children playing at the park, all of them without a parental figure. Such a sight was common in Berrymount, as the little town was famous for its sleepy and familial nature.

Without paying any of the screaming children any mind, Sophie clambered over the woodchips with great care, praying that none of the jagged wooden pieces would stab her delicate feet. No matter how angry and sullen she was, she did not want to deal with the pain of splinters in her feet for days.

"Hey, look! It's Big Softpaw!" a little bear cub cooed as she walked by. "Are you Clara's sister?"

She opened her mouth to respond, but a tiny vixen cut her off. "Duh, Kaleb! She's a snow leopard, so she's gotta be her sister!"

"Not all snow leopards are sisters," Sophia replied flatly, her sullen mood making her less talkative than usual.

"No, but you two are the only ones I've ever seen!" the vixen replied, grinning to reveal a missing canine tooth. "So there's only one leopard family here, right?"

"I guess," the leopard replied.

"Why are you guys the only ones?" the brown bear cub asked, standing to his huge rear paws. He left his action figure—a lion superhero Sophia recognized as the titular character of *The Mane Event* comics Clara loved so much—forgotten in the woodchips.

"We like the cold. It's too hot here."

"Then why'd you want to come here?"

"I didn't. My parents made me move here when I was a cub."

"Do you miss your old home? The savannah, right? That's where leopards are from."

"There are leopards from all kinds of places," Sophia sighed bitterly at the common misconception. "And no, my family is from the Far North."

Kaleb's eyes suddenly widened, becoming big brown discs that seemed to blend into his fur. "Why don't you...uh..." He paused to think for a moment, conjuring a big kid word from the back of his mind. "...Uh...*migrate* there for the winter? You could see the snow!"

The little vixen gasped, clasping her tiny white paws over her mouth as she made an accusatory *ooooh* noise from between her fingers. "Leopards don't migrate for the winter, dummy. Only the vermin with wings do!"

Sophia winced at the loose usage of such a horrible name to describe the Migratory Birds. The little fox had unknowingly exposed her family as the bird-haters they probably were. Not that such sentiments were uncommon. The Great Migration was coming up, and the anti-avian sentiment in Berrymount was beginning to increase, as it did every year at that time.

"Oh, look, Miss Leopard!" the vixen called her over as she walked to the other side of the playground, pointing one little claw towards the ground. Rolling her eyes, Sophia followed her and crouched down beside the slide to see what she was pointing at.

There, nestled deep in the woodchips beneath the tall slide, was a huge, sky blue egg.

"What the…?"

"It's been sitting there all afternoon," Kaleb muttered tensely, as if just looking at the egg were a sin. "Rachel didn't even see a mommy or daddy when she came here after school."

The little vixen shook her head fervently. "It's been alone the whole time."

Sophia slid under the slide carefully, making sure not to press her weight down on the delicate egg as she tried to balance on her toes in an awkward crouch. Before touching it, she inspected all of its visible areas for any cracks or sign of hatching soon, since she had heard that some Migratory Birds left their eggs while they hatched. While she didn't think she would want to miss the birth of her child, Sophia could see why a single parent would need to leave to make sure they had enough food for the new baby.

Nah, what was she saying? Even Breezy had admitted it was a weird custom.

But when she touched the surface of the robin egg, she knew it was not part of any custom. The egg was cold to the touch, and there was no hint of movement underneath the shell. It had been dead for a while now, and had been abandoned. Sophie's heart ached.

From the look on the leopard's face, the children had surmised what had transpired.

"Dead, huh?" Rachel, asked callously, bending forward and putting her paws on the cold shell. The little girl knocked on the egg with a firm flick of the wrist, leaning forward to hear the dull thud that answered her. "Bummer. I thought I'd get to see a Hatching. It's so weird to think about."

"Yeah. Coming out of a rock like that?"

"It's not a *rock*, Kaleb."

"It looks like one, *Rachel*."

"No one comes out of a rock! But you must live under one!"

Sophia, quickly losing patience with the little children's bickering, stood to her feet and dusted her jeans off absentmindedly. An abandoned egg was not unheard of around this time, since the first Migratory Birds were beginning to fly to Berrymount and the surrounding areas for nesting season. But to leave one so out in the open? Disgusting.

"Hey, Kaleb..." she heard the little vixen whisper, as if Sophia were already out of earshot. "...I dare you to smash it."

The little bear cried out in shock at the horrible request, and took several large steps backward. "Nuh-uh! It's a baby!"

"It's not a baby! The baby forms inside the egg. If it's a dead egg, there's no baby."

"But...why smash it?"

"'Cause I wanna see what's inside!"

The bear cub crossed his large arms over his chest, his large lower lip quivering. "No."

"Fine. Then I dare Softpaw to smash it!"

Sophia laughed bitterly, stopped, and turned around to look at the little girl. "No way," she hissed, making a dismissive motion to the children. "Go home and leave the egg alone."

"You afraid to hurt your paws or something?" the vixen spat, growing increasingly frustrated. "Just crack the egg, will you? I'm too weak! I'd do it myself if I could!"

A growl rumbled in the leopard's throat, and she cut her eyes threateningly at the little brat. "Leave. The egg. Alone."

Suddenly enraged by Sophia's less-than-ideal response to her demands, the little fox whirled around and began assaulting the egg with a flurry of kicks and scratches. Small distress marks began to lace their way across the shell, creating the illusion of rifts in a sunny blue sky. Sophia responded reflexively, bounding over to intervene and snatch the girl away from the unborn child.

"You little—!"

But just when Sophia finally wrestled the girl out of reach of the egg, the vixen forced her hands forward, shoving the larger girl away from her with all her strength. The egg's protector had crouched down on her haunches to get a better hold on the little girl, so the small burst of force from the girl's push was enough to send her teetering over. There was a horrible crackling noise, and Sophia found herself covered in cold goo.

Rachel and Kaleb's eyes widened. Sophia was frozen in horror.

Before she could regain her composure, she saw a blur of movement, a quick flash of light, and the two children were sprinting off toward the street. Sophia lurched forward to pursue them, but slipped on the slippery goo all around her feet, and found herself face-down in the woodchips. Suddenly alone with her thoughts, she wept uncontrollably, crying out into the darkening sky in sorrow. Her hand brushed against a small, cold, and soft mass that lay, encased in liquid, beside her.

That night, a friendship had died. And so had a child.

Going to school the next morning was easily the most difficult mundane task that Sophia had ever experienced. She was barely conscious, as she had failed to sleep at all the previous night. The backs of her eyelids did not provide restful darkness, but instead, flashed images of the dead unborn child into her mind, pelting her with guilt incessantly. She could still feel the slip of the embryonic fluid on her fur, even though she had showered for nearly an hour when she got home. She could smell the repugnant odor of the child's corpse. She could see the look of horror on Clara's face when the little girl had seen her come in the door.

The only bit of luck that seemed to be on her side was the fact that her parents had been in the backyard when she came inside. She managed to dash up the stairs and into her bathroom before they could return from their quick stroll through the garden. And judging by the perfectly ordinary way they had both conducted themselves toward her this morning, she could only guess that Clara had not told them what she had seen. Perhaps she did not even know what she had seen.

But they would know soon.

Her entrance into the school building was met with silent stares and hushed whispers from the majority of the other students, so she did her best not to look anyone in the eye. Their intense gazes burrowed holes into her fur as she forced herself to walk with a normal gait, though each step felt too measured and artificial to appear natural. She almost tripped over her slippers each time her feet made a labored movement forward.

Keep calm.

Rachel had taken a picture on her phone before she and Kaleb ran away.

Calm.

She had probably shared it online.

Calm…

And now everyone knew.

"Heeey, Tenderfoot!" a familiar voice called out. Sophia turned to see Daryl, one of her classmates in physics, waving to her from his locker. She slipped over to him, grateful to have someone to talk to. Trying to will away the stares of her classmates had begun to drain her energy already.

"'Morning," he grinned, exposing his large front teeth. "You okay?"

"Yeah," she replied, running her paw down the back of her neck to smooth down the fur that was standing on edge. "Just…rough night."

"Yeah, I know." She winced. The hare was staring at her evenly with his dark gaze, a smile creeping up his muzzle. "Damn, Soph…I didn't know you were like that. I mean, I think I'm speaking for everyone when I say that your feelings are justified, but *damn!* That's hardcore." His tone, to her horror, seemed approving. A small group of other mammalian classmates had gathered around, and a few of them even patted her on the back.

"I hate Migration Season as much as the next guy, but man...I'm not that ballsy," Trevor added, barking a small chuckle. "You look mad as shit in the photo too. Really showing your leopard side!"

"You did us a favor, really," purred a feline voice in the crowd. "Always making such a huge mess of the city when they come to town. They're just a bunch of squatters we can't get rid of."

"Fuck avians!" exclaimed a gruff boy from somewhere.

"Not all avians are part of the Migratory Flock," a voice muttered softly.

"Most of 'em are," another voice scoffed. "So having one less is like having one less cockroach. It's nice, but we're still infested."

A quiet mutter of agreement passed through the crowd. A flood of "thanks," and "thanks, Softy," followed as the students went about their business in order to make it to class before the bell. Several of them punched her shoulder amiably as they passed, grinning.

"Hey, come sit with us at lunch, Softy," Daryl added before leaving, saluting her casually with two fingers. "We wanna hear the story."

Sophia watched them go, waving occasionally to whoever wished her a good day and smiling in spite of herself. Her stomach churned with shame, but she had not found the words to stop them as they spoke so horribly about avians. Many eyes were still on her as she made her way to class, but she walked a little bit more easily, with less of a weight on her chest than before. It looked like nothing bad was going to happen so far, so it would be an easy fix to explain the situation at lunch. Word would carry soon enough, and the whole thing would be forgotten.

She spent the day going from class to class, feeling the eyes of hundreds on her. More high-fives and fist bumps were given to her within the first few hours than she thought she had received throughout her entire life. A few students even went so far as to thank her for her bravery, and even gave her small trinkets. A pair of earrings, a barely-used bottle of perfume, a few holographic trading cards, and even a small roll of money was given to her before she even had the time to turn them down. They all commended her for her modesty, but insisted she take them without question, as tokens of their gratitude.

By the time lunch arrived, the story had taken on a life of its own. The two small children had been replaced with two avians that were picking a fight with her when she went to take a break from her walk. They tried to fight with her, but she had slipped away using her superior agility. Still they pursued her and—to get them to leave her alone—she ran over to a mother robin and snatched the egg from her arms, threatening to smash it if they didn't back off. The birds backed down begrudgingly, but Sophia had allegedly smashed it anyway, even in sight of the mother, to teach them a lesson.

She had pieced the story together slowly through the bits she had heard here and there from others throughout the day. The story was always told in hushed tones, with wide eyes and toothy grins. The story in its entirety was retold by others at the lunch table, and each time they asked for Sophia to corroborate their words, they became overzealous and continued talking before she could explain. She sat quietly as her legend began to grow, attempting to assert herself with an occasional "um" or "wait," but her soft protests were easily ignored by the passionate crowd.

"All hail Softpaw!" a wolf on the soccer team shouted. Everyone turned to look whose endorsement their new hero had received. When the crowd realized that it was Austin, one of the school's star athletes and the current holder of the regional record for most goals in a single game, the sentiment spread like the smoke from a wildfire. Soon, the entire lunchroom was cheering, and the sternest lunchroom monitor—an older elephant woman with a voice to rival a thunderclap—had to rush in to quiet the rabble.

In the chaos, Sophia made her escape into the hallway, enjoying the silence and lack of watchers for a brief moment.

"Hard being a celebrity, isn't it?"

She jumped, and turned to face the source of the sudden voice. It was Mr. Collins, her homeroom teacher from the previous year. Sinking down reflexively, she readied herself for the berating that was inevitably coming.

But instead of raising his voice, the old tiger raised his paw. And placed it right on her head.

"Take care," was all he said. And he gave her a wink.

She watched him go in silence, her thoughts suddenly quiet. In his approval, she recovered her peace.

A few days of praise, gifts, and popularity flew by in a flash, and Sophia found herself to be perfectly content in her new role as the school hero. Wherever she went, younger admirers followed or watched, and classmates asked her out left and right. Even the gorgeous lioness she had been secretly admiring from afar for years had approached her and asked to hang out sometime. She had struggled to remain calm when she accepted.

In the rose-colored haze of her status, it had taken her a full week to notice that she had not seen Breezy at school at all. While it was common for avians to take a few days off from school to welcome their migratory family members into their homes and communities, an entire week was unusually long. Besides, Sophie knew for a fact that they only had one small group—a cousin and her four children—that flew with the Flock each year, and an entire week of preparation was not needed for their arrival.

While collecting her books from her locker the following morning, she heard a quick rustle of feathers and felt a cool breeze, prompting her to turn around suddenly. She had hoped to see Breezy standing there, so that she could explain what was going on before she began to hear the hearsay that was floating around the school. However, instead of a sparrow, a startled crimson cardinal stood there, gawking at her.

Though she recognized him from English class, but she could not remember a time when they had actually spoken. If she had already been nervous about talking to a stranger, the hostile look he gave her when she spun around made her even more nervous.

"H-hey," she stammered, feeling the extreme weight of his gaze. "D-do you know if Breezy's okay?"

He did not move to speak after she finished her question. Instead, he stared at her coldly for a moment in silence, leaning forward slowly until his sharply pointed beak was only inches from her muzzle.

"She ain't comin' to school today," he growled, the bright feathers on his chest pluming outward threateningly. "'Cause of you." He leaned forward so far that she could smell the seeds on his breath. Quietly, in not much more than a whisper, he hissed, "Fuck mammals."

The sound of his talons clipping on the tile floor thundered in the corridors of her mind.

Getting home that evening offered a level of relief that she had not experienced before. Though she was still surrounded by praise and reassurance from the majority of her classmates, the cardinal's words would not leave her mind. They had sent her stomach churning with shame the second that the words left the cardinal's beak, and the uneasy feeling had not left her throughout the day, making even the most menial exercises of classroom functioning nearly impossible.

Finally away from the prying eyes of the student body, she slid down into her bed with a deep sigh, only to have to stand again to empty her pockets of that day's gifts. Since the newness of her heroic act was beginning to wane, so too was the quality of the gifts, as it seemed that only those who had neglected to show their gratitude beforehand were straggling in to give her tokens. These tokens, it seemed, were more so given out of obligation—the need to appear to be in agreeance with the majority of the student body—instead of out of a genuine gratefulness of her bravery. As such, these items were relatively cheap, useless, and lackluster. In fact, they reminded her of the odd kitschy objects that suddenly appeared for sale at every store close to Christmas.

A contact case that had paws painted onto the lids. A cheap pair of kitchen towels that were embroidered with an intricate pattern of leaves with metallic thread in an attempt to make them appear premium. A can of soda with limited edition label art. She sighed, casting the junk onto the floor with the other gifts that had piled there over the last several days. If the stragglers were not even going to put forth any effort into their gifts, she didn't want them.

Maybe Clara could at least use the towels for her dolls... She did so like to tie hand towels around their necks to make them superheroes, but their mother had long grown tired of entire stacks of kitchen towels missing. Much to the tiny leopard's chagrin, those towels were now stored in a higher cabinet, where only their parents could reach. She felt a small grin creeping up her lips. Looks like it would be Sophie to the rescue once again.

Distracted by her plan to turn such a disappointing object into Clara's saving graces, Sophia's mood quickly began to improve, and she busied herself by searching for a little box in which to hide the superhero capes. Her eyes wandered back over to the chaos that had started to take over an entire corner of her room. After sifting through the cheap watches, piles of earrings, digital music download cards, and dollar store teddy bears, she finally found what she was looking for. Removing the box from the stack of goodies proved to be a perilous task, so she was forced to slowly wiggle it out from under the copious amount of junk that had been piled on top of it.

This gift was given on the second or third day after her fateful encounter, and thus, was one of the more expensive gifts she received. A girl in the grade above her—Caroline, a sleek and gorgeous gray fox who always painted her claws a neon shade—had given them to her with a wink and a smile. Caroline was in the same homeroom class as Max, the lioness with whom Sophie would soon be having a date. Apparently

Max had been talking about having a date with "the hero," and Caroline—being a hopeless romantic—had given Sophie a pair of shoes to wear for said date.

Sophie had never owned a pair of shoes so beautiful in her life. They were petite sandals with intricate cord braiding and small fabric leaves poking out here and there. If one was not particularly observant, the shoes could be mistaken as being held together by tiny vines. Such sandals were all the rage among the canine community due to Mia Howless—an incredibly popular lupine singer known for her light, whisper-like singing voice—wearing a similar style of shoe on stage while on tour earlier that year. Though Sophie had always admired the shoes, she had thought them too extravagant to grace a Tenderfoot's paws. These shoes were made for the paws of confident young mammals who didn't need shoes, but chose to wear them on occasion just for the extra flare to their look.

But they suited a hero's paws just fine.

Giddy with excitement, she slipped the sandals on for the first time, feeling the soft, cottony sole under her pawpads. It was the first time that she could remember since moving to Berrymount that she willingly chose to wear shoes.

With the box freed, she slipped the future capes inside, scrawled a little note to Clara from "The Hero," and placed it on top of the towels. She would sneak the box into her sister's room before she and her mother pulled up into the driveway.

Feeling much better than she had for most of the day, Sophia descended the staircase with more of a spring in her step. Like she did every day when she arrived home before the rest of her family, she stepped outside to make the short, leisurely walk to the mailbox. However, when she opened the front door, she had to clasp her hands over her muzzle to keep herself from crying out in shock.

Suspended from the outside rim of the doorway was a small stuffed cat doll, its wrists and ankles tied together with yarn, and a noose around its neck. Red liquid—what Sophia presumed to be ketchup due to the acidic odor—stained the fur in massive patches, and was dripping slowly into a small puddle on the front porch. She thrust her head out of the doorway to look around cautiously, before cutting the doll down with a flick of her claw. She immediately shut the door and locked it, withdrawing back into her room to dispose of the doll before her parents could find it.

The doll had not been there when she arrived home from school not even thirty minutes earlier, meaning that someone had obviously known she was home, and that she would see it. Meaning that someone had followed her. With shaking paws, she locked the door to her room and hastily checked that her windows were locked as well before taking a seat on her bed to inspect the cat.

It was a small, flimsy toy, its stuffing squeezed out of the neck area and legs from much love and use. Its fur—aside from being saturated with condiments—was matted and filthy, and smelled of many long days of play with a young child. She wiped the crimson tomato sauce off of the doll's face and—to her horror—realized that one black, beaded eye was missing. This was not just any stuffed cat. It was Clara's doll, Missy, which was usually kept outside. The doll had been taken into the pool too many times to ever get rid of the mildew smell completely, so she had been banished to live in the toy trunk outside a couple of years ago. Missy had not been missing recently, as Clara had played with the doll just a few days prior, while taking the last swim in the family pool before their father covered it up for the cooler months.

But, then, how could someone have known to find the doll in the container outside?

Her paws shook with more force as the weight of the threat began to sink in. Rattling in her terrified grasp, the toy began making a quiet clinking sound along with every jerking movement of her paws. Sophie's eyes shot down to the source of the unexpected noise, as if readying herself for a sudden attack.

Around the toy's neck, on the string that had been used to hang her from the doorframe, was a small bell in the shape of a hollow mushroom.

She kept to herself the next few days of school. Every set of eyes that laid on her was a potential spy that could be funneling information about her habits and whereabouts to others. Every echoing footstep was the gait of an avian coming to end her.

Despite her mind being logically aware of the unlikeliness of that last scenario, her anxious thoughts could not be bothered to stop conjuring dark wings from every shadow. None of the avian students had been in school for a couple of days now, most of them citing the need to welcome their extended families back from their yearly migration. But Sophia knew better. In previous years, there was not a single day of the Flock's arrival that called all of the avian students away at the same time. Word had gotten out about rising tensions within the student body.

Though her parents had not said anything direct, she could tell that they were on edge the previous night, looking between themselves with a reserved mood that was uncharacteristic of the two spontaneous adults. They had tried their best to seem normal, no doubt, as they mulled over what they were supposed to do about the situation. She wondered just how much they knew. Neither of them used social media, so the likelihood of them seeing the photos of her and the shattered egg were very slim. It was more likely that the school had made calls to all of the parents to warn them of the mounting hostilities. That would most definitely explain why all of the birds had disappeared.

After another day of anxiously ducking and dodging, jumping at every cheery "hello" from another mammal, and imagining all the horrors that could befall her while sitting in classes, Sophia slowly lumbered over to her locker, sandwiched between a small group of new admirers. She had found that keeping to groups kept her mind at ease, and it was so much better to speak to someone else instead of letting the shadows at the fringes of her thoughts run rampant. That, and it was much less appealing to attackers to take on an entire group at once.

She walked with them out of the school, her heavy backpack slung across one shoulder in an awkward attempt to trick herself into believing this was nothing more than a casual walk home. All was well in their small bubble, with the topic of discussion drifting through various popular video games and comics. Sophia had just made an off-color joke about *The Mane Event* when Daryl, unfortunately, changed the subject to match what had been running through her head all day.

"So did you hear that Flock groups camping out in The Heights were attacked last night?" he asked the group, snickering. "They're saying a huge group of mammals stormed them while they were sleeping. I don't know how much of it is true, but that's what you get for camping out on public property."

Sophia swallowed hard. The Heights was the colloquial term given to the rolling hills that lay just outside of the northern edge of town, where large numbers of avians had set up their homes in the ancient redwood trees. The Flock tended to camp out on the hills en masse, in order to stay close to their families dwelling in Redwood Hollow. In previous years, law enforcement had attempted to convince the nomads to move elsewhere or even to rent camping lots at the national forest park just beyond Redwood Hollow. However, the park was in disarray, and often had serious problems like water main breakages due to the very old piping that ran through the property. It was a better bet, it seemed, to stay on undeveloped open land, but with easy and fast access to the Redwood commercial district that ran along the base of the trees. There, the nomads could find everything they needed during their long winter's stay. Thus, The Heights had earned a reputation of being prime real estate to repeat-offender squatters.

"The police didn't come to help them?" asked Caroline, frowning. "That's terrible…"

"They responded to the report of the violence," Daryl corrected her. "They chased off the ruffians causing the trouble, but they can't guarantee the total safety of a large group camping out in the open. That's just not feasible."

"I guess."

"And that attack wasn't even the first one. Avian kids are getting jumped at school. Last week, a little fox beat the shit out of a lark in her class. The news even said the little bird was bloody. Said the attacker was only in second grade."

Sophia clenched her jaw. She wondered if the attacker was Rachel.

They continued to walk further into town, their numbers dwindling as they started branching off from the main road to return to their respective homes. As they got into more populated areas, they reflexively lowered their voices, just in case there was someone within earshot that would not appreciate their charged conversation.

"I saw on the news that a couple of wolves got jumped on the way home from work last night," Caroline muttered grimly. "They found several torn feathers at the site where they were recovered, unconscious. It's starting to spread…"

"That's just what's gotta happen," Daryl cut in, spatting toward the ground. "We've never gotten along, and it was just a matter of time before things boiled over."

"Look, I don't agree with what happens in our town around Migration Season either," Caroline snapped, shooting the boy a warning glare. "But this isn't the way to go about to fix it. When people think in such a black-and-white way…us-versus-them…It's dangerous, Daryl! How can you not see it?"

"I agree that it's dangerous," he nodded, then flashed a threatening grin, his large teeth shimmering in the dim autumn evening light. "Dangerous for any damn wing-beater that tries to cross me."

Caroline made a furious scoffing noise, and then stormed off down the street, electing to walk alone for the rest of her journey home instead of listening to Daryl prattle on. He watched her go irritably, his long ears laying down flat against his head.

"Is there something wrong with me having pride in my city?" he finally said after several long minutes of silence. His voice was thick with fury, and Sophia thought it best not to cross him.

"N-no," she replied hesitantly, as if waiting for others to chime in first. But no one else was there.

"Good. I didn't think so." He shoved his paws into the pockets of his jeans roughly and scowled ahead as he stomped along. Sophia remained quiet, not wanting to anger the hare further. "I mean...look at *you*, Sophia! And for her to say that in front of you? That's so wrong!"

"She has a right to—"

"But you're a *hero*, Sophia! For the same damn cause that she's spitting on! Doesn't that just make you mad?"

Oh. She hadn't thought of the situation from that angle. Since the incident had been an accident, she had never thought about what others might think about the rhetoric that she would be angry about. She kicked herself internally for being so unobservant. It was too late to act angry now, though.

"H-hey..." she started shakily, swallowing hard. The hare's dark eyes fell on her, still seething with fury. Seeing the resentment in his eyes, she immediately backed down from considering a confession. Maybe that was for the best...The school would hate her forever if she revealed she had been reveling in false pretenses. It had gone on too long already.

And she doubted Max would have much interest in dating a nobody.

"H-hey, are you heading home right now?"

"That's the plan. Why?"

"Well, my little sister had dance practice tonight, and I was supposed to walk her home. If it's not too much trouble..."

"Oh, yeah, sure! The attacks got you nervous?"

"Y-yeah, kind of."

"Sure, I can walk you the rest of the way. I live close to the dance studio."

"Oh, me too!"

"Great!" he smiled, the irritation in his eyes dissipating. "That worked out."

They walked in relative silence, only occasionally swapping details about school events and gossip. Daryl brought up Caroline several times, and Sophia just played along, hoping he would burn off his irritation soon enough.

When they arrived at the dance studio, the sun was just on the horizon, making patterns of pink and red in the darkening sky with the last of its strength. Daryl bid her good night, and headed on his way as Sophia dashed inside to collect Clara. The little girl wanted to dawdle about to say goodbye to all of her little friends, but Sophie snatched her away after letting a few precious minutes pass.

"What's wrong, Sissy?" Clara asked, frowning as she flattened her frilly tutu against her leg as much as she could.

"We need to get home before dark," Sophie replied tersely, dragging the little leopard behind her. Instead of leaving the statement open for questioning from the child, she gave her sister a serious look and added, "Mom said so."

Clara nodded obediently, and quickened her pace.

As they shuffled along the sidewalks, Sophie wished that the day had not been so warm...She would have given anything to take off her noisy sandals. Clara's slippers made rhythmic tapping noises against the pavement as well, and the volume of their journey made her even more nervous. They needed to get off the pavement.

"Come on, Clar," she said, forcing a smile onto her muzzle. "Let's take a shortcut and surprise Mom with how fast we are!"

"Like cheetahs!" the little girl cheered, to which Sophie replied with a soft hushing sound.

"Yeah, like cheetahs!" she whispered. "Follow me! This is a shortcut!" The little girl giggled quietly and bounded after her into the grass.

It was an easy path. They would just cut through the backyards of this row of houses, jump the last fence on the street, and enter the cul-de-sac where their house lay in wait for their return. It would only take a few minutes...

As they cut through the second unfenced backyard on their street, a sound of rustling up above them caught Sophia's attention. Clara, oblivious to the need for anxious attention to detail, continued on, skipping across the grass.

"Clara!" Sophie whisper-called, not wanting her little sister to get too far ahead.

And suddenly, she was on the ground.

A large, heavy figure dropped out of the tree above her, pinning her to the grass with long talons. The shape made no attempt to catch only her clothing, and latched onto the flesh of her ankles with a crushing grip. She could feel hot liquid flowing down her paws and into the grass, but found she could not scream, as a giant, feathery wing had been pressed against her muzzle.

The leopard snarled and struggled, lurching this way and that to loosen the avian's grip on her, but its talons were wrapped too tightly around—and in a few places, *into*—her flesh. Each movement proved to be more painful than the last, and swinging her arms up to lash at the dark figure with exposed claws only got her a sound pecking to the face. The bird's sharp beak sliced a stinging, bloody line into her face, just below her right eye, blood beginning to trickle down her face and into her mouth.

"Hey, hero," growled a low voice from above her. "Nice to see you again." She recognized the avian's accent as one that came from Migration-heavy families. There was only one year-round student at their school that spoke in such a manner: the cardinal. "You surprised us by comin' this way tonight. Don't you take a walk every night *startin'* at your house?" he snickered, squeezing her ankles tighter. She made another muffled attempt to cry out, thrashing her head from side to side to get out from underneath the huge wing. He pressed down harder onto her head until she could feel a sharp pain lacing through the back of her neck. He had pressed her into the stones that lay littered in the yard.

"Ringer, stop," another voice snapped from nearby. Despite the distortion to sound that the cardinal's massive feathers caused, she recognized the voice in an instant.

Breezy pushed the cardinal's wing down far enough to reveal Sophia's large, dark eyes. "Ah, *there* you are," she spat. "Feeling proud of yourself now? You didn't really think you could get away with what you did, did you?"

Sophia opened her mouth to speak, but got a mouthful of feathers instead.

"*How* could you do something like that, Sophie?" she demanded, her voice heavy with betrayal and tears. "I was angry but...seriously? You went out and smashed a *baby* over it? You're a fucking monster!"

Sophie shook her head as much as she could, but Breezy was not paying attention to her.

"If you know what's good for you, you should skip town. You don't know what you've started. Things are going to get worse from here."

Sophie stopped struggling just long enough to meet eyes with Breezy. Her head was lowered in shame, and her beak made a harsh frown line across her face. But her eyes—the same serene, passionate eyes that had looked on her with friendship for so many years—gazed into her with a mixture of anxiety and sadness.

"The *HELL?*" Ringer squawked, suddenly thrashing his wings about angrily. "THAT's what this is about? You're WARNIN' her? You—"

Sophia used the few seconds of the giant wing's absence to wrench herself free of the distracted bird's grip. Ringer reacted immediately by pivoting around and bringing his talons down on the back of her neck.

"Oh fuck no. I didn't come out here for this. I'm takin' one down. Even if I have to settle for the little brat!"

She heard a tiny gasp from somewhere nearby as Ringer raised a wing to point at the source of the noise, a twisted smirk making its way up his beak. "You stay right there, or I take her instead," the cardinal cooed menacingly, leaning forward to practically whisper the threat into Sophia's ear.

Rage.

Sophia spun around, jerking free of the avian's grip and pummeling him with a rain of strikes from her paws. As she continued, her frenzy mounted, her fangs gnashing as she dug into his feathers. Breezy screamed, and the sound of panicked wingbeats signaled her sudden departure.

And in a few moments, it was over. Ringer's struggling stopped. Sophia slumped into the grass, panting. She heard Clara whimpering softly from a hiding place nearby.

The lights had come long before even the neighbors had noticed the scene. Sophia kept her head down as she was led away to the sound of her mother's hysterical sobbing.

Once she had been restrained, an officer stooped to chain Ringer's wings, but paused and beckoned the paramedic over instead. He carried a white sheet in his arms. Sophia averted her eyes.

She heard furious shouting from all around her. The racket of the sirens and the large group of officers prowling around in the dark had attracted a large crowd. Many of the voices she heard were demanding her immediate release, since the officers did not know the scenario that had brought forth the violent encounter. Other voices, however, screamed for her eternal damnation. Someone threw something round and heavy at her face. It struck her, but she felt nothing but numbness.

As the car door closed behind her with a bang, she knew only one thing for sure.

Everybody knew her name.

Furry Confessions

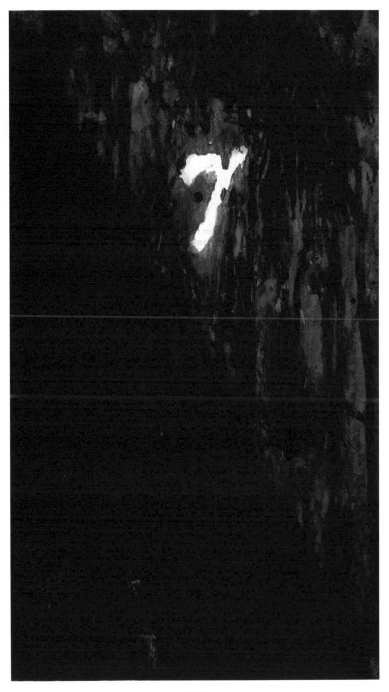

Interlude

"Well," Barba said. "We are done with that." He turned his head over his shoulder and saw rays of light beginning to drift into the room, piercing the panels of glass and painting the room in the different colors.

Zinc walked over to join Barba's side, his tail still curled between his legs, hiding the line of blood that trailed down his leg. "Yeah, I guess we are."

"All seven deadly sins," Barba said, lowering his head and shaking it in disbelief. "What a crazy night." He looked down at another piece of jagged wood near his feet. His ears pricked as he heard the German shepherd moving quietly behind him. In one sudden movement, Barba rushed to the floor, grabbing the wood as he rolled to face Derek. Somehow, the canine was now holding a long, triangular piece of glass. The sharp blade had missed Barba's neck by inches.

Derek growled in a deep voice, "Come now, Barba, we know you're the demon."

Barba found himself growling back, "Dogshit, Derek." He stood, holding the wood in a position to fight. Then, he noticed that Zinc was holding a thick splinter of wood too, and it was also pointed at Barba. "Zinc, what the hell? You don't think *I'm* the demon, do you?"

Zinc snarled, "What Derek did back there was usual for him...but it wasn't usual for you."

Taking a few steps back, Barba's heart thumped in his chest. "I swear to you I'm not the demon. I believe in God; I *love* God."

"Then, why did you do nothing when Zinc branded me?" Derek cried. "You let him *hurt* me. Out of all three of us, you are the only one who did nothing. You corrupted us both, and then you just snickered and made us keep playing your stupid fucking game."

"No!" Barba pleaded as the two started to advance, pushing him back against the clay wall, a couple of feet beneath the stained glass windows. "I'm not a demon, guys! Don't do this!" His eyes darted between the two figures, and he alternated the target of his stick, first at Derek, then at Zinc, and back again. His voice went low, "I'm warning you both. Stay back."

The two stopped, hearing the fire in his voice. Zinc nodded to himself, "Yeah, you are the demon. You even *sound* different!"

Derek agreed, nodding. "And if killing you is the only way we can get out of here alive, that's a risk I'm willing to take."

"Guys..." Barba started, and then he froze. His eyes stared hard at Derek's paws. "Zinc...look at Derek's hands."

All eyes looked at the canine's paws. Now, in the light of the rising sun, they saw that his paws were covered in red. "Well, shit," Derek growled.

Barba's eyes went wild. "See! I told you he was the demon!"

The German shepherd's eyes turned red, and he lunged at the horse. Pressed up against the wall, Barba reached out for Derek's glass-wielding hand even as he slashed at Derek's hip. The dog anticipated the move and grabbed Barba's wrist. The two were holding each other's weapon hands, keeping the dangerous points at bay, although both of them struggled for leverage. Barba's whole body pushed against Derek's as he stared into the glowing red eyes of the demonic canine.

"Zinc, help!" Barba hissed.

"I'm coming!" the feminine tiger said.

He could see the tiger coming closer over Derek's shoulder. He prepared to strike once Zinc attacked, but Derek's strength never wavered. Barba lifted his head, and a bolt of blinding pain near his stomach. Looking down through the blurs in his vision, he saw a massive wooden cross impaling his abdomen, blood leaking from the three-inch-across wound. Holding it in place was a paw striped with gray.

His grip faltered, and he dropped the wooden stake. Instantly, he felt the glass shard pierce his right lung. His head crashed backward against the wall, and as he looked down, his energy draining, he saw two pairs of red eyes now.

"Wha...what?"

The crimson-eyed Zinc replied, "Wasn't hard to scratch myself up."

Derek, horns rising from his skull, added, "Nor was it hard to wipe out the 'S' at the end of the word "demon" on the door. Fucking ghosts trying to ruin our fun."

Tightening the cross into Barba's stomach, Zinc said, "Wasn't hard to lie about there not being any phone service either, right?"

"Right," Derek smirked. "Same with lying about the door being locked."

"And it seems the cards *do* know what we are."

"And the ghosts here gave you every clue, too."

Barba croaked, blood trickling from his mouth now, "W...why?"

Derek curled his snout into a growl, showing his teeth, as he pulled the glass from Barba's chest, grabbed one of the horse's hooves, held it high, and then pinned it to the wall with the glass. "Because you're one of God's little fucking cocksuckers."

Barba screamed, but weakly, "Please, let me go!"

Zinc leaned forward and pulled the cross out of the horse's abdomen. The blood began to pour down his legs. Barba felt his other hoof rise up to the level of his other, and then his eyes widened as the splintered cross was rammed through that wrist, nailing it to the wall as well. "We thought tonight would be perfect to add another spirit to our collection here. A place where we can keep Lucifur's enemies for a while."

Barba's strength left him, and his head hung. "I...I..."

Zinc and Derek turned toward each other, and Zinc said, "Let's get out of here. We need to go catch up on sleep."

"Don't...don't leave..." Barba muttered.

Derek leaned toward the horse, pushing his body close to Barba's, his chest inches from his, his fur tickling the gaping wound at his side, his cock brushing against his. "Aw, don't be that way," he breathed against the horse's tear-stained snout. "Be a good little crucified horse and take it. Dying from blood loss is fairly painless."

"Yeah," Zinc said, his ears perked up in agreement, "but wait till his body is found in a week or two. Imagine how his family will feel when they see this!"

The two giggled and began walking out the door, paw holding paw, and tail curled around tail. In the light of the sun, they were just two ordinary people, young lovers in the fall.

Author Notes

T. Thomas Abernathy is a multimedia artist residing in Knoxville, TN. When he's not covered with various art supplies, he can usually be found underneath a blanket of flour in the kitchen. He's not very good at writing about himself in third person, but he is nonetheless incredibly excited to have his stories published for the first time.

Tristan Black Wolf was writing stories almost before he could read. Since his first publication in 1977, he has published nine books, a score of produced screenplays, and literally hundreds of stories, articles, interviews, reviews, blogs, and general miscellany. Since 2010, his work has been almost exclusively furry, as it is a genre he finds particularly rich in opportunities for unique and vivid characterization. Much of his work appears exclusively on the SoFurry website, which he proudly calls home. In the allegedly real world, he lives in Syracuse, NY, where he is a full-time writer. Having recently earned his PhD, he seeks a collegiate teaching post in literature, where furry writing will be a recommended part of the curriculum.

Stephen Coghlan writes from the oft-frozen capital of Canada. He has an upcoming novel, *GENMOS: The Genetically Modified Species,* which is coming soon from Thurston Howl Publications. His website can be visited at scoghlan.com

NightEyes DaySpring is a known troublemaker who is rumored to have a penchant for coffee and an interest in dead, ancient civilizations. He has been actively writing since 2010. Recently his stories have appeared in *Gods with Fur*, *FANG*, and *Knotted*, along with other anthologies. Currently he resides in Florida with his boyfriend, where in his spare time he masquerades as an IT professional. For day-to-day nonsense, follow @wolfwithcoffee on Twitter.

Originally from Charlottesville, Virginia, **Dax** is currently attending East Tennessee State University in his second year as a biology major who also plays in the University's percussion and African chamber ensembles. In his free time, he enjoys working with animals, especially horses, and hopes to continue working toward his career goal of becoming the owner of a training barn. When he isn't working with horses, he can often be found reading realistic fiction or writing short stories.

Varzen Dralmort acknowledges that too great an amount of pride could make one's eardrums pop faster than an a skyward-spiraling Icarus flight, but nonetheless wonders at what height does happiness turn to hubris. Be it a cheap expedient, he admits we could solve our altitude calamity if we drag Heaven down or raise Hell. Through Thurston Howl Publications, Varzen has also published a harrowing Holiday action tale in the excellent anthology *Wolf Warriors III*. When not flapping around the occasional convention as a giant bat, Varzen lives somewhere and works somewhere else, begrudgingly tolerating a life of normalcy.

Dwale is a poet, author and musician who exists in the Mojave Desert. Its works often touch on themes of spirituality, addiction & mental illness, and are influenced by Japanese aesthetic precepts. Its stories have appeared in various anthologies, such as *Claw the Way to Victory*, *Hot Dish*, and *The Furry Future*.

Faolan is a black wolf from the south of the Netherlands. English teacher by day, and jewelry maker, dancer, gem collector, occultist, and singer in his spare time. Owner of Black Wolf Jewellery. Big fan of furry literature, Pokémon, and K-pop. "Devil's Snare" is his first published story, but he hopes to be able to entertain you with more in the future. Find him in Eurofurence's dance competitions or at Furaffinity.

Searska GreyRaven has been writing ever since someone accidentally gave her a crayon. When she isn't coveting a shiny new idea, she can be found mucking about her South Florida swamp with her partner-in-crime, tending her beehives, and occasionally howling at the moon.

Gullwulf is a seagull wolf who dreams about being a werewolf, and being a famous writer some day as well. She's probably closer to the latter than the former. Hailing from California but currently in migration mode to move, she splits her free time between writing a lot, video gaming a lot, and cooking when she can spoil her friends. She also has a story in Fred Pattern's *Dogs of War* if you want to see more of her stuff. You can also find her on Twitter @Gullwulf and on FurAffinity and Furry Network under Gullwulf.

Thurston Howl is the editor-in-chief of Thurston Howl Publications. He received his Bachelor's degree in English from Vanderbilt University, and his Master's in English from Middle Tennessee State University. He specializes in critical animal studies, and he has several publications to his name, including the novel series The Spirit Sword Saga, various short stories, edited anthologies (namely *Wolf Warriors* and *Furries Among Us*), and even a few poems. He lives with his partner in Knoxville, with their dog Temerita curled up at the foot of the bed, insistent that she is, in fact, a cat.

Hypetaph is a Southern writer who enjoys fiction and horror, and in his rare free time spends it reading and writing these two topics while relaxing with his cats. He has a Bachelor's in English, with focuses in Queer Theory and Women's and

Gender Studies, and finds it easiest to write with a cup of tea and a relaxing video game soundtrack. His first publication appeared in *Furries Among Us,* and he has since written a freelance piece for the Tennessee-local zine *Panacea,* while occasionally reviewing publications when able. He plans to pursue a Master's in English, and write all the while.

Rayah James is a bunny with a Bachelor of Arts in English from Middle Tennessee State University. During her college career, she worked on school newspapers and as a writing consultant. When she is not immersed in writing or reading, Rayah enjoys being on the back of a motorcycle and ballroom dancing.

Bill Kieffer was born in Jersey City, NJ. He never fully recovered. A brain injury at an early age left him with some mild issues and just enough aphasia to be amusing at parties. One of those issues is prosopagnosia (face blindness), which is not so amusing at parties. He's happily married to a woman who encouraged him to discover and explore his sexuality. They both dabble in writing erotica. When he is not looking in the mirror, Kieffer is actually a 6-foot-tall gray anthropomorphic draft horse that types as Greyflank. He is a member of the Furry Writers Guild and has recently published a novella via Red Ferret Press, *The Goat: Building The Perfect Victim.* He is also a columnist for Underground Book Review, a website dedicated to Indie authors and their works.

Billy Leigh likes to prowl the internet as a Wolf and create stories in his spare time. Having obtained a history degree, he has a particular interest in writing period pieces featuring gay anthro characters, partly for the setting but also for the added suspense of exploring characters in eras where homosexuality was frowned upon. When he is not writing, Billy is often found with his boyfriend hiking, dog-walking in the park, or using any excuse to get outdoors. His hobbies also include playing guitar and traveling, whether it be walking in the Australian outback or sampling the nightlife in Prague.

TJ Minde grew up as a military brat who jumped around between Northern California and Southern California before moving to Ohio, where he found the furry fandom. He has been in the furry fandom for over five years and has been writing off and on for about as long. He is incredible grateful for the community of artists, writers and fans, as they helped him find something that he cares about—the written word. TJ has grown to become more passionate about the craft of writing and enjoys creating new worlds and aiding his friends with projects of their own.

J. A. Noelle is a businesswoman during the day, but her real passion has always been storytelling. Through writing, artwork, and costuming, she strives to bring the characters and worlds that keep her distracted most of the time alive to others. She primarily writes fantasy and science fiction, since these were the genres that inspired her to try her hand at writing as a child. When she is not dreaming up new worlds, she is normally doing studio and digital art for her online art business, or entertaining others as a giant blue goat. Visit her online at @RootGryph on Twitter!

BanWynn Oakshadow has been an award winning writer and poet since 1978. He loves to use the unique adaptations and characteristics of animal species as the core of many character personalities in his speculative fiction and poetry. His first novel, *Cheshire's Legacy*, will be coming out in late 2017.

Sisco Polaris has been a part of the furry community since the late nineties and a writer since he was old enough to hold a pen. He started writing furry stories before he even knew what a fur was, or that he was one. Now he has written several popular short story series, and in 2015 he published his first book; *Dyeing to Be With You*. He is the writer behind the popular furry comic *Lost and Found*. A lover of romance, characters, world-building, and erotica; more of his short stories can be found on his SoFurry, or FurAffinity pages, as well as his Patreon. https://sisco.sofurry.com/

Evelyn Proctor grew up in Tennessee, shuffled between several cities there, and eventually moved to California after obtaining a degree in economics. She is the author of the novel *An Aesop in Broken Glass* (under the name Adam Proctor), and may someday finish her second novel. A writer, pianist, gamer, and student of economics in that order, she spends much of her free time working. Her other hobbies include tabletop roleplaying games, drinking whiskey, becoming too excited about the elasticity of demand, and swearing profusely.

Teiran is the furry author behind the series High School Days, the novel *The Hero*, and has stories in *ROAR* volumes 2 and 3 and the upcoming anthology *The Fortune Teller's Poem*. He lives in Texas with his mate Fuzzwolf, and helps run FurPlanet Publishing. You can follow his work current work at https://www.patreon.com/Teiran and on Fur Affinity.

Avin Telfer is a software engineer from San Jose, California, the heart of Silicon Valley. He is passionate about creating games and interactive experiences, as well as storytelling in all its forms. Whether it be books, interactive fiction, live theater, or everything in-between. Currently, Avin works for a major software company enabling other developers to create their own games. In his spare time, he enjoys writing fantasy and sci-fi stories that feature anthropomorphic animals. You can read more of his stories on his website: http://www.AvinTelfer.com/

Weasel is a degenerate writer who received his Bachelor of Arts at the University of Houston-Clear Lake. He currently uses it as scrap paper to fuel his publishing business Weasel Press and Red Ferret Press. www.poetweasel.com

Zarpaulus, sometimes writing as "Joel Kreissman," is the author of the novella *The Pride of Parahumans* and creator of the Para-Imperium universe. He has a degree in Cellular Biology and applies his knowledge to his writing whenever possible. You can check out his work at https://paraimperium.wordpress.com/ for the Para-Imperium specifically and http://zarpaulus.livejournal.com/ for those stories and his other original and fan-fiction.

About the Artists

Joseph Chou created the cover for this book as well as the fronts of the Tarot cards used in the book. The editor for this collection stumbled across Joseph's previous art based on the seven deadly sins on FurAffinity and contacted the artist, requesting permission to use the images. Joseph, however, wanted to create new images, and we could not have asked for a better artist to create the cards and the cover.

Joseph is a hobbyist illustrator who lives in sunny Southern California. He specializes in pencils, acrylics, and oil paints, but has recently picked up digital mediums for convenience's sake. He is fairly quiet within the furry community, and goes under the guise of a red fox dubbed "Fenrir." His works usually focus on landscape/mood pieces, or fantasy/medieval settings. Joseph enjoys online gaming with friends, collecting board games, reading novels, and cooking new recipes.

T. Thomas Abernathy designed the cover and turned Joseph's sin images into the well-designed cards. He is THP's wonderful new graphic designer and marketing expert, and many of the design elements in this book are testament to his skill. For his full bio, see the Author Notes above.

LETTER FROM THE EDITOR

While such letters are typically placed at the beginning of an anthology, I felt, given the nature of the interludes and the atmosphere the piece gives, it would be best to reserve as much non-sinful things for the end of the collection.

With already existent "divine" furry anthologies, such as Fred Patten's *Gods with Fur* and Kyell Gold's *Ten Commandments* anthology *X*, the anthology *Seven Deadly Sins* was meant to be a sharp contrast to the positive collections, being the first furry anthology to showcase the darkest side of furry literature. We wanted to see these characters at their worst, submitting to the foulest of sins. Now, you have seen characters raped and castrated for their Lust. You have seen dead bodies pissed on and ex-lovers assaulted by their memories, all recollections of Wrath past. You have squirmed as bodies are collected and sons are murdered in the attic, examples of our inherent Greed. Wicked, green Envy displayed itself through one's self-amputation for cosmetic beauty and another's wearing the skin of a rival. You have felt Sloth creep in as you watched your lover turn into a bearskin rug or as you heard whispered in your ear, "Tomorrow, lover." Your own stomach grumbled with Gluttony when you heard our tales of cannibalism and hoarding. And I guarantee you beamed with Pride that you were not one of the filthy avians or one of those types who picked up hitchhikers. You've walked with us through tales of these sins, but let these stories be cautionary for you—if you fall to their power, these things could ՝ to you, and only the Nine Circles of Hell will await you.

What was meant to be a playful collection based around the sins became one of the darkest volumes I have ever read, and I am honored to have worked with such wonderful writers. I truly appreciate all the writers' patience and diligence in working with me, and their efforts have created a truly sinful anthology.

I also must thank the two artists for the collection, Joseph Chou and T. Thomas Abernathy. Joseph has been more than gracious with his illustrations of the sins and his work on the cover. And Abernathy did a splendid job with designing the cover elements and placing Joseph's work into a card format.

Thanks also to the proofreaders, Alli Thurston and Weasel. Also to the book reviewers whose blurbs appear on the back of the volume, Kirisis Alpinus and Kit-Karamak.

Through the pits of Hell, ever onward.

Made in the USA
Columbia, SC
07 October 2017